I0646182

EYE OF CHARYBDIS

STEVE WILSON

A Michael Neill Adventure

EYE OF CHARYBDIS

Published by White Feather Press. (www.whitefeatherpress.com)

ISBN 978-1-61808-157-5

Printed in the United States of America

Cover design by Steve Wilson

This is a work of fiction. The characters and incidents are not to be construed as real. Any resemblance to actual events or persons, (aside from historical figures mentioned) is entirely coincidental. No part of this book is intended or should be interpreted to represent the views or policies of the Department of Defense or any other government agency. While some technology is grounded in reality, certain liberties have been taken in the interests of creating a compelling story.

For more information, visit the author's website at www.stevewilsonauthor.com

Reaffirming Faith in God, Family, and Country

For my brother, Mike,
and the Port Dawgs of the 70th Aerial Port Squadron

EYE OF
CHARYBDIS

PROLOGUE

The Bering Sea
Northeastern coastline of Russia,
June, 1985

THE PATROL BOAT BUCKED an angry wave, and the officer steadied himself and squinted ahead. What he saw wasn't surprising, given the weather; the sky was a colorless palette, blotted by mist, and the horizon was far too distant to be seen. He dropped his gaze. The troughs between swells were empty, and this pleased the Russian. They were entirely alone in this patch of ocean, with not a single hazard to navigation—nothing man-made, at least—and free to maneuver as the Soviet captain saw fit.

It was mid-morning. The winds from the north were bitterly cold, and a gray rain blended with the boat's neutral hues. The squall above seemed to conspire with the sea, threatening to swallow the small ship; swells lifted on either side of her bow, symmetrically spaced, but the keel and rudder were strong, and the corvette's triple screws pushed through to find steerage from one crest to the next.

Sleek and trim, the *Admiral Gromov* normally plied the waters that hugged the Kamchatka Peninsula. Her assigned patrol route traced the length of the Kuril Trench, a deep underwater ravine, from the southernmost tip of the headland to the northern mouth of the Karaginsky Gulf. But today's tasking was different, and on this occasion she had sailed into the broad, easterly expanse separating the Pacific Ocean from the more shallow depths of the Aleutian Island chain.

Of medium height, and with a bantam waist, Grigori Kamken squared his shoulders and peered forward, considering his next course of action. There were no shortcuts here, he reasoned. The port of Petropavlovsk was far to the west. Making for home waters now would require resolute seamanship, and simply turning in that direction would mean catching the surging sea on his starboard side, risking catastrophe.

And don't forget—these waters have teeth, Kamken cautioned himself.

"Helmsman," he barked.

"Yes, comrade Captain." The pilot's reply was swift and respectful.

"Increase to flank and bring us about." His words sounded crisp in the enclosed space of the bridge.

The pilot gauged the approach of the next swell, and the order was repeated. "Increasing to flank, preparing to come about."

"Smartly now, Valentin." Kamken thought to smile, but something about this place produced a tangible dread, causing him to shiver beneath his serge greatcoat. "Put the winds to our back."

The seasoned helmsman gave a curt nod and swung into action. Reaching the top of the mountainous wave, he drove the bow across and brought the *Gromov* to a new course, placing the ship's stern squarely before the seas rising behind them. Just as quickly, the falling rain turned to sleet.

"Reduce to one-third." Once more the words were

echoed. The captain eyed the navigational display, a series of analog dials clustered near the compass. "Steer one-eight-zero."

"Aye, sir. Steering due south to one-eight-zero. Helm is answering."

"*Kharasho.*" *Very well.* "Maintain this track until the storm abates."

The pilot's face begged a question. "And then home, Captain?"

"And then home," Kamken nodded. A fresh thought came to mind, one with sober importance. "Oh, and Valentin—keep an eye out for other survivors. I'm going below to see to our passenger. You have the conn, *tavarisch.*"

He braced. "I have the conn, comrade Captain." A wan smile appeared. "Please give my regards to Captain Pavlenko."

There was sarcasm in the pilot's voice, thinly veiled. An able seaman standing nearby flashed a grin.

"I will do just that, Valentin." Kamken's expression was tired but amused. He chose to tease the young officer. "You would like one of his educational pamphlets, *mozhet bit*? Or perhaps a preview of his next indoctrination session?"

"I do not expect special treatment, Captain," the pilot deflected. "The State has many children."

"And each with one allegiance, Valentin," Kamken extolled. "We live to serve the *Rodina.*" He referred to the Motherland, adding, "Our new political officer only seeks the common good—as do we all, *da*?"

Valentin searched for the hem of the sky, but it eluded him.

"*Kanyeshna.*" *Of course.* "My heart is warmed merely by the thought."

The captain could recognize cynicism when he heard

it and let the comment pass. As *zampolit*, the ship's political representative, it fell to Captain Pavlenko to ensure discipline and morale aboard the *Gromov*. The concept stirred an old debate, one that Kamken sometimes puzzled over. Officers like Pavlenko were necessary fixtures; Party doctrine insisted that was true, and Party doctrine was, of course, superior to the tenets of the West—or so Grigori had been taught—but if that were the case, why did the military invest itself so heavily with such proselytes? To be sure, a system of government that exceeded all others needed no inducement to loyalty. Its virtues alone should be enough to instill patriotic fervor.

Pavlenko's rank was equal with Kamken's, and he commanded just as much authority. It was a practice almost unique to the Soviet Navy. Grigori mused on that. The Chinese employed a similar hierarchy, with directors and instructors filling the top echelons of their ranks. Both superpowers had their own political directorates, with commissars dictating Party policy from the top down. Controlling the thoughts—or the actions—of the people was the ultimate goal. Herding a compliant populace to follow the dictates of the State required persuasion. To that end, the threat of overwatch was very real, and was the unspoken duty of the *zampolit*.

Valentin had been right. The State did have many children. Captain Pavlenko was one of them, but he was also more. It was no secret that the man was a uniformed officer of the GRU. Fiercely independent, the GRU was the Soviet Union's largest foreign security branch. Indeed, Kamken's ship had been designed from the keel up as a platform for intelligence-gathering, but there was a difference. While other vessels in this class were built for the KGB's Border Guard, the *Gromov* fell under the GRU's jurisdiction, charged with protecting State property—and guarding her secrets—along the forbidden stretch of the desolate Kamchatka coastline.

Kamken smiled grimly at that, mindful of his footing as he descended the *Gromov*'s ladderwell. On either side of the narrow passageway were other reminders of the corvette's mission. Cramped compartments housed cryptologic gear, hull-dipping sonar suites, and a host of equipment attuned to intercepting signals traffic. Arguably, the patrol boat was one giant ear.

Or several, for that matter.

The comm shack came next. Coded messages—to Pavlenko, no less—streamed in from the admiralty on an hourly basis. Naval Command had dispatched them here, and now they wanted updates. The fact that Kamken's superiors chose to collude with the *zampolit* was inconsequential. That was the order of things, and Kamken knew his place in the food chain.

Topside, the exposed deck spaces bristled with sensors and processing systems, maintained by technicians with shadowy credentials. Taken together, Grigori's boat was crawling with spies, operatives of rival agencies, and distinguishing between simple sailors and the more reticent members of the Soviet *intelligentsia* was no mean trick.

•　•　•　•

Kamken was amidships now, proceeding aft. His ship seemed alive and fairly breathed around him. The sharp clatter of tools rang from the engineering spaces, and the pungent odor of diesel filled his nostrils. Running the length of the boat, the central passageway had become a busy place; wide-eyed seamen darted urgently past their captain, singly or in pairs, seeing to the *Gromov*'s needs and ready for anything the storm might bring their way.

At length Grigori reached the stern, descending one more deck to the infirmary. The hospital berth was the last compartment on this level, and shared space with the medical officer's cabin. The captain was met there by the first officer.

"Report, Pavel." Kamken wished for an update of his own. "Ship's status first."

Senior Lieutenant Pavel Teplov was an intense man whose features masked a jovial personality. Teplov would one day earn a command in the Soviet Navy, but for now Kamken was thankful to be paired with such an officer.

"The engineer reports no problems, Captain. Propulsion is sound, the pumps are online and our electrical systems are functioning normally." A pained expression, and then he continued, "However, fire suppression suffered a leak overnight—"

"*Halon*?" Kamken frowned. The flame retardant was effective as an extinguisher, but could also be deadly.

Teplov gave a nod. "In the forward spaces. Very minor; one of the release valves failed. The discharge was quickly shut off."

"*Kharasho*." That was satisfactory for the moment, but safety was paramount, and the system would need a second look. "And fuel?"

"We have sufficient stores," the first officer replied, "Provided no other rescue missions become necessary."

Kamken was quick to answer. "The *Orsha* has signaled us. We rendezvous at noon." A replenishment tanker shadowed the boat. "And our small craft?"

"She is astern. Secured to her davits." Teplov smiled broadly. "The crew fouled her lines during recovery, but the bosun managed." The rank on his shoulderboards still glistened; overseeing deck operations had left the lieutenant's uniform damp.

The officers' eyes were abruptly drawn aft. The surgery's hatch eased open, and a tall figure entered the passageway. Kamken glanced behind him and imagined that he saw Captain Pavlenko inside.

"*Dobre ootra*, Captain." *Good morning*. It was Petr Bobrik, the *Gromov*'s Chief Medical Officer. Grigori returned the greeting.

"What have you discovered, Doctor?"

Bobrik closed the door behind him. "Each answered question brings a new mystery." He shook his head. "One man, comrade Captain—alone, in a life raft intended for six."

"What of his injuries?"

"His leg is broken, a compound fracture. I've set the bone and given him something for the pain."

"Morphine," Teplov mused.

"*Da*, Lieutenant, morphine," Bobrik answered. "Administered cautiously. He suffers from exposure—hypothermia—but his vitals are returning to normal."

"How long was he adrift?" Kamken asked.

"That is difficult to say." The doctor pursed his lips. "But I would estimate less than eighteen hours."

"Roughly the same time we received our orders," the first officer observed.

Kamken agreed. "The admiralty expected us to find something here."

"Then he will survive?" Pavel always sought clarity.

Bobrik bobbed his head. "Oh, yes, he will survive. It's his mental state that concerns me—the man was very agitated."

"The morphine, perhaps?"

"No, Lieutenant. The analgesic has a sedative effect. For now the drug has calmed his tortured nerves," Bobrik explained.

"He's conscious?"

"He fades, conscious one moment, out the next—much to Captain Pavlenko's consternation, I'm afraid."

The doctor's voice dropped. "The *zampolit* is not pleased with his ramblings."

Teplov's stern look returned. "Has the patient identified himself?"

Bobrik shook his head again. "He wears the uniform of our own navy. His nametape reads Zhukov—nothing more."

The first officer persisted. "And his rank?"

"He wears no rank, Lieutenant," the doctor replied. "And there are no patches or insignia on his tunic."

"*Interesna*," the captain muttered. "So where is his ship? The presence of a raft would suggest an accident of some kind, but we've found no wreckage since entering these waters."

"Maybe he's a naval aviator," Teplov suggested.

Kamken grunted a response. The puzzle gave way to more practical concerns. "Has he taken any nourishment?"

A shrug. "Hot liquids only. Tea and broth. He refuses food from the galley."

Teplov was grinning again. "Perhaps his faculties are *not* so impaired."

Bobrik forced a smile, but the captain ignored the remark.

"Describe this agitation, Doctor. What has comrade Zhukov said since we fished him from the sea?"

"Nothing of substance." The medical officer looked uncomfortable. "And he is very fixated on something clutched in his hand—he calls it his talisman."

A religious symbol? Teplov blinked. Another reason for the *zampolit*'s displeasure. "What kind of talisman?"

"I haven't seen it; the man won't turn it loose." Bobrik dredged his memory to answer the captain's question. "He repeats certain phases over and over. And his accent is Ukrainian."

"What were these phrases, Doctor?" Kamken asked. "Can you recall his words?"

"I will try, comrade Captain." Bobrik paused; the steady *thrumm* of the *Gromov*'s power plant was constant, and the doctor shifted on his feet. "He said that the sea had swallowed his sins. He was quite clear on that point."

"What else?"

Bobrik's eyes narrowed. "He also referred to 'the beast'."

Kamken's head came up. "The beast?"

He nodded. "He told me that the beast had slipped below the waves. And he was now free of its grip."

"Just a bit dramatic, don't you think?" Teplov asked. "Sounds like an old Russian epic."

The Chief Medical Officer disagreed. "No, Lieutenant. I saw the fear on his face. And before the morphine took his voice, he whispered something else."

"What was that, Doctor?"

He swallowed hard, not wanting to sound too theatrical.

"Well, comrade?"

Bobrik's reply brought a chill to the others, reviving the dread Kamken felt in the wheelhouse.

"He gripped my arm and told me that *the eye has closed—pray that it never opens again*."

· · · ·

The mystery facing Captain Kamken and the *Gromov* had begun the day before.

Fog had covered the Commander Islands, a normal occurrence during the summer season. Bering and Medny lay in the shadow of Kamchatka, and while part of the Aleutians, these narrow spits of land were claimed by the

Soviet Union.

The hunter battling the sea was past exhaustion. Using an alternating rhythm, he drove his oar down and back, propelling the hide-covered *baidarka* forward. He was called Anax, but that was just an abbreviated form of a much longer name. To his people he was known as Katmai, a title that brought to mind images of snow-swept Alaskan plains and the brown bears that lived near the top of the world.

Katmai and his fellow tribesmen were Aleut, a label supplied long ago by the Russian pelt and fur traders of the eighteenth century, but the islanders preferred a different name, Unangan—meaning 'seasiders' or 'original people'. This was a nod to their way of life.

Despite their hearty constitutions, the Unangan had suffered under the Russians. Disease brought by outsiders ravaged the population, a consequence not uncommon when two diverse peoples met. Exploitation and hardship imposed by the trading company—a Russian entity—also took their toll. Not even the Unangan homes were sacred; in ages past, the company had uprooted entire families, relocating them to the Commanders as little more than slave labor—

Katmai shook off the fatigue gnawing at his bones. The gale sent spray into his face, and salt stung his struggling eyes. He had rowed twenty-five kilometers south of Bering Island, the largest in the Commander Chain, and now, thankfully, he was almost home again. He had little to show for his efforts. It was unseasonably cold—too much so, in fact, to hunt or fish, or be successful at either—and the shoals of the treeless archipelago would be a welcome sight.

To the west, a pod of six orcas harassed a bowhead whale. Katmai watched but felt no fear. These powerful beasts were his brothers, and were much more interested in prey below the waves. At length the bowhead broke the surface for air, but the killers' tactics proved their intellect. Swarming the victim, the orcas piled on, covering the larger animal's blowhole. She could do little more than fight for her own survival, leaving her newborn calf to fend for itself. Even Katmai felt pity, but the outcome was nature's way, and sunset would find the pod with full bellies.

The sudden change in weather took him by surprise. One day earlier he had stood on the roof of his house, tasting the morning air and reading the winds. No warning touched his senses. The sky was clear and the sea calm. There was nothing above or below to suggest the threat of an impending storm.

Only one explanation remained, and Katmai knew what that was.

He had begun his journey by embarking on a simple hunting trip. But the Spirits had other plans. They had drawn him away for another purpose—to bear witness to a spectacle no one else had laid eyes on. It was an event he would not soon forget.

Katmai almost missed it. The humidity contributed to that. The last bands of fog hugging the Commanders billowed south, following the warm currents fed by volcanism below the waves. It was the Unangan's keen hearing that alerted him first. A deep and constant roar sounded from the west, muffled by the mists hanging low on the horizon. He thought it to be a ship at first, and then his eyesight was challenged. A broad, dull shape stretched across his field of vision—darker than the fog roiling around him—and in an instant, the winged monster ripped through the vapors masking its approach.

He had never seen anything like it. Massive in size, its speed was like something from a dream. Flying at sea level, just above the water's surface, it was visible for scant seconds, with what appeared to be huge horns on either side of its head. The hunter felt a crushing pressure, and passing in front of him, the beast's breath and forward momentum threatened to capsize the small kayak. Had he been just a dozen yards closer, Katmai would have been swept away.

An ear-splitting voice rose in pain as the monster skimmed the waves, and then came the sound of the sea entering the beast's throat. A wrenching din filled the air; Katmai likened it to the cry of a dying animal, and then his view was hidden once more by the veil covering the waters like a shroud.

Blue and green lightning erupted behind the shifting cloud bank. An intense flash of orange appeared briefly before being snuffed out by the combers washing over it. Katmai could hear the leviathan's death throes as air escaped its lungs and was replaced with brine, and then all was quiet as the beast was claimed by the sea and slid reluctantly below the waves.

Katmai steered away from the angry waters and pointed the *baidarka* north. He rowed through the night, his strength waning, his arms and shoulders taut as the storm began to build. By dawn the fog had long since lifted, and the breakers fought against him, becoming gray and lifeless as he drew closer to the shoreline of Bering Island.

The Unangan snorted under his breath. He knew why the ocean paled. The sea had been disturbed, and digesting the mortal remains of the beast had soured her belly. Not everything was meant for the dark halls of the ocean floor, and there were many things, some evil, that would never find rest there.

Katmai retrieved the seal bladders he'd left behind

to mark his path. His actions had become rote. The sun hid its face, and he was chilled to the bone and numb from his experience. In the solitude of the return trip, the hunter tried to shut out the memory of the monster that had nearly claimed his life. He had no interest in sharing his story with anyone. Ultimately, he would speak of what he had seen to only a few in the village.

Some of his people would see his encounter as simply happenstance. Others would view it through a different lens and call it Providential. It never occurred to Katmai that he had been singled out for a greater purpose, and that one day the account of his voyage might save lives.

The hunter harbored a secret. The sea did likewise, but that was the way of things. Something so vast could do no less, and was the perfect place for concealment. The ocean floor was the abode of riddles. Far below the surface, the unyielding depths held many mysteries.

Now they contained one more.

OUTSIDE INFLUENCES

Part One

1

ALIASES

Kiev, Ukraine
Late February, present day

"**S**TILL SURE YOU want to go through with this?" The earpiece crackled, and the voice asked the question for a second time. Sitting at the bar, the man in the leather jacket sipped his drink and smiled. In front of him was a mirror, and his reflection stared back with no small measure of confidence—and an abundance of resolve.

"An American died for this treaty, Dmitri; let's make sure his sacrifice counts," the Ukrainian breathed. "Besides, it's a little late to back out now." His tone suggested a smooth, experienced disposition, but the reality went much deeper than that, touching instead on the spiritual. He stared at the glass in his hand. "How do you drink this stuff?"

Again, the wireless device sounded deep within his ear. "It's an acquired taste, Oleg." Dmitri Yaroslav enunciated carefully. He had to force himself to use the name *Oleg* only. "Was it expensive?"

He was frowning. "Just a few *hryvnia*," he answered.

"Why?"

"Cheap stuff," Dmitri snorted. "Drink it slowly. The alcohol content is probably more than you're used to."

"Don't make fun," Oleg warned. "When this is all over, I'll buy you a round."

"I prefer beer, *tavarisch*," Dmitri shot back. A case officer with Ukraine's security services, Yaroslav was a native of Kiev, and his accent confirmed it. "Is Pyotr in place?"

"He's in a booth," Oleg replied, "nursing a whiskey."

Dmitri's voice rose slightly. "And our other friends?"

The frown gave way to a smile. "They're close."

"*Kharasho.*" *Very well.* Yaroslav sighed. "Now stay sharp—your contacts are just coming in."

"So I see."

The conversation had ceased. Boris Isakov has arrived, the Ukrainian thought silently, with a bit of eye candy on his arm, it would seem.

He looked ahead, and never turned, but his eyes followed three men and a woman as they entered the bar. Each man was dressed in a dark suit; the woman wore a short, black skirt, split on one side with a scalloped neckline. She was clearly proud of her long legs—among her other ample assets—and Oleg allowed himself a moment to take in her beauty.

He identified the woman instantly, having seen her photograph during the morning briefing. Nadia Kolvec was Boris' consort and technical associate, serving as the Russian's number one. And Nadia wasn't just a pretty face; she was suspected in the deaths of two Ukrainian police officers. Dmitri recognized her as well. He was growing nervous, but kept his emotions in check.

The group of four began the long walk from the entrance to Oleg's stool. Two of the men peeled off, taking positions at each end of the bar. Boris moved casually to Oleg's three o'clock, awkwardly close. *A tactical consideration*, the Ukrainian mused; most shooters were right-handed, and Boris must have felt that planting himself there would give him an advantage, should gunplay break out.

"Oleg Kerensky?" Boris muttered. He sounded perturbed, upset that Oleg hadn't spoken first.

"Oleg *Avarysius* Kerensky." He never looked up, but scrutinized the woman's features as she found a seat. The bartender instinctively stayed away. "Boris Isakov?"

A grunt; there would be little in the way of pleasantries. "Are you ready to do business?"

"What's your hurry?" Kerensky paused for effect. "I am ready to *consider* doing business," he answered. "And what of you? Did you bring the sale item?" *Merchandise* sounded so cliché, and trite terminology was something the Ukrainian wanted to avoid.

"Possibly," Isakov hedged. "Are you armed?"

Oleg laughed softly, and then lowered his voice. "Of course I'm armed; I have a Glock on my right hip. And we all know your men are carrying."

Boris raised an eyebrow. His precautions would do him little good; Kerensky might, under ideal circumstances—circumstances that favored him—draw a bead before the Russian could pin his shooting arm.

"Let's keep things civil, shall we?" Oleg advised. An admiring glance went to the lady, but he displayed more interest than he really felt. "Aren't you going to introduce me to your friend?"

"Nadia Kolvec, my chief of staff," Isakov told him smugly. "You may *look*, Oleg Avarysius Kerensky—just don't touch."

The Ukrainian's eyes bored into Nadia's. He wore a four day-growth of beard and drew a hand across his chin. "You have property I covet. But I have no interest in your woman."

"A pity." Nadia was not one for wasting words, and Oleg saw her smile. She liked what she saw, and if conditions were different, she would have enjoyed this handsome foreigner.

Game on, Kerensky decided. For the first time Oleg turned his face toward the Russian mafia boss. "Shall we commence the transaction?"

"Now who is in a hurry?" There was an edge in his voice, but Isakov seemed to relax. "I require more confirmation. How do I know you are who you say you are?"

Oleg heaved a weary sigh. "Let me put your concerns at ease, *Pan* Isakov. You received a promise of payment—a back channel pledge of reward. You came here expecting to find Oleg Kerensky, and here I am. I was told to meet with Boris Isakov, and here you are. For my part, I represent the Polish government, and they are very eager to know your employer."

"But you're Ukrainian," Boris deflected.

"That is correct."

"And you don't like Russians, do you, Kerensky?"

An odd statement, Oleg thought. He gave Isakov an icy stare. "They have not been kind to my family, no."

"Why is the Polish president so interested in what I have to sell?" Boris was fishing.

Oleg shrugged. "His role in this has been withheld from me."

That much was probably true, Boris decided. Damning evidence of any kind would be compartmentalized, and not even the messenger would be privy to much more. But Isakov wasn't through yet.

"And why send a Ukrainian to broker the deal?"

"So many questions." Oleg's gaze fell on the woman's legs. Nadia Kolvec was undeniably beautiful. "Why hire a Russian to fence the sale item? And why here, on

Ukrainian soil?"

Boris was quick to answer. "Probably so that no one party has the advantage."

Oleg nodded. "A fair assumption." *Easy now*, he cautioned himself. "And how do you know I'm Ukrainian?"

"Your accent. You're from Kiev." That was also true, but there was so much more to Oleg than met the ear.

"I was born not far from here, on the outskirts," he answered truthfully. "If that is not enough, I can tell you more—my village, the names of the schools I attended. Anything you like—but I should warn you. Your resistance to this arbitration is embarrassing the lady."

Boris reddened, but Oleg's prodding had the desired effect. For all his protestations, Isakov was being drawn into this charade. The Russian turned to his left and nodded, bringing one of his associates from the far end of the bar. As he approached, the man retrieved something from his coat pocket.

"A padlock storage device," Oleg observed with a smile. "You take security very seriously, my Russian friend."

"All in the name of protection," Boris answered. "Do you know what's on this drive?"

He shrugged it off. "Does it matter what I know?"

Isakov sneered. "It would matter to me—if my life was on the line."

There was an interested light in Nadia Kolvec' eyes. "I think *Gospodin* Kerensky knows exactly what's on the drive." She smiled, and the intensity behind it was more than alarming. "Don't you, Oleg?"

"*Steady*, everyone," Dmitri's voice whispered in Kerensky's ear. "Something just happened—don't let them put you on the defensive."

The Ukrainian kept his cool and decided honesty was the best policy. "Information regarding the new Polish defense shield," Oleg answered quietly. "Firewall proto-cols for the software; I am no expert in this new digital age, but in the wrong hands, the warheads of SMOOTH STONE could be rendered inert—"

"—allowing my country to decimate anyone who stands in our way," Boris announced.

Oleg smiled again. "Are you a patriot, Boris Isakov?"

"More like a venture capitalist," the Russian replied. "If I were a patriot, I wouldn't be selling it back." He turned the drive over in his hands. "But this seems a fool's errand. The Poles could just as easily reconfigure the codes and protect the missiles' integrity."

"They already have." Kerensky smiled broadly, the dimple in his left cheek barely visible beneath the stub-ble.

"So what's the point of all this?" Boris asked.

Nadia stirred atop the barstool, crossing her legs and allowing the hem of her skirt to ride higher. "To entrap those who stole the codes," she purred. From her clutch she withdrew a revolver and leveled it at the Ukrainian's chest. "Put the drive away, Boris."

"That's not friendly at all, Nadia," Oleg said even-ly. The pistol was close enough that she wouldn't miss. "And I thought the two of us were getting on so well."

Nadia continued to stare at him, but said nothing. She reached out, squeezing Oleg's thigh.

"What's going on?" Dmitri's voice came again. "I don't like this."

"Looking for something, *Pana* Kolvec?" Oleg asked.

"Firearms." Her hand moved forward.

"Easy, Nadia," Kerensky's voice nearly caught in his throat. "You won't find any there."

Smiling wickedly, she ignored Oleg's warning and tightened her grip. "Look closely, Boris." Her palm lin-gered before grasping Oleg's Glock. She worked it free and laid it in her lap. "Don't you recognize him?"

Isakov looked again. He was confused, but he trusted the woman's judgment. A hand went into his jacket, and the bodyguards assumed a more defensive posture.

"This is the champion of Poland's agreement with the West," Nadia continued. "The American Marine turned diplomat—Captain Neill, is it?"

"If you say so," Kerensky smiled

"You're sure—he's an American?" Boris asked. "His command of the language—"

Nadia sighed heavily. "Try watching the news, Boris. He's a bit scruffy—but it's definitely him." She lowered herself slowly to the floor, eyeing the four corners of the bar. "I think it's time we leave."

Boris' own sidearm was now out and on full display. "There's an exit in the rear—"

"—and we'll be sure to take *Kapitan* Neill with us," Nadia licked her lips, "to ensure a safe departure." The revolver was still pointed at Neill's chest. "There's a price on his head in Moscow."

"On my head?" The Marine looked surprised. "I'm flattered—but I think I like it right here. Besides, my friends would hate to see me go."

Boris and his men traded glances, their heads turning in every direction. "He's not bluffing, Nadia."

At this late hour, the bar was filled with the criminal element. Drug dealers, thieves and prostitutes. And the setting was becoming more fluid. From the shadows of the darkly lit room, Isakov saw movement. Pyotr Stanislaw—a lieutenant in the Polish Army—rose slowly from his table and edged out onto the floor. On the opposite end, more men stood, concealing their flanks, arms hanging loosely at their sides.

There was a wild look in Nadia Kolvec' eyes. She kept them on Neill and seemed frozen. Etched on her face was a cold determination; a boiling anger intent on recovering control. This was not what she and Boris had planned. The reward was out of the question now, but escape was still a possibility. As the bar's 'patrons' circled closer, she decided it was time to change the circumstances.

It was time for a distraction.

"*Da svedanya, Kapitan.*"

The .38's report was much louder than expected, but it did the trick. The first round struck Neill center mass. The second went high, over his shoulder, striking the far wall. Neill fell back and landed on the bar room floor. Nadia thought to fire again, but Boris grabbed her arm and pulled her away. His henchmen brought up machine pistols—one held an Uzi—and began to fire into the air, inciting chaos. There were screams and the clattering of chairs as customers began a frantic search for cover.

"*Mischa!*"

Pyotr abandoned the use of Neill's alias. He crouched and returned fire, hitting one of Isakov's men in the thigh. More shots erupted, splintering the bar's oak panels and shattering the broad mirror. The Russians used the tumult to mask their retreat, herding their wounded comrade toward the back of the room.

"*All teams converge.*" The bedlam spurred Dmitri Yaroslav into action. "I say again—*all teams converge.*" He removed the headphones he'd been wearing and jumped from the van in the street.

Pyotr heard a flurry of acknowledgements from his earpiece. His first concern was for his friend. Clutching his sidearm, he bounded to Neill's side, thankful to see him beginning to stir.

"Are you all right?" he asked Michael.

Neill winced as he sat up. The tactical vest had done its job. "Which way?" he grunted.

"Out the back." Pyotr offered a wry grin. "You have the luck of the devil, Mischa."

Neill struggled to his feet, eyes raking the saloon's rear exit. "I prefer the grace of God."

"You sound like your father."

Neill grinned in spite of his discomfort. He saw his pistol beneath a stool and retrieved it. "Let's go—we still need that drive."

Both watched as Dmitri's team flanked the narrow hallway, the back door having slammed shut behind the Russians. His ribs smarting, the captain joined the agent in charge. Pyotr was right behind him.

"What now, Sergeant?"

"They must have a car in the alley," the young operative told him. He nodded toward the door. "Our people should be in place. I say we go through and clear it."

"Fortune favors the bold," Neill replied. "If they're waiting for us on the other side, they won't expect a move like that." He shot a glance at the NCO. "Ready?"

The Marine didn't wait for an answer. He charged ahead, ignoring the sergeant's protests and then gripped the door handle. Throwing his shoulder against the hatch, Neill twisted the knob and burst through to the other side.

He found himself in a cold, narrow back street, melted snow between the cobblestones. Neill kept his head on a swivel and looked to the left. Parked twenty meters away, a car roared to life, painting him in the glare of its headlights.

He instinctively ducked as a shot rang out. A bullet whizzed past his ear, followed by another. Neill crowded against the wall and took a knee, sending two rounds in reply. Pyotr and the agent in charge came through next and turned to face the sound of gunfire.

The Russians' car jolted into gear and raced in their

direction. Neill lifted his piece to fire, but was pulled back by Pyotr. The Pole's actions saved Neill's life, and all three men flattened themselves to the deck as the sedan sped past.

The sergeant was quicker than the officers. He led with the muzzle of his carbine and squeezed off a burst. The sedan's rear tires exploded, sending the vehicle fishtailing into a dumpster less than a block distant.

Neill took off once more, staying low while advancing toward the car. All four of the vehicle's doors now swung open, and each of the Russians leapt into the alley with their weapons drawn. His adrenaline flowing, the captain covered the distance just as the gunmen took aim.

More gunfire. Sparks danced off metal and brick as hollow points filled the air. The volley from Isakov and his team forced Dmitri's men to seek cover, with Neill in between. He did a tuck and roll, crouching beneath the rear of the car. Steadying himself, he bided his time as a figure cleared the sedan's taillight.

Aiming low, Neill's leg shot out, his boot crunching against bone. The Uzi clattered on stone as the shooter toppled to the ground, crying out in pain. The Marine whirled without pausing. Nadia leaned across the sedan—her eyes held a deadly persistence—and once more the revolver was pointed his way.

She didn't hesitate at all; Neill was just faster. As he reached forward, he could sense her muscles tighten. This was no time to behave like a gentleman. He clubbed Nadia with his Glock—hard—stunning her briefly. Dropping his pistol, he gripped the woman's forearms and wrenched the gun free, then pulled her across the trunk to land at his feet.

Time compressed and had no meaning. A dark presence filled Neill's peripheral vision. He turned to see Boris leering at him, his semi-automatic inches from his face.

"Time to die, *Kapitan*."

The Russian's hand twitched as he began to squeeze the trigger. But other players had entered the game, and he never finished the act.

From behind came the sound of troops. Neill heard the distinctive click of a rifle's safety. The Ukrainian trigger pullers were brutally efficient; two shots rang out in rapid succession, and the top of Boris's head became a reddish-pink mist, splattering the nearby wall.

In that instant, Neill tensed. He crouched lower to give his rescuers a clear shot at the remaining gunmen. Isakov remained standing for mere seconds, and then crumpled, falling forward, his lifeless body now draped across Nadia's. She was well acquainted with death, but the heartless woman screamed as blood poured from Isakov's misshapen skull and pooled around her.

The tempo in the alley had shifted. There would be no further gunplay. By the time Dmitri's men swept in, all fight had left the Russians, and they lay down their weapons—rather than suffer Boris' fate.

Half of Yaroslav's security team had gathered inside the bar. The rest mingled with Kiev's *militsiya*, policing shell casings and collecting evidence from the crime scene. An ambulance had arrived, ostensibly to cart off the mostly headless body of Boris Isakov.

"What took you so long?" Neill asked. He looked down to see that his hands were shaking.

Xander Voskov—Captain Aleksander Voskov, operations officer with the Ukrainian State Security Directorate, and former member of the Berkut—smiled before answering.

"Such bold action, Mikhail. We weren't expecting it. But I should have known that Marines rush to danger." A frown creased the officer's face. "You've been hit."

Voskov inserted two fingers into the ripped leather of Neill's jacket. The captain winced as he probed.

"Just a scratch," Neill replied. "Anybody else hurt?"

Sergeant Yuri Tereshenko, Voskov's colleague in the SSD, joined them. His rifle was slung across his back, while Voskov's was held in the ready position, the barrel pointed down. "Boris Isakov is not likely to recover," he deadpanned. "His associates are being treated for minor wounds. And *Pana* Kolvec has a broken nose—" he gave Michael a wink, "—we aren't sure how she sustained such an injury."

Pyotr was at Neill's side. "Mischa—" the lieutenant stared into his friend's eyes, "—let the medics examine you. A fire-fight is no small thing to endure."

"You should know, horsefly," Neill shot back. The Pole had taken a bullet just months before. "Any damage on your end?"

"I'm fine. Everyone was shooting at you. Oh, and Nadia was right—you do appear to be scruffy." Pyotr opened Neill's jacket, inspecting his friend's torso. "And your chest?"

"My ribs, actually," Neill answered. "A layer of Tev-lite took care of that." He looked up at the ceiling. "That Uzi packs a punch."

"And thankfully it wasn't pointed in your direction," the Pole returned. "I know a certain *serzhant* who would prefer you alive."

Pyotr knew just what to say to shift Neill's think-ing. "She feels the same about you," the Marine grinned. "Told me to keep you out of trouble."

"She said that?" The lieutenant was warmed by the thought of Christina Arrens. "Maybe there's hope—"

Neill faced Yuri. "What about the drive?"

"We found it in Boris' coat," Tereshenko told him. "Completely intact."

Pyotr offered a puzzled look. "Was Nadia right, Mischa? Will the drive point to those who stole the data?"

"Moles can't stay in the shadows forever." Neill removed his coat, inspecting the top of his shoulder. "In this case, we've got some help. The mainframe housing the protocols has a built-in safeguard. It's called Apocrypha—identifies source codes and IP addresses. It's not enough to determine exactly who the thief is, but it should get Dmitri very close."

They watched as Yaroslav's agents brought Nadia in from the alley, her hands bound behind her back.

"Maybe she can help," Pyotr offered.

The Russian woman was worse for wear. Her skirt was soiled, stained with Isakov's blood. Nadia's hair was damp and frayed at the ends, with a bruise darkening the bridge of her nose. One cheek sported scrapes and an inch-long gash where the Marine had introduced her to the pavement.

Neill raised a hand as she was led past. "Things might go easier if you choose to cooperate, *Pana* Kolvec."

She paused in her tracks, and part of her reply came as she spat at Neill's feet. She had one weapon left, and Kolvec wasn't anxious to give up her advantage.

"Don't be naive, *Kapitan*—" she snarled, "—this is far from over."

"It is for you, *zhinka*," Neill replied. "Ukraine's laws can be quite harsh. I'd consider that."

Nadia was gorgeous, even in defeat.

"Enjoy your victory, Captain Neill. You will find it to be short-lived. In time the Kremlin will hunt you down—you and everyone you hold dear." A menacing look spread across her face. "Moscow knows what you did in Odessa—and they won't soon forget."

• • • •

The agents of the State Security Directorate trundled Nadia through the front door. She was placed in the back of a car, just as dawn's first light colored the sky. Pyotr watched her go.

"I wouldn't be too concerned, Mischa. She boasts an idle threat."

The Marine's hands had stopped shaking, though he felt no less apprehensive. "I'm not so sure."

"Nor am I," Voskov added grimly. He gave Neill a hard stare. "She mentioned Odessa. I wonder what she meant by that."

"It's—kind of a long story. Remind me to fill you in sometime." Michael didn't like being evasive, but in this case it was necessary. "I do find it odd, though; a mafia lieutenant colluding with the Russian government."

"And that surprises you?" The former Berkut's face was set like flint. Circumspection was his trademark, and at present, Xander Voskov had no words of comfort. "Nadia was right about Moscow's long memory, Mikhail. May I pose a question?"

"Shoot."

"I visited the port early last year," Voskov began. "There were rumors—tales of a stolen weapon. Something monstrous."

"That's not a question," Neill pointed out.

"Let me be more direct, then," the officer pressed. "A nuclear warhead—used to threaten innocent lives. Can you elaborate on that?"

Neill shook his head, but offered a knowing smile. "I'm afraid I can't," he answered, spying Dmitri across the room. "Maybe you should ask Major Yaroslav. He was stationed there about that time."

Voskov pretended to be hurt. "You don't trust me, Mikhail?"

"It's not about trust. This is about confidence—in Ukraine's government. Your country's suffered hard times of late. Some information needs to be kept under wraps. And then there's the subject of protection."

"*Protection*?" Xander cradled his rifle more closely. "Ours or yours?"

Neill had a faraway look as he considered Nadia's threat. "I was hoping for both," he said at last.

"You will return to the United States now?" Pyotr sounded disappointed.

The question brought Neill back to the present.

"Not just yet," he said. The captain turned to face the bar. The mirror before him was shattered, but Michael's drink was right where he'd left it, unharmed by the violence that had gone before.

"I promised Dmitri a beer."

2

STATE OF THE UNION

Bethesda, Maryland
Three months later

T HE SMELL OF HASH BROWNS, bacon grease and eggs
hung in the air, and while the aroma was enticing, it
did little to calm the young man's nerves.

The circumstances were certainly familiar. The old
woman recognized that immediately. Seated three tables
away, the anxious customer was most likely Russian,
given his mannerisms and phrasing. He read items from
the breakfast menu, speaking in a thick accent and delib-
erating over pronunciation.

The tortured words came slowly, and the waitress
frowned. She tried to interject, wielding a carafe and
pointing to his coffee cup. He shook his head. Tea was
his beverage of choice, and he struggled to find some
way to communicate that preference.

Natasha Lenkov sipped from her mug and leaned
forward, straining to catch the fractured conversation.
Only a few years earlier, she had faced a similar predicament. In that instance, language wasn't the problem,
but the emptiness of her change purse was, until some-

one stepped in—an American Marine, whose name, she would learn, was Michael Neill.

"May I be of assistance?"

Free of her booth, Mrs. Lenkov stood at a respectable distance and smiled at the server. Before the waitress could answer, Natasha gave the gentleman at arm's length a polite glance and greeted him in her native tongue.

"*Dobre ootra*," she said pleasantly. "This might be easier if you let me help."

A blank look. He felt out of place, a stranger in a strange land. And the spotlight continued to shine on him.

"*Spaseeba, moi prepodsha*." The young man blushed and stood to his feet, the response a common one for his generation. A relieved smile was now on his face. "I feared I might starve before I could place my order."

Natasha slid into a chair across from him. She turned to the server. "A moment, please, miss?"

The waitress moved quickly to the next table, coffee at the ready. Mrs. Lenkov watched her go before speaking again.

"You address me as *teacher*. You are right. I taught school in Moscow."

"I thought so." His awkwardness melted away. "You remind me of my own *uchitel*."

"You flatter an old woman." His courtesy didn't go unnoticed. "Natasha Lenkov." She extended her arm, and alone with him now, she lowered her voice. "These menus have pictures, you know. When in doubt—"

"*Kanyeshna*," he answered sheepishly. *Of course.* "I must seem an idiot." A shake of the head as he gently took her hand. "I needed only to point. And my name is Malyevo; Igor Malyevo."

"*Preeyaht-nah poznikomitsa*," she said in return.

Pleased to meet you. "How long have you been in America?"

"Two weeks," Igor lied. It wasn't his first deception; as it was, the surname he used was also a fiction. "I've come here from Kursk to study medicine. I want to be a doctor."

Mrs. Lenkov considered that slowly. She was struck by Igor's name. *Malyevo*—so close to Malyev. Could there be some family connection—a link to her one and only student? The CIA had told her only what she really needed to know, but the old woman had figured out much on her own.

Ivan Orlov was the name of her pupil now. He had once mentioned that he, too, was from Kursk. And his real name, before being spirited out of Ukraine, had been Malyev. Maybe if they talked long enough, she could learn more from this stranger—determine if the two men were somehow related—and arrange a family reunion, of sorts.

But she'd have to be cautious. First things first.

"I'd suggest the Hungry Man's breakfast," Natasha said. Her index finger tapped the appropriate spot on the menu.

"Please; help me order, Mrs. Lenkov." Igor was politely insistent, and his eyes quickly scanned the nearby tables. His actions didn't draw her attention; the black-garbed handlers from the Central Intelligence Agency— or Secret Service?—were nowhere in sight. Not an unexpected development, Igor assured himself. Today was the woman's day off, after all.

Natasha Lenkov was hardly a trusting soul. But she'd been in America long enough to forget Soviet paranoia, and the man across from her was gaining her confidence.

"I could do with more tea," she plied.

"Then you shall have it," Igor said quickly. His face

broke out into a broad grin. He would cultivate his new friendship, and in time the old woman would lead him straight to his quarry.

This could turn out to be easier than he thought . . .

Ronald Reagan National Airport,
Near Washington, D.C.

"Recognize the glide path?"

Michael Neill raised an arm and pointed toward the river. Beyond the terminal windows, a wide body twin-jet drifted over the Potomac, landing gear deployed, and then began a slow descent on the northern end of Runway 19.

Standing at Neill's side, Staff Sergeant Christina Arrens looked up. Her eyes followed the officer's hand, and then a smile appeared. Wearing her service uniform, the young woman was impeccably turned out, every bit the professional NCO.

"The River Visual approach," she answered. "And I suppose you know why it's called that."

Neill gave a nod. "It's the scenic route. Follows a path from the Capitol building, the Washington Monument—"

"—and the White House."

"Yes, and the Pentagon, too. Plus half a dozen other landmarks. That airspace was ruled out of bounds after 9/11."

"But that was only briefly," Arrens said. "Those restrictions were lifted years ago."

The captain was well aware of that. He just wanted to draw her out. She seemed to relax, and Neill was thankful to see her smile. Since breakfast, Christina had been far too quiet, and her mood became sullen as the morning wore on.

"Ever considered becoming a pilot?" Christina asked.

"That sounds like a recipe for disaster." He dismissed the question with a shake of his head. "Can you picture me at the controls of an aircraft?"

She didn't answer, and the two were silent for a moment as they watched the jet touch down. "They do make it look easy, though, don't they?" Neill remarked.

"Which part? The landing or the flying?"

Michael shrugged. "Either."

"You can't have one without the other. But how hard can it be?" She was being facetious now. "You go up, you come down. Millions of parts, all working together to counteract gravity."

Neill was impressed. "Good choice of words, since you can't *defeat* gravity. Circumvent it, maybe. Apply maxims of nature that postpone its effects. But everything about flying conforms to physical law. Otherwise it couldn't happen."

Facing the Potomac, the captain's eyes scanned the runway. At the opposite end of the field a 727 picked up speed and leapt skyward. The bird struggled at first, its wings dipping to each side before catching more lift in the warm, spring air.

Keep her up there, Lord.

The prayer was uttered softly, a concession to habit, but not without heartfelt concern. The faithless might have scoffed at Neill's simple words, denying that the petition could have any effect in keeping the aircraft aloft. Michael was, of course, familiar with the principles of powered flight. Growing up in Ukraine—he'd been born near Kiev—his attention had often been drawn to the skies, watching as the planes of Eastern Europe soared above. He knew that with sufficient acceleration and lift, even Ukraine's awkward airliners could take their place in the heavens, their contrails scratching a path in the blue vault high overhead.

On a wing and a prayer, his Dad would say. Neill had adopted the phrase for himself.

"Thanks for the briefing." Christina's eyes narrowed, her voice bringing him out of his trance. "You're just trying to distract me. Make me feel better about all this."

"How am I doing?"

A playful glare. "I'm not impressed."

"So you *don't* want to go through with it," Neill observed with a grin. The color of his own uniform gave his eyes a hazel look.

"It's a little late to change plans now," Christina answered. There was a hint of annoyance in her voice. "It's a TDY, Mike. *Temporary* duty. I'll be back in ninety days. Just keep working on your Polish while I'm gone."

"You're avoiding the issue, Christina," the captain pressed. "Wasn't this whole thing your idea?"

"Not exactly. More like the First Sergeant's. To protect us, I think. He's been suspicious ever since we got back from Poland."

Neill laughed. "Etheridge was suspicious long before that. There's a lot of experience behind those hash marks."

"It did cross my mind," Christina admitted. "And the colonel?"

"I think both of them have expectations," Neill said slowly. He offered a different perspective. "Look, Warsaw wasn't just a chance for us to prove ourselves. It was something more. A way to separate our emotions and get the job done—and we did that."

"So it was a test?"

"More like an opportunity. To do the right thing," Neill's eyes met hers, and he lowered his voice, "—and come to terms with what we really want."

Christina didn't look away. "I know what I want. I always have."

Her comment stirred his blood. "Well, Terryton's no dummy. And since you're his favorite—"

Christina's face brightened. "Not me. That would be you, Captain Know-it-all."

Another shrug. "The colonel looks the other way on your account." Neill was amused. "And I still think this was your idea."

A sigh, and she turned her head. "I just need time to figure things out. Poland made me realize I can't run anymore."

"Run from what?" He smiled again, and she noticed. "Are you saying that you'll miss me?"

She returned his expression and parried. "Absence makes the heart grow fonder, Captain. And Etheridge gave me a choice. Germany or the Pacific. Naturally, I chose Hawaii."

"Berlin might've been nice," Neill suggested.

Christina shook her head. "I needed a break from that part of the world. Besides, three months in paradise might help my tan." She paused for effect, adding, "I even bought a new bikini just for the occasion. Maybe I'll send you a picture."

The comment was meant to ruffle him, and Michael feigned embarrassment. "I'm growing a little uncomfortable with this discussion."

"You love it," she prodded, "but you are turning red."

Travelers with boarding passes streamed by. An airline attendant fielded questions at the gate, bringing a new thought to mind.

"What did that TSA agent say to you, back at the x-ray line?"

"He called me a 'ground-pounder,' " Neill said. "The same term Willis Avery used the first time we met."

"I remember that day. And how is the new Secretary of Defense?" Christina asked.

"Busy. The past four months have been a whirlwind." Neill chuckled quietly. "His was one of the fastest confirmations in history. Didn't hurt that the president has a clear majority in the House and the Senate."

"That's not what I meant," she told him. "I'm talking about personally, not professionally."

The captain had a faraway look. "I don't think he can tell the difference," he quipped. Still, Neill understood her meaning. "Richard's death shook him up—"

"Shook all of us up."

Neill's head bobbed. "True. Some more than others."

She had a feeling he'd go there. "Don't start, Mike. Ilya Maersk pulled that trigger. It wasn't Crockett's fault, and it wasn't yours, either."

"But I was the O. If I'd insisted—"

"You're second-guessing yourself. Richard did just what you or Nate would have done. He thought an awful lot of you and just wanted to help—and he did. But sometimes things go bad." She reached out and touched his sleeve. "You warned him twice. I was there, remember?"

His memories of that night weren't all painful. "The lady in red. Now how could I forget that?"

Christina let him linger over that thought and then switched it up. "So how's the SECDEF adjusting?"

"I think it's safe to say that he's thrown himself into the new job."

She gave a crooked smile. "Men are like that. It's a defense mechanism, part of your DNA."

Neill dropped his tone, bringing every bit of polish to his words. "I must admit, at this moment I'm on the defensive. Right now I'm fighting the strongest urge to kiss you."

"Be careful, Marine. Those urges can get you into trouble."

"Then maybe we should talk," he conceded.

"We have talked," she reminded him. "There aren't many ways around this. We've discussed a few. We both chose this life, and I refuse to let you walk away from your career. And I'm not walking away from mine, either." She looked over his shoulder. It was time. Christina retrieved her boarding pass and carry-on. "They're seating first class and military. Gotta go."

"Wait a sec." Neill started to reach out. This was happening much too fast. "What's behind all this? And why are you really leaving?"

She faced him now, with the strongest of emotions shining in her eyes.

"Because you took me someplace magical, Michael Neill. To a world of castles and treasures and sacred relics—a fairy tale come to life." Her tone was soft, patient. "On Christmas Eve, you stole my heart—and you've done that with every kiss since then. Europe was something I'll never forget."

Every kiss. The words inspired action he couldn't resist. "I don't think either one of us will." Neill reached out and took her hand. "Now close your eyes."

"Mike—" her chest rose and fell as she fought for breath, "—not in *public*."

Neill didn't wait for compliance. He slipped his arm around her, pulling her close before placing his lips on hers. Everything about the embrace intoxicated him. The act was brazenly physical for each; she returned his passion, and after a moment, he reluctantly released his grip, leaving both Marines wanting more.

"Aren't you the bold one."

"I want you to hang on to that."

"Count on it," she breathed. Her voice caught in her

throat, and her eyes grew moist. She pulled a sealed envelope from nowhere, thrusting it into his hand. "This is for you, but don't open it yet."

Neill turned it over, reading the ink. His name was written on the outside—a small, hand-drawn heart dotting the 'i'.

"Well—*when*?"

"You'll know." As an afterthought, she added, "And don't go to Russia while I'm gone. You're not very popular with the Kremlin."

Apparently not, he didn't say. "Trust me. I'm staying right here."

Christina brushed past, but then turned. "I love you, Michael Neill." Leaning forward, she squeezed his arm and kissed him briefly on the lips.

In an instant she'd entered the bridge to the aircraft. The scent of Neill's cologne lingered for some time. Her words to him lasted much longer.

And so did the kiss.

The Pentagon

The responsibilities of the office were much greater, to be sure. And so were the potential headaches.

Just months after confirmation, late nights and weekend work were common. Travel went without saying, and crisscrossing the country would soon become the norm. There were, of course, visits to foreign nations—coalition partners, allies, and the occasional junket to third-world backwaters—but it had only been a short time, and those trips hadn't made a big impact on the schedule just yet. Overall, most frustrations were lessened by seeing prudent advice give rise to meaningful action.

It was a step up, the man in the rumpled suit decided.

Once upon a time he'd been the president's national security advisor, and for Willis Avery, accepting the role of Secretary of Defense was a lot like his old job. To do one or the other required a broad understanding of the issues. These were many, but in his new job, Avery not only advised the president, he also had the authority to implement policies to defeat America's enemies—and protect her shores from credible threats.

There were stark differences, of course. Dealing with an industrial complex hawking weapons had come as something of a surprise. Many systems were unneeded or redundant; some overlapped existing programs, and were luxuries at best. Avery suspected that their revenues were intended solely to line a contractor's pockets. Politics always reared its head. Pushing back against various government agencies and the vestiges of the last administration was also distasteful. What galled Avery the most was the fact that so few in either group had ever really worn the uniform.

The best part of the job was being in the thick of things. SECDEF enjoyed 'touching the mission'; meeting with his commanders, or better yet, rubbing shoulders with the troops. He was slated for a trip to southwest Asia soon, Kuwait first, and then a stop in northern Iraq. The Kurds had established a base there, and Avery was gratified by the support offered by western allies. After years of neglect, the presence of peace—enforced by the provisional army—was reassuring, and the U.S. now had a new partner in the region.

The man felt fresh on this particular morning. It was a common misconception that a position in the highest echelons of government robbed an individual of rest. That wasn't the case for Avery. Being bone-tired at the end of the day meant that he'd given his all, and sleep came easily. Nor was stress much of a problem. The new

SECDEF was a hands-on manager, but he was well-adapted to delegating responsibility.

Assistants and under-secretaries focused on the small stuff, leaving Avery to manage the bigger picture. Two aides alone were charged with his daily calendar, coordinating a shifting priority of appointments. SECDEF liked to spread the wealth, so to speak, and with a full-on staff, he could set the tone and then simply turn his people loose.

The Secretary seemed born to the job.

His day started early. The Pentagon loomed large, its limestone façade catching the first rays of morning sunlight. Built largely of concrete—steel was in short supply during construction, and there was no marble, as Italy was an Axis nation—the massive office complex had a very large footprint on the banks of the Potomac, and was practically a stone's throw from Reagan airport.

Avery's driver bypassed the building's southeast side and chose the river entrance, delivering his charge to the basement parking garage. Guards at the entry control point alerted additional agents, and within minutes, the Secretary and his protective detail breezed through the executive tunnel and arrived at the office. Avery greeted his administrative assistant (in another time, she would have been his secretary), quietly thanked his escorts and then slipped inside the door.

"Time to start the day, Cull." The big man shed his coat, draping it over the back of a chair. "Now please tell me the coffee's ready."

Cullough McKeckney, Special Assistant to the Secretary of Defense, sized up Avery as he entered the room. He was rarely surprised by the SECDEF's appearance, and his day-to-day apparel was completely predictable. Case in point, the man disliked pinstripes, preferring solid col-

ors—white, powder blue, or even gray—and his choice
of dress shirts leaned toward cotton Oxfords, usually the
button-down type. Contrasting slacks, tastefully styled
shoes and a fashionable tie completed the look, but his
cufflinks called attention to the worn edges at the sleeves,
and McKeckney was reminded that the Secretary could
be very hard on his wardrobe.

"Fresh and hot, Mr. Secretary." Cull took a step toward the credenza, lifting a bottle of flavored creamer.
"But I'd be careful with this. My wife says it's only a few
atoms away from being plastic."

"I like plastic in my coffee."

McKeckney poured the dark liquid into a mug and
handed it over. "You've had breakfast?"

SECDEF nodded and began doctoring his brew. "Mat-
tie couldn't sleep. She got up when I did." He checked
his watch and then parked his frame behind the desk.
"So—what's on the docket for today?"

The younger man could hear enthusiasm in Avery's
voice. McKeckney rifled through a few notes and then
selected the appropriate folder from one of the chairs.

"SECAF's not too happy," Cull began, referring to the
Secretary of the Air Force. He straightened his tie and
took a seat. "Neither is her chief of staff."

"Do you always start Fridays with bad news?" Avery
grinned and sipped from his mug. "And how have we
ruffled their feathers?"

"You rescinded an Air Force policy."

"I do that on occasion," the Secretary snorted. "Twice
this week, in fact."

McKeckney smiled. "You're on a roll, then."

Hanging on the wall behind Avery was a life-sized
portrait of Ronald Reagan, flanked by an equally impressive oil of George Patton. "Which policy are they carp-
ing about?"

"The one requiring NCOs to have a degree, for promotion to the next rank. SECAF thinks you're meddling."

A frown. "Did she say that?"

"Not in so many words."

Avery waved his hand. "She'll get over it. Zoomie leadership was using that as a force-shaping tool, ostensibly to reduce manpower in the Reserves. We're way past that now." The Secretary leaned back in his chair. "Most senior sergeants came up when high school diplomas were the norm. Prior service guys from other branches." He looked thoughtful. "Penalizing people with experience isn't the tone I want to set."

"You want to roll back the clock." He wasn't really asking, and there was a glint in McKeckney's eye.

"You were Army, Cull. I thought you'd appreciate that."

McKeckney had, in fact, served eight years, starting out as an infantryman and moving on to cannon cocker. His current employment was part of SECDEF's new program, designed to include veterans in government service. President Charles Cassidy had a similar initiative, quietly encouraging returning service members to consider politics at the local level as well as in Washington. Each recognized the managerial skills and work ethic fostered by the military, and as a result, a fresh crop of clear-eyed enthusiasts waited at the door, promising to revitalize both political parties.

Avery didn't wait for an answer, and offered a remark that was completely cliché. "There's a new sheriff in town now. And he wants to shore up the military, the same way Reagan did. As you know, SECAF was appointed by the previous administration."

McKeckney reflected on that. "And her father was a big donor to Mark Breese. I think I see the connection. Do you want to push the issue?"

SECDEF nodded. "A standard press release. Send it through DoD channels. The usual thing; how I'm pleased to ensure equal opportunity for our senior enlisted ranks. That'll play well with our friends across the aisle. Compliment SECAF's willingness to join in those efforts, and direct her to broadcast a similar message—with my endorsement."

"Draft by Monday?"

Avery's head wagged. "Timing is everything, Cull. I want it on her desk by close of business *today*. That way it flies under the radar, but it's still out there."

McKeckney made notes. "That might be embarrassing."

"But that's the point." Avery considered the woman a political hack, but kept that to himself. "She'll cool off over the weekend." He sipped his coffee, signaling an end to the discussion. "Anything else?"

"Eight-point covers. Some airmen don't like the current headwear."

"I don't either. Those things look like potato sacks," Avery chuckled. "Morale is one thing, but fashion's another; I'd rather talk about the Hellcat. Where's the prototype today?"

"Proto*types*," McKeckney gently corrected. "YF Alpha and Bravo arrived last night. They're over at Andrews, prepping for the air show next weekend."

"Schedule?" Avery asked.

"They'll be flying hops—*sorties*?" He wasn't sure if that was the correct term, "—all next week. Maximum exposure, up and down the coastline. The media will eat it up."

"They have been somewhat curious. By week's end our squadron out west will become common knowledge."

"Holloman?"

Avery answered with a nod. The base in New Mexico hosted four of the birds, parked on the same tarmac with jets from the German Defence Ministry. It wasn't widely known, but Luftwaffe pilots had trained there for years. It was believed that the presence of the Hellcat wouldn't raise any eyebrows.

"It's just as well, I suppose. We can't keep secrets forever. And if this airframe delivers as advertised, the American taxpayer—and our allies—will get quite the bang for their buck."

"Is that the driving consideration?"

Avery saw the cautious look on his face. "You want the speech?"

The younger man shrugged. "Might as well. You are getting pretty good at it."

"All right, Cull." Avery settled back in his chair and drew in a breath. "This country's coming off eight years of cut-backs and fiscal misery. We can counter that— with emerging technologies and a private sector hungry for expansion."

"Aileron Dynamix," McKeckney volunteered.

"Incorporated," Avery added. "They've chewed up the market share once dominated by MDI." He was al- luding to McBride Defense Industries; that contractor's heir apparent had squandered the government's trust by selling secrets to the Chinese. "Aileron's been build- ing relationships for years, and has an excellent rapport with a host of suppliers. And they're not re-inventing the wheel. It's smarter to utilize existing systems—to wrap those around your hardware. Keeps costs low so you can maximize your budget in other areas.

"That kind of thinking has also streamlined produc- tion. The F/A-38 Hellcat was airborne in less than three years. Her avionics and mechanical systems are nearly identical to an F-22, which makes it easier for the pilots and the airmen turning the wrenches."

McKeckney grinned at Avery's use of gender. "How is she in flight?"

"Very nimble, according to the reports. A tactical fighter suited for multiple roles; overwatch at sea, border surveillance, even non-linear warfare, with impressive sensor capabilities. The price tag is reasonable, too, and gives us affordable options. At $26 million per copy, it comes in way below the budget of a Raptor or an F-35."

"Are you thinking of replacing those platforms?"

He shook his head. "Those fighters are the backbone of western air interdiction. The need for proven systems isn't going away. But we can use the Hellcat to supplement our shortfalls, fill in the gaps left by the last administration's austerity measures."

"So the president's policies weren't all that bad, then. Is that what you're saying?"

"You can only spin that so far," he chuckled. "Mark Breese left a trail of broken promises. A crisis of confidence in the federal government. We have to restore faith, Cull, build trust again with the American people. That's been the president's plan since day one."

"The so-called Cassidy Mandate," McKeckney supplied. "What's next for the squadron?"

Avery shifted in his seat. "They've done very well in arid climates. The Joint Chiefs think they should be tested someplace else. I agree."

"Hickam, maybe, in Hawaii?" The American military's pivot toward the Pacific was well-known.

"That's definitely on the short list, but let's see how they do in a different environment, exposed to freezing temperatures and salt air."

"How about Alaska?" McKeckney's brow wrinkled. "They've got Eielson, but Elmendorf's closer to the sea."

"Elmendorf. It's an en route base." Avery thought it

over. "Elmendorf it is, then. We won't tell the flyboys that their tasking was just accomplished by a former artilleryman. Who's the squadron commander?"

"Chris Prentice, full bird colonel. He was the flight lead for RESILIENT EAGLE in Poland." He saw that register in SECDEF's eyes. "The colonel showed considerable restraint, too—managed to shoot down only one Russian pilot."

"That wasn't Colonel Prentice. His wingman was the one who splashed Ivan," Avery corrected with a smile.

"In any case," McKeckney went on, "The man flew twenty-one missions over Eastern Europe and then transitioned back to Nellis after the inauguration. Which brings us to the next topic."

"Lead on, McDuff."

"Polish missile defense." McKeckney referenced his list once more. "Construction on the last emplacement site is nearly complete. The first four are prepped and have power. The ordnance is crated and should be delivered by Tuesday."

"Full complement?" Avery asked.

"Sixteen rockets per battery."

The SECDEF muttered under his breath. "Russia won't be happy."

"The Russians enjoy being unhappy," McKeckney replied.

"Got an update on tensions in the region?"

"Moscow has backed down, and there appears to be two reasons for that. The first one's obvious. They've achieved their short-term goals in Ukraine. The second's a bit more intangible."

"I can't help but think they're up to no good," Avery growled. "But let me hazard a guess. It's all about deterrence. Poland has stood up to the neighborhood bully, and Ivan respects that. What's more, the Poles have added teeth to their resolve. A fully-functional missile shield can't be ignored."

"Your friend in counter-intelligence seems to agree with you," McKeckney said with a smile. He stood, retrieving a bottle of water from the fridge. "That's not to say that things haven't been a little frosty. Moscow, Kiev and Warsaw are haggling over natural gas shipments. Each concession they make is countered by an impasse. It would help tremendously if they could just agree on *price*." He sighed. "Am I in the weeds yet?"

"Keep going," the boss directed.

"Falling oil futures have put the squeeze on Russia, and their economy is spiraling in the wrong direction. At the current rate, inflation will spike at ten percent by the end of the quarter. Consumer prices are already in the double digits—and that doesn't bode well for the common man."

"It's already taken a toll," the Secretary said. He began ticking off a list of woes. "Stagnant growth. Reduced consumer demand; and wages and pensions haven't kept up. All of that makes for a potentially explosive situation."

"The Kremlin's still got the advantage." McKeckney wasn't ready to bury Mother Russia just yet. "They're using energy as a bargaining tool, leveraging resources against their neighbors in Eastern Europe."

"Happens every year," Avery shuddered. "Things got pretty bad last winter—riots in the streets, civil unrest. Ukraine hasn't forgotten that."

"Well, they do owe Moscow billions. Now the EU's gotten involved. They've offered long-term loans to Kiev, provided the central government uses that money to repay their debts."

Avery visibly winced. "That's a best-case scenario. Vast sums of cash flowing into that country presents its own set of problems; Pavlovsk has made tremendous reforms, but corruption's still rampant."

McKeckney agreed. "The man won't survive politically if something isn't done." He took a long sip. "The State Department thinks he'll get it right by the end of summer. That should get Russian gas flowing again and ease disruptions come October."

"It's late spring, Cull. Come winter—"

"Yes, sir, I know. The problem becomes more acute," McKeckney finished. "Poland can't help, and Hungary and Germany are hard-pressed too. They have their own problems. Ukraine needs fuel. Her citizens have to heat their homes—just like we do—and hot water's very important. Especially when you don't have it."

"We've discussed a few contingencies," Avery volunteered. "This problem has evolved into a national security concern. The president wants to make a goodwill gesture, sell a percentage of our surplus at a greatly discounted price—a *quid pro quo* gesture, I might add."

McKeckney's gleam returned. "While sticking a finger in the Kremlin's eye?"

"We have a few things on the table," Avery evaded. "Let's track west to the next trouble spot—and our fractious cousins in the not-so-United Kingdom."

"Ah, Scottish independence." A different folder now. "The polls are updated on the hour. It's a very big deal over there."

"It's a very big deal here, too, Cull," Avery grumped. "They tried this just a few years ago, and now it's back. Which way are they leaning?"

"The polls swing back and forth. I thought the Chinese were inscrutable; but the Scots—" He let that hang in the air, plucking a loose sheet from the binder. "The *Daily Mail* says the secessionists are gaining momentum, with fifty-one percent of the populace ready to vote yes. Most pundits agree that the tea leaves are somewhat difficult to read."

"For us, maybe. But it's hard to begrudge anybody a chance at freedom. A couple centuries ago we did the same thing."

"And broke away from merry old England?" McKeckney adopted a British accent. "That turned out rather well, wouldn't you say?"

"Two centuries have come and gone," the Secretary declared. "The passage of time has dulled our collective memory. We tend to forget the pain. Keep in mind that things were a little messy at first. Independence is like that, and it's usually preceded by something called *revolution*."

"So—broadly put, you're concerned with 10 Downing Street."

"And broadly put, you're correct," Avery came back. "The ramifications are enormous, and most people don't get that. My objections are purely selfish. Don't get me wrong; I applauded BREXIT. And I'm not a big fan of the EU, either. But from a military standpoint, it's a bad move." SECDEF's color darkened. "If the Scots get their way, the United Kingdom will suffer economically—and that could force Lord Mallory to step down."

"That's the part I'm a little fuzzy on," McKeckney admitted.

"Consider what happens if the secessionists rule the day," Avery began. "The Crown would lose between seven and nine percent of its taxable base. A lion's share of their oil revenues would go with it. Now suppose that Scotland decides not to honor its share of Great Britain's financial obligations. That would ramp up the debt-to-GDP ratio—which, in turn, would raise costs on just about everything else. See where I'm going with this? A classic domino effect. The economy constricts, and growth grinds to a halt. Ultimately, it all trickles down to the individual shop-keeper, the bobbie on the street, or the factory worker in Southampton—the people paying the government's salaries—and they might have something to say about that. The PM could be out of a job. And if that happens, the Brits will have to form a new government.

"In the long term, we'd have to sort through a disheveled ally's resources. Then come the other complications. The pro-independence group wants a nuclear-free Scotland. That means we have to figure out where to park our attack boats when it's time to rotate crews or do maintenance. There aren't a lot of options along their coastline. The port in Faslane is nearly irreplaceable—and we can't just bring them back to Kings Bay every time a part goes bad."

McKeckney waited for the Secretary to take a breath. "It's like a wool sweater; pull one loose strand and the whole thing begins to unravel."

"Not a bad analogy." Avery got out of his chair and moved toward the coffee. "They don't just live in neat little hedgerows across the border; Scottish citizens are intertwined with life on both sides. Many have civil service jobs, and there's no telling how many make up Her Majesty's armed forces."

"The UK was our best ally in Iraq and Afghanistan."

"And our alliances militarily are still just as crucial." The Secretary refilled his mug. "Intelligence-gathering is a shared responsibility. A government shake-up puts all our collaborative efforts in doubt, and restructuring who-does-what in a transition becomes dicey. Between us, we operate a joint base in Cyprus. What happens there?" Once more his head went from side to side. "Changing horses in mid-stream doesn't fill me with confidence."

McKeckney noted Avery's penchant for metaphors.

"Who-does-what goes hand in hand with who-gets-what—am I right?"

"Now you're catching on," SECDEF confirmed. "The new government in Edinburgh would want to retain some assets, things like tactical equipment, or a percentage of weaponry to shore up their forces. That diminishes the Brits' capabilities. And on paper, the Scots' military would resemble something out of the EU's playbook—a smaller defensive force, a lot like what we see in the northern Scandinavian countries."

"A blunt spear?"

"Simple, but accurate. They wouldn't be able to project force—not in the same way the UK of old did. And you can't overlook their nuclear arsenal. The Brits maintain a fleet of subs armed with Trident missiles. Those would face relocation, just like ours." He stirred his coffee and returned to the desk, eyeing the stack of folders next to his subordinate. "I'm hoping you've got better news in there."

"That's not unfounded. Congress has started working with the administration to craft laws for a change—promising, effective laws, I might add. The higher courts have been relatively quiet. They've been largely squeezed out of the equation."

"That's what happens when Congress finds common ground with a sitting president."

"There's good news on the domestic front," Cull put in. "Opening the pipeline from Canada has jump-started the economy. Employment out west is trending upward. Even ANWR's getting a strong look." The Alaskan National Wildlife Refuge held vast oil resources, but so far had been politically out of bounds. "Additionally, the president's reinvigorating the coal industry, reducing the EPA's footprint through executive action—"

"—and savvy legislators," Avery grinned.

McKeckney continued. "The environmentalists are screaming, but West Virginia's seeing a huge surge in jobs—and nobody's complaining about that."

"Ideologues rarely see the value of compromise. For that you need a politician. Not much point in going down that rabbit hole. Anything else in your bag of tricks?"

"Just this." The Army veteran produced a thin portfolio. He opened the cover to reveal a photo clipped inside. The image was familiar. "The Office of Personnel and Readiness finally got back to me. They're balking at the salary, but with a little English on the ball, I think we can get it through." He tilted his face to one side. "You think a lot of this kid, don't you?"

"I'll let you read his file sometime." It was another vague response.

Cull breezed through the contents. "Mad language skills. Could be useful, I guess."

"It's not just language. He's culturally savvy, too." Avery had a question. "Did you mention my name?"

McKeckney's head shook. "It's flagged as a simple DoD request, with no references to any specific office— but it's bound to come up sooner or later. Want me to go harder?"

Avery appeared indifferent. McKeckney knew better. "Let the process play out. No need giving the impression we're in a hurry. Any other objections?" ,

"They've got a Navy JAG advising them. He's nit-picking the job description—doesn't seem to like the title, either. Suggested we work in *for the office* instead of *to the office*. I agreed. Figured it was best to pick our battles wisely."

"Smart move. Any other pushback?"

"The JAG is also questioning the organizational hierarchy. Wants an additional layer in between."

"The Department of the Navy?" SECDEF grated out.

"Too restrictive. The buck stops here, Cull. The Department of Defense. Make sure they understand that."

"And if they resist?"

Avery offered a mischievous smile. "Cassidy owes me a favor or two. If need be, I'll request a presidential finding. Those are a little hard to turn down."

"What sort of timeline were you looking at?"

"Roughly a year, but I want to make the offer long before. The headhunters will be sniffing around—"

"—and you don't want to lose the opportunity."

"Hang on just a sec." SECDEF's phone buzzed on the desk. Avery picked it up and checked the display. After a moment's study, his expression soured.

"Cull—turn on the television."

McKeckney's hand went to his belt, where his own cell had begun to trill. He was up in an instant, crossing the floor. "I'm on it, Mr. Secretary."

He grabbed the remote and the plasma came to life. McKeckney toggled through the channels and found a news feed. The images displayed were disturbing; pitch black waters, calm as a mill pond, yet dotted with floating debris—much of it quite grisly—pierced by searching beams of light and a host of watercraft bobbing nearby. The crawl at the bottom of the screen was irritatingly slow, but its message was both predictable and familiar. The men were silent for a full twenty seconds, and Avery's first response was a mournful groan.

"Dear God," he muttered. "It's happened again."

• • • •

Plans would change in the next hour. Clearly the media was jumping through hoops, and the airlines would also be scrambling for details. At some point—sooner rather than later—the State Department would begin quietly working up scenarios while giving their full attention to the possibility of a terrorist attack.

There was no such thing as a typical Friday for the Secretary of Defense. Avery watched as the video looped through once more, soberly concluding that the aides charged with his schedule were about to earn their pay.

Sydney, eastern Australia

Her position was a fluke. Contingent on the board's whims. And her stake in the game depended on how well the professor used her waning influence and played politics.

In plain language, keeping this job was purely conditional.

She decided that contemplating career options was best left for another time. The hour was late, and the lights were burning bright in the University's science wing. The school's grounds covered the suburb of Camperdown, below Dawes Point and Darling Harbor, filling a niche near the coastline between the Coral Sea, to the north, and the Tasman, to the south. The campus itself was dotted with neo-gothic sandstone and brickwork, evoking images of Great Britain's Dartmouth and Cambridge colleges. Imposing structures in the quadrangle completed the staid but scholarly look.

There was a fourteen hour time difference between Sydney and Washington, D.C. It was already Saturday morning in this part of the world. Dr. Taylor Brisbane, titular head (how she *hated* that word) of the Applied Physics department, was in charge now. The previous department head—Dr. Price was the old man's name— had died months earlier, the victim of both a heart attack and a stroke. His unexpected departure left the big chair empty, and Brisbane was the logical choice to fill the seat. Eminently qualified and thoroughly tenured, the scientist had established her bona fides at a young age, and now, pushing thirty-eight, her climb to the top could hardly be ignored. All of that was based on hard work, cogent scientific analysis, and academic achievement.

And that in spite of her less admirable qualities.

It was Brisbane's lack of interpersonal abilities that threatened her career. People skills ranked low on the list comprising her impressive résumé. She was known for her forthright character, speaking empirically from established facts, with little regard for others' feelings or observing the niceties of cultivated and polite discourse. Her colleagues urged deference, but the good doctor, her intentions pure, found it difficult to hold her tongue.

Brisbane moved from one set of instruments to another. Each was tied to a monitor, parsing datum into categories that could be used to determine frequencies. None of these were technically receivers, *per se*. Those were downrange, in places like Mindanao, in the Philippines; Tokyo, in Japan; various shipboard platforms (the Australian Navy was very cooperative); Guam, and even Hawaii—although the emplacement site on Hilo was a little too distant to be reliable. Taylor had argued against that one; for one thing, it was on the wrong side of the mountains, and without a proper line-of-sight—

"I can't watch anymore, Doc." The voice came from Dr. Brisbane's research assistant, Bailee Russo. The television before her was alive with stark, contrasting images; bright lights, black water, and jolting camera angles that focused on the flotsam of tragedy.

"Nine News?" Brisbane sounded detached.

"Yeah." Bailee had an uncommon gift, and could wedge two syllables into a word designed for one. Such was the dialect of Oz. "And the first reports were right. It's near the Philippines."

The volume was low, barely registering, but Brisbane recognized the program's hosts. Reporters were called *presenters* in Australia, and newscasts were known as *bulletins*.

All of one hundred and five pounds, Bailee was ten years younger, with a bleach-blonde pixie cut and bangs that obscured the horn-rimmed readers perched on her nose. "Flight 778, bound from Luzon to Anchorage. Two hundred and sixty-nine souls." She didn't finish the sentence, and didn't have to. "The transponder went silent an hour after take-off—just like the plane that went down months ago."

"Any witnesses?"

The petite woman read the crawl and waited. "The crew of a cargo ship saw part of it—oh, *geez*! Now they're pulling more bodies out of the water." The limp torsos on the screen, most wearing life vests, and some obscenely twisted, belonged to civilians. Russo hid her eyes—before turning back again, overcome by curiosity. "Wouldn't they still be strapped in their seats?"

"You don't have to stare." Brisbane's accent was entrenched, but no less than Russo's. Emerald eyes flashed, and the Aussie's olive complexion became ruddy. She was scarlet-haired, with a smile that dazzled when she chose to share it. "I could use a little help establishing the waveguides."

Russo scanned two monitors at once. "Spectral peak confirmed by all stations. That was three hours ago."

"Same time that plane dropped into the sea," the doctor observed. "What's the spike-to-inferior noise ratio?"

The research assistant had a quick answer. Perky and cute—in a way the university boys loved—she was still clad mostly in pajamas. "Off the chart. And the boost in resonance is distinctive. Definitely not part of the background clutter." That bit of confirmation was only a formality.

Brisbane crowded into Russo's space and studied her monitor. "Ripples in the ELF band have completely dissipated." Not unusual. The phenomenon that had set off their instruments must have bounced around the globe. The ionosphere was a closed cavity, trapping waves of all types, but even one as powerful as this would eventually fade.

"There's nothing there, Doc," Russo answered. She cross-checked her equipment once more. "The signal's long-gone. It's easy-peasy now. All downhill—we wake up the servers at the remote locations and cross our fingers."

"You haven't done that yet?"

A sly grin, and Bailee brushed the hair from her eyes. "Oh, we're up and running. Just waiting for the software to tabulate the results."

Taylor smiled. For all her whimsy, Bailee knew her job, and could sometimes anticipate directives like a mind-reader.

Brisbane was drawn to the newscast, absorbing what she could of the faraway tragedy. Planes falling from cruising altitude rarely produced survivors, and presumably, every passenger aboard the doomed aircraft was now dead. It was a reasonable assumption. That outcome was painfully obvious, especially to the crews of the flotilla snatching wreckage and bodies from the water.

Broadcast live, the images on the screen mirrored those in Avery's office. The debris field littering the surface was largely filled with unidentifiable objects. Only the corpses of men, women, and children were recognizable. Still, hope found its way into the most unlikely of circumstances, and it would be several hours before the rescue operation shifted to something far more realistic.

• • • •

"Here it is, Doc."

A new display filled Russo's screen. Featured prominently was a map of the Bering Sea, bracketing a wide swath of the Pacific Rim and a stretch of ocean that included the coastline of the Kamchatka Peninsula. Bailee reached out a hand and stabbed the monitor with her finger. "And there's the point of origin."

Brisbane was silent. Her father's words echoed in her memory, taking her to a time before she was born, and to an event that was still classified by the governments of several nations. The mystery had haunted her for years.

Occasionally, her father would retell the story. Alton Brisbane gave her the standard line about accurate charts and safe passage, and how less than halfj of Australia's waters had been properly surveyed. It was necessary to send a mapping vessel, the *Canberra*, into the Indian Ocean, to scour the seafloor between Wharton Basin and the Broken Ridge, far afield of the Australian Current, on a line that followed the Tropic of Capricorn.

While the purpose was rational, there were questions. *Why had the ship wandered so far west?* Rumors persisted that the *Canberra* had sailed to Prince Edward Island, between South Africa and Antarctica. But those waters were not a part of the normal trade routes. Another story had it that the ship lost all power. There was no clear explanation, and at the time—and in the days since—the Australian Chief of Navy declined to comment.

The lack of transparency disturbed the leftenant's daughter. Delving into official records only added more frustration. Hearsay was rampant. Taylor became unconventional in her search for the truth. She poked her nose into some inconvenient corners, and when doors began closing, she knew she was getting close.

She brushed those thoughts aside and focused on the

present. Death had reached out its hand, cruelly wrenching two hundred and sixty-nine souls from the sky. The causative agent had appeared briefly and then vanished. Brisbane compared the effect to the aperture of a camera lens, filled with light before closing; or an eye that had opened and then snapped shut.

The facts pointed to only one conclusion. The normal function of the plane's avionics had been disrupted from an outside source. That was a game-changer. Someone had deployed a weapon of phenomenal power. The list of likely suspects was short, and Taylor Brisbane had a gnawing feeling about who that someone might be.

3

UNDERCURRENTS

Warsaw, Poland
Five days later

SHE WOULD HAVE PREFERRED a more residential address—Ursynow would have been a good choice—but the woman had taken a flat in the city's Praga district instead. While not the most desirable of neighborhoods, and once the poorest, that part of town was experiencing a revival of sorts, rejuvenated by clubs, bars, and restaurants, and quickly populated with an influx of musicians and writers—the culturists of the new eclectic. Split into northern and southern sections, this once-neglected warren was expanding, promising growth for the old city.

But the fiery journalist wasn't interested in Praga for its Bohemian attractions. Born in Kiev, she spoke Ukrainian, Russian, and French, and a sizeable percentage of the borough's residents were French-speaking expats with whom she could converse and blend in. The cozy nightlife was simply a plus, and the presence of her peers gave the reporter a certain anonymity.

One that she hoped would keep her alive.

Viktoriya Gavrilenko, now Viktoriya Turandot, had almost reached her second floor apartment, eyeing the well-lit corridors and peering around corners to get a sense of her surroundings. The carpet was new and the cove-ceiling overheads freshly painted. The wrought-iron heater at the far end of the hall was silent—although not so much during the winter months, when it had a tendency to rattle. Taken together, everything was as it should be. Nothing seemed amiss; no partially opened doors, no tell-tale movement, and certainly no strangers present to give the woman pause.

There was a mirror by the fire escape. Always conscious of appearance, Viktoriya glanced at her reflection. She was dressed for summer, dazzling in a floral skirt and bright red heels. But the look was different. Her crimson hair, a trademark during President Dobrogost's summit, was gone. Now she was strikingly blond. This, too, was a step toward obscurity.

Crossing the floor, the journalist tapped her earpiece and waited for a response.

"Clear."

Viktoriya smiled. The man's voice gave her comfort, and the simple reply was at once distinctive and familiar. Xander Voskov was somewhere in the building, moments away if needed, surveiling her movements with equipment that Viktoriya could only guess at.

Yuri Tereshenko would be close, as well. The senior sergeant was the other half of her protective detail. *Before* and *After* were their code-names, labels picked by Viktoriya herself. In public venues, one scouted ahead while the other trailed behind. And she had picked up on some of their terminology. The one in front walked 'point'. The man who followed had her 'six'. All of that to safeguard one woman's life; and so far, they had been very successful.

A second unit worked the night shift. At times they switched places. She couldn't be sure, but she was convinced that the two man teams shared rooms on the third floor, although they rarely surfaced. Viktoriya hadn't seen Yuri for days. Xander was even less visible, and had only shown his face that morning before fading into the background.

And what a face, she mused.

The man had an angular jaw, deep gray eyes and a hooked nose. His penetrating gaze could set her heart racing, and at the same time chill her very soul. Voskov's aloofness had put her off at first, until personal magnetism won the day, compelling her to draw near. And being close to him now was what she really wanted.

"Thirty minutes?"

"*Zhinka*!" Voskov cautioned. "This is no game. Have I not told you—"

Viktoriya cringed. Xander had warned her about using measurable units of time over an open channel. Even without a context, it might provide signals intelligence that could be mined for relevance.

"*Prosty minya.*" *Forgive me.* "Sometimes I forget."

"Have a care, woman."

Her tension eased. She could hear the bridled irritation, but his voice carried something else. The stony officer normally masked his feelings, but when it came to Viktoriya, he had only her best interests at heart.

The apartment didn't really belong to her. It was Voskov who paid for the flat—not directly, of course, and under an assumed name—and the rent was split between the American CIA and Ukraine's clandestine services. The collaboration was intended to offset expenses, and the return on investment was priceless.

Both East and West had benefited from her investigative reporting, and Viktoriya was well-compensated for her work. Her contacts helped gather intel that was crucial. The results were startling. Arkadi Murovanka, president of the Russian Federation, was toppled from power through the journalist's efforts, with Ivan Malyev also playing a role. Pairing the two created an unlikely combination—reporter and reformed terrorist, seeking the same end, and achieving a goal that was arguably beyond reach.

But the risks were undeniable.

Just last winter, before the New Year, two attempts were made on Viktoriya's life. Assassins on General Karpenko's payroll had been retained to kill the woman. The first was an amateur; the second, Ilya Maersk, was much more formidable, yet the outcome was the same. In both instances the Berkut had intervened, using their signature tradecraft. Voskov and his team had been there to stop them. Viktoriya was quickly spirited out of Ukraine, and Maersk and the other gunman were now dead.

Viktoriya removed her makeup and earpiece and headed for the shower. Hot water and soap were an afternoon ritual, and she used both to wash away the day's concerns. Fifteen minutes later she closed the valve and grabbed a towel.

She dried herself and pulled on a thick robe, a gift from Voskov. A mischievous smile appeared; it was much shorter than what she would have chosen. But that was what her protector had intended.

Standing before the bathroom mirror, Viktoriya regarded her reflection once again. The woman staring back was browned and vibrant. The sun was a good friend, a 'boon companion', she'd once written. Winter had been slow to loosen its grip this year, but with warmer weather, Viktoriya spent many afternoons outdoors. Warsaw's parks were perfect for crafting features, and she would happily perch on a bench for hours. The payoff was evident, and spring and summer were her favorite seasons of the year.

Drying her hair came next, followed by some blush for her cheeks and a touch of eyeliner. Her lips and lashes were naturally full, a trait passed down from her mother. She wanted to look her best, which wasn't difficult. The Ukrainian was blessed with an exotic appearance—many Eastern European women were—and with one more glance at the mirror, she bounded into the front room to check the door.

Viktoriya stared through the peephole. Xander wasn't there, and the hall beyond was empty. She'd given him plenty of time. He should be here by now. Occasionally he stopped by to give her an update or to share a meal. Of late, their time together had grown more intimate—and that was something both of them looked forward to.

She sighed. Maybe the man was simply being unpredictable, for security reasons. She found her cell and made a call, but that went directly to voicemail. A second attempt, with the same result.

Viktoriya waited ten minutes, looking at her email. On the third try, Voskov's grumbling tone came through loud and clear.

"Something has come up, *moya lyubov*."

Now she pouted. "Are you canceling our date?"

"A postponement. Until tomorrow."

"But we've seen so little of each other." Her disappointment was heavy.

"The price of doing business, *zhinka*. Have a little patience."

The call ended without goodbyes or sentiments, but that was Voskov's way. Tenderness was hardly a Berkut trademark. Viktoriya laid down her mobile and wore a wry grin. There would be no hearts and flowers in this relationship.

The two had certainly begun on an unconventional note. Muslim fanatics brought terror to the streets of Warsaw, and Viktoriya found herself in the thick of it. Xander had been there to protect her, shielding her body with his own. She was impressed and instantly smitten. His was a chivalrous act that spoke of honor. A more formal introduction came later, but that was contentious, to say the least.

She was reminded of the past. Beauty was a tool, one that Viktoriya used to get what she wanted and advance her career. She learned that some men—most men, in fact—could be easily manipulated, given the right influences. Coldly dispassionate, she was always in control of her emotions. Then she'd met Michael Neill, and her perspective was altered.

Michael was cut from a different cloth. Faith was a moral compass for the American Marine. Personal integrity guided his actions, so much so that he'd refused her bed. His gallant rejection of intimacy was somehow appealing to her; he was steadfast and unmoved by distraction (or nearly so) and those distinctions separated him from every other man she knew. She was loathe to admit it, but those were the qualities that had pulled her in, threatening to undo her objectivity.

Viktoriya was drawn to Xander in the same way. He, too, was sworn to duty. That spoke to his strength, and if she couldn't conquer him, she could at least respect his resolve.

Headquarters Marine Corps

Halfway around the world, the International Operations and Intelligence Office—Russian/Eastern European branch—had become a lonely place. Less than a week had passed, and Christina's absence was keenly felt. Neill missed her terribly; for professional reasons, of course, but deep down, the separation was personally unbalancing.

Normally cluttered with dispatches of raw data and CIA assessments, Christina's desk now had an empty look. The office was just too quiet, and it wasn't natural, the captain concluded. He was in a reflective mood. Six months earlier Neill had spent time at the Foreign Service Institute, immersed in Polish. Arrens had shouldered much of the daily responsibilities while he was gone. Now the tables had turned, and Neill could sympathize.

There was a television mounted on the wall next to the cubicle. The Marine stepped forward and powered it up. It was a poor substitute for his colleague, but he welcomed the company the flat-screen provided nonetheless. He leaned in and increased the volume.

"Of course, in the aftermath of this horrific tragedy, the investigation has shifted to forensics." The news anchor became somber, staring into the camera. "Our own Nash Allen is on location with more."

The image on the screen jumped to a waterfront in Quezon City, the Philippines. The view was split; a map on one side, a reporter on the other. In the background, ships and small boats filled the harbor. Nine News in Australia had done yeoman's work covering the crash, and over the past few days, the network had laid out an impressive timeline of events, complete with animation and graphics.

"That's correct, Roland." The man touched his earpiece. "Agencies from at least five separate nations have converged on Luzon, each bringing their own experts to piece together what happened to Flight 778. This follows the loss of the Borneo Air Transport plane, which crashed in the Bering Sea last March."

Neill noted each man's sedate tone. Roland's accent reflected the so-called Received Pronunciation heard in Great Britain. Nash Allen's voice was less refined, and more in the General category. Both brought a certain dignity to their speech, and their careful handling of the English language invited a viewer's attention.

Off-screen, Roland offered murmured agreement. "One hundred and eighteen deaths in that crash. Naturally there are questions regarding each accident. Have the authorities given you any explanation, any sense of what happened to cause these aircraft to fail in flight?"

Nash furrowed his brow. "There is widespread speculation here, but few answers. Much of the wreckage has been recovered, and more than ninety-five bodies have been accounted for. Representatives from the ICAO—the International Civil Aviation Organization—" he enunciated each word, relishing the opportunity to expand an acronym, "—have joined with the American-led National Transportation Safety Board to determine what happened to each airliner."

"And are those agencies cooperating?"

A nod. "The NTSB has assumed the lead in this inquiry. Of course, the U.S. is an ICAO council member state, and the plane was an American carrier."

"What can you tell us about the plane's final moments?"

Nash continued. "Radar indicates the plane began to descend, as if on final approach. At six thousand feet, she started to tumble—before cartwheeling into the sea."

The presenter in the studio broke in. "Was there any apparent structural damage as the plane lost altitude? Anything to suggest a mechanical failure?"

Nash shook his head. "Roland, witnesses aboard the

merchant vessel say 778's lights had already winked out. The crash site is one hundred kilometers north-east of the Philippines." The map now filled the screen, a large circle enclosing the recovery area. "At eleven p.m., it's naturally quite dark, and very difficult to see those kinds of details."

"What about radar?"

Yes. Neill sat on the corner of his desk. *What* about *radar*?

"Secondaries interrogated the plane's transponder as a matter of course—minutes before loss of radio contact. Just a routine handshake request at the next waypoint."

"For the benefit of viewers just tuning in, could you explain that terminology?"

Nash Allen was pleased to be of service. "Control sectors shift responsibility as aircraft transit from one zone to the next, Roland. They do so using a number of navigational aids—things like GPS, satellites, and radio beacons. Waypoints are connected by routing paths fixed in three-dimensional space. These become the reference coordinates used to determine position and destination." Nash gave a visible shrug. "The data collected at the last waypoint was normal. Altitude was correct, and nothing bounced back to suggest anything was awry."

"It's as if the plane lost all power." Roland's frustration went beyond simple theatrics; this was no attempt to gin up ratings. "Has there been any success in reaching the plane's black box?"

"The U.S. Navy's lending a hand." The reporter's mouth became a thin line. "But given the depth of the sea, investigators think it will be quite some time before that happens."

Neill muted the plasma and pulled up a chair, surfing a few websites. Notions explaining the crash—or attempting to—were abundant. Then came the conspiracy theories. Many of these were plausible, and most were grounded in the realm of possibility. Others were more far-fetched.

The conjecture ranged from other-worldly vortexes to anti-gravity particle beams. Chinese hackers and encounters with aliens were also popular concepts. Captain Neill dismissed the outrageous and searched for more conventional answers. The most likely scenarios were also the most reasoned, and fed Neill's own evolving suppositions. The media in most cases was not to be trusted. Resources available to the intelligence community were a big help, and after studying maps of the Pacific Rim, he had a working hypothesis that made sense.

He suspected malice, but a little confirmation was in order. He turned next to audio intercepts. Neill's methods were a bit unorthodox. On a day to day basis, much of his time was spent sifting through radio traffic—benign stuff mostly—eavesdropping on frequencies used by the Russian military. At-large broadcasts were collected by listening posts on land, at sea, and by satellites orbiting the Earth. Software screened out the unintelligible signals, preserving voice patterns and conversations that might net useful information. Ordinarily, the data would then be passed on to stations around the globe, where experts analyzed the feeds, interpreted their meaning, and then rendered their own judgments. This was the accepted practice.

Neill bypassed all that. He preferred to hear the intercepts without a filter. His understanding of the language (or languages) didn't come from a classroom environment. The son of American missionaries, Michael had been raised in Ukraine. He could pick out the nuanced differences in regional dialects, and recognize the subtle inflections of accent from one province to the next. Learning Ukrainian, Russian, and English—all at the same time—certainly had its advantages.

He had spent years monitoring Russian chatter and could identify half a dozen dispatchers from their voices alone. On rare occasions, a name would rise to the surface, and on very rare occasions, it might be repeated a second time. That was a breach of protocol, a lapse in operational security, and what happened next was always predictable.

The radio operator would catch the error, or more often than not be admonished by a superior (Neill's ears were always attuned to those conversations). Additional transmissions would then be clipped, with strict adherence to discipline pushing aside the sloppiness that had gone before. And since the crash of Flight 778, the very rare had occurred on two separate occasions.

The captain slipped on a pair of ear buds. He queued up the links for the last ninety-six hours and pulled out a lined pad. Collating software had digitized the transmissions and arranged them in chronological order, and while it was impossible to comb through each one, Neill relied on a system that focused on specific blocks of time.

He was making a leap of faith, and quite possibly prejudging the evidence. While the presumption of innocence was a guiding tenet of civil jurisprudence, that dog didn't hunt in the world of counter-intelligence. Expecting an adversary to misbehave was an analyst's bread and butter. On the other hand, convincing yourself that something was out of place meant that you'd eventually find it—even if it wasn't really there.

And in that, balance was everything.

Neill chose the hours right after the crash as a starting point. The beginning of an operator's day was the best time to eavesdrop. If the Russians were involved, there would be telltale chatter worth dissecting. But then Neill considered that Flight 778 had gone down at night.

He mulled that over. Not much point in monitoring that crew's broadcasts. They were, after all, the late shift for a reason, and not top drawer personnel.

He skipped around a bit and then jumped ahead to the morning shift. Clearly something was going on. Another jump, later in the same day. Both the high command and the admiralty—on the Kamchatka Peninsula, not surprisingly—had begun issuing directives. In some cases, Neill could hear tonal stresses. Excited voices. The broadcasts tried to impart orders without the standard reliance on coded phrasing.

An odd reference followed. Something from classical literature. Was it Greek? Roman? The captain wasn't sure. A very long pause, and then the traffic resumed. That was when the operators slipped up. Not once.

But *twice*. And then silence.

"You in bed, Dmitri?" Neill checked the clock. It was nine p.m. in Kiev.

There was a pause before Dmitri Yaroslav answered. "I find that to be a very personal question, Mischa," the officer teased. "And if I was the shameless type, I would offer a more colorful response."

"You're too much of a straight arrow for that," Neill told him. "Is this a secure line?"

"All of my phones are encrypted. How may I be of service?"

"I need a favor."

Ah, an opportunity—and that was not at all unexpected. Ukraine's clandestine services were good; the SSD had been listening to the same chatter, and now a counter-intelligence officer from a foreign nation—the United States, no less—was asking for help. Dmitri considered that. Even if it wasn't a *quid pro quo* request, the inquiry would be telling, and offer insight into what the

West did or didn't know. Yaroslav was inclined toward cooperation, and his friendship with Neill was just another inducement.

The major spoke again. "I'm listening."

Neill referred back to the notes on his pad. "I have a name. And a nationality."

"Ukrainian?"

"That's why I called you."

"What else?"

"Something that sounds like a code-word, or a project designation. I'd really appreciate the insight of Ukraine's foremost spook."

"Then I'll ask when I see him," Dmitri grinned. "You should know that flattery will not help you, *Mischa*."

"But it doesn't hurt."

"Of course not." He grabbed a pen. "Give me this name."

Neill supplied the information. He waited while the SSD agent wrote it down, and then repeated the presumed citizenship. It was a stretch, but the pertinent facts might help determine background. In a best-case scenario, they could possibly clinch it.

A new thought came to mind. "Have you found our mole yet?"

"We're closing in." Dmitri's next comment surprised the Marine. "I should tell you that I've been expecting your call."

"Oh?" Neill's response was laced with mild curiosity. "Is it your birthday?"

A soft laugh, but Yaroslav refused to take the bait. It was time to return to the subject at hand. "And the other term—this project designation?"

"Charybdis."

"*Kah-rib-diss*." The major sounded it out phonetically. A question followed, spoken very slowly. "Can you give me some context, Michael?"

"I'd prefer not to. Run everything through your database. If there's anything to it, the context should make itself apparent."

"And you're sure about this project's title?"

"You seem reluctant to repeat it," Neill observed.

Yaroslav wouldn't offer a comment. "I'll see what I can find, Michael. Call you tomorrow?"

"Sounds like a plan," Neill answered, and with that he ended the call.

4

THE ASSASSIN

"I CAN UNDERSTAND MRS. LENKOV'S CONFUSION," CULL McKeckney muttered, scowling at the report in his hand. "Malyev; Malyevo—Russian-sounding names, with only a one letter difference." There were others on the list as well. Some were familiar to him, but most were not.

Willis Avery smiled, peering at Cull from the other side of his desk.

"And what makes you think she was confused?" He shook his head. SECDEF wasn't buying that. "She's cagey, that one. Intrigued, maybe. But I doubt that old schoolteacher was confused."

Cull raised a brow, his eyes never leaving the memorandum. "Well, it appears that her instincts were correct."

"Doesn't surprise me," Avery replied. "She grew up in a different era. Stalin's purges were still fresh in the minds of most Russians, so she learned to test the waters very carefully."

"*Trust*—but verify," McKeckney injected.

"To borrow a phrase, yes. That was the way of things

back then," the Secretary added. "Soviet citizens accepted *nothing* at face value. Sloppiness got you an invitation to the gulags—or worse."

"What about the rest of the players?" Cull asked. "Eisenhower Gleeson; Sasha Kobrin, Andrei Ulyanov, Viktoriya Gav—Gavri—"

"*Gavrilenko,*" Willis finished for him. He rose from his chair for a better look at the file Cull held. "Is her photo attached?"

"It's not here."

Avery waved his hand. "Not important. Google the name when you go back to your office."

McKeckney pressed on. "All part of Captain Neill's universe, no doubt. I realize I'm no Richard Aultman—" the boss winced at the mention of that name, "—but it might help if you brought me up to speed."

Avery drew in some air and leaned back. "All right," he began slowly, with a heavy dose of sarcasm, "For the benefit of all the *late-comers* in the room, let's review.

"Michael Neill you know. Three years ago, the good captain—" a pause, "—he was a lieutenant then—was tasked with verifying the disarmament of some leftover nukes. The collection point for those weapons was a certain port city in Eastern Europe."

Cull had a knowing grin. "Odessa? In Ukraine?"

Avery responded with a frown and another wave of the hand. "I can neither confirm nor deny that—short of a presidential declassification."

"Go on."

"Should have been routine—but you can never make those kinds of assumptions in the former Soviet Union."

Now it was the younger man who was intrigued. The story had all the earmarks of a spy novel, and Avery had just started.

"Things got a little dicey," the Secretary continued.

"We hadn't counted on Ivan Malyev and Sasha Kobrin—Russian terrorists bent on . . . *disrupting* the social order." Avery shifted in his chair. "And that's putting things mildly."

"Does this have anything to do with Russia's president, Arkadi Murovanka?"

A nod. "Then-president Murovanka longed for the old days. Still does, by most accounts. Anyway, he employed some rather shady tactics, trying to force the Republics back into the Federation's sphere of influence."

"And Ivan and Sasha; I take it they were part of that plan."

"Until Michael Neill happened along," Avery supplied. "Kobrin was killed—shot from the sky by Russian commandos—but Malyev survived the attack. Of course, his reaction to that was somewhat predictable." A dark expression crossed his face. "But Captain Neill managed to persuade Ivan to stand down and play ball with us."

"I imagine that's a long story."

"Indeed it is. Suffice it to say that he's been helping us ever since—*without* the Russians knowing about it."

"Until now," the younger man offered.

Another nod. "The Russians thought Ivan was dead. But recent events would seem to cast some doubt on that assessment."

Cull glanced back at the report. "And Eisenhower Gleeson?"

"Ike's the CIA's case officer. Helped us recruit Natasha Lenkov, someone to nursemaid Ivan along, teach him the language, ease his transition to life in the West—and keep a watchful eye on him."

"And Viktoriya? The report says she's a journalist."

"Viktoriya was instrumental in helping the CIA build a case against the Russians. She had contacts in Ukraine, and used them to trace a lot of the evidence back to Murovanka."

"*And* General Karpenko?"

"That's right."

McKeckney caught on fast. "Malyev turned on his handlers, is that it?"

"In a nutshell," Avery answered. "It helped that Viktoriya asked all the right questions." He became thoughtful. "It would seem that reporters and intelligence officers are cut from the same cloth."

"Elderly Russian schoolteachers, too," Cull grinned. "Didn't take Mrs. Lenkov long to bring this to the CIA's attention."

"That's what she's been instructed to do," Avery shrugged. "Igor Malyevo was taken in by her age. He didn't expect she'd have a mind like a steel trap."

"That's not his real name," McKeckney said, referring back to the sheet. "Well, it's *half* right; the FBI ID'ed him as Igor Nemesh. He's been under surveillance for the past eight months."

"The reason?"

"Suspected ties to the Russian mafia. They're big up in Virginia, the Fort Lee community." Another glance at the intel. "Interpol tipped us off. And given Igor's background, Gleeson thinks he's here to kill Ivan Malyev."

"That's where my money is." Avery's face became a smirk. "By the way, his name's Orlov now."

McKeckney rolled his eyes. "Good Lord, how do you keep all these people straight?"

The Secretary laughed aloud. "Takes practice. Let's get back to Igor; how'd he get here?" Avery asked.

"Came across the border from Canada—with a bogus passport. Customs and Border Patrol could have nabbed him then, but figured he might lead them to bigger fish." McKeckney considered that. "It's all a game, isn't it?"

The boss frowned. "Come again?"

Cull shifted in his seat. "The Russians. The Ukrainians. It's all part of the game, and even after the fall of the old Soviet system, they're still playing it."

"Well, we both know things haven't changed much. Old habits die hard." Avery checked his phone. "What time does this op kick off?"

The younger man's eyes tracked to the clock above Avery's head. "Thirty minutes. Nemesh thinks Mrs. Lenkov has arranged a little get-together to probe ancestral ties."

"A good cover," Avery acknowledged. "Where's this meeting taking place?"

"Jefferson Memorial. A public location, out in the open. Mr. Gleeson's the agent-in-charge, with DC Metro providing back-up."

"Good. Then let's reel this punk in."

Cull teased a suspicion in the back of his mind, one that found a voice. "Gavrilenko and Neill; each is Ukrainian by birth. Both are young, and by all accounts very bright." He leveled his eyes on the boss. "Do those two share more than just a common language?"

Avery mumbled something about international relations before rising from his chair. He stretched, thoughts racing back to Warsaw, and his stance was oddly similar to the one struck by General Patton in the painting behind his desk.

• • • •

North of the Washington Channel

Nemesh/Malyevo's cell chirped as he steered west onto D Street. The assassin plucked the phone from his belt and read the display.

Change of plan. Meet at the Westmont Suites. There's

a cafe, ground level, near the Waterfront Metro station on M Street. Do you know the place?

Igor smirked. This was not unexpected. The dossier provided by General Karpenko's staff described Ivan as a master of tradecraft, well-versed in keeping pursuers guessing. Switching locations was something Nemesh would have done had he been in Malyev's shoes.

He wheeled the car south—it was a late-model sedan—and headed toward his new destination. He was driving into the mid-morning sun, and a quick glance in the rearview revealed no tails or suspicious behavior among passersby. The Russian needed to get close to Malyev in order to carry out his mission, and so far there was nothing to indicate that he was being watched.

Igor kept a garrote under the seat, a tool of the assassins' trade, but as he approached the Westmont it became obvious that he wouldn't be able to use it here. As effective as it was, the garrote was best suited for missions where stealth was critical, and an open air bistro didn't fit that bill. Too many witnesses, and a murder in such a setting could hardly be mistaken for anything less than an intentional and heinous crime.

He made another left and recognized the place immediately. An outdoor cafe, with uniformly spaced tables that stretched the length of the patio. A broad awning skirted the building's facade, sheltering customers from the sun or inclement weather, and there, seated at the far corner, were the two people he'd come here to meet.

And to kill.

The woman in the overwatch position surveiled the scene from across the street. Sharp-eyed and alert, Special Agent Denise Gustafson—a Marine Corps veteran—had a direct line of sight with her charges and every approach leading up to the Russian couple.

Agents of the CIA now had the advantage. This new rendezvous point was a last minute alteration, intended to throw Nemesh off his game, and the flat Gustafson held was scouted days earlier, all part of a contingency that gave law enforcement teams the upper hand.

"CRAFTSMAN's in sight," Gustafson spoke aloud. The tall, black woman's hand went to the sidearm concealed beneath her jacket. "Rolling in from the west."

"Got him." A score of voices came from the earwig Denise wore. One belonged to Ike Gleeson, and she recognized the small talk of the two down in the cafe.

"Stay focused." Gustafson watched as Nemesh motored closer, slowing as he approached the corner. "He's going to turn, people."

She was right. The assassin edged toward the next street, his head never turning, showing no interest at all in those he intended to harm. He sensed the targets nearby. Mrs. Lenkov wore a scarf and sunglasses; Ivan Malyev's head was covered by a hat with a narrow brim. They faced each other, directing their eyes away from the street.

"Where's he going?" The voice came from the woman seated with Malyev.

"There's no place to park," Gustafson replied evenly. "He'll circle around, maybe find a spot near the alley. Team Two?"

"In my sights, MOTHER HEN." There was silence, followed by muted chuckles.

Gustafson squinted. "Something funny, IVANHOE?"

"Negative, boss." A pause. "CRAFTSMAN is tapping his brakes—just turned, headed north, coming back to your vantage point."

"He didn't park?"

"No, ma'am."

That was odd. "No vacancies?" Denise asked.

"Plenty of vacancies. He rolled past all of 'em.'"

"Roger that," the woman answered. She looked below, reacquiring the target. "Everybody stay sharp. Either he's hoping for an open space in front—"

Another possibility came to mind, and her blood ran cold.

The assassin angled the car carefully toward the crosswalk. His marks were right where he'd left them, seated at their table sipping icewater.

Nemesh sized up the obstacles that lay in his path. He could determine only one; the corner jutted out from the lane of horizontal parking spaces, presenting a barrier that would impede the car's progress. But the Russian judged that with enough acceleration he could jump the curb, careen from the street onto the sidewalk, and smash the vehicle into the unsuspecting customers.

Timing was critical; Igor needed to gun the engine, but doing so too early would draw unwanted attention and only serve to warn his targets. Waiting too long could also be fatal to his plan, reducing the chance of building up the required speed, and in this instance, speed was most certainly required for a successful outcome.

Ultimately, Igor relied on instinct. Coasting past the Westmont's entrance, he gripped the wheel and pressed his foot hard against the accelerator, white-knuckled as the car surged forward.

Denise Gustafson sensed Igor's murderous intent just seconds before he stood on the gas pedal.

"*Abort!*" she ordered. "All teams, *abort!*"

In the street below, the sedan's engine roared as it barreled toward the corner. Igor had never pushed the vehicle so hard, and the fuel seemed to catch in the lines, unaccustomed to the demands being placed on the aging motor that rumbled under the hood. At the last instant, Igor turned sharply to the right. The front end bounced as the sedan hopped the curb, sending the Russian forward, where he smacked his head against the steering column, splitting the skin at the hairline.

Everything happened in an instant. Even as the blood began to run, Nemesh could feel the patio table crumple as it was crushed beneath the axles. The Russian thought he heard screams. Customers who had been enjoying the spring weather jumped to their feet, stumbling, falling, and diving clear of the juggernaut that slammed through the Westmont's plate glass window.

But what of his mission? Had he succeeded in wielding the car as a weapon—killing the treasonous expats who had turned on the *Rodina*?

"*Hands on the wheel*!"

The voice was muffled. Igor blinked, turning to his left.

Mrs. Lenkov?

Nemesh was staring into the muzzle of a semi-automatic pistol. The woman with the gun held a passing resemblance to the old schoolteacher—until she reached up and pulled the sunglasses and wig from her head.

'Ivan Malyev' was also an imposter; the spry young man who easily avoided the advancing sedan stood off to one side, in front of the windscreen. He'd also drawn a sidearm, and leveled the business end of the weapon at Igor's chest.

Even in his addled state, things were now becoming clear to the Russian.

He'd been had.

But Igor was determined not to be taken alive. And maybe he could wreak a little havoc before he went—

• • • •

The female agent was tense but calm. Drawing a bead on the car's driver, she could see a hand slip into his jacket, a fluid movement that could only mean one thing.

"Don't do it!" she ordered.

Too late.

Nemesh tried to withdraw the gun concealed in his clothing. The pistol never cleared his coat. 'Mrs. Lenkov' opened up, two rounds in succession, followed by two more. Igor's eyes went wide as the window was punctured, the glass shattering in a way that obscured the agents' view of their would-be killer.

"Why?" The agent's hands were shaking. "He couldn't hope to escape."

Denise tossed a glance at the crosswalk. "There's an alley back there. He probably thought he could bolt from the car and just slip away." She smiled. "And remember, he wasn't expecting to go up against armed agents."

A dark suited man flashed his credentials and passed through. He received deferential nods from the first responders and was allowed a closer look.

"Nice shooting, Vasquez." Ike Gleeson peered into the car, his praise seemingly out of place. The agent's marksmanship was impeccable—a nice grouping, drilled right through the Russian's forehead. There was blood, but most of that was a result of Igor's impact with the steering wheel.

The assassin wasn't the only casualty. Falling glass and debris injured two customers inside. Four people were hurt in the scramble to escape the vehicle as it leapt across the sidewalk.

Fortunately, no one else was killed.

Gleeson shook his head, surveying the damage. The look on his face was somewhat mournful.

It didn't have to end this way.

Agents of the CIA and Metro Police encircled the crime scene, policing brass and taking photos and measurements of the skid marks left by the car. Within an hour they had confirmed that Nemesh/Malyevo intended to kill both Lenkov and her student—a manila envelope beneath the car seat contained glossies of both Russian *émigrés*.

This crime scene would bring Gustafson back to Nemesh's apartment. It would take another few days of digging, but as the lead investigator, she would find evidence confirming the Russian's ties to organized crime. Before they finished scouring Igor's flat, her detail would uncover another image, this one in full color, the photo taken in resplendent surroundings. The setting had the appearance of a European ballroom, and the subject was a woman of striking beauty, her gown giving every agent pause.

They didn't have her name—at least not yet—but she became known among Gustafson's team as the woman in red.

5

SHOOTING FROM THE HIP

Headquarters Marine Corps

A LOT WAS EXPECTED from the career planner's office. Most days were filled with difficult options. The specialists holding the billet were charged with recruitment and retention, and it was the latter of the two that sometimes made for hard choices.

As one of the smallest branches of the American military, the majority of Marines were under the age of twenty-five—and that was just the way senior leadership liked it. An infantryman over thirty was practically an old man. Breaking down doors and blowing stuff up was a vocation for the young, so one-term enlistees—and occasionally the ultra-fit second-termers—were the preferred choice for membership. The Corps saw it as their duty to produce Marines who would serve their country well, and then live out their civilian lives as good citizens. And they were good at it.

There was always the need for those with maturity to assume supervisory roles. A smaller percentage of Marines made up the NCO and Staff NCO ranks, and only the cream of the crop reached that level. The Corps identified hard-chargers early on and cultivated them for greater responsibility. High standards ensured the best leadership, and there was room at the top for only a few.

That was exactly where men like Master Gunnery Sergeant Owen Etheridge came in. It was his job to advise those with potential and channel them into an ever-narrowing chute of opportunity. Etheridge and career advisors like him grew the Corps by winnowing its ranks; herding qualified applicants upward to fill needed slots. The master gunny had developed a discerning eye for spotting exceptional aptitude. It was his responsibility to strike a balance between supplying the needs of the Corps and enhancing and nurturing the careers of men and women who re-enlisted—without letting talented individuals slip through the cracks. He did that in a variety of ways; using tests, interviews, recommendations from an individual's chain of command—and of course, his own gut feelings and instincts.

His practice of passing judgment on the character qualities of Marines started at an early age. Etheridge had grown up in the low country of South Carolina and was steeped in the culture of the Corps. The son of a Baptist preacher, the master gunny had grown up in a modest home between the Marine Corps Air Station in Beaufort and the Recruit Training Depot at Parris Island. He had always admired the way most Marines carried themselves; firm but fair, stoic at times, and uncompromising in their commitment to their core values. Etheridge wasn't completely naïve, though. Every barrel had a few bad apples, and he'd seen his share of those who didn't embrace that heritage. He also took note that for those, their time in the Corps was usually short. And that stuck with him.

It was his parents' upbringing that imparted a deeply-felt integrity in the man. His family's work ethic had left a mark. Owen's mother was a cook revered in the black community for her take on southern cuisine. By the time Owen graduated from high school, the family had taken a step of faith and bought a small diner, and now, nearly thirty years later, his mother and father—with a lot of help from the master gunny's siblings—owned and operated three restaurants that dotted the South Carolina coastline. One of the food networks had featured the chain on their broadcasts, and with a glowing endorsement, business was booming.

Ain't nobody can cook like a woman from the south, Mama Etheridge was fond of saying. The slogan had found its way onto the chain's menus, and over the doors of each establishment. Etheridge smiled at the memory. He kept a calendar by his desk, and looked forward to the day sixteen months from now when he would retire. He planned to return home to take his place helping his brothers and sisters in managing the operation.

It had been a good run. Owen took great satisfaction in knowing that he would leave the Corps in better shape than he'd found it, and a share of that credit rested on the efforts of senior enlisted men—and women—like himself. He thought back to the years he'd spent in his primary MOS, his military occupational specialty, and the work he had accomplished in this office. More than a few jarheads had benefited from his experiences, and mentoring gave him insights that he hoped to carry with him into his next stage of life.

Etheridge left his office and moved down the hall. The IOI shop was just around the corner; the first cubicle there belonged to Staff Sergeant Arrens, but the chair was empty, and the desktop monitor was dark.

"That's gonna take some getting used to."

Neill glanced up. The senior NCO had eased into the

room and leaned against the door frame.

"Come on in. I could use the company."

Etheridge found his way behind the desk and planted himself. "You have that look on your face, Cap'n."

Neill blinked. "That look?"

"Like a pit bull with a soup bone. Would you like to share a few thoughts?"

Neill relaxed and tossed aside the ear buds. "It's just some new intel. Chatter being passed around between the Russian mainland and Kamchatka."

"Does it have anything to do with that plane crash?"

The captain nodded, leaning back in his chair. "It might. I've reached out to someone in Ukraine's security services. The intercepts I've heard suggest a possible link."

A frown. "To Ukraine?"

"I've asked the SSD to shake a few trees. We'll see what falls out."

"How are the Russians involved?"

"That's not clear," Neill answered. "Their networks came alive right after the crash. Now they've dried up. I'm a little suspicious, given the amount of chatter. Could be they're just interested. Either that—"

"—or they're somehow responsible," Etheridge finished. "What's the connection? And why would the Russians risk an international incident by downing a passenger plane? You're too young to remember, Captain, but they did that back when Reagan was president. Things didn't turn out so well."

"I can't see a logical rationale, either," the officer admitted. "But Moscow gets squirrely sometimes. A tendency toward specific behaviors, especially when they're trying to overcome setbacks."

"What types of behaviors?"

"Think back. A few years ago Ukraine was edging

closer to NATO. They were also ready to strike a deal with the EU. And on the world stage, more and more European nations were cozying up to the West. Remember how Russia responded?"

Etheridge didn't hesitate. "They invaded. Took the Crimea and gobbled up big chunks of eastern Ukraine."

"Consider the present. What kind of pressure is the Kremlin facing now?"

The master gunny's brow arched. "Poland's missile shield is nearly functional, for one thing. And falling oil prices are pushing Russia's economy toward recession. How am I doing?"

"You've been paying attention. Keep it up and Sergeant Arrens could be out of a job," Neill grinned. "Now expand on that."

Etheridge's face became a scowl. "Okay, I'll go out on a limb. Let's get back to your line of reasoning. You said they exhibit certain behaviors. The most recent example is their land-grab in the Crimean Peninsula. Are you suggesting the Russians want to invade somewhere else?"

Neill looked pleased. "That was Peter the Great's strategy. Acquiring territory to expand his empire. Murovanka, Karpenko and Rurik have seen one setback after another. They've been squeezed. I think they might be squeezing back."

"Like they did in Kiev?"

The captain blinked. "You slipped that in without missing a beat."

"You're not an operator, Cap'n. Technically you belong here in this office."

"Every Marine's a rifleman, Master Guns," Neill replied. "I cut my teeth in the field."

"In some rather unorthodox ways." Etheridge's expression was now blank. "The C.O.'s still not happy about Ukraine. You could have been killed."

"Colonel Terryton reminds me of that on a regular basis."

Etheridge dismissed the comment. "He cares about you, kid. We all do."

"Don't get sappy on me, Master Guns," Neill teased. "Now where were we?"

"We were discussing a potential invasion. And I was about to say how unlikely that seems."

"But that's what the Ukrainians thought," Neill began. "Look, the Russians don't always play it smart. Calculated moves work well in chess, but this is different. Sometimes Moscow shoots from the hip. They might try a political solution, but the old guard likes to bludgeon their way through problems." He took a breath and let that soak in. "Think about what they gained in Crimea. Territory and military installations, including the naval base at Sevastopol. The population in the east is largely ethnic Russian, so they've got support from the people. Expanding west, things get a little dicier, but they *could* seize Odessa—if they have the political will. From there it's just a hop, skip and a jump to the interior, where the bulk of Ukraine's resources lie."

"But their biggest problem isn't territory," Etheridge said. "It's fuel. They've got lots of it—"

"Do they?"

The big black man wasn't prepared to be challenged on that point. "Well," he recovered, "that's what the CIA keeps telling us. Do you know something different?"

Neill was guarded. "I have a theory. But since it runs counter to recent assessments, I'll hold off on sharing it. You were saying?"

"Fuel. Yeah," Etheridge muttered. "Okay, let's say they've got lots of it, just for argument's sake. But it isn't fetching the prices it once did. Fracking in the U.S. is reducing our dependency on the Middle East. The oil producing nations are reeling."

"Makes for a lively discussion, doesn't it?"

"That it does," the master gunny agreed. "But that's not the reason I'm here." He handed a folded slip of paper to the captain.

"What's this?"

"An email from your other boss. The one at the Pentagon."

Neill read the first line. "Secretary Avery?"

"He's requesting a meeting. Friday morning, his office. And no uniforms, just civvies."

"Who's invited?"

"Good grief, but if you aren't full of questions," he assailed with a grin. "The colonel's on TDY in Germany. Arrens is soakin' up the sun in Hawaii. So it's just you and me—and Lieutenant Crockett."

"Nate?" The thought of seeing the sniper again was a happy one, and Neill absorbed the rest of the message. "He's in Lejeune."

"That was Mr. Avery's call. Crockett's flying in tonight." Etheridge drew in a breath and asked calmly, "How's he doin', by the way? After Warsaw, I mean."

"He's exorcising his demons," Neill replied. *Both of us are*, he didn't add.

Etheridge detected an edge in the officer's voice, and silently gave him credit for wanting to protect his friend. Nathan Crockett had been at Neill's side on the Chinese-controlled island of Huo Shan, but that wasn't his last rodeo. In Poland, the lieutenant's role was to add an additional layer of security to a very delicate diplomatic mission. Between the two Marines—three, counting Christina Arrens—they had helped to blunt an aggressive Russian push against Central and Eastern Europe.

But their efforts weren't without a considerable degree of loss.

Neill felt true remorse over Richard Aultman's death, and not just the regret that came from grief or heartache. Since Ilya Maersk had shot Avery's assistant, Neill's pain had been replaced with guilt. What he'd told Christina was the truth—he had been the officer in charge. It was his responsibility to ensure the safety of those around him, and in that, the Marine had experienced his first major failure.

He and Crockett were riflemen. Despite his stint in the Army, Richard Aultman was not. He never should have stood in Maersk's path. Nothing could have prepared him to face one of Russia's most lethal assassins. Michael should have insisted that Aultman stay by Avery's side.

Had he misjudged that situation? The short answer was *yes*. The young officer had made a critical error in assessing the outcome of that night's conflict—and a man's life was forfeit as a result.

There were times when the anguish over Richard's death stole his focus. Those instances were never more real than when he sat in this office, his mind wandering after hours of inactivity and analysis. That truth was revealing in itself; Neill had grown dependent on field work, where the constant shift between tangible needs and changing conditions dulled the boredom of a desk job.

But hindsight would always be 20/20 when you sat on your backside. Neill breathed a heavy sigh and tried to clear his head, attempting to shake off the past and the things he couldn't change.

He returned to the subject at hand. There were two other names on the missive. American, or possibly British by the looks of them. Neill recognized neither, and there was nothing to indicate their fields of expertise. He put those out of his mind and checked his inbox.

The officer had even more questions now.

"Why wasn't I copied on this?"

"Operational security," came the answer. "Don't get your tinsel in a tizzy, Cap'n. You're too old to pout. This stuff is need to know—and now you do."

"Not everything," Neill ventured. His default setting was to probe. "Guess I'll just have to wait till Friday."

"Yes, sir. I guess you will."

Ordinarily an intuitive individual, Etheridge couldn't guess at the turmoil in the younger man's heart. Had he known, the master gunny might have tried to ease his torment. Neill had been noticeably stern of late and hadn't opened up to anyone. For his part, the senior NCO wasn't above keeping a few secrets himself. The captain had the rank, but Etheridge had the authority, and sometimes you just had to let these kids know who was boss.

• • • •

Neill held the cell in front of his face, the fading dusk quickly yielding to twilight. "Can you check on something for me?"

Nearly five thousand miles distant, General Andrei Ulyanov stirred from sleep and growled into the phone.

"Do you know what time it is, little Michael?"

"What—the sun's not up yet?"

Andrei muttered something about impertinent Americans, which was only partly true. Michael let it slide.

"Is this personal or business?" The general ran a hand across his face, stifling a yawn. "For anyone else—"

"I know, you'd tell me to call back tomorrow," the Marine gloated. "Let's just call this a favor."

Andrei grumbled again. "Tell me what you need."

Neill did, chiding himself for not calling from a more secure line. He spoke in Ukrainian. After a few minutes, the general grunted a reply, recording the Marine's request on a pad he kept on the nightstand.

"I'll have to call in a few favors," Ulyanov reflected. Lying next to him, Irina turned on her side, annoyed by her husband's late-night conversation "What you ask is no simple thing. Why don't you just talk to Dmitri?"

"I've already got him working on something else."

"At least you're honest," Andrei grinned. "Anything else?"

"That should do it," Neill told him.

"You're going to owe me for this," the senior officer told him.

"Just put it on my bill." And as he said it, his tone reminded both men of Michael's father.

6

MISSION PARAMETERS

Aboard the USS Meyer

"**S**HE'S STILL WITHIN SIGHT." Captain Robert Beacham gripped the field glasses and studied the wide expanse. To the north, the gray hull of a Russian ship raced along the horizon, breaking the line between sea and sky. "Care for a look?"

Senior Chief Petty Officer Malcolm Richey took the binoculars and dialed the focus wheel. In the distance, moonlight graced the Russian's hull, making it stand out from the surrounding sea. Both ships matched speed, but Beacham's penchant for acceleration would kick in soon, and the *Meyer* would begin to outpace the foreigner.

"Intel says she's the *Belousov*, a salvage platform."

"Roger that," Beacham returned. "She's been nosin' around for days. Sweeping with active sonar."

Richey lowered the optics. "What's she looking for?"

"No clue. But she's after something."

"What about that other contact? That research vessel—what's it called?"

Beacham was quick to reply. "The *Pont Claire*. She's due north, making for the Commander Islands."

"Think there's a connection?"

"Not likely. The research boat's probably looking for oil. The *Belousov*? Well, your guess is as good as mine." The captain sized up his counterpart as they stood on the bridge wing. "You losin' more weight, Senior Chief?"

"Some," Richey mumbled. With a square jaw and a salt and pepper flat top, he stood a bit taller, pulling in his gut. "Almost twenty pounds now."

"I could stand to drop a few." The captain turned his head, facing the bridge. "*Mis*-ter Callahan!" he barked.

"*Aye*, Captain!" The ensign standing amidships kept his eyes forward.

"Instruct the Officer of the Watch to signal the Russian. Advise them that we are turning south—and wish them fair winds and following seas."

"Professional courtesy?" Malcolm asked.

"They might be our enemies, but that doesn't mean we can't be nice."

Ensign Callahan bellowed another *aye*. "Officer of the Watch, raise the starboard contact." To Beacham he asked, "Standard Russian, Cap'n?" There were several crewmen aboard who spoke the language.

"English, Mr. Callahan," Beacham called out. "Make him work for it." He flashed Richey a grin. "We don't have to be *too* nice."

The ensign repeated Beacham's order. "What course shall I set, sir?"

"Make your course two-one-zero, Mister."

"Aye, sir, making my course two-one-zero."

"New orders?" Malcolm asked.

The captain nodded, waving a hand toward the *Belousov*. "We're giving Ivan a little breathing room. Maybe he'll tip his hand."

Richey's eyes crinkled. "We could point BABYBLUE his way. Paint the hull for a look-see."

The captain considered it. "Not yet. That contractor from Aileron Dynamix is still calibrating the operating system. Let's wait till he sounds the all clear." Another grin. "Lieutenant Chau seems enthused with the hardware."

"He's all about it," the senior chief agreed. "It's nice to have him back aboard."

Beacham grunted. He'd insisted on having Simon Chau present for BABYBLUE's shakedown. The technicians from Aileron were extremely proficient, but contractors knew which side their bread was buttered on. Most were apologists for the whiz-bang science they shilled, and had a tendency to whitewash system glitches, minimizing problems until the lab geeks could flesh out solutions. But not Simon Chau. The former Chinese national was practically a savant, and could see through the smoke and mirrors foisted by those intent on delivering a payday for their employers.

"Might be worth it," Malcolm continued. "We'd find out pretty quick if the Russians can detect its usage."

"Aileron claims that they *can't*," the captain told him. "But who knows what the tech looks like on their side of the fence." He dismissed the thought. "We'll get our chance. Right now, CINCPAC wants us to provide material assistance. Recovery efforts in the Philippine Sea."

"That plane?"

"That plane's black box," Beacham said. He lowered his voice. "The temperature in the room's changed over the past few days, Malcolm. SECNAV's got a burr in his saddle. The directive from his office was a little terse."

"Must be getting pressure." The senior chief didn't push for details. The skipper would share more when the time came, Richey decided. But that presupposed he knew anything at all.

Headquarters Marine Corps,
Henderson Hall

"Cold already."

Nathan Crockett leaned forward, eyeing the stained mug on the desk. He peered inside and stirred its tepid contents. "You got a microwave in this place?"

"Yeah," Neill grinned. "It's hiding next to the coffeemaker. Want me to draw you a map? Or do you need coordinates?"

"I think I can find it," Nate sneered. He ambled into a nearby cubicle. "When did Arrens leave?"

"Last Friday."

"Dang." The scout/sniper frowned, moving his head from side to side. "I missed her by a week. Good kid, that one."

"The best," Neill allowed. Both Marines wore dress shirts and ties. Crockett's blue blazer hung on the coat rack. Neill's was laid across his desk.

"You worried, Homestyle?"

The captain stared blankly. "Should I be?"

Nate shrugged, punching digits on the microwave. "That's a hard one to answer. Kaneohe Bay, Bellows Beach. I'm thinking bikinis and one whole summer in Hawaii. She'll be bronzed inside of a week. Probably fightin' 'em off with a stick right now."

"Are you provoking me?"

"Just trying to get your goat, that's all."

Neill eyed his friend. "What about tomorrow—you still planning on going through with it?"

A pained look. "It seems like the right thing to do. Don't you agree?"

"I think it's appropriate. But it will be painful. Want me to make a phone call first?"

"Might help," Nate granted. He retrieved his coffee

and sat down again, anxious to change the subject. "This is Arrens' desk, isn't it?"

"That would be it."

"Thought so." A vial of perfume was by the phone, and Crockett picked it up. "There's something about it. Kinda jars the memory."

"Oh?" Neill raised a brow. "Is it ambiance? A certain *je ne sais quoi?*"

"Is that Russian for smell? 'Cause smell's the word I'm looking for."

"I think you mean fragrance."

"That might work too. And don't tell me you haven't noticed." He stirred the coffee once more and laid the spoon aside. "She left this intentionally, didn't she?"

"Put something under that," Mike directed. "Things won't go well if she comes back to a mess."

The lieutenant clucked his tongue. "Hen-pecked already. It happens, I guess. Even to the best of us."

"You could use a little domesticating yourself," Neill observed.

"No doubt." Crockett brought the vial close, a wistful expression on his face. "This stuff brings Warsaw to mind."

Neill looked at his phone. It was time to go, but still no word from Dmitri. He stood and pulled on his coat.

"If you want to keep those memories alive, just dab a little of that behind your ears."

• • • •

The corporal from the Headquarters and Service Battalion approached the river entrance, angling the sedan into the Pentagon's basement garage. Etheridge, Neill and Crockett displayed their IDs at the entry point before exiting by the main elevator. They were met there by a tall man with a close haircut.

"Cullough McKeckney." Avery's Special Assistant greeted Etheridge with an affable smile. "I don't believe we've met, Master Gunnery Sergeant."

The barrel-chested black man was also dressed in civilian attire. He shook hands and introduced the officers.

"You're prior service," Neill assessed.

Cull nodded. "Army. Second Battalion, Eighth Field Artillery Regiment." A frown darkened his face, and he asked facetiously, "Either of you two ever worn the uniform?"

"Boy Scouts," Nate quipped. "And Mike was a Sea Cadet."

"Then your clearances should be more than adequate," McKeckney deadpanned. He reached behind and punched the elevator button. "The Secretary's waiting upstairs. Shall we?"

The doors opened on the second floor, just off the central courtyard. McKeckney led the Marines south to the E-Ring. The corridors within were busy with foot traffic, and as they headed toward the SECDEF's office, Cull spied a café.

"Anybody want coffee? I'm buyin'."

Neill gave Crockett a look before waving aside the offer. "I think we've had enough."

McKeckney grunted. "Just as well. We're hosting brunch in the conference room." He narrowed his eyes, a guarded smile creasing his face. "The DoD knows how to treat its guests."

"I read the Secretary's email, Mr. McKeckney." Neill shared their host's expression. "Something tells me we aren't the only visitors on your list."

"Roger that, Captain—and call me Cull." A USPS worker passed by, stopping to deliver mail, and the group had to adjust their track to avoid an electric cart. "There's a whole slew of DVs here for the briefing. Mr. Avery's entertaining the Australian ambassador as we speak. They've got the inside track on the science, whereas we have the logistics and resources."

"The Aussies are here?" Crockett asked.

The Special Assistant gave a nod. "Things happened fast after that plane went down. Their ambassador called ours, and the Prime Minister got involved. CINCPAC was next," he said, referencing the Commander-In-Chief/Pacific. "Two days later, our allies down under moved Heaven and Earth to arrange transport. Brisbane and Russo have been here ever since."

Neill recalled the names in the email. "Taylor Brisbane and Bailee Russo?"

"Those are the two," Cull replied. "Do you know of Dr. Brisbane's work?"

"Dr. Brisbane?" The captain shook his head. "Never heard of him."

"Apparently not," McKeckney grinned again. "*She's* the reason for today's little get-together."

"Brisbane's a woman?" Nate blurted.

"You're a quick study," McKeckney joked. He lowered his voice, adding, "Very striking, too, but you didn't hear that from me."

The foyer of the Secretary's office was empty. A conference area opened to the left, and as the group filed in from the hall, voices could be heard from within. Avery appeared suddenly, ushered them forward and began making introductions.

"Don't let the shiny stuff dazzle you," the Secretary whispered with a grin.

The officers clipped IDs to their coats and gave the room a once-over. McKeckney had understated things; all manner of VIPs and distinguished visitors filled the long conference area. SECNAV was there; CINCPAC too. To their left, Neill spied several more naval personnel—two rear admirals among them—along with a smattering of State Department bureaucrats. Everyone with an office in the Pentagon was in uniform, and most were Navy men. Those who traveled from beyond the complex wore civilian clothing. The captain filed that away for later; he suspected there was a reason, and his mind was already working on it.

The Australians mingled with a group from New Zealand. It was hard to gauge their number; all sported short haircuts—members of the armed forces, Neill surmised—and those not in military dress had been issued guest badges with their names. Gerald Gillam, the Australian ambassador, emerged from the center of the room and began pressing the flesh with Etheridge and Crockett. He was broad-shouldered with reddish features and an unmistakable accent. He was also postured as if to protect the guests who stood behind him.

Much like a chaperone, Neill reflected.

The tall redhead to Gillam's rear had a commanding bearing. Clearly this was Dr. Brisbane. Intense green eyes darted from one face to the next, as if measuring personalities. Neill had seen that behavior before, practiced by diplomats—functionaries intent on establishing their place in the game.

But there was something more. Her poise seemed forced; the glances stilted, almost furtive.

The other woman in the room was more relaxed, and less pretentious. This was a soul at home in a sweatshirt and sneakers. Shorter than anyone else, she made her presence known with a winsome smile, and depending on how she turned, her features were hidden by layers of blond hair that hung in perfectly straight bangs.

"Dr. Brisbane." Neill waited his turn, taking the scientist's hand. Her grip was warm. The captain started to say more, but Willis Avery broke in.

"If everyone will take a seat, we'll start today's briefing."

The group settled in around the conference table. Crockett pulled up a chair next to Russo. She gave him a friendly grin before looking away. He was staring, and Neill was amused by his friend's obvious attraction.

McKeckney dimmed the lights, but one end of the room brightened. A projector in the ceiling came to life, tied to a desktop computer. Images began to glow on a screen set before them. Avery's assistant held a remote and toggled through to a map of the Pacific Rim, highlighted with locations from the Philippines to the northern reaches of the Kamchatka Peninsula.

Great, Crockett thought. *Death by PowerPoint.*

Neill was thinking the same thing, but neither man spoke.

"History's biggest threat to peace is making a comeback," Willis Avery intoned. There was murmuring from around the table. The Secretary shuffled forward, as if testing the carpet beneath his feet. "That might sound a bit dramatic, but each of us, and our respective governments, need to be circumspect about the dangers we're facing.

"By now the whole world has heard about the loss of Flight 778. Apparently the Borneo aircraft was just a prelude. All told, the death toll is staggering." The screen now displayed photos of both planes. "Each represents a wanton disregard for human life. And there have been other incidents. We've kept those from the public."

SECDEF studied his audience and weighed their reactions. His comment went much further than previous statements and clearly suggested malice.

"You're implying this was all deliberate," CINCPAC voiced. "Propagated, I would assume, by a state actor. Anyone we know?"

Avery stood taller. He looked different, somehow. Neill recognized what it was. Ordinarily, Richard Aultman would have been nearby, and the captain was struck by his absence.

"Only a few nations have the technology to create this type of havoc, ladies and gentlemen. China, North Korea, or possibly Iran. But quite frankly, we're leaning toward—"

"The Russians?" Neill slipped in.

"That's correct, Captain." Avery gave the officer an opening. Neill took it.

"I've gleaned evidence that points in that direction myself," the Marine continued. "You mentioned other incidents, Mr. Secretary. What might those be?"

Avery gave a wordless glance to McKeckney. The younger man used the remote to bring up a new graphic.

"What you see is the Takamori Nuclear Plant, Japan. In February, the entire facility went offline. Knocked out by an outside source."

An assistant under-secretary of State raised a brow. "Were their systems hacked?"

Avery shook his head. "Nothing so elegant. More of a brute-force approach. Fortunately, the plant has a self-correcting power grid, so disaster was averted."

"What caused the shut-down?"

He shoved his hands into his pockets. "We're getting ahead of ourselves. Cull, pull up the next target."

Another image appeared, and Nate's eyes widened. "C-130," he chirped.

"Spent some time on those, have you, Lieutenant?" Avery grinned, but the expression faded. "Air Force cargo plane. Advanced avionics on a fifty year-old platform.

Three weeks ago, this bird's electrical systems were hit head-on and nearly blinded."

"Did it crash?" Etheridge asked.

"Not in this case, no. It was hardened against those kinds of attacks."

Crockett stirred in his seat. "Hardened against what kind of attacks?"

"An electromagnetic pulse." Taylor Brisbane spoke aloud to the group. Every eye turned and locked on the woman. "More commonly known as an EMP."

"The intensity of this one was unlike anything we've seen," Avery added. "Extremely powerful. The aircraft was briefly overwhelmed."

An official from DHS posed a question. "Is that what brought down 778?"

"That's our theory. Anybody flown commercial lately?" Bailee Russo raised a hand. Avery acknowledged her with a nod of his head. "What's the first thing flight attendants tell you before takeoff?"

"Fasten your seatbelts?" Nate offered.

"Nice try, Marine. What else?"

"Turn off your mobiles," Russo contributed. She pronounced the words with a typically Australian lilt.

"Give the lady a cigar."

Neill was intrigued. "Many airliners require computers to fly. Knock those out—"

"Bingo," Avery said. "If a cell phone's a threat—" everyone knew that they weren't— "just consider what an EMP could do."

"Where was the C-130 when it was hit?" the captain asked.

"Close to Kadena Air Base, on Okinawa." McKeckney brought up a map. Points of interest were clearly labeled, including 778's crash site, the Japanese power plant, and a spot marked for the Borneo plane in the Bering Sea.

Crockett was skeptical. "Aren't those locations beyond Ivan's reach?"

"Hang on, people. We're starting to chase rabbits," Avery cautioned. "Let's focus on the threat." He smiled at the Australian contingent, drumming his fingertips on a sheaf of notes. "And for our guests, please keep these non-disclosure agreements in mind.

"Our presenter today chairs the applied sciences department at the University of Sydney. She's an expert in the field of radiophysics. Her research assistant, Miss Bailee Russo, is a doctoral student, and given their credentials, these two ladies can explain this a whole lot better than I can." SECDEF took his seat. "Dr. Brisbane?"

"Thank you, Mr. Secretary." Taylor Brisbane stood, partly out of respect and partly to be heard. There was polite hesitation, or an awkwardness of sorts. She was putting her best foot forward, Neill decided. But it was clearly an effort—

"A preface first, followed by a simplified explanation. Glimmers of an EMP weapon cropped up earlier this year." Brisbane launched into an instructional tone, overcoming her tentative start. "My research is focused on Schumann Resonances—the study of low frequency disruptions in the Earth's magnetic field."

Crockett leaned forward. "For my sake, I hope that's not the simplified explanation."

Laughter rippled around the table, giving the room a more relaxed air.

Brisbane smiled awkwardly. "These faint disturbances caught our attention—so we fine-tuned our equipment, and by the time the Borneo plane was lost, those 'glimmers' had become full-blown eruptions." The scientist looked to McKeckney. "Frame one, please."

The on-screen image changed, displaying what appeared to be sound waves plotted on a graph. Despite the colorful presentation, Neill couldn't fathom its meaning. It was a sentiment shared by everyone else—except Bailee Russo.

"Much of our work touches on cymatics, a phenomenon that deals with the effects of audio impulses on physical objects. This slide depicts a dampened sinewave pulse. Of course, oscillation is a big part—"

"*Doc.*" Bailee had come to the rescue.

"I apologize—not the explanation Mr. Crockett was looking for, I'm afraid." Even in subdued lighting, Neill could see the professor's face darken.

"Don't sweat it, Doc. And call me Lieutenant," Nate beamed.

Etheridge followed with a question, shifting the focus away from Brisbane's awkward moment. "And you believe this is evidence of a new weapons system? I'm not disputing your hypothesis, Doctor. I'm just trying to be clear."

"This phenomenon does occur naturally," she said. "It's very common in the low frequency band. But in recent cases, we've witnessed electromagnetic energy on a much more powerful scale. The latest pulses were narrowly focused—on a tight beam—leveraging amplitudes that would disrupt normal flight operations."

The senior NCO folded his arms across his chest. "That would certainly suggest a military application," he agreed. "How effective would this weapon be on other types of aircraft?"

Bailee answered that one. "That's hard to say. Sometimes the auto-pilot runs the show—computers take over, eliminating the need for human intervention. In instances where software is used, the risk would be greater."

"What about a small plane?" Crockett asked.

"Single engine aircraft are much less susceptible,"

Brisbane returned. "They don't require computers for flight. That's not to say they aren't vulnerable. But a heavy—carrying hundreds of passengers—that's another story."

"Is this weapon land-based?" Etheridge asked.

Brisbane shook her head. "No—*Master Sergeant*, is it?"

"Master *Gunnery* Sergeant. Just call me Gunny."

"All right, Gunny. To answer your question, it isn't stationary; in fact, it's quite mobile. The last pulse originated—" she shot a glance at McKeckney, "—can you bring up frame two, please?"

Necks craned as the slide was queued up. The display marked a position that was south of Japan.

Crockett whistled softly. "The Philippine Sea. Smack dab in the middle of the ocean." He turned to face Brisbane. "It's aboard a ship?"

"No," Avery answered. "We've ruled that out. A seagoing platform would have been seen by our satellites."

"Has the NRO taken a look at this?" It was Neill who dangled the question; he was referring to the National Reconnaissance Office.

"They've eyeballed the region. Came up with squat."

"What about a submarine?" Homeland Security quizzed. "Something that could maintain a low profile. Pop up out of nowhere—a Russian boomer, maybe?"

Avery dropped his chin. Etheridge saw him give CINCPAC a wink. "Let's just say we've been keeping tabs on Ivan's boats."

"So it wasn't a sub." Neill inferred. "Are you saying it was airborne?"

Avery nodded. "Airborne, yes, Captain—but at very low altitude."

Neill's eyes narrowed. "How low?"

"Thirty-five feet above sea level." The reply came

from McKeckney, and everyone turned in his direction.

"Thirty-five *feet*?" the Marine repeated.

"That's correct, Captain Neill. Dr. Brisbane's data matches our own—what little we have, that is. This aircraft is fast, and it stays low. Probably to avoid radar." Avery stepped toward the screen and raised an arm. "And its hunting grounds are the western Pacific Rim."

"Where does this thing hide when it's not causing disasters?" Crockett pushed past Avery's dramatic statement and was staring at the map. "If the Russians are involved—"

"The intercepts suggest Kamchatka," Neill replied. He got to his feet and gave the corners a cursory look. "Got a yardstick around here?"

The Special Assistant supplied a small fob and handed it off. "Will a laser pointer do?"

"Thanks." Neill thumbed the device, and a red dot appeared on the screen. "Chatter ramped up after 778 crashed. Lots of traffic up and down the peninsula—" he aimed the beam upward, "—primarily between Cape Lopatka—right here—and Karaginsky Island, to the north. Most military operations are controlled from the naval base at Petropavlovsk. Can you pull up satellite imagery, Mr. McKeckney?"

"Give me a sec." Cull slid behind the computer and began tapping keys.

"Kamchatka is roughly the size of California," Neill continued. "Lots of open space and frozen tundra. The eastern shoreline faces the Pacific, which gives this territory its strategic value."

The scene before them changed again. "Is this what you're looking for, Captain?"

Neill studied the display. "That's it. See the topography?" He waved the laser at a vast stretch of seaboard. "Sloping escarpments, mountain ranges, and narrow beaches. Fog covers much of the region, depending on the time of year."

Nate squinted. "Is *Petro*—Petrus—" it wasn't going to happen, so he gave up. "The naval base—is that where this beast lives?"

"We don't think that's the case," Cull replied. "Russian flight ops from the base at Petropavlovsk were negligible at the time 778 went down."

"It's this location I'm interested in," Neill announced, and the red dot danced on the map. "Just northwest of the Commanders—a spit of land called *Ust-Kamchatsk*."

"Do you speak Russian, Captain Neill?" Homeland Security asked.

"Just a little," Mike hedged. "As you can see, Ust-Kamchatsk is right on the water. More of the same, in terms of landscape, but I'm starting to see a connection."

Etheridge asked, "With the Commander chain?"

"It's not really a chain, Master Guns; just two large islands, Bering and Medny. But under the right circumstances, they could create a very nice screen for air operations."

"How so?" Avery prodded. "There's an awful lot of water out there."

"Fair enough," Neill allowed. "But flying low above those waters might confuse an adversary's radar—trick them into thinking you're just part of the scenery. And that strait could be used as a choke point. To get close, a sea-going vessel would have to follow the Kuril Trench—between the Commanders and the peninsula." He shook his head. "That sea lane's only about a hundred miles wide, and with all of Ivan's naval assets—"

"I think I see where you're going," Gillam spoke up. "That approach would be anything but stealthy."

Avery faced CINCPAC. "What's the present disposition of Russia's navy, Admiral Tankersley?"

The officer was quick with an answer. "The waterways along Kamchatka are heavily patrolled. Have been for years. Sub chasers, tenders, support ships and the like." He gave Avery a knowing grin. "The Russians have learned the lessons of the eighties and nineties, Mr. Secretary."

The man with the unruly hair turned back to Captain Neill. "What clicks about this Ust-Kamchatsk region? Was it mentioned in the chatter?"

"No, Mr. Secretary. In fact, the Russians did their dead-level best to avoid it. And to me, that's telling."

"But that doesn't work, Mike," Crockett protested. "Planes need runways or landing strips. This imagery doesn't show any—just a sheer cliff face with no beach to speak of."

"He's right." McKeckney adjusted the view, showing the top of the ridgeline. "There are simple structures along the peak, and a road, but no runway."

"Maybe closer inland; a base on the other side of the mountains—" Neill's voice trailed off.

"Wait." Nate leaned forward in his chair, reaching out to tug on McKeckney's sleeve. "We're making the wrong assumption. Can you zoom in? The shoreline—right along there, on the eastern side."

"Here?" Cull asked.

Crockett gave him a nod. "Check out the base of that cliff—where it meets the beach. See those striations?"

"The straight lines?" Russo put in. "Running out to sea?"

Crockett was like a bloodhound now. "Very uniform. Like tire tracks—something very heavy rolling across the deck."

"The surface there is pretty flat," Neill noted. "Not consistent with the rest of the shoreline."

"That's man-made," Nate crowed. "Butts up against

the ridge. See where the slope begins to climb?"

"More lines," Brisbane said. "But there's no sign of any buildings or structures. Could it be a natural formation?"

The sniper shook his head. "Straight lines don't exist in nature, Doctor. You might see a few—short ones, for the most part. But certainly not half a mile long."

"That's why you're here, Lieutenant," Avery harrumphed. He'd been counting on the sniper's ability to see through the camouflage.

McKeckney brought up the lights. Brunch was wheeled in and served cafeteria style. The aroma of breakfast filled the air, and Crockett proclaimed the sausage gravy to be excellent. Coffee, tea and orange juice were also on hand, and the attendees broke into smaller groups, continuing their discussions between bites of fruit, scrambled eggs and biscuits.

"I think I see it," Neill muttered. Screen grabs from the briefing had been printed and passed around the table. "The flat space at ground level looks like a ramp. And it leads right into the shallows."

Cull squinted at one of the grainy images. "Vertical lines, too. Like a hangar door."

Nate washed down toast with a gulp from his mug. "That's exactly what it is. They've made some attempt to hide it; textured surfaces, irregularly spaced shapes. But you're right, Mike. That apron in front is definitely a ramp."

"Spot on, Sherlock," Neill quipped good-naturedly. "Good thing it wasn't a microwave. You might not have seen it."

The master gunny was confused. "So what are we looking for here? A hydrofoil, or some kind of seaplane—like a PBY?"

"An amphibious aircraft, that's my guess," Neill replied. "Fairly substantial, too, I should think."

"Why do you say that?"

"Has to be. Whatever it is, it's got to be large enough to carry a robust weapons system. And the Russians aren't big on subtlety."

The banter faded as they ate. Along with his meal, Nate was focused on Bailee's needs, refilling her teacup twice, and goading the young woman toward seconds. For her part, she encouraged his attention, smiling coyly as the lieutenant skirted the line between flirtation and simply being helpful.

Neill was preoccupied with the handouts. He studied each in turn before noting the SECDEF's interest.

"What's your assessment, Captain?" Avery asked. Only those seated nearby heard his comment.

"There's not much here for that, Mr. Secretary."

"Meaning?"

He waited before answering. "Clearly you're thinking about reconnaissance. Lieutenant Crockett and I wouldn't be here if you weren't."

McKeckney's interest was piqued. "Reconnaissance? Of Kamchatka?"

Willis Avery drew a hand across his chin. "Within reason, mind you."

"A physical presence—on the peninsula itself?" Neill pressed.

Dr. Brisbane put down her tea and joined the conversation. "Are you contemplating a military operation?"

"Mr. Secretary, that's Russian soil." The alarm bells were going off in Cull's brain. "Sovereign territory of a foreign nation."

"I had a feeling we might be taking a closer look," Nate grinned.

"Trust me, this won't be like Huo Shan," the SECDEF said evenly. He turned to face Neill. "I said within reason, son. Signals intelligence only. We get close; we find out more. If we can save innocent lives by doing so, it's our moral imperative." He gave the Marines a hard look. "But I am not authorizing an incursion on Ivan's playing field. Are we clear on that, Captain?"

"Crystal. And for the record—" he gave Etheridge a stare, "—I take my orders from Colonel Terryton. And I serve at your pleasure."

"Well played, Marine," Avery grated out, "—divided loyalties aside." SECDEF seemed to relax. "In fact, this mission should be a cakewalk compared to your previous taskings."

"Does the president know what you have in mind, sir?" Neill asked. "I'm with Mr. McKeckney. The Russians play rough, and things could get very dangerous on their turf."

"We've got other assets capable of gathering that intel, Mr. Secretary," McKeckney pointed out. "Unmanned aerial vehicles, satellites—"

Nate was shaking his head. "Painting the big picture is an integrated process. It takes more than just having eyes in the sky."

"True. Signals intelligence alone isn't enough," Mike agreed. "I know it's a tired phrase, but you need boots on the ground. Wars aren't won with air power alone. You can soften up a target with ordnance, but to keep territory, you have to be standing on it."

"Surely you're not thinking in terms of a military strike, Captain," Cull asked. "That kind of talk makes me a little nervous."

"Bad analogy. My apologies." Neill's phone chirped where it lay on the table. He checked the display. "Would you excuse me, Mr. Secretary? I've been expecting this."

He didn't wait for a reply. With phone in hand, Neill got to his feet and headed for the door. Avery watched him go, and Taylor Brisbane's eyes also lingered as he went.

• • • •

"I hope this isn't a social call."

"At this hour?" Dmitri fired back. "Sleep is much too important, Mischa."

"That's a relief." The outer office was empty. Neill paced the carpet. "You're late, by the way."

"It took me this long to declassify the material," Major Yaroslav chuckled. "And you'll forgive me when you hear what I have to say."

"I'm listening," Neill answered.

"I understand you have retained the services of an Australian scientist." Clearly Dmitri wasn't jumping right into the fray. "One of great repute, if my sources are correct."

Neill was surprised. It seemed the SSD's intelligence network was broader than even he had imagined.

"Could be. But why tell me that?"

"New considerations have surfaced, Michael. Think of it as a warning. If *we* know—"

So do the Russians, Neill thought silently. The intelligence game could be maddening.

The major continued. "You were right about Charybdis. It *is* a project designation; a multi-faceted program. The Russians have been developing it for several years."

"And you're privy to the specifics?"

There was hesitation. "Your government should be very careful, Mischa."

Neill filed away the Major's warning. "What about that name?"

Dmitri drew in some air. "Dr. Radya Zhukov, preeminent scientist of the former Union of Soviet Socialist Republics. He's not been heard from in quite some time. My government believed him to be dead until now."

"Ukrainian?" Michael asked.

"From Zaporozhye. I can confirm that."

"What else can you tell me?"

Halfway around the world the major shook his head. "Nothing more, Mischa—not without something in exchange. But I can say this; the SSD is very interested in Dr. Zhukov. My director would like to propose a collaborative effort."

Neill wasn't surprised or offended. Among friendly nations, this was how counter-intelligence worked. Dmitri was a good operator, and getting better all the time. Information sometimes came with a price—even if it could be used for mutual benefit. Allies and partners had always played this game. Dmitri had sketched in the basics; he'd told Michael what he was looking for—and also whom—but he wasn't about to give away the store. And it was clear the Ukrainian SSD wanted a return on their investment.

"Set your conditions. I'll see what I can do."

7

BRIEFING THE BOSS

"W HAT DID TANKERSLEY mean, Mike? That stuff about the Russians learning their lessons?"

Neill and Crockett sat behind Etheridge and the driver, and the sniper had been taking in the sights. The lieutenant rarely visited the Capitol, and D.C. was a place he recognized mostly from the evening news.

"A little known fact of the Cold War," the captain began slowly. "Back in those days, the CIA used submarines to gather intelligence—right under Ivan's nose."

Nate raised a brow. "Seriously?"

"The Navy sent their boats dangerously close to Russian shores, right into the Sea of Okhotsk."

"No way."

"Way. Sailors and spooks. They managed to get the goods on the Russian Navy, risking their lives at the same time."

"Spy versus spy stuff?" Crockett was being drawn in.

"Yup," Neill answered. "Remind me to tell you about it sometime."

"Sure. We'll have plenty of time for that in the next

few days."

The corporal from H&S had reversed course, taking the quickest route back to Henderson Hall. Thanks to a tour in Afghanistan he was an aggressive driver, but the junior NCO still had to contend with rush hour traffic. The Marines didn't arrive at the office until late afternoon.

Etheridge rode shotgun. He spilled out of the front seat and stretched before the young officers joined him in bounding up the steps. He reached for the door, but sound and motion coming from behind stayed his hand. Neill scanned left, noting a taxi wheeling into one of the empty spaces. The cab came to a stop and disgorged a single passenger—someone familiar to the Headquarters men.

"Wasn't expecting to see you, Colonel," the master gunny boomed. He turned, and all three descended to the curb.

"Caught a red-eye out of Frankfurt." The colonel's voice was raspy. "Got delayed—had a four hour layover in Ireland. Volcano filled the friendly skies with ash." He shook his head. "Guess I missed the Secretary's party."

"We'll fill you in," the master gunny promised.

The cabbie moved to the rear and began pulling luggage from the trunk. Nate stepped forward, introducing himself to the ranking officer.

"Sir, Lieutenant Nathan Crockett." He felt awkward, prepared to salute, but suddenly realizing he wasn't in uniform.

"Pleased." Nicholas Terryton gripped Nate's hand. "Nice to finally meet the hero of Huo Shan. Bang-up job in Warsaw, too, by the way."

The boisterous officer looked uncharacteristically sheepish. "Not so sure about that, sir."

"Captain Neill says otherwise."

Crockett waved him off. "He's just being nice."

"He has that reputation," Terryton agreed.

Etheridge wrenched the colonel's suitcase from the asphalt. Neill lent a hand with the rest of the bags. "We'll stow your gear in my truck, Colonel. I suspect you'll need a lift home."

"I appreciate that, Master Guns. Let's head inside, I want to hear more about Avery's briefing. Something tells me I'm about to get an earful."

"You don't know the half of it," Etheridge warned.

Neill led the way with Terryton's garment bag. "I'm not so sure we do either," he said.

Bringing Terryton up to speed took longer than expected. Neill proceeded point by point with an assist from Etheridge. Crockett contributed occasionally, showing deference for his seniors by keeping his comments short.

"Sounds like most of this hinges on our friends in Eastern Europe," the colonel said, mulling it over. "How does the Ukrainian fit in? What's his name again?"

"Radya Zhukov—Doctor Radya Zhukov," Neill intoned slowly. "He's kind of a mystery, sir. I haven't been able to determine his specific skill sets."

Terryton was frowning. "Major Yaroslav wouldn't spill, huh?"

The captain shook his head. "I get the impression he knows a lot more than he's willing to share. At least for now, anyway. He said as much, in fact."

"What's he holding out for?"

"Cooperation, sir," Neill told him. "The Ukrainian SSD is willing to provide sensitive information. But they want something in return."

"I'm listening," the colonel muttered wryly.

Etheridge piped up. "Ukraine's security directorate

wants a piece of the action. Two of their operatives will join our team and share intelligence."

"*Our* team?" Terryton asked. "Why are they so interested in Dr. Zhukov?"

Neill waded in. "Radya Zhukov is from Zaporozhye, in Eastern Ukraine. He's some kind of scientific genius—someone the Russians pressed into service back in the early eighties."

That struck the colonel as odd. "And just how old is the good doctor?"

"Close to seventy. But he got an early start. A child prodigy, from what I've heard."

"And the Ukrainians wants us to feed them fresh intel? What do they hope to get out of all this?"

"That's not entirely clear, sir. Dmitri was very guarded on that point. If we play ball, we'll get more. But not until we've reached a consensus on the operation."

The colonel settled into place behind his desk. "Tell me about Avery's plans. And have a seat."

Neill pulled up a chair. Crockett and Etheridge did likewise. "The Secretary wants an American naval vessel to transit the Northwest Pacific Basin, on a northerly course through the Bering Sea," Neill began. "Said ship will pass very close to Kamchatka—between the peninsula and the Commander Islands—collecting SIGINT along the way."

"And what do the Ukrainians contribute to this little voyage?" Terryton's question held a measure of sarcasm.

Neill caught the shift in the colonel's mood. "Dmitri claims they have an asset in the region; a resource that can point out key segments of the Russian coastline—a geographic anomaly that's caught our eye."

"What might that be?"

"Sir, the Russians have an aircraft operating in the Bering Sea," Neill went on. "The Australians have suggested that this plane is a support platform—one used to deploy a pulse weapon. And thanks to Crockett's keen eye, we've discovered what appears to be a hidden base or a staging area of some kind."

"An EMP weapon? Is that the idea?"

"That's correct."

"Why are the Russians doing all this?" Terryton was asking lots of questions, but that was part of his job.

"Prevailing wisdom says that Russia can stick it to Ukraine, and the rest of Eastern Europe, pushing their advantage with oil and natural gas," Etheridge offered. "Captain Neill, on the other hand, thinks otherwise."

"What's led you to that conclusion, Captain?"

"Just a hunch, sir," the young officer replied. "The Russians have been very edgy of late; overly protective of their strategic reserves and oil interests in the region. I need a little more time to research this, but it might just be that their crude supply isn't as vast as we've been led to believe."

"And the personnel—who's on the team?" Terryton eyed Neill warily.

"Ukrainians, Australians, and Americans. Two from each group."

"Well, that narrows it down," the C.O. hissed. "I'm interested to hear about the U.S. contingent. Do those individuals have names?"

Neill looked uncomfortable. "For the record, I did emphasize that I take my orders from you."

"He did say that," Etheridge confirmed.

"I'm sure. Let's have it, Marine," Terryton ordered. "Who's Avery sending?"

"Lieutenant Crockett. And myself," Neill managed. "The Australians have chosen Dr. Brisbane and her research assistant."

The colonel wasn't enthusiastic. "Avery doesn't need

you involved, Captain. DoD has plenty of interpreters. So does the CIA."

Etheridge leaned forward. "That's true, sir. But those personnel don't have a working relationship with the Ukrainians. Neill does; and he knows the operatives being sent by the SSD."

"In case you haven't noticed, people, we're a little short-handed these days." Jet lag certainly hadn't helped Terryton's disposition.

"I'm aware of that," Neill replied. "But I couldn't tell the Secretary of Defense to go pound sand."

Terryton felt chastened. "Who got the tasking from Major Yaroslav?"

"He suggested someone familiar, agents we've dealt with in the recent past." Neill was breathing again. "Sergeant Yuri Tereshenko and Captain Aleksander Voskov, former Berkut officers, now on the SSD payroll."

"The Berkut were disbanded; brutality during the revolution." Terryton had a faraway look. "I remember reading about that. Are those the same two that helped out in Warsaw?"

"And Kiev. Yes, sir, they are," Neill nodded.

The colonel moved on. "Can they be trusted?" It was a trick question. "They're Ukrainian, after all."

"Your chief counter-intelligence officer is Ukrainian, Colonel," the captain said hotly, a little too much so for his own good.

"He's got a point, sir," Etheridge defended.

Terryton raised a hand. "Relax, Neill. I've read your report on Poland. And Ukraine. A number of times, in fact. Textbook international cooperation. If you trust them, so do I."

"Yes, sir," Neill exhaled. "I apologize."

"No need." The colonel stretched in his seat. "What's your role in all this?"

"Avery wants someone who can interpret the chatter in real time," Etheridge said. "Neill will liaise with the Navy's comm and signals people. His language skills make him the perfect fit—and that should put the Berkut boys at ease."

"Sounds like the planets have aligned for this one," Terryton grumped. "And Lieutenant Crockett will go along as Neill's wingman?"

"My pleasure, sir," Nate chirped.

"That was a question, not a compliment." Terryton studied the lieutenant's face, and after a pause added, "Still, I wouldn't begrudge anyone a battle buddy."

"I was hoping you'd see it that way, sir," Neill told him.

"No skin off my teeth. Crockett's not under my command. Now tell me about Dr. Brisbane."

The master gunny spoke again. "The Aussies have sophisticated instrumentation. Brisbane thinks she can locate the weapon."

"Not if it's turned off, I'll wager," Terryton protested.

"Bailee says the device emits a specific signature—even when it's not fully operational," Nate said. "She's convinced they can find it."

"Who's Bailee?"

"Bailee Russo," Etheridge grinned. "Dr. Brisbane's girl Friday. And I believe Lieutenant Crockett was quite taken by her."

Nate blanched. "She's attractive. That might not be entirely germane, but—"

Neill's thoughts went to Christina, a pang of melancholy creeping in.

"Young ladies are always relevant, Lieutenant," the colonel opined, suddenly in a lighter mood. "Isn't that right, Captain?" Neill was struck by the comment, but thought better of pressing the issue.

Just as quickly, Terryton posed a new question. "And what about this resource the Ukrainians have—do we know what that might be?"

"It's not a *what*, sir—more like a who." The captain shook his head. "Beyond that, we don't know."

"More intelligence—contingent on our cooperation," Terryton observed. "What's the projected timeline?"

"The USS *Meyer*'s already in the region, steaming southwest," Neill answered. "She was headed to the Philippines—originally to aid in the recovery efforts for 778's black box."

"She's been re-tasked," Terryton grunted.

A nod from Neill. "She'll lay off the Emperor Seamount Chain and await our arrival. The *Knox* will replace her at the crash site."

What came next was obvious. "When do you leave?"

"We gear up Monday, followed by operational planning. On Wednesday we catch a C-17 out of Andrews. Then it's on to Travis in California, Elmendorf in Alaska, and west to the Aleutians. From there the Coast Guard will chopper us out to the *Meyer*."

Terryton had absorbed as much information as he could, given his fatigue. He stood slowly, and those assembled around the desk got to their feet.

"Then you should enjoy your weekend, gentlemen. I'll see you here first thing Monday morning."

"Roger that." Neill traded glances with Crockett. "We've each got a few things to do before then."

"Oh? What might that be?"

"Lieutenant Crockett has a personal matter that requires his attention."

"What about you?" Terryton asked. "Big plans?"

"A great deal of prayer," the captain smiled. "A few phone calls, maybe some range time with my uncle. And I was hoping to catch up on my sleep."

• • • •

The State Department driver took Brisbane and Russo to the brick-lined streets of Georgetown. Their rooms had been booked at the Avenue Suites. The rest of the Australian contingent traveled separately—and only the young women were shadowed by a Secret Service detail.

Bailee was giddy at the prospect of being in D.C. She'd never been to the U.S. before. Taylor had visited twice, but both occasions included conferences on the west coast, and sight-seeing held little interest for the driven scientist.

"What do you say, Doc?" Russo prodded. "Wanna go nosh on some dinner?"

The lobby was warmly lit as they made their way inside. "The hotel restaurant's closed," Taylor suggested. She tossed a look over her shoulder. "And it's getting dark outside."

The younger woman shifted the backpack on her shoulder. "Oh, be a mate, Doc. Live a little." Bailee had heard of Foggy Bottom's restaurants and was anxious to explore. "You play it safe way too much."

Brisbane raised a brow. "We're going to help the Americans find a weapon of mass destruction—off the Russian coastline, no less. I'd hardly call that playing it safe."

Russo was beaming. "I know. It's exciting, isn't it?"

The doctor dropped her guard. "If it's excitement you want, maybe you should be dining with that Yank *leftenant*." Taylor smirked at her young friend. "I do believe you're quite smitten with him, am I right?"

"Was I that obvious?" She was aghast.

Brisbane gave a shrug. "Only to him, I imagine. I just know you better than most people. He is a cute bloke— I'll give you that—in a round-faced sort of way."

"He's totes mcgotes," Russo gushed. She pushed the bangs from her eyes. "And if questioned I'll deny I ever said that." She decided to press her boss. "What did you think of Captain Neill?"

Brisbane looked away. She switched the satchel she carried from one hand to the next. "A bit young. But competent. I trust he'll get the job done."

"Now that's a ringing endorsement." The blonde's remark was laced with sarcasm. "You should try to put yourself in other people's shoes. And it wouldn't go amiss for you to be friendly, Doc."

"I *was* friendly."

"You were polite," Bailee corrected. "But I think you came across as stuck up."

Taylor seemed flustered. "How should I act, then?"

"For now?" Bailee stepped off toward the elevator. "Like a tourist. Let's drop our kits in the rooms and find some supper."

The Northwest Pacific Basin

Hydrography was hardly a romantic science, but it was useful. Measuring the physical features of waterways was as old as sailing itself. Harbors and coastlines sometimes hid danger, and plumbing the shallows to mark hazards kept ships from running aground. While bays and inland waters were the primary concern, mariners soon turned their attention to the open seas.

Pushing away from land, merchantmen demanded charts that would aid navigation and safeguard their cargoes. Masters of packet ships required surveys to establish the most expedient routes. Naval commanders and strategists were not to be left out, either. They were determined in their pursuit of a military advantage, and without a knowledge of the oceans' characteristics, a nation's ascendancy on the high seas was in doubt.

But hydrography wasn't solely focused on currents and sea beds. It also looked at a coastal zone's landmarks, aids to navigation that could be used to mark a vessel's position. Wise seafarers relied on the science. Ignoring its ordinances could lead to disaster. The tides demanded respect, and a sailor's understanding of the waters beneath his keel ensured success or failure; the sea could be unforgiving, and it was difficult to recover from the latter.

Oceanography had changed dramatically over the course of a hundred years, and markedly so over the past thirty. What had begun with lead lines and depth poles had advanced to sonar, echo-sounding and more modern digital solutions. These included side-scan and multi-beam systems, and the process also utilized remotely operated undersea vehicles and GPS. For shallow water work—known as the littoral zones—oceanographers employed sensor arrays to determine underwater features. Avoidance was the key, but at times, obstructions below the surface proved interesting, or even better, potentially profitable.

And in those cases, the equipment was used to bring searching eyes closer.

• • • •

The big ship churning the waters far to the south of Attu was the R/V *Pont Claire*, an ice-class research vessel owned and operated by Northwestern Challenger Petroleum. Three hundred and fifteen feet long, the double-hulled ship was designed for offshore oil exploration, and was fitted with drilling equipment and a host of cranes and booms. The ship had just transited the International Date Line (which meant adding a day as it traveled west), following that course as it snaked around the Near Islands of the Bering Sea.

Her last assignment had been a geophysical probe of the ocean floor, testing for hydrocarbons. Cap-rock at that site looked promising; oil was buoyant, and the rock acted as a seal. Its presence was necessary before drilling would even be considered.

There were other encouraging signs. Best of all, the data retrieved from the collection point met Challenger Petroleum's criteria. The ship's geologist was ecstatic; the ultimate goal was finding oil, and the cursory evidence supported a very hopeful outcome.

Tall and soft-spoken, Captain Cliff Tucker stood on the bridge. Dawn blazed astern; the sun's rays were a bright orange, and the winds pushing south were kicking up whitecaps. Apart from that there was little to see. The Commander Islands were just out of sight. On occasion, a pod of whales would cross the ship's wake—three times in as many days, by last count—and when they entered some island's shoals, gulls, terns and gyrfalcons would flock overhead, scrutinizing the vessel for the possibility of a meal.

The scenery rarely changed, and after forty-five days at sea it was nearly time to go home. But the *Pont Claire* had one more duty to perform before Tucker pointed her bow north.

"The bosun's on the fantail riggin' the towed array." The voice came from behind, and carried a Scottish brogue. Tucker didn't need to turn. He recognized the man's burr and shuffling gait as he entered the wheelhouse. "So what's the skinny?"

Sean Crackenmoor was a career roughneck, a veteran of the North Sea oil rigs. Known affectionately as the Cracken, he was a big man, given to wearing plaid shirts, earth-tone corduroy trousers and work boots. Weathered gloves hung from his belt. These were always handy, and he rarely lifted a finger without them.

Tucker's response came in a low growl. "I promised Spit Weathersby a favor. Any objections?"

Sean grinned beneath his beard. "None from me, Cap'n. Is Lucky Lance still chasin' ghosts?"

"Not today, Mr. Crackenmoor. That would be us."

Lance 'Spit' Weathersby—Lucky was recent, and threatened to supplant his given nickname—was also employed by Challenger Petroleum. He was the master of the R/V *Dumont*, the *Pont Claire*'s sister ship. Finding oil fields was one of Weathersby's gifts, and he had a remarkable tally of successes. But his fortunes ran hot and cold, and his failures were equally spectacular. On his last trip, Weathersby had thrown a propeller, and the *Dumont* had to be towed back to Alaska.

"It's probably nothing. Spit's not even sure." The captain was almost dismissive. "You've heard the story. Side-scan sonar detected an anomaly, but the images weren't clear."

"Bad sounding?"

"Maybe. I haven't seen the data. And the *Dumont* didn't make another pass." Tucker gave a shrug. "That's the long and short of it."

"And that's where we're headed?"

"Aye. That's where we're headed," the captain repeated, tapping the GPS display. "Should be on-site in another day. Who knows? Maybe Spit's phantom is sitting on oil. Might earn us another payday."

"Sasha the Red won't be too happy about that, Skipper." Sean looked nervous. "That salvage ship keeps pushin' north."

"The *Belousov*? Just a coincidence," Tucker hoped. "We'll make one sweep, then double back and make another. After that, we skedaddle."

Crackenmoor hoped he was right. The recent fuel crisis had made the Russians more aggressive. Sean looked at the plot, checking their destination. It was just south of Medny Island, with Bering to the northwest.

Practically in Ivan's backyard.

8

PERSONAL BUSINESS

The Russian Federation

I T WAS A DRAMATIC skyline in any century. The architecture was instantly recognizable, distinguished by ancient ramparts and blood-red walls; but moreover by the out-of-place presence of spires and cathedrals, each pointing to a Heaven disdained—and always denied—by the former Soviet government.

Moscow had a chill in the air, and her citizens kept their coats and *ushankas* close at hand. Bitter winds gusted through the city's historic districts, their bite keenly felt as they raced between the armories and gatehouses of the Russian stronghold. Weather in this part of the world was always a force to be reckoned with, and rarely an ally—although cold winters had stopped Napoleon's army, and the Nazi war machine in the last World War. Those were oddly providential instances, and divine intervention could scarcely be interpreted without a deeper understanding of the city's background.

A mythic fortress on the riverbank, Moscow's most-visited site was born with a martial soul. Few descriptives could adequately capture its presence in history, and there was no shortage of metaphors for the sprawling structure. The Kremlin was a clenched fist. It was also a place of old world monarchy and the seat of deeply felt religion. The defenses surrounding the ancient redoubt were a reminder of past conflict, right down to the brick-reinforced moat that turned it into an island. In later years, the city would be torched by troops from Crimea and Kazan, but by the early 1500s, the symbol of the Russian state would be safe from horsemen advancing from the east.

Like many landmarks, the fortress's origins could scarcely be traced. The uniformly stacked pile of crimson blocks started out as a simple stockade, and the present fortification was born with a voracious appetite. From the beginning, fire-breaks were needed, and the trees of Moscow's forests were harvested in the interests of safety and construction. Vast swaths of land were cleared of timber, the wood being used for scaffolding and earthworks—the forerunners of what would become the garrison recognized world-over. In the coming years, a second set of walls was raised, plastered with the mud of the Moskva river. With the rise of more effective artillery, these reinforcements were as wide as they were high.

The Ivans of old who commissioned the city's architecture endowed the buildings with an artistic flair. Moscow's jewel, St. Basil's Cathedral, was reminiscent of a fairy tale castle, despite its overtly religious purposes. Within the perimeter of the fortress itself were rusticated walls and domed towers covered with tin. Spires stretched skyward. Regarded as a group, these embellishments, including the Tsar's Cannon and the Royal Bell, gave the Kremlin compound the look of a giant's toy box.

Sixteen towers of varying size ringed the perimeter.

Straddling the brickwork encircling the grounds was a parapet that stood between *krasnaya ploschad*—Red Square—and the bastion's courtyard. The true seat of power was the Kremlin Presidium—once called the Council of Ministers of the USSR—planted high in the northernmost quadrant of the citadel. Three stories tall and having a yellow color scheme, the outer surfaces were painted in hues closer to mustard and exhibited a garish cast when sunlight beat down on the exterior.

Major Alexei Pirogov of the southern military district left Ivanovskaya Square and pushed through the Presidium entrance. Ascending two flights of stairs, he arrived at the control checkpoint and presented his credentials. The watch officer inspected the major's ID, glanced at Pirogov's face, and then wordlessly waved him through to the next office.

"*Dobre dyen*, General," Alexei barked respectfully. He eased the door closed behind him and came to attention.

"Good day, Major Pirogov." Leonid Karpenko stood at the window. From this vantage point he could see the Patriarch's Palace and the Church of the Robe. A little further on, the Bell Tower of Ivan the Great broke the horizon, dominating the view to the south.

Karpenko waved the junior officer toward a chair. Pirogov seated himself, bracing for what was to come. He knew why he had been called. Being summoned generally meant trouble, and once his report had been made, the major would most certainly be called on the carpet.

But there was more to it than that, Alexei reasoned. He'd seen the reports. The news had been splashed across the front page of every tabloid, and the story had been broadcast on the state-sanctioned networks as well. Sanitized or not, accounts of the disaster pointed toward a deliberate act. Pirogov suspected his own government's involvement, and given the pressure Karpenko must have felt, he could sympathize with the general's reflective mood. In fact, he was morbidly thankful for it. Distractions elsewhere would take the focus off him.

There were rumors rippling through Pirogov's chain of command. Most dealt with the eastern peninsula of Kamchatka. The naval headquarters there generated its own share of problems, and the districts swirled with wild tales of aerial prototypes and unrestrained weapons testing. Alexei put little stock in those. Official reports were always more trustworthy, but one thing was certain; far removed from Moscow, Petropavlovsk had disturbed the fragile peace of the Pacific coastline.

The general relinquished his view of the south, taking his seat behind a massive desk. "You've come from Bryansk, *da*?"

"I have indeed, comrade General."

"And what did you find?"

It's what I didn't *find,* the major thought. "I have interviewed each member of the strike team. They all told the same story."

"And?"

"Your suspicions were not ill-founded, comrade General," Pirogov admitted. No point in stringing this out. "We scoured the crash debris and the surrounding forest, and I personally supervised the dig at the gravesite."

"You discovered only one set of remains, *da*?"

"That is true. The grave was shallow; it would appear that wild animals, feral dogs—possibly something larger—made a meal of what was left. You must keep in mind that three years have passed, comrade General. As it was, we found the bones of only one man. That evidence would serve to confirm the testimony."

"Did these remains belong to Kobrin or Malyev?"

"Impossible to determine. I have requested a forensic examination—DNA testing and the like. The results will be available in a few days."

Karpenko snorted. His question had been rhetorical.

"I can provide you with the results now, Major. Sasha Kobrin died in the skies above Bryansk—it was that, or the fall killed him." He produced a thin binder and pushed it across the desk. "You will no doubt recognize the man in these photographs. Keep in mind that they were taken only weeks ago."

Alexei blinked. He opened the folder, and a familiar face stared back.

"Ivan Malyev." He spoke as if he'd seen a ghost. "Where did you get these, comrade General?"

Pirogov's deference was over the top, more so than usual, Karpenko noted. "From one of our operatives in the United States."

Pirogov narrowed his eyes. "An agent of the GRU?"

"The FSB."

"You sent this man to find Ivan?"

"Success was almost immediate. Malyev is alive and well, living in the greater D.C. area, so it would seem." What Karpenko didn't know was that Igor Nemesh was now dead, his body occupying a cold slab in a Washington D.C. police morgue.

The photos showed others surrounding Malyev. They had the look of a protective detail. "Collaborating with the Americans?" Pirogov asked at last.

"That is correct." The general's voice was uniformly calm, and he touched on another topic. "The Ukrainian woman has hurt our cause, Alexei; she didn't come by her information through investigative journalism alone. She had help, and now Malyev is aiding the Central Intelligence Agency."

"They flipped him?" It was all starting to make sense

to the Major. Still, he had questions. "But this isn't possible. How did he survive the crash?"

Pirogov had been there. His troops had done the job, firing on the aircraft as it approached from Ukraine. The shoulder-launched missile had found its mark, and the plane exploded in mid-air. The fireball alone should have consumed both men.

"Suffice it to say that he did," Karpenko pointed out. "We tasked our agents to spread fear throughout the republics. The plan nearly worked, but now it has begun to unravel." There was a rising edge in the general's voice. "Holcek failed, Major. Not even Ilya Maersk could staunch the flow of evidence. Both are now dead—at the hands of a disbanded Berkut squad, no less. We followed by pressuring Warsaw with the threat of military action, but Dobrogost found the resolve to accept NATO's protection—and Poland's missile shield stands watch over our western approaches."

Alexei's pride smarted. He'd recruited Sergei Holcek himself. The gunman was hardly a novice, a blunt instrument at best, but he proved unequal to the task of killing Viktoriya Gavrilenko. Ilya Maersk was a seasoned veteran of such work, and he, too, had failed. Alexei took some solace in that, yet failure of any kind—regardless of who did the vetting—was unacceptable to a general officer like Leonid Karpenko.

"I find it hard to believe that Malyev would resort to treason, comrade General."

"Truly, Major?" Karpenko snarled. "You lack imagination then. What incentive would he have to remain loyal—after his own countrymen tried to take his life?"

"But that's just the point, General." Pirogov's anger began to boil. "You assume that Malyev was aboard that plane."

Karpenko squinted. "Haven't you also made that assumption?"

"Until this moment, yes. But we must now consider another possibility, that only Kobrin flew the aircraft."

"Did you not order both men to return?"

"I did," Pirogov admitted.

"And did Malyev confirm those orders?"

"Yes, but he must have defied—"

"Come now, Major. Let's reason this out. Why would Malyev remain behind in Odessa? The *militsiya* and state security services were almost certainly looking for them. And what profit would either man find by staying in Ukraine?" Karpenko dismissed the notion. "The point is moot, Alexei. Perhaps he did survive the crash. Or it's possible that you're right, and the two split up before the plane left Ukrainian soil. The fact remains that Malyev is now in America."

"He must have had help." Pirogov's backbone stiffened. "Someone from Ukraine, perhaps. Someone—"

"—a Ukrainian, yes, that's quite correct." Another folder was pushed toward the major. "At my request, the FSB has initiated a case file. This dossier contains a complete biographical sketch."

Pirogov flipped through its pages. There were several loose sheets, with more photography in the sleeve.

"A *Ukrainian*?" Alexei asked. The man in the photo wore an American uniform.

"He was born in Kiev," Karpenko explained. "Our agent in the U.S. has done some digging of his own. We have determined that this man is Malyev's western ally. Keep reading—the father's background is quite telling."

Pirogov was surprised to see other names listed. "The circle completes itself," the major offered. "If Remora was unsuccessful, then this American must be quite formidable."

Karpenko mulled that over. "Resourceful, at the very

least. He has surrounded himself with some very capable associates. Men and women, it would seem."

"Including the American president's security advisor." Alexei held up the picture. "Where was this photo taken?"

"Warsaw."

"At the Polish summit. Last January—"

"December," Karpenko corrected.

"You're sure? This man has aided Malyev's defection?" Pirogov was starting to connect the dots. "Does he also have some link to the journalist?"

"We can place both in Odessa at the same time."

The major considered that. "Malyev, Gavrilenko—and this American, a Ukrainian by birth. Their combined skills have hurt us indeed." There was one more picture. "And this woman?"

"A separate issue, but connected, nonetheless."

"I see," Pirogov mumbled. He lingered over the last photo in the stack, and for the first time that morning, the major had a reason to smile.

This could be useful, Alexei judged.

Operatives of the intelligence services were always looking for pressure points; circumstances, situations, and certainly individuals that could be manipulated to gain a tactical advantage, and after studying these images, it was clear to Alexei that the general had found one.

Eastern Virginia,
Across the Potomac

From Neill's apartment, it was a forty minute drive to Anacostia. The two officers endured a little Beltway traffic—not bad for a Saturday—with Crockett repeatedly checking his phone as their destination grew closer.

"Expecting a call?" Mike grinned.

"Keeping an eye on the time, grandpa," Nate teased.

"Relax. It's only eight-thirty."

"Yeah, but I don't want to be late. And I've watched paint dry faster."

A familiar neighborhood came into view; split level ranch houses on either side of the lane. Crockett released his seat belt as they wheeled into a driveway.

"C'mon, c'mon, I've got people to see and places to go."

Neill killed the engine. "Gotta observe the pleasantries, old man; the master gunny stands on ceremony."

"You did call, right?"

"Guns knows we're coming."

"I wasn't talking about the gunny," Nate protested.

The captain stifled a laugh. "You were there, moron. Of course I called." Both men exited the car. "Don't forget your stuff."

Nate wrenched open the rear door, retrieving a garment bag from the seat. "Did she sound okay? I mean—"

"I know what you mean. She sounded fine. Now let's go inside and say hello." He held out the keys. "Here, I'll trade ya."

"Where's he off to?" Master Gunnery Sergeant Daniel Gavin Neill—medically retired—grumbled under his breath. He watched as Crockett eased the car into the street and sped north.

"Wait one, Master Guns," Mike told him. Nate's bag was draped over one arm, a change of clothes zipped inside. "Let me ditch this first."

The senior NCO sighed heavily. "Nobody ever wants to stop and visit."

"Cheer up. He'll be back later." Seconds went by and

the younger Neill emerged from the guest room, inspecting the kitchen as he passed. "Any coffee left?"

"Help yourself." Daniel moved from the window. He grinned, and asked, "And why was Nate gussied up in his alphas? He looked like he was dressed for a funeral."

"That's close." Mike found a mug stamped with the Third Battalion, Fifth Marines emblem and poured coffee.

"Is this about a woman?"

"Yeah, but it's not what you think."

"You're not being very forthcoming." As an afterthought he added, "Ever since Kiev, come to think of it."

"I'm all about accommodation." He stirred in cream and sugar. "And since you like to complain, I just thought I'd meet you halfway."

"Okay, Academy boy. Crockett can fill me in at dinner." The master gunny slipped on a pair of readers and powered up his desktop. "Get your butt in here. There's something I want you to see."

Mike sipped from the mug. Satisfied with the taste, he left the kitchen and wandered into the den. "Ah, the magic box glows." He feigned surprise. "Are you still using dial-up?"

"Don't be a smart aleck," his elder groused. The retired NCO pulled up a chair. "Christina hooked up the Wi-Fi. Are you getting forgetful in your old age?"

Mike smiled at the name. "Why are you so grumpy today?" He planted himself on the ottoman. "Do I bring that out in people?"

"The great Michael Neill, irritant-at-large," Daniel chuckled. He favored his left arm, and Mike spied a brace on his wrist. "Are you referring to me alone, people in general, or maybe a certain Staff Sergeant Arrens?"

"Bingo," Mike allowed.

"Called you, did she?"

The captain's head bobbed. "We talk every morning around breakfast time."

"And she was anxious, I'll wager." Daniel shrugged. "Well, can't exactly blame her. She's left her boyfriend behind—without getting him to commit."

Michael parried. "Commitment isn't the issue. This is all about timing. And it's not just me." He watched as Daniel began tapping away at the keyboard, bringing up a trusted news site.

"How's the coffee?"

"Stronger than last time. Different brand?"

"From Hawaii." Daniel wasn't quite ready to leave things alone. "You know where that is, right?"

"I've seen pictures. A bunch of islands, I think."

"Very good, junior. And unless I'm mistaken, that's where Christina is." He turned and gave his nephew a scowl. "By the way, you're an idiot."

"What was I supposed to do? She needed to clear her head. And I'm some kind of distraction."

"Narcissist."

"You're full of compliments. How would you have handled things?"

Daniel stopped and peered over his frames. "For one thing, I wouldn't let that girl slip through my fingers. And don't start with the regulations again. That argument's getting stale. Women like her are hard to find— hence my bachelor status."

"That has more to do with your bubbly personality."

"Hardy har har. Piercing insults. But you're dodging the issue." He was staring now. "I've seen you two when you're together. You've been drawn to her since day one. Admit it."

"Oh, I admit it." His candor surprised the gunny.

"What about your other girlfriends?"

"What's that supposed to mean?"

"That Russian woman. The journalist." He raised an eyebrow. "I've seen her pictures—she's very nice."

"Viktoriya's Ukrainian."

"Whatever."

"And she's not a girlfriend." Neill frowned. "Can we move on?"

The master gunny refused. "Answer a serious question first; do you think your feelings for Christina will change?"

Neill sighed. "No. I can't see that happening."

"Then you've got some decisions to make."

The reply came in a measured tone. "The Corps has put limits on my personal life. And I'm not about to re-sign my commission. The ball's in Christina's court, too, and she doesn't want to leave her career. Like I said, it's all about timing."

Daniel peered at his nephew. "I get obligation, Mike. But there are other ways to serve. Once a Marine, always a Marine. You'll always have that."

"Any other words of wisdom?"

"That girl needs to know that you care."

"I'm pretty sure she does. And trust me, I know what I've got in her."

"So don't lose her." NCOs could be blunt, and senior NCOs rarely sugar-coated things. "If you're smart, you'll start making an effort. There's too much focus on the physical. Not enough on what you look for in a serious relationship."

Neill eyed his uncle shrewdly. "And when did you become such an expert on women?"

"I've been reading stuff."

"What stuff?" A thin paperback rested on the coffee table. Mike picked it up. "Oh, this looks deep. *Women Love Conflict, Men Prefer Beer*. You're kidding me, right? Who wrote this?"

The master gunny brightened. "A buddy of mine. A Marine." Daniel shrugged. "He should know, too. The guy's been married three times."

Neill tossed the book aside. "So he's an expert."

"Here, have a seat." Daniel rose, protecting his arm. He was unsteady at first. The veteran of Iraq also had a prosthetic leg, courtesy of an insurgent's IED. His halting movements were familiar, but the bum wing was a recent condition.

"That wrist still bothering you?"

The elder Neill waved him off. "It's been worse."

"Have you seen the doc?"

"There's no point in that—he'd just refer me to an orthopedics guy, or a bone-cracker. Besides, the VA's backed up."

"What a coincidence." Michael pulled out his wallet and handed over a card. "I made an appointment for you with a chiropractor. A functional specialist."

"I'm not forkin' over money to some civilian doc."

Mike ignored his uncle's protests. "A consultation first. And they'll probably do x-rays. That could get expensive, so bring your credit card and some chickens. Or whatever it is old jarheads use for cash."

Daniel ignored the razzing and studied the appointment time. He was ready to walk back some of his earlier wisecracks. "It does hurt," he confessed. "And it doesn't feel like it's getting better. You don't think it's broken, do you?"

"That's for the doc to decide. Now what was it you wanted to show me?"

Daniel pulled off his glasses. "Halfway down. Left side. See that thing about Russia?"

Mike clicked on the link. "This uranium story?"

"That's the one. Is it accurate?"

"Let me read it first." He sped through the first paragraph, and then the second, shaking his head. "It's accurate, all right. Another foreign policy blunder—courtesy of the Mark Breese administration."

"What's it all about?"

Mike waded in slowly. "For years, the Russians have been buying up uranium assets. A lot of it's in the northern hemisphere; mostly owned by a Canadian company across the border, but on land in the U.S."

"Doesn't the State Department have to approve stuff like that?"

"They do and they have. After the deal was made, the Canadians donated a hefty sum to Breese's re-election campaign."

"That should be illegal."

"You'll get no argument from me." Mike scrolled through the rest of it. "They worked some financial sleight of hand, and now the Russians have the rights to a boatload of our heavy metal deposits."

Daniel whistled softly. "Lately Ivan seems pretty focused on generating kilowatts. What's Moscow up to?"

Neill considered that thoughtfully. "They've decided to make energy the new coin of the realm. It's been used to great effect in Eastern Europe. Look at how they've manipulated Ukraine and Poland. Think about it; next to food and water, what else do you need to survive? And what does any sovereign nation require to secure its infrastructure?"

"Power," Daniel answered, a gleam in his eye. "Hydroelectric, nuclear, gas, and oil—emerging technologies are nice, but too many of those are pie in the sky concepts."

"Exactly." The younger man sat back in the chair. "And it's got me thinking, too. Ivan doesn't do anything small. My guess is that Moscow's got a master plan. On the outside is their obsession with energy. But they're hiding something."

"Hiding?" Daniel frowned. "I don't follow you."

Mike had a peculiar look. "I've got to work it all out. I don't know enough yet." He looked up at his uncle, his expression softening. "I'm not trying to keep you out of the loop; I just need to learn more."

"You'll get it, Mike."

"In time." He stared out the window, and then back again. "You really need to keep that appointment, Guns."

A smile. "Don't tell me you're worried about me."

"You're all the family I've got left," Mike told him. "Somebody has to worry about you. As it is, I haven't been around much the past few years. I regret that."

"You've got responsibilities, Mike. Big ones."

Neill shook his head. "That's no excuse. And neither of us is getting any younger."

Daniel had rarely seen his nephew wax emotional. "Listen, life's thrown you some curve balls lately. Take some time off. Fly out to the Pacific. Surprise Christina. She'd like that."

"Can't do that right now, Gunny."

Daniel stared. "Oh? And why not?"

Mike looked out the window again and said nothing.

"You're going somewhere." He caught on fast. "All right, Marine, spit it out."

"You know I can't do that. It's classified."

Daniel's expression turned. "Must be the Russians again." He swore out loud, and his face became stone. "This Ilya Maersk—" he growled. "Are we sure he's dead?"

The younger Neill nodded. "Ukraine's state police confirmed it. Two of their agents gave him a taste of his own medicine, from what I've been told."

"Polonium," Daniel shuddered.

Mike thought about Kiev, and the Berkut's actions

that night in the alley behind the bar. Since Warsaw he'd come to know Yuri Tereshenko and Xander Voskov much better. Both men were calculating individuals, capable of taking lives—but not indiscriminately. And each had taught Neill something about human nature.

There were those who could deal the hand of death without compunction. Some for good and some for evil. Neill counted the Berkut officers in the first group, while Boris Isakov and Nadia Kolvec—they were far less reputable, there was no doubt about that. The Marine had been shaken by Isakov's death, but Xander Voskov was as cool as a cucumber.

He considered that carefully. Where did he fall when measured against such men? Neill had a conscience, and being a combat-trained Marine and a follower of Christ had honed his scruples.

Sometimes it wasn't easy to balance morality with duty—especially if there was a fine line separating the two. Such actions required strength of character. Could he pull a trigger to save a life? Of course he could; he had fired on Ivan Malyev in Odessa. He was ready to do the same while protecting Christina in Warsaw. But in those instances he'd never actually killed anyone.

And what if he had? Once the deed was done, could he justify it without regret? Those were questions that presented themselves each time a judgment call had to be made.

Something else occurred to him, and Mike thought about his dad. What would he do under such circumstances? David Neill was a man given to sacrifice, putting the good of others first, but that argument worked both ways. Taking a life to save one still involved killing, and doing so meant playing God. Unless, of course, the Almighty was using the participant for His will—and how did that factor into the equation?

Mike broke from his reverie, sure of one thing; he could trust his new-found friends from Ukraine. They served under different flags, but just like Crockett, Tereshenko and Voskov had his back, and their brother-hood had been formed in the heat of battle.

Remorse aside, that was all that mattered.

• • • •

Crockett took the Anacostia to John Hanson Highway, proceeding northeast past Prince Georges Country Club. From there the car's navigational system directed him to follow Annapolis Road, and within twenty minutes of leaving the freeway, the Marine coasted through a neighborhood of neatly manicured lawns and comfortable homes nestled near Edgewater.

He slowed his approach. It was a quiet street. The nav system announced one left turn after another, until Nate recognized the numbers on a house at the end of a cul-de-sac.

This was it, all right.

His palms were moist as he edged off the road and into the driveway. The young officer shot a glance in the rearview; fresh haircut, a clean shave—even by Nate's standards, he looked more than presentable.

The air was cool as he stepped out of the car. This should have been easy, but a nervous hand went to his collar. The Marine took the unnecessary step of straightening his tie once again. He drew in a deep breath, perched the barracks cover on the top of his head, and with one more look at his reflection, Lieutenant Nathan Crockett marched up the steps and tapped gently on the front door.

The woman who answered was younger and prettier than expected, and Nate found himself looking into the crystal blue eyes of Amber Aultman.

Richard's widow offered a polite smile. "It's good of you to come." She was looking over Nate's shoulder. "Is Captain Neill with you?"

"No, ma'am." Nate removed his cover. "He offered, but I thought it best to come alone. I hope that's all right."

She nodded. "Oh, yes, it's fine. Please come in."

They moved inside, entering a room off the foyer. Crockett's eyes followed her as she went. Mrs. Aultman displayed great poise, something the Marine hadn't counted on in a woman so recently visited by grief.

"These are for you." Nate held a small bouquet. "It's kind of you to see me, considering the circumstances."

She turned. Yellow roses, with white carnations. Her smile widened. The young officer seemed to struggle with his words, and she was both touched and amused.

"That's very thoughtful." She reached out, accepting the flowers. "Won't you sit down?" Nate settled into a chair, and the young woman asked, "If you don't mind— I was wondering—"

"Yes, ma'am?"

"Did you practice that line?"

Dry wit. The weight on Nate's shoulders was much lighter now. "Yes, ma'am. Half a dozen times. But just since I left the highway." He returned her grin, but cautiously. "Did it sound forced?"

"You can drop the *ma'am*, Lieutenant—my name is Amber." She brought the arrangement close to her face, enjoying the fragrance. She was partial to roses, and the scent reminded her that spring had arrived. She recalled the numerous occasions when Richard—

She hadn't planned for this. *Keep it short*, she'd told herself. The Marine's visit was sure to open fresh wounds, and she was still dealing with the pain of Richard's death.

"Amber." Nate spoke off the cuff and uttered the first

words that came to mind. "That's a very pretty name."

A reflexive cringe. *Dumb jarhead*—he chided himself—*what are you, in high school?*

The young widow was caught off-guard. She'd half-expected a brash, cocky gunslinger—with a subdued outer shell, in deference to her recent loss—yet the lieutenant seemed genuinely sensitive, and without a hint of bravado, masked or otherwise.

Small talk was automatic. Common courtesy came first, followed by simple questions and comments. Nate noted the features of the Aultman home, complimenting Amber's taste in furnishings but stopping short before the conversation became shallow. She returned the favor, exchanging more pleasantries, asking about his deployments and where he was stationed before thanking him for his service. Then she mentioned something that took Crockett back to Warsaw's Royal Castle.

"You might not be aware of this," she started, "but Richard served in the Army. He was very proud of that."

The conversation had shifted to Amber's slain husband. Both knew that it would. She'd found a context Nate could identify with, while at the same time steering the discussion toward some familiar and bittersweet territory.

"So he told me. Did you two know each other then?"

She shook her head. "He got out just before we met. Finished his degree, and then went to work for the State Department." Her voice was low, faltering. She stood, moving toward the kitchen. "Would you like something cold to drink? Or maybe some coffee?"

Amber served iced tea, sweetened, and Nate filled in a few gaps while they sipped.

He began slowly, and reliving the story was painful. Crockett took the young woman back to the night of the dinner, telling her about REMORA's attempt to poison the delegates, and the chaos that ensued when the assassin stole a policeman's pistol. She'd heard this tale before, but her eyes brightened as Nate offered new details. He was well-placed to do so; the Marine was trained to observe the incidentals—what others might miss—and he provided a different perspective on what happened that evening.

Ilya Maersk had given them the slip. He was loose in the Castle. Searching for the gunman, Nate and Richard separated so the sniper could clear one of the galleries. Amber hung on every word, holding her glass tightly as the story progressed.

"I'm sorry," Nate abruptly caught himself. "Do you want me to stop?"

She shook her head, sitting a little more erect. Her eyes were moist. "Keep going."

Crockett paused, choosing his words carefully. He hadn't been in the chapel when Richard was shot, and sitting here now, Nate was thankful for that. The finer points of Maersk's handiwork weren't important. Amber was only interested in hearing about her husband's final moments, and by the time Nate finished, the tears were flowing freely.

This was difficult for both of them. Amber dabbed at her eyes, and Nate remained silent, hoping for composure. But then a sob escaped her lips, followed by several more. He spied a box of tissues on the end table and handed them across. Without clear training to fall back on, he resorted to simple human compassion.

He reached out and placed his hand on hers.

"So you never saw Maersk leave the building?"

"No," Nate breathed. "I never saw him again *period*—not after that." His chin dropped to his chest. "Some scout I turned out to be."

Amber's frown took nothing away from her beauty. "And you blame yourself?"

"I can't think of a better candidate."

"You didn't shoot Richard, Lieutenant. Maersk did that." The widow's expression became a smile. "It sounds like we're both confused."

Nate started to speak, but Amber cut him off.

"You're angry—with yourself. And I'm mad at my husband. Don't you see? We're both awfully selfish to be dishing out blame like this."

Crockett wasn't quite ready to be assuaged. "I should have made him come with me. He had no business going up against a trained assassin."

"Probably not. But from what I've heard, he gave as good as he got."

He blinked. For the first time since the shooting, a simple fact was staring him in the face. Cornered by three trained marksmen—Marines, no less—it was Richard Aultman who'd bested the Russian, putting a round through Maersk's leg—an injury that slowed the shooter, giving the Berkut squad a chance to catch him.

And what she said next caught Nate completely by surprise.

"Captain Neill told me that he prayed with Richard, before that night," Amber said calmly. Without hesitation, she posed a question. "Are you a man of faith?"

"Mike drags me to church when I'm in town. I'd like to think I'm a better man for it."

He rarely discussed spirituality with anyone except Neill. Mike had an easy way of talking about religion. Amber seemed equally comfortable with the subject. He decided to turn the focus elsewhere.

Yet at the same time, Nate was strangely warmed.

"I came to share parts of the story you might not have

heard," he resumed. "And that's not the only reason I'm here. I wanted to offer my condolences." His next words held great respect. "To tell you that I'm sorry."

The moment faded. Neither one of them could tell how long it lasted before Crockett's eyes brightened.

"And I have a first name too, Amber. It's Nate."

The two stood at the front door as Crockett prepared to leave. "What's next for you?" she asked.

He drew in a deep breath. "A new assignment. Mike and I leave soon." He winced. "Sorry—I shouldn't have said that. Kind of a 'need-to-know' thing."

"You sounded just like Richard then," Amber smiled.

His face reddened. "I should probably go. Too many painful memories. And I've made you cry."

"Those tears needed to flow."

Nate pressed on. "You mentioned being angry with your husband," he reminded her. "I can understand that. It's only natural—something to do with the stages of grief, I suppose." He was staring at her again. "Pain doesn't last forever. You'll get through this. And when you do, you'll find hope. And friends to help you enjoy it." He moved toward the steps that led to the driveway. "There's only one more thing I came here to say."

"Oh?"

"You didn't see me at Richard's funeral."

She nodded. "Captain Neill told me you had to get back to Camp Lejeune."

"That's what I told him. And it's true—but I could have pushed it back another day or so."

"So why didn't you?"

Nate hung his head, but brought it up again before speaking. "The truth is I just couldn't face you. I couldn't look you in the eye—until now."

"Feel better?"

A smile. "Maybe." He retrieved something from the pocket of his trousers. "I want you to hang on to this."

Her hand went out. "What is it?"

"Cell phone number. And my address at Lejeune. If you need anything, and I mean *anything*, you pick up the phone and give me a call."

Nate gunned the motor and edged into the street. He gave her a wave—a salute, really—then accelerated through the intersection and sped west. Her eyes followed the car until it disappeared, and with her world quiet once more, Amber stepped across the threshold and back into the house.

She felt raw inside, emotions kindled by the lieutenant's account. Since Richard's death, grief and loneliness had been her nearest companions. Images of her husband swirled in Amber's head; his face, the scent of cologne on his hands, and his touch, brought to life by Nate's words, and the memories washed over her in waves. Crockett spared her the unnecessary parts of the story, painting a noble yet accurate picture, but the pain had resurfaced, and the widow could only steel herself for another empty day and bear it through more tears.

An aching heart knew no quick remedies, but at the same time she felt unburdened. Mike Neill had described Lieutenant Crockett as 'high speed, low drag', a man of war, and probably accustomed to taking lives, but today, he'd shown only tenderness and compassion, shattering her stereotypes of what a sniper could be.

It wasn't reasonable to think such men were always gentlemen. Nations relied on rough individuals, operators skilled at visiting violence upon their enemies. War was a dirty business, and those who got the best results were warriors released from their chains, determined to bring peace through the most decisive of methods.

She was focused on the other side of the coin. Nate's gentle spirit had clearly made an impression. In the stillness of the big house, Amber reflected on the Marine's self-conscious manner, the careful way he presented his story. The recollection brought a smile.

Amber busied herself in the sitting room, straightening cushions and collecting empty tumblers, then made her way to the kitchen. The Marine's flowers lay on the countertop, and after placing the glasses in the sink, she transferred the bouquet to a vase filled with water. It had been a while since she'd received such a gift, and she took her time arranging the stems and enjoying the fragrance.

She closed her eyes, considering her guest. Nate's features drifted into view. Turned out in dress greens, his bearing was impeccable. Three rows of ribbons—decorations for Afghanistan, the Navy and Marine Corps Commendation Medal, along with the Combat Action Ribbon—spoke of service, a résumé denoting battlefield accomplishments. Yet given his experiences, the lieutenant's face betrayed no hard lines. His round looks gave him a youthful appearance, younger than he probably was. On top of that, he was annoyingly handsome, and for the briefest of moments—

Amber caught herself. She refused those thoughts, calling on her husband's memory to replace them. Nathan Crockett was like any other man; better than most, maybe, but still fallible. Her anger flared, a fire erupting in her wounded and lonely heart. Two facts were quite clear. In spite of his skills with a weapon, the Marine had failed to protect her husband.

She moved to the next room, eyeing the card in her hand. The solace it promised was now gone, stolen by an impulse of emotion, and as she exited the kitchen, she tossed it toward the waste basket. Her aim was clouded by tears. It struck the rim, bouncing in the opposite direction, and Amber never saw it come to rest against the baseboard next to the fridge.

COLD ARSENAL

Part Two

9

COMMISSAR

Aboard the R/V Pont Claire
Three days later

CLIFF TUCKER CURSED aloud and lifted a hand to shield his eyes. He needed sleep, but wouldn't relax just yet—and probably couldn't, given his agitated state. His senses were on high alert for good reason. Since dusk of the previous day, the Russian Navy had gotten frisky, pursuing the *Pont Claire* east, and giving Tucker's crew a restless night as they tried to avoid the warship bearing down on them.

The chase began when Tucker's men retrieved the sonar array, just as darkness fell. A patrol boat appeared on the horizon, pacing the *Belousov* and then heeling to starboard in hot pursuit. They were driving him, Captain Tucker reasoned; a show of force to send a message, and only a landlubber could miss its meaning. These waters were very close to Russian territory, and Ivan wasn't keen on entertaining guests so near his shores.

This was typical behavior, and Tucker tried hard not to be concerned. The skipper had seen these corvettes before and recognized their tactics. The Russians weren't known for their manners, after all, and often ignored the time-honored traditions of the sea, bullying smaller craft that were less heavily armed. In some cases, they crowded another vessel's lane just to make a point. They could have easily overtaken Tucker's ship, using their bulk to threaten him, but as morning dawned they slowed their pace and stayed dead astern.

A thin smile crossed his face. Some conflicts never changed, and this one harkened back to the days of the Cold War. The Russian word for *courtesy* was probably very difficult to pronounce—if it existed at all.

The glare hurt his eyes. Patting his pockets, Tucker realized the shades he relied on were still on the bridge. He cursed again—more loudly this time—and started back up the steps.

Tucker found his sunglasses right where he'd left them. He snatched them up as the first officer jammed the bridge phone back in its cradle.

"Angie needs you in the Scif, Cap'n." He referred to a sensitive compartmented information facility, a common enough term in military circles.

"We don't *have* a Scif, Cal," Tucker replied tiredly. "What we've got is a sonar van." He shook his head. A high-resolution mapping specialist, Angie enjoyed throwing out acronyms, and was part of Challenger Petroleum's geek squad. "Is that where she is?"

The first officer nodded. "Says it's urgent."

Urgent? The skipper considered that. She must have pulled together some data from the sonar sweep.

"I'm on my way."

Tucker moved back through the hatch and down the ladderwell. Reaching the main deck he continued aft and ambled around crewmen as they secured cables. By the time he reached the stern, Sean Crackenmoor stood in the van's doorway, blocking the view inside.

And the Cracken looked excited.

"Skipper, you've gotta see this."

"So that's Spit Weathersby's phantom. What the Sam Hill is it, Angie?"

The air conditioner chugged, keeping the sensitive equipment cool. It was dark in the van and Tucker shivered as he stared at the big-screen plasma affixed to the bulkhead. The visual was monochromatic, and depicted something he'd never seen before.

"Two thousand images to come up with this composite, Captain." Angie never took her eyes off the display, studying it for whatever she could glean. "The new software stitched this together in less than an hour. And I was hoping you could tell me."

The ship's pride and joy was a underwater vehicle dubbed Elvis, equipped with echo-ranging equipment and 3D imaging sonar. Dual sounding gear mounted in skids could ping simultaneously, returning images in a stereographic display.

And what a display it was.

"Submarine, maybe?" the Cracken offered.

Angie shook her head. "It's too big, Sean. Wrong shape, too."

Tucker frowned, studying data embedded within the black and white frames. "Have you got dimensions on this?"

"Eighty meters long," she replied. "Fifty-five meters wide—" she traced a finger from the top of the screen to the bottom, "—from here to here. And given the symmetrical shape, it appears to be relatively intact."

"How long has it been there?"

"Hard to say, Cap'n. It's in a hundred and sixty feet of water, and the seafloor is constantly shifting. Depending on the duration of its stay, this thing might have been covered a hundred times over by sediments."

"Any markings?" Tucker asked.

"None that I can make out."

"Is it radioactive?"

"Should it be?" Crackenmoor asked. He considered that an odd question.

"Probably not. And if it ever was, seawater has a diluting effect. Acts as a shield, too."

Elvis looked down on the object, providing an overhead view. Tucker took a step toward the screen. He'd come to his own conclusions.

"Those are wingtips," he announced.

Angie agreed. "I was thinking the same thing."

The Cracken studied the monitor. "It's a plane?"

"What else could it be? The configuration looks odd, I'll grant you—short, stubby airfoils." Tucker pointed ahead. "But this thing was built to fly."

Angie leaned forward in her seat. "But what are these things—on the front?" If that is the front, she didn't add.

"Looks like a moose rack," Sean quipped. "You know—horns or antlers."

"Planes don't have antlers, Sean."

"I know that," Crackenmoor assured her. "Has to be some kind of structural feature. So here's the next question—who does this thing belong to?"

"It's not American, I can tell you that," the skipper snorted. "My vote goes to the Russians. Judging by their behavior, I'd say this is what that salvage ship was looking for. They must've figured we'd found it, and decided to follow up."

"And that's why they chased us off?"

Tucker didn't give an answer. "Is that Navy ship still in range?"

"The *Meyer*?" Angie asked. "She's well over the horizon. Headed southwest, I think."

"Send her a radio message. Include the data on this thing—and make sure they get the imagery." Tucker tapped the screen.

"I'll bet the U.S. Navy will be mighty interested in this."

Arkangel Base Plateau,
Kamchatka Peninsula

The admiral's driver steered the Land Rover to the east, through the compound's living quarters, climbing the bumpy, rock-strewn road to the pinnacle's crest. Only one route led to the mountaintop; narrow and barely paved, this single lane path was carved out of uneven granite terraces, a testament to the skills of the Soviet engineers who labored here thirty years before.

The journey to the top had begun far below, stretching from Ust-Kamchatsk, the Russian Navy's outpost that lay to the west. It was hardly the scenic route. Nothing grew on this windswept highland. The terrain was a study in gray and white, dusted with crushed slate and a recent snowfall, and winter would not release her grip for another month at best.

Taras Pavlenko, admiral of the Navy—the Military-Maritime Fleet of the Russian Federation—sat in the back as the car rolled to a stop. Thirty meters away, the summit's peak broke the skyline, and beyond the ridge was a view of unparalleled majesty.

"Brace yourself, Captain," the officer told his aide. Pavlenko's face was pitted, ravaged by years at sea. "It is not so warm here as your office in Petropavlovsk."

"Probably no more than eight degrees, comrade Admiral." Captain First Rank Nestor Tamarkin was refer-

ring to the temperature in Celsius, not Fahrenheit. He
turned, watching as the protective detail pulled along-
side. They had been following in an identical car. Six
members of the naval infantry—Russian Marines—immediately spilled out, stamping their boots in an effort to
warm themselves.

"Their vehicle has no heat, Admiral," Tamarkin observed. "Unfortunate."

"I should have warned them," the officer chuckled.

Pavlenko and Tamarkin got out as well, and the admiral stretched. His joints were stiff after the long drive,
and he trudged closer to the top of the summit. Snow and
gravel crunched underfoot. Spread out below them was
a wide expanse of ocean, and from this vantage point,
the new arrivals could see the horizon thirty kilometers
away, the vista dotted with naval vessels and merchantmen plying the waters of the Pacific.

Taras sifted memories. He had a personal connection
to this coastline, and to the frontier of waves that beck-
oned in the distance.

"I want to keep a small detachment of troops here,
Captain Tamarkin," the admiral said abruptly.

"Some of our Marines, Admiral?"

Pavlenko nodded his head. "Six should be enough."

"We have that many already."

"Those troops are *above*. I want a smaller contingent
to remain below, securing the lower levels."

"Are you expecting trouble in the labs?"

"We're getting closer to the final outcome, Captain. I
simply want to be prepared."

Tamarkin decided to change the subject. "One can almost imagine seeing the Commander Islands, *tavarisch*,"
he mused. The precipice dropped away to the shoreline,
and scudding clouds lingered far out to sea. Tamarkin
squinted, his gaze sweeping the horizon. It was nearly

noon and the sun was exceptionally bright.

The admiral shook his head. "They are too distant, comrade Captain." The cold pinched moisture from his eyes. Gusting up from the beach, the sea breeze lifted his words, threatening to carry them away. "Besides, Arkangel has other wonders—far beneath our feet."

A domed pillbox atop the ridge was camouflaged to match its surroundings. The two officers descended a series of steps, and reaching the landing's base they were stopped by a heavy door. A keypad was mounted on the frame. Pavlenko reached out a gloved hand, punching in digits, and the two men listened as a servomotor growled to life behind the walls and over their heads.

In short order the door slid open to reveal the narrow confines of an elevator compartment. The conveyance was large enough for only four men, and Captain Tamarkin waved for two of the Marines to join them as they stepped inside the car.

"It smells of diesel," the captain muttered. "And jet fuel."

The admiral nodded. "Not surprising." With a touch of a button, the door slid closed again, and the steel-reinforced cage lurched and began its descent.

They rode in silence. The frigid temperatures at the surface were forgotten, and a damp humidity could be felt as the lift slipped deeper into the mountainside. The elevator controls displayed six choices, along with a floor plan of the base. One of the elevations—at sea level—was wide and expansive, and at least five stories tall. It was easy to guess the intended purpose of that space. Tamarkin had never visited Arkangel, but surmised that the last level had been constructed as a hangar, a facility for the outpost's power plant, with additional room for machinery and parts storage.

The car stopped halfway down and the door opened to a narrow corridor. Security personnel waited for them on the other side, checked their credentials, and guided the senior officers to a conference room at the far end. They were met there by the duty officer, a stout man with a thick beard, who came briefly to attention before showing them into the base commander's office.

"Gentlemen." The man in charge scurried about, concerned with his visitors' comfort. In doing so, he showed proper deference, Tamarkin judged. "Some tea is in order. Something to warm chilled bones, yes?"

A former aviator, Colonel Utkin dismissed the guards and closed the door. He allowed the officers a chance to remove their cold weather gear, and after the customary introductions the lanky pilot waved them to a set of chairs. As they settled in, Utkin began pouring from a *samovar* close at hand.

The office was small. Tamarkin was struck by the confined spaces he'd seen so far. His eyes traveled to the wall behind Utkin's desk. Photos hanging there depicted a wide variety of aircraft. One image in particular captured the captain's interest.

The colonel noted Tamarkin's disdain with a smile. He had seen that look on the faces of other guests. "You expected more from Arkangel, Captain." He handed the admiral a cup of tea, and another for his aide.

"I expected to find a hardened facility—safeguarding state secrets. I am not disappointed."

"A clever answer," Utkin allowed. "But nothing important happens on this level. The real work is done in the labs—and in the hangar below."

"The admiral has briefed me on this hangar." The senior captain sipped from his cup, and his mood brightened as they broached the subject. "I understand you call it the *Nest*."

"*Da*, comrade. An appropriate nickname, don't you think?" He regarded Pavlenko with a calculating eye, anxious to touch on another topic. "The message from Petropavlovsk. It was intriguing, Admiral. I take it your team has found something worthy of our time?"

"Captain Tamarkin's team." He turned. "*Tavarisch*?"

"We are optimistic. Recent events have provided— shall we say—a boon of information."

"Regarding Charybdis?"

A nod. "The schematics of the weapon exist only in Dr. Zhukov's mind, but comparisons can be enormously valuable. The American airliner, the Japanese nuclear plant. And the Air Force cargo plane. That incident was most illuminating."

Utkin's brow furrowed. "The turbo-prop aircraft?" His interest was now piqued. "I thought that attempt was unsuccessful."

Tamarkin was forced to concede. "The results were less than expected, that much is true. But sometimes we learn more from our failures than our successes."

"And in this instance?" Utkin pressed.

Tamarkin began slowly. "As you know, the doctor has been reluctant to reveal the workings of his operational hierarchy—the so-called *system linkage dependency*. A clever safeguard, intended to ensure his survival—"

"And that of his team," the colonel volunteered.

"*Da*," the captain agreed. "Each link is a closed entity, functioning perfectly within the whole. But divorced from the sum of their parts, these links are useless. An examination of the separate components has so far yielded nothing."

"Until now," the admiral offered.

"We are much closer," Tamarkin hedged. "The computer models are promising. A full test of our prototype will provide a more concise answer."

"I'm interested in your comparative studies." Utkin narrowed his eyes. "Can you elaborate on those?"

"We focused on the sinewave present in each incident—a three-dimensional approach to the problem, if you will." The captain drew in some air. "Establishing a baseline came first, followed by a review of the amplitudes used to bring down the other aircraft."

"And the American transport— the C-130?"

"Ironically, that was our most useful test case. We compared the power deployed by Charybdis, and then evaluated the American's response." The captain gave a shrug. "Against the civilian airliner, we were able to extrapolate on a series of scenarios."

"Defensive scenarios?"

"Yes. That is correct."

"So the secrets of Dr. Zhukov's monstrosity are now open to us?"

"Time will tell, Colonel."

"How much time?" Utkin was anxious.

Tamarkin was irritated by the probing. "Perhaps as little as two or three days."

Pavlenko shifted the focus with a separate question. "And the doctor?" he asked.

The base commander drew back. He seemed wary.

"Dr. Zhukov has asked for you, Admiral. He requests an audience."

Colonel Utkin led the visitors back to the elevator and the three descended. Even before the lift reached the first floor, the visitors could hear men's shouts, the clanking of tools, and the whirr of heavy machinery echoing in their ears.

The noise grew louder as the door slid back, but this was not the hangar. Finding themselves in an anteroom, the officers' senses were greeted by warm air and the stench of diesel fuel. Tamarkin wrinkled his nose and caught something else—the hint of brine and seawater. It then occurred to him that most aerodromes weren't built next to shorelines, and the scent in his nostrils probably came from the tides hidden somewhere out of sight.

"And the sea, Colonel? This refuge provides secrecy, but how does it affect your instruments?"

"Corrosion is a problem. We are constantly fighting the elements," Utkin confirmed.

The room was crowded with technicians perched on top of stools. They seemed oblivious to everything except the computer screens before them. Narrow windows were set near the ceiling; these afforded little view of the areas beyond, but it was clear that the workshop was comparatively small.

On the other side a welder's torch flashed, illuminating steel girders high above. Tamarkin stepped back; it was difficult to see, but the glare reflected off something sleek and aerodynamic, a flat, horizontal surface that appeared to stretch across his entire field of vision.

One of the reasons for their visit stood in the center of the room. Pavlenko saw him first. Radya Zhukov was a tall man, older than the others, with close-cropped, graying features and deep-set eyes behind wire-rimmed glasses. Wearing a soiled white lab coat, he leaned on a cane, supervising a young woman seated at a lathe.

"Come with me, Captain." Utkin edged toward a set of double doors. A keypad and a palm print reader were mounted on the wall. "It's time I gave you a tour of the Nest."

The officers watched as Pavlenko skirted around workstations. He wore a smile, but his expression was cold.

This was to be a contest of titans.

"Dr. Zhukov."

"Admiral," the doctor replied. "To what do we owe the pleasure?"

The man clutching the cane regarded Pavlenko with little emotion. A unique tension existed between them; the two had met long ago, years before the collapse of Soviet Russia, on a stormy sea not one hundred kilometers away.

Pavlenko's words were smooth. "I was curious. Have you reconsidered my offer?"

Zhukov answered him with a question of his own. "Has my work displeased you, Admiral?" he asked with a thin smile. "You have your weapon, do you not?"

The girl at their side looked away, and technicians close by lowered their eyes.

"That is true, Radya—" Pavlenko raised a brow and stopped mid-sentence, "—but we don't yet know how it works."

Zhukov played a different card. "And I wonder how short my days might be if I were to hand over its secrets."

The officer pretended pain. For the first time he deferred to the woman in their midst.

"Perhaps we should discuss this privately, Doctor. Your daughter need not be concerned with our deliberations." Another plastic grin. "Don't you agree?"

Tanya Zhukov sat motionless. She felt dread whenever Taras Pavlenko visited Arkangel. As long as he was absent, she could focus on her work, care for her father, and pretend that her future might one day be normal. That wasn't likely, but she kept the hope alive in spite of her current circumstances.

• • • •

"*Bozhe moi.*" *My God.*

Captain Tamarkin stared upward. Lighting affixed

to the ceiling's metal framework cast shadows on the ground. The outline on the floor was dramatic, but no less so than its source.

"She is the largest in the world," Utkin smiled. "Is this the first time you've seen the *Commissar*, Captain?"

Standing beneath a horizontal stabilizer, the officer took a moment to absorb the view before finding his voice.

"Aside from photos, yes, comrade Colonel."

"Very few exist," Utkin replied. "And photographs don't do her justice, wouldn't you agree?"

"I cannot argue that point."

A massive aircraft dominated the space before them. Clearly a cargo plane, it was impressive from the ground up, squatting on six sets of double tires and matched by an equal number on the opposite side of the fuselage. With a breadth of nearly three hundred feet, the plane's wingtip pontoons seemed to reach for the far walls, and the tail section towering above them cleared the girders by mere meters.

There was activity all around them. Technicians used a ladder assembly to access a wing strut, while on the ground, others turned wrenches beneath the wheel well. All wore red coveralls. A maintenance stand sat nearby, and a portable generator was positioned next to the row of colossal tires. Power cables snaked across the floor, connected to glowing, open panels in the *Commissar*'s fuselage, and the plane's APU—the auxiliary power unit—hummed in the background.

There were other features. Covered by steel grates, recessed trenches ran the length of the hangar. These depressions contained a shallow level of dark liquid, probably oil or hydraulic fluid, judging from the color, and water pooled in various spots on the floor. Giant fans were set within the walls; a few were turning now, providing a constant flow of air that wafted across the room. These were intended to control humidity, preventing the build-up of condensation on machinery and critical components.

Tamarkin stepped forward, moving laterally to get a measure of the bird's mass. Judging from the exterior, the cargo hold within must be cavernous, commanding most of the space fore and aft, and the power-plant was equally impressive. Twin turbofan engines hung on each side, and the roots of both wings were reinforced to carry their weight.

As he approached the right side of the aircraft, his eye was drawn to the front, where huge nacelles sprung from the nose. These dual surfaces served as platforms for additional thrust, supporting eight more engines. With four mounted on each, the oversized extensions gave *Commissar* the appearance of some otherworldly mythical beast.

These features grew larger as Tamarkin walked beneath the wing. He was struck by something else. The bow of the *Commissar* dipped lower than her stern. The plane's nose-gear was designed to kneel—cargo was loaded through the front—and in this crouching position, the aircraft resembled a bird of prey, and it was easy to imagine that she was almost ready to pounce.

Tamarkin smiled, but at the same time was confused.

"The landing gear," he began. "Very sturdy. But I thought this to be a seaplane. Is the aircraft capable of tactical airlift?"

Utkin shook his head. "She is not intended for short-runway operations. Her size precludes that option." He waved a hand. "But even a bird needs feet. These wheels are required to bring the *Commissar* back into her nest."

"And what a nest it is," Tamarkin observed. "Your testing is done in this facility?"

"This is where we see to the *Commissar*'s needs."

The voice came from behind. Tamarkin turned to see Admiral Pavlenko, with Dr. Zhukov at his side.

"Testing is done in flight—far out to sea, and under cover of night," the senior officer continued. "As you might guess, this aircraft would be very conspicuous in the light of day."

"Darkness covers a multitude of sins," the doctor was quick to add. His tone was derisive. "Isn't that true, Taras?"

The admiral was not put off by the comment. "Radya has suffered a change of heart, it would seem," he chuckled. "He is now more interested in benevolent causes. But he cannot deny his involvement in these sins, as he calls them."

"Benevolence is a difficult concept for you, isn't it, Admiral?" Zhukov snorted, clutching something in his free hand. With the other he leaned on his cane.

"Not when it concerns the State, Doctor," Pavlenko shot back, "—and the freedom to protect the interests of the *Rodina*."

"I have found such freedom to be an elusive goal." Zhukov tightened his fist.

"I know that you've *tried*." The admiral was eager to exploit a vulnerability. "Do you still carry your talisman?"

Zhukov looked away. "I pray to it daily."

"Has it brought you any peace?"

Radya's head came up. "I am convinced that hope remains."

"Tell me, Doctor; if one were *truly* free from sin—how much could he accomplish?"

Zhukov gave a quizzical look, thinking the question to be rhetorical. He started to speak, but the admiral cut him off.

"I'm only trying to prove a point, Doctor. You have already achieved much. Sin is a myth—like the God revered by those who created Him. And such is the concept of our shortcomings."

"Is that your definition of the word, Taras? Simply a shortcoming?"

"Like weaknesses, those are meant to be *overcome*, Radya." A smile. "But to fail? That is the real sin."

In the skies over Alaska

She was a C-130 Hercules, a J-model, with twin propeller mounts on the leading edge of each wing. This aircraft was a last minute replacement, and not the larger and more stable Globemaster originally planned for the mission.

The pilot pointed the nose southwest and increased thrust. The four engines roared, spewing exhaust as they climbed, and the plane followed the narrowing land mass that would become the Aleutians. Kodiak Island fell away to the east, and soon nothing but the wide expanse of the Bering Sea, to the right, and the northern Pacific Ocean, on their left, lay on either side of the plane's underbelly.

Three pallets crowded the cargo deck. Two carried heavy equipment, while the last one was laden with electrical gear and baggage, secured in the ramp position at the rear of the plane. Nearby were the American/Australian team, sitting shoulder to shoulder, occupying the inboard-facing seats that lined the bulkheads.

Neill was enjoying the turbulence that rocked him to sleep. Crockett snored beside him, and Brisbane and Russo were closer to the forward crew door.

But the doctor was having a rough time—while the

Marines had grown used to the aircraft's gentle, unpredictable motion, the disturbance affected the women differently.

Nate woke to the sound of gagging. He looked to his left to see Taylor doubled over, filling a paper sack with the lunch she'd eaten hours earlier.

"Sounds like the doc's losin' her cookies," Crockett observed loudly.

Bailee caught Nate's comment. "Turbulence. Havoc with the inner ear." She hugged the scientist's shoulders, offering comfort whenever the plane dipped or pitched to one side or another. "Can you find another barf bag?"

"Hang on."

Neill released his belt and bounded toward the front of the plane. He was met there by the loadmaster, a petite Air Force staff sergeant who anticipated his needs, providing the captain with a bottle of cold water and two small bags that looked woefully inadequate.

"She's a greenhorn?" she asked, wincing at the Australian's discomfort.

"Not used to gray-tails," Mike answered.

"Looks like the first-class type."

"Roger that."

Neill returned to Russo's side and broke the seal on the water. Brisbane handed off the bag she'd been using and grasped the bottle with both hands.

"She looks better," Nate said. He gingerly dropped the airsick bag into the plane's trash receptacle. "Never seen anybody get that bad before."

"It's over-pressurization," the loadmaster told them. "The nausea's just a symptom—some people experience severe pain, inner ear problems—"

"—and vomiting," Neill finished for her.

The sergeant gave a nod. "It's worse for some. We've had troops in so much pain they couldn't function."

"And that's all caused by overpressurization?" Nate asked.

"Yes, sir," she answered. "The guys down in Keesler figured it out. Metal particles in the air lines. They come from a corroded rivet. Every time the system's used, the shavings get pushed forward and play against the check valves. Most of 'em have been replaced—"

"—except on this plane?" Neill grinned.

"We're working on it," the staff sergeant replied. She looked up and added, "But maintenance is spread pretty thin these days."

Mike wasn't about to bust her chops. "Aren't we all," he quipped, and then glanced forward. "Can you check on something for me—what's your name—?" he read her Velcro uniform patch, but she was too quick.

"—Staff Sergeant *Jeeves.*"

"Jeeves." The captain smiled again. "Seriously?"

They flew straight and level for the next hour. The cargo deck had turned frigid, and the group donned gloves and cold weather gear. Dr. Brisbane's condition improved with the drop in temperature. Soon she was talking with Captain Neill and the others after one last trip to the 'honey pot'.

"That was embarrassing." Her tone was subdued, her face pale, and she clutched a pack of disinfectant wipes. "I don't normally get airsick."

"These cargo planes aren't known for their creature comforts, Doc," Mike allowed.

Brisbane's head went from left to right. "You mean this isn't a seven-four-seven?"

"That's good, Doc," Neill chuckled. "So you *do* have a sense of humor."

"Bailee says I should try harder."

It's a start, Neill decided. "Just hang tough. We'll be landing on the island of Attu before you know it."

"And then?"

"The Coasties have choppers. We'll hitch a ride with them out to the *Meyer*."

"A helicopter?" Taylor's eyes widened.

Bailee crowded in. "Ooh, never rode on one of those before," the young woman gushed. She was enthused, but Taylor wore an alarmed expression. Mike saw the scientist's look and tried to change the subject.

"What got you started on those Schumann Resonances—audio impulses—whatever." His question earned a laugh.

"Ever hear of the Vela Incident?" Brisbane asked.

Russo withdrew. She'd heard this tale before. Neill shook his head. "Can't say that I have."

"In 1979, a Vela satellite detected an anomaly over the Indian Ocean—an atmospheric double-flash, characteristic of a nuclear detonation."

Neill had a questioning look. " 'Characteristic' of a nuclear detonation. Was it ever confirmed?"

"The data at the time was inconclusive. The blast—if there *was* one—stirred controversy." Brisbane took a sip of water. "To this day, no one has claimed responsibility."

"And does Dr. Taylor Brisbane have any theories?"

"She does indeed, Captain," she said with a smile. Her color had returned, and her green eyes flashed. "It's possible South Africa was involved, but my vote goes to Israel."

"Why Israel?"

"Three reasons, really. Reports surfaced that Israeli ships were seen in the area. Now that's circumstantial, but no one's been able to discount their presence. The second is related to the first; Israel doesn't have a nuclear test range within their borders. Weapons testing would need to be performed elsewhere."

"And the Indian Ocean fits the bill?" Neill wasn't convinced. "That's a pretty long haul for a small, green water navy."

"No argument there," Brisbane replied. "But it's not that far-fetched. Back then, the intelligence community believed Israel to have a large weapons program—quite sophisticated, in fact, and they can be very focused when it comes to their nation's defense."

"I'm guessing that's reason number three. So why haven't I heard of this before?"

"Politics," Brisbane said in a measured tone. "An Israeli test would have been awkward for the U.S. government. A panel of scientists later decided that no such test took place—saving face for the American president."

Neill recalled his studies at Annapolis. "Back in the day Carter was heavily invested in non-proliferation. And he was facing a tough re-election campaign. A nuke test by the Israelis would only stir the pot."

"There was some additional evidence. Are you familiar with the big radio telescope in Puerto Rico?"

"At Arecibo?"

"That's the one." She was impressed. "Arecibo detected an atmospheric wave traveling northwest, *on the same day*, something researchers hadn't seen before."

"Sounds like a stretch to me, Doc—but you're the expert."

"Call me Taylor."

"All right—Taylor." Neill could see Brisbane's passion for the subject. "Do you have some personal connection to all this?"

"My father was an officer in the Royal Navy," she explained. "He was at sea, and on the day of the blast, his ship experienced something very much like an EMP. They drifted for days, powerless in the Indian Ocean."

"And you think this Vela Incident had something to do with that."

"That's my guess, Captain."

He stared for a moment. There was a cold light that shown behind Taylor's eyes, as if to suggest emptiness. Yet there was fire, too. Growing up as an MK—a missionary kid—Neill had seen that look before, and learned to pick up on the traits that spoke of spiritual need. He could tell she was trying; her faltering attempts at humor, and the intensity she displayed for her work. The good doctor was also vulnerable, but bounced back quickly after succumbing to nausea. With tongue in cheek, he decided she was human after all.

"Call me Mike." He was smiling again.

"Very well—Mike." There was an awkward pause, and she offered a gloved hand. "Nice to meet you, by the way."

Neill laughed and reached out. "We've already met, Doc."

"I know," Brisbane said, recalling their first meeting. "But that day at the Pentagon—I probably seemed like a cold fish. I regret that."

"No worries. You were dealing with new surroundings. Jet lag, too. And there's nothing like the prospect of facing down a mystery, is there?" Neill observed with a faraway look.

Especially when your father's involved.

• • • •

Russo pulled Nate closer. "Is he chatting her up?" she asked.

"Chatting her up? You mean hitting on her?"

"Yeah."

Nate glanced their way. "No. He's already involved." He was amused by the thought. Christina was off-limits, but Captain Straight Arrow was bending the rules—and so far, the brass seemed to be ignoring their affections. Either that or they were completely unaware. "What's the doc's story, anyway?"

"Simply put? She's lonely. And a broken engagement hasn't helped her confidence." Russo sighed heavily, although the effect was lost in the drone of the engines. "Classic situation. A brilliant scientist absorbed in her work. And her father died last year, so she's got no one left."

Nate gave a nod. "I get it. She's a little fragile."

"Yeah."

"And all these planes falling out of the sky—will this give her the chance to prove her theories?"

"She's got a personal and a professional stake in all this." Bailee relished being close to the American lieutenant. "And yes, it should. She's always on go, never stops. I was hoping—"

Sergeant Jeeves emerged from the flight deck. She waved to the Marines to get their attention, and then the sure-footed NCO made her way aft, undaunted by the bumps and variations in altitude.

"Attu Station sent this, Captain Neill." She handed the officer a folded note. The message was brief and told him just what he wanted to know.

The Marine appeared relieved and gave his comrades a thumbs-up. "The other team arrived two hours ago," he told the Australians. He avoided any mention of their nationality—a detail Jeeves didn't need to know. "Which means we're that much closer to solving our enigma."

"And hopefully saving some lives," Nate chimed in.

"Roger that," Neill agreed. He gave Nate a curious

look. "Got time for a sidebar, Lieutenant?"

Crockett blinked. "Operational planning?"

"Something like that." Neill moved forward. A single window was on the starboard side, and the sun gave the compartment a warm glow. "You okay?"

"Who, me?"

"Yeah, you." He shot a glance over his shoulder. "I thought you wanted time with Bailee—but you seem reluctant."

"I hadn't noticed," Nate deflected. He was suddenly concerned. "I haven't been rude, have I?"

"No, but I think Miss Russo was hoping for more. What gives?"

Nate's features darkened. "Just a little preoccupied, that's all."

"Ever since the weekend. Does this have anything to do with Amber Aultman?"

Crockett was silent, choosing his words. "I suppose so."

"I should have warned you," Neill said with a grin. "You put on the uniform—to impress *her*—but it ended up being the other way around. Am I right?"

"She wasn't what I expected." Nate stared out the porthole. The Bering Sea lay beneath them, stretching out to the horizon. "She's a nice woman. Tough, too, but wounded."

"A nice woman. And what about your Aussie friend?"

Nate soured. "You ask a lot of questions."

"Just helping you sort it all out, Lieutenant."

"So now I'm conflicted?"

"I'd say you're being pulled in different directions."

"You should know something about that," Crockett teased. "Christina on the left hand, Viktoriya on the right. How many other chicks are vying for your attention?"

"Don't go there," he warned good-naturedly. "And

take things slow. Amber's fragile right now; she probably doesn't know her own feelings. Give her time to heal."

"Trust me, I'm not rushing into anything."

"Glad to hear it," Mike said. "I need you focused."

"Focused is good," Nate grinned. "What's the plan once we get to Attu?"

"Gather our gear; get something to eat. After that we load up for the flight to the *Meyer*."

"Probably best if we make that happen quickly."

"Agreed," Mike said. Having Ukrainian operatives around would invite questions, and that was something Neill preferred to avoid.

The hill country,
Northern Georgia
Near Fort Gordon Army Base

"Scotch?" Hayes asked.

"Kentucky bourbon, if you've got it."

Willis Avery took a turn around the den, staring wistfully at the photos hanging before him. Many were just like the ones that adorned his predecessor's office, and a few even featured Allan Hayes, crouching on a tank, or standing with a group of soldiers. In those pictures, the former Secretary of Defense was younger and leaner, diamond sharp in an Army officer's uniform.

"M-60 battle tank," Avery noted, tapping the glass on one of the frames. "Not long before the Abrams was put into service. Am I right?"

"The proverbial good old days." Hayes poured two glasses and handed one to Avery. He frowned as he tried to attach context to the image. "That one was taken in

Germany. Can't remember exactly where."

A playful smile. "Memory's the *second* thing to go," Avery chided. "I wouldn't know about the first."

Hayes ignored the taunt and studied the pictures, his thoughts racing to the past.

"Being a soldier was easier in those days. We played by the rules. So did the Russians. Our enemies now are far less chivalrous. And the mission tends to be compromised by the politicians." He shook his head. "Sometimes I'd like to go back."

"No point traveling that road," Willis observed. He sipped his drink and tugged at his collar. "Feels a little warm in here, don't you think?"

Avery's former boss moved to the thermostat, then touched a keypad mounted beneath it. Cool air began to flow from vents overhead, and Hayes offered his friend a knowing smile.

"The scrambler's on, Willis. You can speak freely now." Hayes' grin widened. "Even in retirement, I find it necessary to immerse myself in cloak and dagger."

"Something for me to look forward to?"

"You'll never retire, Willis."

Avery grunted something and eyed the device on the wall. The fixture was a simple affair, a plain, white box, with few buttons, and a small, green bulb that glowed softly when the system was active. "DoD put that in?"

A nod. The two men were now bathed in a net of electrons that would defeat any listening devices. "NSA. A team from Gordon installed it. Those boys know all about encryption."

"No doubt," Avery said. He swirled the drink in the bottom of his glass. "The stakes are too high to leave things to chance."

Hayes considered his friend's words. "Agreed. And what we're about to do has never been tried."

"What's the verdict? You ready to get back into the game?" The question was rather pointed.

There was a gleam in Allan's eye. "I say we roll the dice."

"I've briefed the president on the broad strokes. But what about your teaching position at the War College?"

"That's just part-time," Hayes answered.

"And your health—how are you feeling these days?" The question was posed with mock gravity.

"My prostate troubles? That was just a ruse, Willis." Hayes lowered himself into a chair and clicked his heels together. "A story to keep the focus off my new job. In fact, the prognosis is quite good—almost as if I'd never had cancer."

Avery's response was laced with sarcasm. "A miracle of modern medicine."

"Something along those lines, yes." Another thought came to mind. "And Captain Neill's party—are they on their way?"

"En route as we speak. They'll be aboard the *Meyer* soon." Both men were staring at the wall, drawn to a single image. The photo depicted Hayes with a younger man, one who looked strikingly familiar. "Hard to believe, isn't it?"

"What's that?"

Hayes paused before answering. "Our current enterprise. Inspired by an American missionary—"

"Now furthered by his son, and someone within the People's Republic of China," Avery finished for him. He raised his drink high. "To White Dragon. May God protect him."

Their glasses touched. "Was that a prayer?" Hayes asked.

"Absolutely."

SECDEF downed the last of his bourbon. Their new

friend in Beijing would need some divine intervention. Involving himself with the West would be deemed treasonous, and China's reward for traitors wasn't a pleasant one to consider.

10

CAPABILITIES

Above Joint Base Elmendorf-Richardson, Alaska

TWO IDENTICAL HELLCATS jumped from the runway, climbing into crystal blue skies and speeding west, following the Alaskan coastline as it curved in an arc beneath them. Dubbed HELLCAT Flight, today's second sortie would take the planes more than one hundred kilometers in several directions, on a mission designed to test the new aircraft in roles that went far beyond their tactical warfighting capabilities.

The lead jet dipped its wings and banked abruptly to the south. The second plane did the same. Both dropped to an altitude of five thousand feet and were now headed out to sea, hopping over the Gulf of Alaska on a track far from the southwest corner of the Yukon Territory and due east of British Columbia.

Chris Prentice had command of the flight. A colonel in the U.S. Air Force, the officer bore the call sign HELLCAT Lead, an unimaginative title that left no doubt about his place in the pecking order. Prentice was an extremely capable pilot and squadron commander, a hard-charger who had proven himself many times over in the past few years, and more recently in the skies above Kaliningrad, the Red Army enclave north of Poland. During his TDY there, the colonel had taken a foreign pilot under his wing, a young lieutenant who got twitchy and shot down a Sukhoi-27. The Russian had breached Polish air-space and provoked the coalition squadron.

"It's like driving a sports car." The voice of HELLCAT One crackled in the colonel's headset. "But you already know that. You're a veteran." Major Nick Tate had been Prentice's second-in-command in Central Europe, and had followed the senior officer to Elmendorf. Things were different here. The ops-tempo in Poland was admittedly more stressful, but testing a new jet over the American homeland carried its own set of concerns.

The lead pilot shrugged within the confines of his cockpit. "I've only been flying these things a few weeks longer than you have." And that made Colonel Prentice the most experienced Hellcat driver in the U.S.—after the test pilots at Aileron Dynamix, of course.

HELLCAT Lead surveyed the open skies around him. This assignment was a reward for his efforts in staying Ivan's hand in Europe. He and Tate had been chosen for a new phase in fighter history, both tasked with evaluating the Hellcat's capabilities for the Air Force, the branch of service most likely to take first delivery of the new fighter—*should* the airframe pass final muster, the colonel mused.

"Any complaints so far?" the colonel asked.

"Flaps were a little tight on take-off—but the trade-off was more control. I actually prefer it to the Raptor."

"Smooth and strong," Prentice concluded. "Like a middleweight." That made sense. Neither aircraft carried ordnance for this mission, which decreased their overall load considerably. "Reminds me of the convertible I had back at the Academy."

The sky was a canopy of sapphire over their heads. "Wanna put the top down?" the major teased.

Prentice smirked. "I'll pass. I'm more interested in putting these birds through their paces."

The feed from HELLCAT One was clearer now. "Roger that, Lead. What's first on the agenda?"

This afternoon's tasking included tests intended to showcase the F/A-38's intelligence, surveillance and reconnaissance suite—or ISR—with the primary focus on SIGINT, or signals intelligence. The colonel checked his radar, noting several commercial airliners far to the south, lifting high above the waters covering the Cobb Seamount on their way north to Anchorage.

"Climb to angels thirty," Prentice directed. "Put your ears on; we'll take a stab at intercepting their radio transmissions."

HELLCAT One waited for the colonel to add thrust.

"Head-on—or variable orientation?"

"We'll rotate through the points of the compass. Avionics on these planes are top-notch, if the brochures are to be believed. Let's put them to the test and see if they function as advertised." Prentice lifted the nose of his aircraft and began a swift ascent. "We'll look down on 'em first and see what kind of a return we get." He dialed in the commercial frequency used by the airlines. "I'll send the pilots a text."

"Warn 'em?" Tate asked.

"Let them know we're in the neighborhood. Everybody up here's a little jumpy these days. No need panicking a group of sightseers on holiday." Prentice looked to his right, where Tate had taken a tandem position off his starboard wing. "After that we'll jump to twenty thousand feet and have some fun—in-flight engine cut-off and re-start."

"Now you're talkin', boss. Pushing the envelope on

the ol' pucker factor." Tate craned his neck and took in the view below, where the ocean sparkled in the afternoon light. "Is the Coast Guard on station?"

"Should be," Prentice answered. The Coasties were their partners for some of the testing. A mock tanker disaster had been slated for today, with HELLCAT Flight providing search and rescue support and analysis of the simulated spill. But the morning sortie had crowded it out. "That phase of the op will take a few hours, so we'll adjust the schedule and start fresh after breakfast tomorrow."

"What about ARCTIC WRATH?" Tate asked. "The wing commander should be clearing us to receive ordnance."

"Wouldn't be much of an evaluation without live-fire. But that's *next* week—after we've taken care of the checklist."

"Back to work?" the major sighed.

"Back to work," Prentice repeated.

He put on his game-face, focusing on one of the Airbuses directly ahead. It was time to cut the chatter and see if they could figure out what the in-flight movie was.

Northwest Pacific Basin

Fifteen hundred miles distant, the USS *Meyer* sailed west by northwest, true and steady—haze gray and underway, in naval terms—her bow pointed at the Commander Islands, and the Kamchatka Peninsula beyond that. A tropical storm was building to the south, just north of Midway, and the cruiser raced at twenty-two knots, driving ahead of the squall that dumped rain in her wake.

The developing gale had given the sea a mild chop, with broad swells lifting and falling beneath the *Meyer*'s keel. Fore and aft, the skies were a study in contrast;

sunlight blazed to the north, as far as the eye could see, but astern, gray clouds gathered and grew darker as they formed near the horizon.

A day had passed since Neill's team, the Ukrainians included, left Attu for their rendezvous with the warship. Captain Beacham welcomed them aboard, eyeing the Eastern Europeans and their rifles warily, and then made sure the newcomers were properly situated, handing them off to Senior Chief Richey for stateroom assignments.

Neill's people were glad to have a solid deck beneath their feet. Brisbane managed much better, her nausea a thing of the past, and seemed to be getting her sea legs.

"Does the sun *ever* set around here?" Neill observed.

"We get lots of daylight this time of the year," Richey chuckled.

"You losin' weight, Senior Chief?"

Malcolm sucked in his gut even tighter and returned the compliment. "You're looking well yourself, El-Tee," he gushed, shaking Neill's hand. Simon Chau stood at his side as the introductions were made.

Neill fingered the rank on his collar. "It's *Captain*, Senior Chief." He faced Chau with a sympathetic look. "How's married life treating you, Si?"

The lieutenant smiled. "I recommend it."

"Give it some time, junior," Richey muttered with a grin. He regarded Taylor and Bailee with interest. "I understand you two are here to help us sort out this mystery."

"We'll do our best," the scientist replied, her accent crisp in the ship's corridor.

The group peeled off their gear, stowing jackets and parkas away in their rucks. Malcolm saw to their creature comforts with berths in Officer's Country. The men shared one cabin, while Brisbane and Russo bunked next door. A few able Seamen were tasked with carrying the Aussies' luggage.

The Ukrainian men hung back, with Neill bringing up the rear. "Captain Beacham will want us to secure our weapons in the ship's armory," he told Voskov. "You okay with that?"

"Perfectly acceptable. We are guests, after all. By the way, Viktoriya sends her regards, Mikhail."

"I was starting to wonder. It's been weeks since I've heard from her."

"A little jealousy, perhaps?"

"Not at all," Mike said with honesty. He looked Voskov squarely in the eye. "I had a feeling you two would become an item. In fact, I'd say the best man won."

"Glad to hear it," Voskov smiled.

"Major Yaroslav also sends greetings."

Mike's head swung around. "You're English is improving, Yuri." The Marine was impressed, but then lowered his voice. "Dmitri tells me you bear good tidings—not to mention some important intel."

"Yes," Yuri confirmed.

"Concerning Radya Zhukov?"

Neill detected a flicker of interest on Voskov's face. Tereshenko became tight-lipped, but nodded nonetheless.

The officers from Kiev relaxed after reuniting with Mike and Nate. But they were still the odd men out. The *Meyer*'s crew were attentive to the international guests, doing their best to extend the ship's courtesy, and the Ukrainian contingent doubled up with the Marines. It made for cramped quarters, but ensured that the former Berkut officers weren't intentionally segregated.

And that wasn't all. Simon Chau, ordinarily reticent, was thrilled by their arrival, going so far as to reserve the Officer's Mess to celebrate a reunion of sorts for the Colonial Rifles.

• • • •

"A toast," Richey boomed, raising his glass, "To successful missions, past, present—and future."

"Hear hear," Neill agreed.

Drinks were brought close, clinking and spilling. The group recovered quickly enough. "Easy, boys and girls," Nate teased. "That's some vintage ginger ale you're wasting."

"Not exactly my brand," Neill said, winking at Taylor. "What do they serve in Oz, Doctor?"

Bailee nudged her boss. The Aussie blushed.

"Soda's are common, but the science is in on sugar. It's entirely detrimental on human physiology."

Crockett and Russo weren't having it. The two pelted the doctor with crumpled napkins and popcorn. Neill interpreted for Xander and Yuri, who followed with boos of their own, joining in with a second wave of snack foods hurled in Brisbane's direction.

She flinched, quite surprised by the sudden assault.

Taylor pulled Mike aside after the luncheon broke up.

"That was all in fun, right?" Taylor had that look on her face, the one she'd worn that first day at the Pentagon

"Come again?"

The redhead's eyes grew wide. "They were throwing food at me," she blurted. "That was a joke, am I right?"

Neill grinned. At least she'd grown to trust him—a little.

"They like you, Doctor." He brought up his hand, removing popped corn from her hair. "I'm not sure *why*, exactly—"

"Neither am I," she snapped testily. The scientist received more than a few second glances from sailors moving along the corridor. "I've always had trouble getting on with people."

Neill had been poking fun, but now he regretted the remark.

"Hey, I was kidding. Dale Carnegie aside, nobody's quite got the lock on winning friends and influencing people."

"You seem to do all right," she sulked. "Your friends were awfully glad to see you—," she dropped her voice, "—even that somber Ukrainian."

"Xander? Ukrainians have always frowned on Western humor. Remind me to tell you about it sometime."

There was a pause. Brisbane's next question came from the blue.

"You miss her, don't you?"

"Excuse me?"

"There's someone in your life—someone you've left behind." Her head came around, and she looked into his face with interest. "A woman can sense these things."

"Woman's intuition?" Mike asked. *Not too bad for someone lacking social skills*, he considered.

"You aren't denying it, are you?"

He hesitated. "It's not exactly authorized, Doc. I'm an officer—"

"—and she's not. Is that it?" She sympathized with his predicament. "Don't forget that I'm a military brat. I know a little about fraternization between the ranks."

Bailee and Nate had long since slipped past—headed who knew where—leaving Taylor and Mike alone in the passageway. He decided it might be best to change the subject.

"Hey—I'll let you in on a little secret."

Taylor viewed him suspiciously. "I'm listening."

"People are generally good sports. And they usually respond to kindness."

She bristled. "What do you suggest?"

"A little friendliness wouldn't hurt."

Taylor's chin dipped. "Bailee told me the same thing. Anything else?"

"Step outside of your comfort zone. And give people something they'll give back."

"What's that?"

"One of these." Mike was grinning broadly.

"A smile." The corners of her mouth went up.

"See?" Neill chuckled. "Works every time."

"That's always been a little hard for me, Captain."

He started to answer, but Senior Chief Richey rounded the corner and waved for attention.

"Cap'n Neill? Skipper wants to see you in the CIC."

"Can Doc Brisbane tag along?"

Richey surprised them both with a nod of his head. "Ever been privy to a classified briefing, Doctor?"

"Secret squirrel stuff," Neill explained.

"Secret—secret *what*?"

It was early afternoon when the three made their way back to the Combat Information Center.

"Festivities over?" Captain Beacham asked. He was intent on the *Meyer*'s navigational display.

"Aye, sir," the senior chief grunted. He cleared his throat, and Beacham realized the Australian scientist had joined them.

"Dr. Brisbane," Beacham said in greeting. He gave Neill a friendly glance. "I see the Marines have authorized you to receive sensitive information." She was ready to leave, but the captain waved her off. "No matter. Your expertise might be helpful as well." The officer walked to a filing cabinet, secured with a combination lock. He turned the dial and retrieved a folder.

"An American research vessel just discovered something on the ocean floor," Beacham handed over two of the images. "I'd like Captain Neill to take a look."

The Marine was drawn in. "Any reason why?"

"Several. For one thing, your roots go back to the old country. Secondly, you're SECDEF's expert on all things Russian." He stopped, thinking about his next comment. "And lastly—" his voice trailed off, "—from what Avery says, you have a great deal of experience with Soviet superweapons."

Malcolm held back a grin. He'd been there on Huo Shan when Neill faced off against a crack squad of Chinese commandos. That mission uncovered the Tempest torpedo and Admiral Xian Lee's secret Navy. What followed was a desperate chase deep in the South China Sea, where Mike's snap judgment had saved the lives of the Colonial Rifles, along with the entire crew of *HMS Bradford*. Their adversaries had not fared so well.

What Richey didn't know was the extent of the Marine's first assignment in Odessa, or his subsequent accomplishments in Poland. Of course, the Navy man had the requisite clearance, but his 'need to know'—

Neill studied the photos from the *Pont Claire*. They were a little grainy, composites pieced together from dozens of other images. And the photography was undeniably shot below the waves.

"When were these taken, sir?" he probed.

"A couple of days ago."

"Can you tell me where?"

Beacham turned to the display, tapping a spot close to the Commander Islands. "Not seventy-five nautical miles from our position," he answered. "Do you know what this is, Captain?"

Neill nodded. "Yes, sir. Classic Russian lines; hardly

elegant, but functional." Mike traced a finger around the object and was ready to offer his opinion. "It's a little far from home, Captain Beacham, but I'd say someone's found themselves a Caspian Sea Monster."

"That's what I was thinking." Beacham's eyes went back to the plot board. "In a few hours we'll survey the coastline. Do you need assistance in setting up your equipment, Professor?"

"Bailee can give me a hand. We'll require a bit of room, and a clear line of sight to the target zone."

Beacham smiled. "You're starting to sound like a real tactician. What about you, Captain Neill? Are you ready to brief your team?"

The Marine braced. "Just give the word, sir."

"Very well then. The word is given."

11

COASTLINES

Oahu, Hawaii
Bellows Field Beach Park,
Eastern side of the island

ONCE THE SOLE PROPERTY of the U.S. Air Force—and the Army/Air Corps during World War II—vast chunks of Bellows Field had recently been gobbled up by the Marine Corps, used for exercises that didn't include live-fire activities. For the artillery side of the house, that was disappointing; but the island *was* a tourist mecca, and you couldn't have everything.

But it would've been nice, the cannon-cockers had grumbled.

It was early afternoon, and Christina Arrens squinted beneath blue-framed sunglasses and peered out to sea. Her eyes followed the Waimanalo coast as it angled north. The Mokulua Islands—the *Mokes*, as they were known to the locals—sat just offshore, a nature preserve and popular destination for kayakers, bird watchers, and paddle-board enthusiasts.

The woman at Christina's side broke her contemplation of paradise with a question.

"Thirsty?" Mary Margaret Stillwell reached into a small cooler and produced two bottles of water.

"I'm in." Reclining on a towel-draped beach chair, Christina wore her new bikini, every inch of exposed skin covered in oil. She looked to the horizon. "Which one is Moku Iki?"

Maggie handed off one of the bottles. It was cold to the touch. "The closer one. It's currently off-limits." The two women, roommates at Pearl, opened the bottles and slaked their thirst. "Moku Nui is the bigger island. Some people swim there, but I'm not that daring. Tomorrow morning we'll drive over to Lanikai and rent a couple of kayaks, if you're up to it."

Christina tried judging the distance from shore. "It's about half an hour away—am I right?"

"Good eye," Maggie beamed.

"Good PT," Christina quipped.

Maggie sat up and pointed to their right. "See that spot? Back in 1941, a Japanese mini-sub washed up on the beach. There's a picture of it on the wall in lodging."

"History's at every turn," Christina answered. The scent of coconut butter filled the air, and she stretched, digging her toes into the warm sand beneath her feet. "You've been to the North Shore?"

A smile. "Honey, I practically *live* on these beaches."

"I don't doubt that." Christina eyed her friend with envy. Stillwell was practically bronzed, and in another week, Arrens would match her friend's skin tone.

Maggie turned. "Okay. Chit-chat's over."

"What does that mean?" She looked south. Rabbit Island and Makapu'u Park lay in the distance, and young men stole admiring glances as the two Marines soaked up the sun.

"Meaning it's time for you to come clean about this boyfriend of yours." Maggie wanted dirt. "C'mon, start dishin' ."

"He's not exactly—"

"Knock it off," Maggie barked. "And give me your phone."

Christina giggled—not something she did often. But she relented, handing over the cell. "Think you can find the photo directory?"

"C&E School taught me *some* things." Maggie was a sergeant, one stripe below Christina's rank, and rode a desk at the NCIS Field Office. She toggled through the phone's settings, careful not to mar the device with oil. "*Aha*—I think I've found him." She dried her fingertips and pinched the screen, enlarging the image, then held it up for Christina to see. "Is this your dreamboat?"

Arrens' grin got a little wider. "Mag-pie, that's no dreamboat. That's my love boat."

Maggie was shocked. "Get out. You did not just say that." She scrolled through a few more photos. "Island life has certainly loosened you up."

"You don't approve?" Christina teased.

"Oh, I definitely approve," Maggie declared, staring at the phone. "There's just one problem."

Christina's smile gave way to a frown. "I know. He's an officer."

"Which is fine," Maggie shrugged, "if you're planning to ruin his career, or yours."

She stared into the distance. "There are ways around that."

"Not many. Check the regs. It's detrimental to good order. Especially within the same chain of command." Maggie took another drink of water. "Now, officer to officer, that's a different story. We both know it happens. Sometimes the rules are enforced very strictly. Sometimes not." She shook her head. "Things get a little squishy at that level. Best thing to do is steer clear of this guy. That, or tell him to resign his commission."

"Not an option."

"Okay, then," Maggie said. "Tell me about school."

Christina blinked. "School?"

"Those online courses. I know what you're up to."

"There's not much to tell," she answered. "Advanced calculus is a pain, but I'm doing really well with German."

"*German*?" Maggie's eyebrow went up. "You work the Eastern European desk, don't you? Wouldn't Russian, or maybe Polish—"

"Mike's fluent in Russian," she told her friend. "And I needed an elective." The enormity of her efforts were creeping up again. She shook it off, eager to get back to the topic at hand. "I really thought I could handle more of a workload, but I had to drop my technical writing class. I just couldn't keep up."

Maggie wasn't sure, but it seemed that Christina's voice cracked just a bit. "Sometimes we expect more from ourselves than anyone else. My advice to you is to go easy on that woman you see in the mirror." She gave her a compassionate smile. "Writing class can wait till next semester. What's your GPA right now?"

Arrens' face brightened again. "It's pretty high; I just aced all my mid-terms."

"So there you go," she said. "You're doing fine."

"Sometimes it's just so *difficult*." Christina seemed a little embarrassed. "I don't mean to get emotional; sorry about that."

"No need to apologize." Maggie was very intuitive, and considered the long range goals Christina was striving for. "Is there anything else you'd like to talk about?"

The woman in the vibrant blue bikini smiled. "Up to this point, that's all it's been—just talk." She took a deep breath and exhaled slowly.

Maggie had been expecting this. "The job's not done until the paperwork's finished."

"It's in the pipeline," Christina assured her. She went through a mental list before continuing. "Statements of eligibility, end of active service; commanding officer's checklist." She skipped ahead. "High school transcripts; and I've already got most of my college courses out of the way. So the initial stuff is done."

Talking about it helped. But Maggie wasn't finished with her subtle interrogation.

"Has he told you he loves you?"

"Who—Michael?"

"I'm not talking about the commandant of the Marine Corps." Stillwell shook her head. "Of *course* Michael."

"In his own way," Christina replied, mustering her conviction.

Maggie stared at her friend as the sun beat down on her browning skin. "Has he seen you in that bikini?"

"No." Christina had an idea. "Do you think I should send him a picture?"

"Might sweeten the pot."

"Stop it."

"And you two still haven't . . . *you* know—"

"No. Not that we haven't *wanted* to." Christina knew what she was asking.

"Sounds like he's got commitment issues," Maggie decided. "Have you talked to him lately?"

"He's away from the office," came the answer.

"How *far* away?"

Christina was becoming irritated. During their last conversation, Mike had mentioned that he'd been tasked with something new.

What that was, he couldn't say.

"Well, he's not off with some redhead on his arm, if that's what you're thinking." Christina was eager to change the subject. She removed the scrunchie behind her head, running her fingers through auburn hair. "Now come on. Let's go and get our feet wet."

Aboard the USS Meyer

"Hand-outs?" Nate entered the wardroom, a surprised look on his face. "Dude, you are really slippin'."

Neill shrugged. "No tech support, no slide-show," he grumbled. "My IT specialist is TDY, so we'll do this the old-fashioned way. "

He stood before an Epson printer. The machine spat out a small stack of pages, which were set aside, while on the wardroom table, a chart of the area had been un-rolled, its four corners anchored in place with salt shakers, assorted condiments and napkin holders.

"Does this run-down have color photography?" the sniper asked. "I'm a spoiled child, Mike. I needs my pretty pictures." Crockett was just getting spun up when Brisbane and Russo popped in, with Chau, Richey, and the Ukrainians not far behind.

"Take these and staple them," Neill directed. "The pages are numbered."

Crockett clutched the still-warm sheaf in his hands and smiled. "I knew all that public education stuff would come in handy."

From the passageway, an unfamiliar face appeared, wearing a nervous expression. "Captain Neill?"

"That's right." Mike stuck out a hand. "Are you the linguist?"

"Meteorologist, primarily, but yes, sir. Ensign Antonio Vespi at your service."

"Welcome to the club." Neill's eyes swept the group, zeroing in on Xander and Yuri. "Ensign Vespi speaks the language, and he'll be interpreting for our guests from Ukraine."

Nate gave a frown. "You couldn't do that?"

"I can't do *everything*," Mike fired back. "And this will make my life easier. Everyone take your seats, please, and we'll get his party started."

"We're here," Neill began, an index finger stabbing the chart. "Near the Kamchatka Peninsula, due east of Petropavlovsk, about fifty kilometers from the coastline." Nods from the Ukrainians as Vespi translated. "We'll be in a position to begin our survey in short order—while avoiding unwanted scrutiny from the Russians."

"Easier said than done, Cap'n," Richey supplied with mischief. "But you just leave the driving to us."

Neill lifted his notes from the table and stepped off toward the center of the compartment. "You've all seen our area of responsibility. Flip to the second page." Papers ruffled as the team found a map. "We've identified this part of the shoreline as an area of interest—possibly a staging point for military operations."

"Amphibious operations?" Crockett asked.

"Yes."

"You sound pretty sure of yourself," Nate pressed. "That wasn't the case at the Pentagon. Has something happened to confirm your suspicions?"

Mike approached the table. "Just this."

He paused for effect and held the last page in the printed presentation. There was a collective gasp.

"Is that an airplane?" Bailee asked, voicing the question while the others simply stared.

"That it is," Mike replied with a grin. "Sort of."

"Looks like a *photograph* of an airplane," Crockett managed to say.

"You're both right. The image you see was supplied by a research vessel—the *Pont Claire*, out of Anchorage. They were looking for oil—"

"And found that?" Brisbane finished. "An aircraft?"

"*Underwater,*" Russo threw in. "At least it looks like it's underwater."

"Right again. Not far from here, actually. Just to the north. And technically, this image is a *mosaic*; a composite pieced together from hundreds—if not thousands—of images."

"Was thermal imaging used?" Chau posed the question.

"Not in this case. The vehicle wasn't emanating any heat."

Richey sat back in his chair. "Not surprising. You say it's not far? The water's pretty cold in these parts—even in the Spring."

"The ship used thermal data from the surrounding seabed, but there were other metrics available. Given current technology, it wasn't too hard to capture a high-definition image."

Chau liked what he saw. "Fairly smooth modeling, too. That's a digitally collected sonograph. Variations of light and dark give the impression of three-dimensional shading."

"How does this relate to Flight 778?" Richey asked. Everyone at the table now pored over the printed pages.

Neill began slowly. "We all need to understand just what this aircraft is, and how it found its way to the ocean floor."

"My guess?" Crockett broke in. "I'd say it crashed."

"There's a stunning hypothesis," Neill said. Nate's comment got a few laughs.

"And how long has it been there?" Chau asked. "The control surfaces appear to be—well, *old.*"

"I was getting to that. The *Pont Claire*'s specialists have had several days to interpret the data. Based on the build-up of sediments, the rate of decay and other factors, they estimate that it hasn't been disturbed for over thirty years."

"That's about right; I'd say closer to forty," Malcolm added. "It's Soviet, isn't it, Cap'n Neill?"

"There are no external markings, Senior Chief, but its design matches the characteristics of a wing-in-ground effect vehicle—an *ekranoplan*."

"A Caspian Sea Monster."

All eyes turned to stare at Richey.

"What the Sam Hill is a Caspian Sea Monster?" Nate wanted to know.

"Prototypes of this aircraft were tested in the Caspian Sea, north of Iran," Neill explained. "Spy satellites captured the first images. The CIA noted it's odd configuration but they were stumped." He tapped the page and gestured toward the middle of the plane. "See the appendages on the front? Those are jet engines."

"Looks like rocket launchers." Nate gave the sonograph a sideways look. "I know Ivan's a little squirrely, but why put jet engines on the nose?"

"It's is a *sea*-going craft, and Soviet engineers wanted to minimize exposure to salt water."

"What's this wing-in-ground effect?" Taylor asked.

Mike eyed Malcolm. "Correct me if I'm wrong, Senior Chief, but the closer the wing is to another surface— such as the ground, or the sea, in this instance—the more efficient it becomes. A wing passing through the air creates pressure beneath it; but forces acting on the upper surface are decreased. The high and low pressures are channeled across the top to the ends of the wings—" Mike demonstrated using his hands, "—creating drag, which inhibits lift. The Russians got around that by using shorter wings. But there's a catch."

"There usually is. You just can't go around breaking the laws of physics."

"But you can bend them," Neill said. "This plane—for want of a better word—is a nap-of-the earth vehicle, and it can only make use of this principle at very low altitudes, say, a dozen feet or so."

"Like a hovercraft?" Bailee asked.

"Something like that."

"What did the Russians use it for?"

"Search and rescue, for one thing. Cargo transport. Any number of missions," Mike replied. "And these beasts have tremendous airlift capabilities. Consider the 747, which can hold over 460 passengers. The Airbus seats 500. But *these* leviathans—" he eyed the page, "—can carry upwards of a *thousand* Soviet infantry."

"It's a big troop-carrier," Nate snorted. "Perfect for invasions."

"And flying low, Ivan avoids radar detection," Malcolm reminded them.

"Is that what the Russians had in mind?"

"Makes sense to me. It's stealthy and could be used to deliver combat-ready troops to locations without airstrips."

"So this thing lands in the water—is that what you're saying?" Crockett had pen in hand and was doodling in the margins.

"It's water-borne. It starts from a ramp, like the one you discovered on the shoreline of Kamchatka. Builds up speed, lifts off and skims across the surface, before coming back to rest in the same place."

"It's a *chimera*—a mash-up, if you will." Simon had to admire the Russians' cleverness. "This machine is neither fish nor fowl."

"But it does incorporate the most efficient features of each," Malcolm pointed out. "This one must have ditched during landing, or suffered some kind of accident."

Crockett leaned forward. "You think the bodies of the crew are still aboard?"

"That's a good question." Neill nursed that thought, and turning to Xander he spoke in Ukrainian. "Captain Voskov, does the SSD have any reliable data on this aircraft?"

The officer appeared reluctant at first. Yuri was visibly uncomfortable. "I suspect that this vehicle is part of the Charybdis project," Xander relented at last. "Major Yaroslav has mentioned this to you, yes?"

"He has. Can you elaborate further?"

"Charybdis was the brainchild of Radya Zhukov," Xander told them slowly. "During the eighties and nineties he was one of the Kremlin's top scientists. It was his team that perfected aspects of this vehicle for military purposes."

"So Charybdis is the code-name for this flying monstrosity?" Crockett was getting antsy.

Xander eyed the sniper, waiting for the translation. "Charybdis is the *project* designation. But there's much more to it than just this vehicle."

"How much more?" Nate shot back, "I thought Dmitri sent you two to give us a hand. So far you've been pretty tight-lipped."

"Like your State Department," the Ukrainian grated out, "when the Russians annexed the Crimea and the eastern part of my country."

Even without the benefit of a translation, it was clear that Voskov was bitter.

"Don't blame me for *that*, comrade," Nate said angrily. "Given all the carnage we've seen lately, I'd say your Caspian Sea Monster is a weapons platform."

There was a pause as Vespi filled in the gaps. "It's not *mine*, Lieutenant," Xander growled.

"There have been whispers about this," Yuri spoke

up, anxious to quell hard feelings on both sides. "These vehicles have been mothballed—is that your term?—for quite some time. Accidents, cost over-runs, *et cetera*. These types of aircraft fell out of favor. And when the Soviet Union collapsed, Zhukov went missing."

"Maybe he's turned up again. And he's got a bigger boat this time—a plane like the one on the seabed."

Yuri tried a little peacemaking. "*Gospodin*—excuse me, gentlemen. Bickering amongst ourselves will not help."

"Ease up, people. Yuri's right," Neill chided softly. "We're all friends here, don't forget that. Working toward a common goal. Whatever role Zhukov's played, this aircraft is *Russian* in origin—not Ukrainian."

The awkward moment passed, and Malcolm spoke up. "I've seen that look before, Cap'n Neill. You're a big picture kind of guy. Would you care to share an opinion or two?" The light in the wardroom shifted as the sun began to slide slowly to the west.

"When I first laid eyes on this, it got me thinking; what's it doing on *this* side of the world—in this ocean? Could it somehow be related to the planes falling out of the sky? Is there some nexus with what we're seeing today?" He gave his audience a chance to answer those questions on their own, but when no one spoke he continued. "What's the reason for testing a big prototype like that here in the Bering Sea?"

"Ask the question slowly," Malcolm responded, "and it almost answers itself."

"Exactly," Neill lit up. "Think about it; before this plane ended up on the seafloor, it was headed someplace. It's a prototype, or else we would have seen more of them in service. And what do you do with prototypes?"

"Test their limits?" Nate volunteered.

"Yes—and gauge their ability to accomplish the mission."

"And what was this plane's mission?"

"You said it yourself. It's a troop carrier. That's an assumption, I'll grant you, but it makes sense. Now let's carry it further—to the present day."

Nate had a dubious eye. "You believe there's a link between our flying fish—" he held up the image from the bottom of the sea, "—and the weapon knocking planes out of the sky? These aircraft are a generation apart, Mike. I don't wanna rain on your moment, but where's the connection between the two?"

"How quickly you forget."

"Okay, then. Refresh my memory."

"Think back to the Pentagon." Neill shuffled through his notes. "Remember this?"

Understanding filled Crockett's eyes. "That hidden base—the hangar on Kamchatka?"

"That's the one."

Bailee made a contribution. "Two separate aircraft. Forty years apart—"

"—but each one tested and developed *here*, on the eastern shore of Kamchatka."

"What's special about Kamchatka?"

"The peninsula's strategically located," Neill told her. "Remember when I said this Chimera was going some-where? Take a look at the map." He gestured toward the chart spread out before them. "The plane ditched here. What's the nearest location where Ivan would want to land an invasion force?"

Nate reached out a hand and traced a line from the Northwest Pacific Basin to the Aleutian Island chain— and beyond.

"Holy Moley," he breathed.

"Alaska?" Chau blurted. "What's in—" Simon's eyes widened.

"Oil," Vespi joined in. He stopped there, concerned that he'd overstepped himself.

"Oil indeed," Neill replied. "And lots of it. The Alaskan National Wildlife Refuge. Ivan's coveted that resource for years. He's certain we won't touch it, which makes it all the more enticing."

"But Russia has plenty of oil and natural gas. Don't they?"

"That's what we're supposed to think," Mike said. "But what if they're facing a shortage? With fracking and other assets, the paradigm seems to have shifted."

"And not in the Russians' favor."

"Where'd you come up with this?" Nate quizzed. He was wary of the old Red bear, but even this theory gave him pause. "Do you think they'd really consider it—invade our shores?"

"From the Pacific, Alaska's the first stepping stone toward sovereign U.S. soil."

Nate's eyes were glued to the image of the plane ditched on the seafloor. "Might be helpful to get a closer look at this bird."

Neill shook his head. "No chance of that, I'm afraid. After this was taken, a Russian salvage ship arrived on the scene and chased the *Pont Claire* away."

"The *Belousov*," Yuri supplied innocently. He spoke in English. "Ukraine has been monitoring her progress in the region."

"Not much gets by the SSD," Neill observed.

Yuri gave up more information. "We have a reliable source—right under the Russians' noses."

Neill narrowed his eyes. "Major Yaroslav hinted as much. But we'll get to that later." He was ready to lay all the cards on the table. "Let's be clear on this mission, people. We get close enough to discover what we can do to blunt this weapon's effectiveness. In that, we're in full support of Dr. Brisbane and her magic decoder ring—" a rueful smile, "—or whatever it is she's brought to flush out our quarry."

"So what's next?" Bailee asked.

Neill used a grease pencil and marked a spot on the chart. "We start here, first thing tomorrow morning. The *Meyer* will lay off the coastline—not too close, mind you—following a track north-by-northeast. The good doctor will pull out all the stops—"

"—and we'll go monster-hunting," Bailee gushed.

"Won't the Russians be suspicious; having an American warship so close to their shores? Won't they be watching our every move?"

"That can't be helped. And it's not without precedent. Ivan sends his bombers into our backyard, encroaching on our airspace. We've come to expect that and so have they."

"What if we're challenged? Anybody thought up a good cover story?"

Richey leaned forward. "We've got an asset coming up from Sapporo, a Japanese science ship with lots of gadgets on board. We'll be working with them to uncover evidence of woolly mammoths on some of the outer islands."

"Naturally," Nate said. He glanced at Bailee, flirting. "Mammoths, sea monsters, and salvage ships—"

"—oh, my," she winked back, an amused expression on her face, and the lingering look she gave him hinted at more than just humor.

Anacostia, Maryland

"And how did you get this injury?"

Daniel Gavin Neill tugged at the strap and loosened

the Velcro brace, testing his forearm for pain. The wrist was sore, but the level of discomfort had actually started to fade.

"Too much PT, most likely," the Marine piped up. Staring into the doctor's face, he was silently thankful that Mike had arranged this appointment.

"PT?" Dr. Carolyn Osbeck's hands glided gently up to Daniel's shoulder, resting there as she gently manipulated the arm in its socket. In her late thirties, the tall, pretty osteopath wore her hair in a bun atop her head, giving the woman an even more graceful stature. "In my line of work, that means physical therapy."

Daniel drew himself up to his full height. He was enjoying the doc's touch. "PT stands for physical training in the Marines, ma'am," he said proudly, "and it truly is physical therapy, as you put it.".

"So you're a soldier, then?"

"Oh, no, ma'am," the master gunny told her. "Just an old jarhead. There's a difference."

Carolyn had stopped listening. She took hold of Daniel's arm and turned his palm face up. "Describe the level of pain; one being the least, with ten as maximum."

Daniel thought about it. "I'd say three to five, most days."

"Sharp, dull, or throbbing?"

"All three, sometimes."

"All right." She released his arm and jotted down a few notes. "Let's check your neck alignment next, then get you back to x-ray and see if we can rule out a fracture. We'll need to focus on C-One and Two also. With the amount of wear and tear you've had, that could be responsible for a lot of your pain."

"Maybe an MRI?"

"That's for soft tissue, Mr. Neill. But it might come to that." She cradled his head in her hands, drawing closer, feeling the vertebrae in his neck, and then smiled for the first time. *God, she smells good*, and Daniel thought he was looking into the face of an angel. "We'll take this one step at a time."

"You're the doc, Doc," he beamed. "One step at a time it is."

12

EYEBALL TO EYEBALL

*Kamchatka Peninsula,
Twenty-five kilometers offshore*

"**B**ASELINE TRACK established," the Officer of the Watch sang out. "Present course is zero three five; first pass is complete and the scope is clear."

"Right ten degrees rudder, Mr. Callahan. Come to zero seven zero," Bob Beacham answered. "Lay in second track and commence your southerly run."

"Aye, sir, right ten degrees rudder," Callahan repeated. "Helm is answering, coming to zero seven zero."

Lookouts posted on either side of the bridge turned to port and scanned the coastline. So far, Ivan had kept a low profile, with little or no naval activity detected by the Americans between the *Meyer* and the distant shore.

"Heads on a swivel, gentlemen," Beacham ordered. The able seamen with the field glasses swept the horizon. "They can come at us from more than one direction."

"Kinda quiet, Skipper," Malcolm Richey observed after a moment. "*Spooky* kinda quiet."

"They know we're here, Senior Chief."

He shifted his attention to the tactical display dominating the center of the compartment, and then picked up a hand-held mike—known as the 1MC, or one main circuit, to address the ship's company. Richey could guess what was coming.

"This is the Captain speaking," Beacham said over the intercom, his voice echoing in the enclosed compartment. "As you all know, we've entered waters that are considered by the Russians to be theirs. And while we are far outside the limits of their territorial claims, you can be sure that Ivan won't be quite so understanding.

"I'm directing every member of this crew to maintain a heightened sense of vigilance. Compare notes with your shipmates; if something doesn't look right, bring it to the attention of your supervisor. If something doesn't square with your instincts, then by all means, don't keep it to yourself.

"The Russians, the Chinese—hell, everyone in this part of the world, for that matter—has a different value system than most of us. And for that reason, I am ordering new protocols to keep us safe."

A collective groan rippled throughout the ship. Sailors and old salts—many who had been with the skipper when the *Meyer* escorted the arsenal ship through the South China Sea—could guess what those protocols might be.

"We'll conduct steering casualty and chemical/biological drills, alternating every four hours. In short order, I will test our responses, and I would remind all lookouts to be wary of any surface vessel or aircraft approaching our position. Said vessels and/or aircraft are to be considered hostile, and appropriate action will be taken to safeguard the integrity of the ship and continue in the performance of our mission. Since yesterday, spotter aircraft have loitered just beyond our radar nets, and you can be sure that the Russians are *werry* interested in our travel plans.

"That is all."

"Any returns on Front Door, Mr. Chau?"

One compartment away, Simon checked the instruments and issued his report.

"The Russians are serving up static, sir," he replied, speaking into the handset. "The *intentional* variety."

Beacham smiled. "They're jamming us. What's the source?"

"Bearing is three one five, west by northwest. There are several broadcast points, but they overlap and originate from our target zone," Chau answered. He had become quite efficient, and would earn a promotion very soon.

"Very well. Mr. Callahan, slow to one-third, turn to starboard and bring us to two one zero."

The Officer of the Watch repeated the order, and the helmsman eased the ship into a quarter turn to the right, bringing the *Meyer*'s bow into the rising sun. The change in course bisected the swells rolling below them and altered the rhythm of the ship as it rode the waves.

The skipper was back on the phone. "Do you have what you need, Lieutenant Chau?"

"Aye, sir." A pause. "If you'd like an overview—"

"I'm on my way." Beacham laid the phone in its cradle, directing a glance at the OOTW. "Ensign Callahan, you have the conn."

The Annex was located next door, an anteroom of the Combat Information Center, and as such was part of the *Meyer*'s nervous system. Situated behind the bridge, this rectangular compartment was filled with instrumentation stacked floor to ceiling—or, in nautical terms, from the deck below to the overheads above.

The narrow alcove hummed with the electronics gear that supported the ship's mission. Internally, the environment of the Annex was chilled to sixty-five degrees. This protected the delicate computers from overheating, and the brisk compartment gave rise to another name, *the Reefer*. Some forward-thinking individual had also designed the berth to protect against electro-magnetic pulses, and with that in mind, the bulkheads were heavily shielded to guard against external assaults.

"*Attention on deck!*"

Everyone in the room stirred as Captain Beacham eased through the hatch, his eyes roving the length of the space. Commander Towle, the *Meyer*'s executive officer, followed the captain, clipboard in hand, glancing left and right. Suddenly top-heavy with rank, those assembled in the Annex seemed to brace. Beacham removed his cover and ran a hand through his hair before turning to face Towle.

"Report, Commander," he growled. It was not a request.

"Defensive systems are all online, Skipper," Towle returned. He hesitated. "Phalanx is a little sluggish, but Weapons has a crew looking into it."

Beacham frowned. "The hydraulics, you mean?"

Towle shook his head. "Negative, sir. *Sluggish* in the way the interface operates. The radome doesn't seem to be talking to the tracking antenna. We ran multiple tests before we entered these waters." He lowered his voice. "Twenty-two percent of the dry runs came back with no joy."

A frown darkened the skipper's face. "That percentage is unacceptable, Mr. Towle."

The close-in weapons system, dubbed Phalanx by the manufacturer, protected the *Meyer* from anti-ship missiles. Utilizing a radar-guided Gatling gun, it was a last-ditch measure against sea-skimming killers that might cripple a surface ship.

"No worries, sir," Towle said reassuringly. "Lieutenant Sanchez is working the problem. He's making considerable progress—" a quick look at Lieutenant Chau, "—with an assist from our resident savant."

Beacham grunted, and the message was instantly received. First-line of defense—or last—the Captain didn't cotton to unreliability aboard his ship, and he wouldn't rest until Phalanx was running at top efficiency.

Another thought came to mind. "Mr. Towle, instruct the Intel department to provide regular updates."

"On the hour, sir?" The skipper's mood wasn't one Towle was anxious to test.

"As warranted." Beacham offered a tight grin to his XO. "I'll let you decide how often that might be."

Nearby, Bailee Russo huddled over a desktop computer parked at a central console. Taylor Brisbane was on her right, glued to waveforms that traveled across the screen of an oscilloscope. Both women wore warm clothing; the petite assistant had been swallowed by a large, fleece liner, borrowed, the skipper wagered, from Lieutenant Crockett, and a knit watch cap was pulled down over the woman's head and ears.

Dr. Brisbane was similarly dressed, but instead of a ski cap, one of the officers had gifted the Aussie with a baseball hat embroidered with the ship's name and number. Her long, red hair was gathered in a pony-tail and trailed from the back. The captain smiled to himself. He imagined that both women had been on the receiving end of a great deal of attention, and word of the young ladies had spread throughout the ship.

The compartment was crowded, but the Ukrainian contingent was noticeably absent. Neill and Crockett sat nearby, doing nothing in particular. Nate stole glances at

Bailee, while Simon Chau was seated directly behind, intent on the console that hummed before him.

"Sir," Chau began, rising from his chair, "the jamming transmissions are varied and overlapping, ostensibly to protect a 'sweet spot' at the base of these cliffs." He pointed to a spot on the chart, a broad map fixed to the bulkhead.

"Same location identified by Lieutenant Crockett," Beacham muttered. "What's BABYBLUE got to say about this?"

"BABYBLUE requires command authority. The mains are online, and the dish is pointed in the right direction. I just need you to give the word."

"Proceed, Mr. Chau. Let's throw the switch and interrogate the eastern escarpment, one quarter power."

Chau wore a question on his face. "Sir—"

"Something on your mind, Lieutenant?"

"The system is state-of-the-art. Aileron Dynamix claims it *can't* be jammed. So what gives?"

"We're a good twenty-plus miles offshore, Mr. Chau. Maybe we should add more gain to BABYBLUE's output." His hand gestured toward the shoreline depicted on the display. "We need to get a peek inside that mountain, and short of landing on the beach—and knocking on the front door—BABYBLUE's our only option." Beacham dredged his memory, trying to come up with an analogy. "Look, Aileron has made lots of claims trying to sell their products. The whiz-bang stuff is probably true, but only under optimum conditions. *Officer of the Watch*—" the captain called, picking up the ship's phone, "Have we returned to Track One?"

"Aye, sir.".

"Skipper," Simon was puzzled again. "Are we retracing our steps?"

"That's correct, Mr. Chau."

"But we've zeroed in on the target." From the corner, Neill watched the exchange with mild amusement.

"Think it through, Lieutenant," Beacham said. "Ivan knows we're looking for something. If we discontinue our sweeps, what will that tell the Russians?"

"That we've found what we're looking for." The realization was sinking in. "And that there's no need to continue."

The captain smiled. "Do we really want to telegraph that message, Lieutenant?"

"I guess not, sir."

Beacham nodded. "Very well, then. Let's go through the motions and keep our Cold War friends guessing."

Neill stood and stretched. His presence in the Annex wasn't really required, but he stuck around anyway, just to keep abreast of any new developments. Moving past Dr. Brisbane, he tapped the scientist on the shoulder.

"Smoke break, Doc?"

Taylor looked up and blinked. "I don't smoke, Captain Neill."

Mike grinned. "It's just a euphemism. But I did see your eyes crossing. Let's step outside and get some fresh air."

Sunlight dazzled the two as they exited the compartment. Neither expected such intensity, and a stiff north wind stole their breaths. Neill produced a pair of sunglasses while Brisbane squinted.

"How about an adjustment?" The Marine reached out and tugged on her cap, pulling the visor down and shielding the Aussie's eyes. "Better?"

"Much, thank you." Neill took hold of the railing, steering the scientist closer to the bulkhead. "It's nice to get out of there. I haven't had a break since dawn."

Taylor's brow furrowed. "You know, it's just occurred to me; I haven't seen Aleksander and Yuri all morning."

"They're around." His reply was a bit off-handed. He didn't offer any other explanations.

"They wouldn't be in the comm shack, would they?"

"They might be."

"But why?" she pressed.

He offered his most conspiratorial look. "I think Yuri misses his mother."

"They're working on some kind of contingency plan, aren't they?"

Neill was taken aback. "Nothing personal, Doc. It's just—"

"—need to know?"

"Exactly."

Taylor allowed a little exasperation to creep into her voice. "Two weeks ago I was tucked away at the university. Now I'm staring down one of the world's most dangerous adversaries. It's all a bit much to take in."

Mike considered things from her point of view. Military operations were part of his everyday life, but not so with Taylor. He tried a little empathy.

"You're not alone here, Doc. This is a team effort. Many members, one body; all pulling together, each doing their part." A verse from the New Testament came to mind. *"Now if the foot should say, 'because I am not a hand, I do not belong to the body,' it would not for that reason stop being part of the body."*

"Is that from the Bible?"

Mike nodded his head. "First Corinthians. Chapter twelve, I think."

Taylor smiled. "I see the analogy. My father would often quote Scripture. His way of taking my mind off problems. He was fond of telling me, *Today's worries don't measure up to the power of the Almighty.* I'm afraid I've wandered from that simple faith, Captain." She stared out to sea, past the horizon. "Too many disappointments."

This woman had her own set of complications, he decided. She could ask questions round-the-clock, but the minute she got an answer that didn't square with her philosophy she became evasive.

"God could solve all of our problems with the wave of His hand; but that wouldn't teach us to face those challenges as adults. And it would make it an awful lot harder to trust in Him."

Brisbane sized him up carefully, gauging his motivations. She thought she'd figured out this American, but now she changed her mind. Was Michael Neill a cold, calculating intelligence operative—or an impassioned zealot with an ulterior motive?

"You make this faith of yours sound almost cerebral. I wasn't expecting that."

"There are aspects of Christianity that are very cerebral. It's always been a thinking person's worldview. But it's also experiential."

"What does that mean, exactly?"

"That's just a fancy way of saying that without heart, beliefs only add up to facts. You know, head knowledge."

"Does faith guide your actions, Captain Neill?"

"Yes; I'd be lost without it. Much like your academic training guides your steps." He decided to change the subject. "By the way, your equipment back in the shop is pretty impressive."

It wasn't really, but he had to start somewhere. The discussion had become much too philosophical, and he was eager to put things back on a more down-to-earth level.

Brisbane looked into his eyes. "O-scopes and high-voltage probes?" She shook her head, pony-tail bouncing from side to side. "You really need to get out more, Captain."

"No, seriously. The way that little . . . wave thingy goes up and down—what's that called?"

"Oscillation?"

"Yeah. What exactly are you looking for?"

"Sinewave signatures." She was indulging him now. "You know, the kind of evidence that might point to a weapon of mass destruction."

"And how's that coming along?"

She sighed. "The instruments have detected strong impulses in the background." Brisbane stopped there, recalling the last time she tried explaining the phenomenon. "I'd say it's a good start. Once we've discovered the weapon's secrets, I think we can find a way to counter its effects—is that what you're getting at?"

"Not exactly. I guess I'm asking how *you're* doing."

Beneath it all, she was touched by his concern. She stepped back a little, deciding that maybe she was allowing anxiety to crowd out her manners.

"I'm a little bit nervous about all this, Captain. Our search was just academic a few days ago; now we're here, eyeball to eyeball with the Russians." The *Meyer* had completed her turn, and the sun was now over their left shoulders. "I'm not like you military types. Conflict isn't something I'm comfortable with."

Mike grinned, recalling the title of the self-help book his uncle was reading. "I understand, Doc. But it's not like we're about to pick a *fight* with them." To the east, a low fogbank was rolling their way. "We stay here on the ship, gather the intel, and *boom*—we save the free world."

A sly look spread across the young woman's face. Neill had made it sound so easy, but a chill ran down his spine, and he was reminded that very few strategic goals were ever achieved quite so easily.

Military Stockade,
Chernihiv, Ukraine

Nadia Kolvec was alone in her cell—the same one, oddly enough, previously occupied by Major Vadim Mayakovsky. That Ukrainian officer had been arrested in the theft of a nuclear warhead, and had given the West a taste of international intrigue, Eastern European style.

Nadia's incarceration began the day after her conviction. There were only a few women in the stockade, and none with her stunning good looks. Since arriving, she had become Chernihiv's most infamous resident, tempting the prison guards with her alluring appearance and using her varied skills to bend men toward her will. And in that she was very successful.

In any culture, rich or poor, materialism was always an inducement toward cooperation. Nadia needed many things, and she knew how to get them. She knew how to apply pressure to achieve her goals. And Nadia was not without her contacts. The woman's life in prison did almost nothing to curtail her criminal activities. It simply opened up avenues for new ones.

Her jailers could be persuaded to provide contraband for those willing to pay the price. And pay they did—Ukraine was still a poor nation. It would take decades before the effects of communism would be eradicated, and even those with the least influence could be leveraged to bend the rules, or break them outright for power and position.

Tangible commodities were always in demand. Nadia traded in cell phones and drugs, and learned that if she could identify a need or desire, the rest came easily, and for those who craved a different experience, she found a willing market, and a captive supply of 'resources' to satisfy her varied clientele.

"You're new here," she purred.

Nadia's cell was in an isolated wing of the stockade. Visitors here were the exception.

The man in the uniform approached without a word. He had a chest full of ribbons and badges, more so than the jailers who walked the halls on a daily basis. And his rank was much greater, as well.

But the officer said nothing.

"I know who you are," Nadia continued. "Colonel Topol Raviche, the new commandant. Your predecessor told me you were coming."

"Nadia Kolvec. The madame of Chernihiv." His eyes lingered. "Also known by other names."

A smile. "I've heard them all."

"Then you know why I'm here." Raviche produced a key and slipped it into the lock. "We should become acquainted with each other. Our association might be regarded as mutually beneficial." He turned the key and opened the door, his hand loosening the tie at his neck.

Colonel Raviche entered the cell. He looked out of place behind bars. She lifted her hand and pulled him closer. The guard at the end of the corridor kept watch, and for the next hour he made sure the two weren't disturbed.

Nadia saw this as an opportunity to gain the colonel's trust. She took the long view, thinking two steps ahead. Of course, Raviche wasn't of the same mindset, and while he was focused solely on other things, Nadia's schemes were more diabolical.

Somewhere out there was an American, a Marine, a

man who had helped to crush her schemes and put her in prison. There was no doubt that he had gained the upper hand months before, but that wouldn't last. Nadia's plans dove-tailed nicely with those of the FSB and the Russian Federation, and if she had her way, *Kapitan* Michael Neill wouldn't survive the summer.

13

PRECEDENTS

Washington, D.C.

"**B**REAKING NEWS as we begin tonight's broadcast," the camera pulled back, revealing the anchor's features and affable smile. "I'm joined here in the studio by Defense Secretary Willis Avery, for a frank discussion of American naval activity near the Kamchatka Peninsula, and what that might mean for Russian interests in the region." The newsman turned to his right. "Mr. Secretary, thank you for being our guest."

"Always a pleasure, Brent," Avery answered.

"Queue up camera two," a voice drawled off-screen. SECDEF's face filled the monitor. The program producer was left to wonder why make-up hadn't done anything to tame that shock of hair on the Secretary's head.

"Mr. Secretary," Brent began, "not to put too fine a point on it, but our sources tell us an American warship has been cruising the Russian coastline, ostensibly to send a message to the Kremlin—and President Rurik." A pleasant smile, revealing perfect teeth. "What say you, Mr. Secretary?"

Avery beamed right back. "I'd say you have pretty

good intel, Brent. And if your people get bored with Beltway politics, send a few of 'em our way. We could use their talents over at Langley."

The anchor pressed ahead. "So these reports are accurate?"

He nodded. "We do have a naval vessel navigating those waters."

"Does this ship have a name?"

Avery had a shrewd grin. "I'll play a game with you, Brent. Hazard a guess. If you manage to come up with the name, I'll confirm it for you."

"I'll bet that my producer could locate that information in a New York minute."

"I'll bet he could."

In the booth, a well-worn copy of *Jane's Ships of the World* was being scoured, but the reference material was also online, and in far less than thirty seconds an office wag had accessed a list.

Brent tacked in a different direction, using the humor of the moment in an attempt to score more information.

"And this vessel's mission, so close to the Russian coastline? Is this an intelligence gathering operation, or are you simply giving the Kremlin a little heartburn?"

"After they buzzed the *Reagan* in the south Pacific last month?" Avery shook his head. "A little tit-for-tat would certainly be *tempting*—possibly even justified— but we're bigger than that."

Mark that down as a non-answer, the anchor noted.

"So—what *are* you saying, Mr. Secretary?"

"What was the question?"

"All right," Brent chuckled. "Anatoly Bazhenov, the Russian ambassador, has protested loudly—"

"—*very* loudly."

"—that our Navy's presence in Russian waters sets a dangerous precedent—that this move is tantamount to aggression. Would you agree with that assessment, Mr. Secretary?"

"No, I would not."Avery was blunt. "Listen, Brent, any American naval vessel operating in *that* part of the world, would, out of practical necessity, position itself well beyond the limits of Russia's sovereign territory. At present I am aware of only one of our ships, steaming some twenty-five kilometers from the shores of the Kamchatka Peninsula. We recognize Russia's sovereignty, and respect their claims to navigation in the sea lanes surrounding their shores—just as we would expect the armed forces of the Russian Federation to respect our territory and the contiguous zone claims of other nations."

"Including the U.S.?"

"Particularly the U.S."

The anchor stared. "That last statement seemed a bit pointed. Have tensions escalated in the region?"

"I wouldn't say that."

"What would you say, Mr. Secretary?"

"Only that we're cooperating with Japan, looking to uncover evidence of mastodons—" A pause. "No, that's not right—woolly mammoths on islands close to the peninsula."

"Woolly *mammoths*?"

"That's correct." Avery folded his hands. "It's a new world for the U.S. Navy, Brent."

"The Russian press is devoting more and more coverage to what they're calling—" the anchor checked his notes, "the *recent frustrations* between our respective countries. But you're saying that our naval activity has nothing to do with the two aircraft lost there recently?"

A sly look crossed SECDEF's face. "I would certainly be in the best position to answer that, now wouldn't I?"

"What about President Rurik's comments on Wednesday; that the upgrade in Russia's military doesn't signal a new arms race. Are you buying that?"

Avery was thoughtful. "I think the recent uptick in modernization is just their way of compensating for a deferred focus."

"After the fall of the Soviet Union?"

"Yes."

"What do you make of Rurik's other comment; that his country would push back against our missile shield in Poland, by adopting a system capable of piercing those defenses? Do you see that as saber-rattling?"

The Secretary raised a hand of caution. "I prefer less provocative terminology, Brent. In that regard, I think *bluster* would be more appropriate. And every nation has the right to determine how best to safeguard their borders."

"You're being very conciliatory, Mr. Secretary. Does that mean you won't second-guess Rurik's actions?"

"Not at all, Brent." A shake of the head, accompanied by another smile. "Not at all."

• • • •

"So," Nate began, "What's your take on Navy chow?"

Bailee looked across the chow hall, the din of clattering plates and hungry sailors filling their ears. "Your cooks don't believe in seasoning food, do they?"

The two had become inseparable as the mission progressed, and spent every moment of their free time together. "That's usually not a problem for a field Marine. We always carry hot sauce." He unzipped his Gore-Tex and pulled a tiny bottle from inside. "But I'm guessing this is too spicy for your tastes."

"The spicier the better," the young woman teased, a mischievous grin on her face. "But not *too* spicy."

That was too vague for Nate. "Are you qualifying your intentions?" After all, she'd been sending all the right signals, hadn't she? He was confused. Maybe he'd missed something, or maybe this Aussie was more nuanced than he'd supposed.

"I just don't want to give you the wrong idea." Bailee looked from side to side, lowering her voice. "I like you a *lot*, Nathan. I really do. But we need to stay in control. Do you follow?"

"I'd follow you anywhere." He said it with a smile, but the attempt at humor fell flat. Nate shifted gears. "Look, I know what you're saying. If you don't *want*—"

"Desire's no problem." Her voice was full of determination. "You should know that by now. It's just that—I'm waiting on God for this. Things are moving fast, and I want to be sure. Is that a problem?"

"Heck no." His smile returned. "I think I prefer that."

"So you're not disappointed?"

"Are you kidding?" He gave Bailee an exaggerated smirk. "I am a gentleman, y'know—or at least I try to be."

Before heading for the exit Crockett dropped off their trays at the scullery. The air here was thick with steam, but entering the passageway beyond, he thought he saw Bailee shiver.

"Are you cold?" he asked her.

"It's just a chill," she said, clutching her sweater. *Although you could be a mate*, she thought to herself, *and put your arm around me.*

Members of the crew filed past on either side of the passageway, and for good measure, Bailee crowded in closer, pressing against the Marine. Nate got the hint. He pushed open the hatch that led outside and took Bailee by the hand. Frigid sea winds tugged at the couple as they moved toward the ship's stern.

"Feel better?"

"Much," she said, squeezing his arm. Eyes closed,

Bailee tilted her chin up, her face inches from his. She caught the scent of his cologne. "What would you like to do now?"

The voice was enticing. Her accent closed the deal. Nate's heart was racing, and in spite of the cold gusts surrounding them he felt warm. Did Bailee feel the same way? He started to ask, but she pulled him in, halting any further questions.

"*Blokes,*" she chuckled behind half-closed eyes. "You're a dumb lot, aren't you?"

Nate stood taller, giving her a puzzled look. "What's that supposed to mean?"

Bailee stood on tip-toes, melting against him.

"You know what it means, Leftenant," she breathed. "Now hush—and give us a kiss."

Yelizovo Air Base,
Petropavlovsk

The *Beriev* aircraft was an ungainly bird, its appearance made more so by the oversized turboprop engines perched atop its inverted wings. Like much of the technology in this part of the world, this plane was a relic of a different era, and apart from the massive *Commissar* was one of the last amphibious aircraft still in service, having entered the Soviet Naval Aviation branch in the early sixties.

Designed for maritime patrol, the *Beriev* for today's mission would support a flight of MiG-29 Fulcrums as they surveiled the Americans steaming along Russia's coastline. Heavily armed—but not entirely for show—the twin-engine MiGs were fully fueled and waiting on Yelizovo's tarmac, ready to leap into the sky at a moment's notice. But while the Fulcrum was a sleek, aerodynamic fighter/interceptor, the airframe suffered from limitations not experienced by its western counterparts like the F-15 and the F-16.

Fuel capacity was one concern. This limitation kept the MiG from exploiting its on-station time. Loitering above an enemy element allowed pilots the option of attacking at will, or suppressing the opposing force's choices when it came to striking a lethal blow. Nothing was more frustrating to a Fulcrum driver than having to break off an assault due to fuel considerations—or the lack thereof.

Avionics were also less than top-notch. Navigation and radar systems had restrictions not experienced by pilots serving in the air forces of NATO or its client-states. And oddly enough, situational awareness for the pilot was another obstacle. Poor radar representation meant the system had trouble identifying targets in formation, leaving the Fulcrum, and by extension, the pilot, blind to the choices in the skies beyond the driver's seat.

Despite these problems, the Fulcrum was superb for close-in combat. As a rule, the Russians didn't name their aircraft; it was NATO that branded the MiG with the *Fulcrum* moniker. Russian pilots enjoyed the label, flattered by the description, and the name began to stick with the front-line squadrons fielding the planes.

The fighter employed a helmet-mounted sight, giving pilots the appearance of a science-fiction combatant, and the smooth lines of the aircraft made it an exceptional and deadly adversary—one that was difficult to beat in dogfights at altitude.

Lieutenant Tasha Alanova's MiG was crammed with all manner of equipment, much more so than the aircraft she had trained in years before. Tasha was tall, and the Fulcrum's cockpit was intended for pilots smaller than the headstrong native of Zagorsk. Still, the young woman managed to shoe-horn her frame into the cramped space—the ejection seat wasn't exactly molded to her backside—and was in the midst of pre-flight checks when her radio came to life.

"Snapped in, Tasha?"

"*Da*, Niko." The lieutenant looked down and to her left. Her maintenance chief, Nikolai Corbis, stared up at her from below, his features hidden beneath a flame-retardant hood and mirrored sunglasses. "Remove the crew ladder."

Alanova could see Corbis salute, his gesture exaggerated. In response, the lieutenant pulled the oxygen mask away from her face and gave the sergeant a curt nod. She couldn't see it, but he grinned back, and she watched as he wheeled the portable steps back to the apron's staging area.

She signaled her readiness to base operations. Confirmation from the tower came next. Tasha flipped a few switches, shifting the twin Klimov engines from idle to half-power. A glance to left and right confirmed that Sergeant Corbis had pulled the chocks, and from fifty meters away her wingman in FIREFLY One indicated that he was also ready to take to the air.

FIREFLY Lead smiled behind her visor. In another twist of history, women pilots—indeed, women in almost any combat role—were commonplace in Russia's military. The most romanticized of these had taken place among Soviet ground forces, where women had filled the roles of snipers, picking off German troops in places such as Sevastapol or Stalingrad during the Second World War. It was not widely recognized, but the role of sharpshooter fit women superbly well. Assassins were required to be intensely focused. The so-called gentler sex could be very deliberate when it came to scouting and taking out an enemy combatant.

And so the Russian military used women in these roles. War mandated it. With so many men dying hand-to-hand against the Reich, the Red Army didn't have the luxury of chivalry. With their very existence threatened, they trained their women for bomber squadrons, front-line trigger-pullers and tank drivers, taking out the enemy individually or *en masse*. Communism didn't recognize gender, and if an individual, regardless of sex, could be effective against an enemy of the *Rodina*, then so be it.

"Tower, FIREFLY Lead requesting permission for take-off," Tasha announced in a clipped tone. The voice of an air traffic controller followed.

"Copy, Lead. Taxi to runway sixteen and await further instructions."

Warm air lifted from the asphalt in waves, distorting Lieutenant Alanova's vision.

"Taxiing to runway sixteen, Tower." The paved surfaces before her were clear, with no other traffic in sight. "Awaiting further instructions. What of the weather?"

The controller came back. "Conditions are good. A fine day for flying."

"So we are authorized to proceed?"

A grunt of approval. "*Da*, Lieutenant. Start your roll out."

"*Spaseeba*." The sun was still high in the sky. It wouldn't be dark for hours. Tasha applied thrust and her Fulcrum eased forward. "Permission to buzz the tower?"

"Denied," the controller grinned. "Focus on the mission, *moloda zhinka*—and happy hunting."

14

GENERAL QUARTERS

Nate escorted Bailee back to her stateroom. At length they reached their destination, where a light tap on the door revealed that Taylor was inside.

"Date night?" Brisbane asked. She held back a yawn.

Bailee shrugged innocently. "I'll just be a minute," she promised, "so don't lock the door." Turning to Nate, she took hold of his hand. "What about you? Off to Dreamland?"

"I've kinda worked up an appetite," Crockett grinned, pulling her close. "It's been a while since dinner. Come go with me, we'll get a burger."

"Can you get one of those at this hour?"

"The galley serves meals to the late shift."

She shook her head, then kissed him once more. "It's late. Better get some sleep."

Disappointed, Nate answered, "Okay. But you know where to find me."

"I'll try not to forget that," she said with a smile.

Crockett stumbled into the room he shared with the others, kicking Neill's rucksack in the darkness and spilling its contents across the deck. The sniper then entangled a foot in the pack, dragging it halfway across the cluttered floor space.

From the corner, Xander growled beneath one of the wool blankets that covered his rack. He began to stir, his frame curled into a ball and now illuminated by the glow of Mike's cell phone as he held it high.

"Didn't you pick up any skills at sniper school?"

"Point that thing somewhere else." Nate shielded his eyes, and his whisper carried annoyance as he scooted Mike's gear from underfoot. "Sheesh. We *do* have wall lockers for this stuff, y'know."

"Which our guests needed."

Silent until that point, Yuri weighed in by scooping up a shower shoe and flinging it in the direction of the American officers. Neill saw it coming and swatted it away, sending it flying back.

"Where you been, anyway?" Mike grumped. He checked his phone. "It's nearly midnight."

"Just hangin' out. With Bailee." Nate plopped down on Neill's bed, landing on the captain's leg and getting an exasperated grunt in return.

"Off the bed, Romeo," Mike barked under his breath. He freed his leg, shoving the lieutenant with his foot. "You can't waltz in here like some love-struck teenager, disrupting your bunkies."

"Hey, c'mon." Nate pulled at Neill's blanket. "I'm hungry. Let's go for some mid-rats in the chow hall."

"I'll go," Yuri volunteered. "I'm wide awake now."

"What about Xander?" Nate asked.

"*Yes*—he is always hungry," Yuri answered. Mike's eyes adjusted to the darkened compartment, and he could see the Ukrainian's grin. "I wake him."

• • • •

In the darkness of the stateroom, Bailee found it hard to sleep. She tossed and turned in the rack for some time before coming to a decision.

"Where are you off to now?" From across the room, Brisbane sounded groggy.

"Chow hall," Russo replied, pulling on her jeans and a hoodie. "Dining facility. The mess. Where the food is."

"It's a little early for breakfast."

"They have meals at all hours. Want to go with?"

"I'm not hungry. You go ahead."

• • • •

"You really like her, don't you?"

Mike saw his friend nod. "What's not to like? She's cute as a button. Smart, too."

"Smarter than you," Neill agreed.

The four men moved down the passageway, descending two decks on their way to the ship's galley. Lights had been dimmed, more so than normal, and aside from the occasional seaman, the compartments they passed through were devoid of activity. That was fine by Xander, who shuffled along sleepily. Mike wondered why the Ukrainian had tagged along, and finally decided that maybe the cranky officer had begun to bond with the group.

Neill decided to tease Nate. "You sure it's food you need—and not a cold shower?"

"You'd love for me to answer that, wouldn't you, old man?"

"Not really. Contemplating your romantic liaisons is quite enough to put me off food."

• • • •

Thirty kilometers to the southwest, Firefly Lead and her

wingman banked due north, relying on their instruments as they observed merchantmen plying the waters covering the Kuril Trench.

A fog bank pushed in. Lieutenant Alanova dipped her starboard wingtip slightly to the east, pointing her sensors out across the horizon. There were few ships following the coastline tonight, but one stood out from all the rest; the radar signature of the USS *Meyer* was unmistakable, a sleek, swift-moving vessel cutting through the pitch-black swells that rose and fell as the ship sailed on a parallel course with the Commander Islands.

"She's just ahead," FIREFLY One sang out.

"I see her," Tasha replied evenly. "Keep your targeting device off and maintain radio silence."

•   •   •   •

Threat indicators deep in the *Meyer*'s CIC began to emit a soft warbling tone. The sound was insistent but not alarming.

The radar operator noted two targets on his screen, and clicked on the shared view mode, giving the weapons section a heads-up. He'd been watching the aircraft since they popped up over the horizon.

"XO, twin bogeys approaching from the southwest."

"Speed?"

"Twelve-hundred MPH, Mr. Towle." The radar operator's voice rose an octave. "Bearing is two-five-five, closing quickly. Intercept with our position in less than five minutes."

"Sound general quarters." The order was repeated. Towle's eyes swept the instruments at his disposal. "Weapons?"

Lieutenant Sanchez spoke up. "Returns indicate twin MiG-29s, XO—Fulcrums out of Petropavlovsk."

The executive officer lifted the handset for the 1MC.

"Captain to the CIC. I repeat; Captain to the CIC."

. . . .

The alarm klaxon sounded as Neill and company took their first sip of coffee—or tea, in Xander and Yuri's case—blaring from loudspeakers and disturbing the peacefulness of the ship's dining facility.

"This is not a drill; this is not a drill; general quarters, general quarters. All hands, man your battle stations! This is not a drill—"

Personnel filling the broad compartment reacted with uniform urgency, legs and elbows flying as they darted for exits, wolfing down food as they left. To a man, Marine and Ukrainian eyes flew open, casing the room in a natural reaction to danger.

"*Shto pres-khodit?*" *What is happening*? This came from Xander as he stood to his feet, shoved rudely by a slight chief petty officer on his way out.

The klaxon continued, its alarm bells screaming obnoxiously. Nate's blood ran cold, and he instinctively reached for his rifle, but that had been secured in the ship's armory one deck below.

Neill blurted a simple explanation to the Ukrainians before catching Crockett's eye.

"*Find Russo and Brisbane,*" he ordered.

"Roger that," Nate bellowed.

Bob Beacham entered the CIC and immediately sought out the executive officer.

"Report, Mr. Towle."

The XO relaxed as the captain arrived. "Two aircraft approaching, fast, steady bearing with decreasing range, both coming right at us, Skipper."

"MiGs?"

"Yes, sir," Towle replied.

The captain did a quick overview of the Fulcrum's strengths and weaknesses. These fighters had multi-target capabilities, along with their Vympel medium-range missiles. But he'd heard that they weren't as lethal as their menacing looks made them appear; pilots required extensive training, and there were system upgrades on a regular basis. Those refinements worked against seamless flight operations, and the latest inception of the MiG had a mixed history.

Beacham studied the screen. "Attack formation," he grunted. "Advise forward and lateral gun mounts. Tell the crews to remove covers and make the weapons ready in all respects."

"Aye, sir. Fifty caliber gun tubs report all ready."

At the speed the MiGs were approaching, Beacham knew the fifties would be practically useless against fighter aircraft. The captain and crew would have to rely on 30 millimeter chain guns and the ship's close-in weapons system.

"Phalanx?"

Towle nodded. "Ditto, Cap'n."

"All ahead flank." The ship couldn't outrun her supersonic pursuers, but the Skipper knew a moving target was harder to hit than one steaming lazily along on her course. There was no point in making it easy for them.

Evasive action came next. Beacham lifted his eyes from the radar screen and stared out into the night.

He had a bad feeling about this.

Controlled chaos ensued in the passageway. Nate made his way toward the stern, while Xander and Yuri followed Mike toward the *Meyer*'s bow and up ladderwells to the bridge.

"Captain Neill!" Mike stopped and spun around.

"Where's Bailee?" Taylor asked.

"She's not with you?"

"She was going to the galley." The Aussie scientist wore sweats and was out of breath.

"We were just there. Didn't see her." Neill turned in Nate's direction. The lieutenant was nearing the end of the passageway and stopped when he heard Taylor's voice.

"*Nate*—" Mike called, "—take the Doc with you— find Bailee!"

The sniper didn't need to be told twice. He dashed astern, disappearing around a corner.

Taylor tried to keep up.

• • • •

The MiGs were close enough to distinguish the *Meyer*'s portholes, antennae, the curved surfaces of the ship's protected radomes—even the markings at the waterline that encircled the hull.

"Bank to starboard, Firefly One," Alanova directed. Given his current course, her wingman would pass directly over the American ship's radar mast, a provocative action by anyone's reckoning.

Firefly One had anticipated the lieutenant's orders. Almost immediately, he turned hard right, breaking formation and continuing south before executing a loop that brought the MiG back. Neither aircraft flew over the ship, screaming past the bow and stern—in a way that let the *Meyer*'s crew know they'd been discovered.

"Charge weapons," Tasha ordered. "Descend to two thousand meters. Follow my lead on the next pass."

"*Da*, comrade."

• • • •

On the *Meyer*'s bridge and in the CIC, lights flashed and phones rang as updates and status reports were shared between departments.

"They're coming around, Skipper," Radar declared. "Turning tight and low on the deck."

"Are they targeting us?" Beacham wanted to know.

A quick glance at the instrumentation. "Aye, sir!" Weapons answered. "Both aircraft are now painting our hull."

"Pass the word, XO; tell the lookouts to stay sharp."

• • • •

Lieutenant Alanova's fighter approached the *Meyer* from the starboard beam, while FIREFLY One came at the ship from three points off the bow. Screaming in from the coastline, the fighters showed no signs of changing course in what appeared to be a strafing run.

Beacham had the icy feeling that's just what it was.

He watched them closing in on his ship, feet planted firmly on the deck. Should they attack, he knew what the MiGs would do next; they would zero in on the *Meyer*'s bridge, raking the command and control center with can-nonfire—30 millimeter, most likely—in an attempt to disrupt operations and sow confusion. And while Ivan's fighters had acted provocatively, neither had committed a hostile act against the American vessel just yet.

Bailee was on her way to the galley when general quarters sounded. Alone in the passageway, she halted her steps, confused by the raucous alarm and the activity of the sailors rushing past to get to their stations.

Her first instinct was to head back to the stateroom, back to Taylor, but re-tracing her steps would be difficult. The crew manning the fifty cal had arrived, ammo cans in hand; these seamen went about their work me-thodically, and she didn't want to get in their way.

Up ahead, she caught sight of Lieutenant Chau ducking into the Annex. She decided to join him there, spurred into action by the sight of a familiar face. She bolted toward the compartment just as Simon eased through the hatch, dogging it from the inside.

●   ●   ●   ●

Lieutenant Alanova was well within range, her gunsights leveled amidships and pointed at the *Meyer*'s towering superstructure.

Stupid Americans. Always willing to believe only the best of their adversaries. Had their roles been reversed, Tasha would have already opened fire on the advancing fighters, splashing them *before* they had a chance to attack. But the enemy's naivete—and their rules of engagement—worked to the Russians' advantage, giving FIREFLY Flight a tactical edge, one that could spin the outcome of this situation in their favor.

●   ●   ●   ●

Nate looked to the deck above them. Russo was running toward the ship's bow, on the same level as the CIC and the Annex. He spied a ladderwell and pushed in that direction, pulling Taylor with him.

"We have to go up!" At the same time, he became aware of the MiGs zooming in toward the *Meyer*'s starboard side.

The MiGs raced in to the ship's hull. From his spot on the *Meyer*'s bridge, Beacham watched as gunfire erupted from the lead fighter's wing, flashing in a burst. The scene was surreal to the captain; he'd experienced combat in the Persian Gulf during the Iraq war, but hostilities with Russia were hard to fathom, and he was still processing that notion when cannonfire struck the ship.

Portholes along the starboard bulkhead of the bridge

shattered, shrapnel and broken glass exploding within the compartment. The machine gun emplacements on either side of the forecastle erupted in sparks and fire as the rounds landed, shredding deck plates and bulkheads, killing anyone in their path. Those manning the gun mounts were blown apart.

The routine discipline of the ship's company was swept away. Captain Beacham turned his head in every direction. His vision blurred, and he dropped a hand to his side. He felt pain. Blood soaked his uniform, oozing from half a dozen shrapnel wounds, and as he slumped to the deck, Bob Beacham felt life ebbing from his body.

The volley of rounds traveled aft, peppering the bulkhead enclosing the Annex and the deck supporting it. Nate pulled Taylor into a passageway as the ordnance ripped through the hull.

Bailee was not so fortunate. Her search for safety took her to the most dangerous place aboard the ship. The Russian rounds stitched a ragged pattern in the deck plates. Caught in the open, she was struck by cannonfire and flying metal. She collapsed to the deck, barely able to maintain consciousness.

That was where Crockett found her. She saw his face, and the last word to cross her lips was the sniper's name. His heart pounding, Nate scooped her up and ran like her life depended on it.

Commander Towle kept the ship on her original course, following the Russian coastline as the mayhem began to fade. The *Meyer* had been badly hurt, but she could still be conned from the bridge.

The ship's defenses did their work. Firefly One was knocked out of the sky. Lieutenant Alanova's Fulcrum was hit hard but remained aloft. She turned tail, heading back to Yelizovo with impaired hydraulics and one wing shredded.

Aboard the *Meyer*, damage control crews fell back on their training, the deck beneath their feet slick with blood. First responders—firemen and medical personnel— saw to the needs of the injured.

Neill, Tereshenko and Voskov changed their course and headed for the *Meyer*'s sickbay. Located in the bowels of the ship, the facility came alive as the wounded were brought in. They entered the compartment from the port side, while Crockett, Bailee in his arms, burst through a hatch to starboard. Brisbane and Chau were close behind.

"Corpsman up!" Nate yelled. "This woman's badly hurt." A petty officer found an empty stretcher.

Neill stared across the room.

Bailee Russo was white as a ghost.

• • • •

"There was blood, Michael." Taylor's voice was weak. "So much blood." Brisbane's sweats and hands were stained with it, and Neill could see it as he approached.

Medical personnel criss-crossed the deck. Able seamen were pressed into service, lending a hand where they could. The number of casualties was mounting.

"Were you injured?" Neill wanted to know.

She shook her head. "This is all from Bailee."

"Simon?"

"I'm fine, Mike. I was inside," Chau answered. "I heard banging from the hatch—and then machine gun fire bouncing off the bulkheads. I was too late."

But the Marine had stopped listening. The corpsmen tending Bailee's wounds swore. After some effort, Neill watched as an officer reached out a hand to Crockett and shook his head. He mouthed a simple phrase, one that Mike couldn't quite hear—

Nate sank to his knees, bowing toward the deck. A muffled, drawn-out sound escaped his mouth, lifting into the air of the compartment. Neill left the others and walked to his friend's side.

"Get up, buddy," he told him. The corpsmen covered Bailee with a blood-stained sheet and withdrew, giving attention to others still in need. "We need you in the land of the living."

"I never should have left her." Nate refused Mike's outstretched arm and staggered to his feet, eyes on Bailee's still form.

Half a dozen Scripture verses came to mind. Neill kept those to himself. Nate wasn't ready for a sermon on comfort.

Malcolm Richey strode through the sickbay, checking on the men in his charge. The dead were few; the wounded many, but the medical teams were well-trained and managed to stabilize those with the most serious injuries. Richey saw Neill and the others at the far end of the compartment, standing near the body of the Australian woman.

"Dr. Brisbane," he began, drawing close to the huddled group. "I'm sorry."

Taylor started to reply. Nate's voice interrupted her.

"I can't protect anybody, Mike," he grated out. "Not Richard, not Bailee." His head went from side to side.

Simon started. "C'mon, Nate. That's not—"

"True?" Crockett growled. An angry fire burned in his eyes. "You weren't in Warsaw. People die when I'm around—the wrong people."

The lieutenant drew himself up and took a step back. Mike reached out again, but Nate pulled away and headed for the hatch.

"Nathan—*wait*."

"Let him go, Simon," Neill told him. "He's hurt. Let him deal with this on his own terms. At least for now."

Richey was shaking his head. "You know the Russians, Mike. Why'd they do it? Why stage an unprovoked attack on an American warship?"

"I don't have any answers, Senior Chief." He glanced at Yuri, who muttered aloud.

"What'd he say?" Malcolm asked.

"Yuri blames it on bloodlust." Neill could understand the sentiment. There was no love lost between the two nations. "My guess? The Russians think we've found something. And they're willing to risk war to keep it under wraps."

15

BRIEFING

The Pentagon

WILLIS AVERY LOOKED up from his desk as Cull McKeckney entered the room.

"Conference call, Mr. Secretary," Cull informed him. "Separate lines, but both originate from Kiev. I think you know these gentlemen." He checked his notepad. "General Andrei Ulyanov, and a major with Ukraine's Security Directorate, Dmitri Yaroslav."

"Met them both in Warsaw. Good people." SECDEF checked his day planner. His mood was grim. "Has Bazhenov arrived yet?"

"The Russian ambassador's on his way," Cull answered. "Should arrive in the next hour. I would imagine he's already received his instructions from Moscow."

Avery gave a nod, and returned to the sitrep on his desk. "Twenty-one injured, eight dead. And one of the Australians is among the deceased."

"That's quite the butcher's bill," Cull added.

"Quite. This could spiral out of control very quickly, Cull. Anatoly Bazhenov is a spinmaster. He'll try to convince us that this was *our* fault. He has something of a history in that regard."

Avery's mind went back a couple of years, when a new Russian jet fired on an unarmed U.S. Navy plane. Captain Neill's best friend and Academy classmate died in the attack. Avery was the National Security Advisor at the time.

"What's the president saying?"

"The man's understandably upset," Willis returned. "Publicly he's grieving; privately—*politically*—he has to stand up to the Kremlin and call Rurik on this. The ball's already rolling. Cassidy's calling for our allies to impose sanctions, on top of stripping Russia of its G-8 status, and the Joint Chiefs and I have been instructed to explore our military options."

"NATO's been gaming this scenario for over a year," McKeckney reminded his boss. "Facing down a more aggressive Russia. This will just heighten things."

"The top dogs in the Kremlin's military have pushed back against substantive dialogue," Avery added. "This is a test of leadership. The president pledged to shore up our military might and restore America's respect in the world. Moscow's given him an opportunity to do just that."

"I doubt that's what they had in mind."

SECDEF looked thoughtful. "Probably not; we'll pick Anatoly's brain once he gets here. Chuck Cassidy wants answers, and so do I."

"A false flag event, maybe?"

Avery didn't think so. "Those are generally done secretly—designed to make it look like someone else did the dirty deed."

"Well, we've got Ivan dead to rights on this one."

"No doubt about it," Avery said slowly. "Still, it all makes me wonder. What's Moscow up to? Are they trying to draw us into something else—something that gives them the advantage?"

The younger man let that statement lie for a moment. "That's what they pay us to find out. What's next?"

"I've just ordered all U.S. military and DoD installations worldwide to elevate their force protection conditions to the next level—particularly those in the Pacific. If this is part of some broader attack, I don't want us caught with our pants down."

A little late for that, Cull decided silently. He looked at the time on his phone. One other detail remained—

"The interpreter is waiting outside. Want me to bring him in?"

Avery nodded again. The Ukrainians would provide an English-speaker for the Americans' benefit, but for all his trust in Ulyanov—and America's allies in general— the Secretary preferred having someone who could assure him of what was being said in any conversation he was part of.

"Pull up our guests on the plasma after the interpreter's in the room," Avery directed. "And make sure he's out of the camera's view—we wouldn't want to offend the Ukrainians."

Cull smiled. "Gotcha, Mr. Secretary."

• • • •

Communications within the Secretary's office were top-notch, and within minutes, the faces of both Ukrainian officers had resolved and were displayed on the big screen dominating the far wall.

"Captain Neill asked for a favor," Ulyanov intoned, waiting as the interpreter translated for the Americans. "But I have not been able to reach him."

Avery kept his eyes on the wary officer. "Neill's on assignment right now, General. I'd offer details, but at the moment, his mission is classified."

Ulyanov waved a dismissive hand. "No matter, *Mr. Secretar.* I have the information to fulfill his request." He shot a glance to the left side of his screen, where he could see Dmitri's face. "I will disclose it directly to you. President Pavlovsk has agreed that you should know."

"I'd be happy to listen, General," Avery brightened.

Andrei spent the next few minutes briefing the Americans, with Major Yaroslav filling in a few gaps and providing intel from the Security Directorate's case files. The disclosures left them aghast.

"You're sure about this?" Willis asked when the two foreign officers finished.

"I wish I weren't, *Mr. Secretar.* This does not bode well for either of our nations. We must act."

Avery's mood deepened. "Please tell your president that we'll vet this very carefully."

"Trust but verify?" Ulyanov smiled.

The SECDEF mulled that over.

So Ivan's got a secret, he considered. *And now we know what it is.*

McKeckney cut the feed. "What's next?"

"We'll have to move fast," Avery answered. He pondered a scenario. With luck, it just might work.

There were key personnel in the region. He avoided the word *assets*; that term was cold and impersonal, an injustice to the men he'd come to rely on. Neill was practically in place; Crockett, too, and Avery had learned to trust them both.

Ulyanov was right. It was time to sever the snake's head, and a bold plan began to form. An opportunity had presented itself, but it wouldn't last for long.

"Cull, we're going to do something that we've never done before." He spent the next several minutes sharing what he had in mind.

"Will the president buy into that?"

Avery was surprised. He'd expected resistance. The former artilleryman offered none at all.

• • • •

A flight of four F-18 Hornets joined the USS *Meyer* between Ust-Kamchatsk and the Commander Islands, dispatched from the USS *Ronald Reagan*. The big carrier had been cruising near Midway, but was now moving northwest, making her presence known to the Russians.

Not surprisingly, there were no further attacks from Kamchatka.

Neill slept about four hours before giving up on a full night's rest. He awoke at dawn and found a quiet spot in the chow hall for morning devotions. The words he read came from the book of Isaiah;

> *He who vindicates me is near.*
> *Who then will bring charges against me?*
> *Let us face each other!*
> *Who is my accuser?*
> *Let him confront me!*
> *It is the Sovereign Lord who helps me.*

The Captain's thoughts were on the mission, but he couldn't help but be concerned for Nate. The two Marines had shared several taskings together; from their time aboard the *Lexington*, off the coast of northeast Africa; to the South China Sea, and finally to Warsaw, where they had helped ensure the success of an accord between Eastern European nations, banding together to stand up to the Russian juggernaut.

"Lord, so far this hasn't gone as planned," the young officer prayed. "We've suffered losses—terrible losses. I don't pretend to have all the answers, and I can't do any more in my own strength." He stopped, searching his heart, and emptying himself of anything that might stand between him and Heaven. It was not a process that Neill was prepared to rush, but in time he pressed on.

"I'm giving this to You, Father. Your ways are not mine. I'm putting it into Your Hands, and asking You to let me be an instrument of Your will."

Neill continued his meditations.

Who will condemn me?
They will all wear out like a garment;
 the moths will eat them up.
Who among you fears the Lord
 and obeys the word of his servant?
Let the one who walks in the dark,
 who has no light,
trust in the name of the Lord
 and rely on their God.

His mind wandered. He thought of the two Ukrainian operatives that had recently joined the mission. Voskov and Tereshenko had bedded down shortly before Neill. Crockett had stumbled in after four a.m., having spent hours staring out to sea from the ship's fantail. He finally collapsed in his rack, but sleep eluded him, dropping off only after Neill left the small compartment and headed out to start his devotions.

Mike bowed again in prayer, lifting up praise and the needs of his shipmates—Nate and Taylor, primarily—to the Father. The verses he'd read spoke to his heart, and he was ready for the next step in this assignment. The coming days would be difficult, but it was time to press for answers.

"Cap'n Neill?"

Mike looked up from the Scriptures before him.

"Senior Chief," he replied. "Care to join me for some coffee?"

Malcolm Richey shook his head. "Maybe later. Your presence has been requested at the highest level; the Secretary of Defense would like an audience. Secure videofeed. He wants Captain Voskov and Sergeant Tereshenko too."

"Where?"

"We have cubicles in the SCIF," Richey answered. "I'll take you there."

16

MISSION REVEALED

Petropavlovsk Naval Base,
Kamchatka Peninsula

"THE ATTACK ON THE American ship; you chose not to use the *Commissar*?"

Taras Pavlenko considered Tamarkin's question as they sipped tea in the Admiral's office.

"And reveal our hand to the American Navy?" He shook his head. "That day will come, Captain, but not for some time yet. We have managed to further our goals through other means."

"Half a day has passed. Aside from defensively attacking our aircraft, the United States has not responded militarily."

Pavlenko nodded. "But their defensive posture has shifted; threat condition levels have been raised," he told the captain. "President Cassidy will seek the counsel of his subordinates. I am convinced that some action will be forthcoming."

Tamarkin played devil's advocate. "He might not be as hawkish as we were led to believe."

"*Vozmozhnah*," the admiral replied. *Possibly.* "Making assumptions of that kind isn't wise, *tavarisch*. Our operations will depend, to a great extent, on the predict-ability of the Americans."

"Is there a contingency in place to force their hand? Another brazen assault, perhaps?"

Pavlenko chuckled. "Our strategy displeases you?"

Tamarkin was impassive. "I understand that we have little choice, Admiral. We must see to the needs of the *Rodina*. But these tactics smack of desperation. What if the Americans see through it?"

"It's no secret that you've looked on Charybdis as a fanciful venture, Captain. But I had hoped that our suc-cesses would improve your opinion."

"I am not *unimpressed*, sir," Tamarkin countered. "Charybdis is truly a wonder weapon. And to employ it in pursuit of our ultimate goal will save Russian lives, and undoubtedly ensure an outcome in our favor."

Tamarkin surprised him. "That is my hope, as well," Pavlenko said. "And what of your team's efforts?"

"One last test today. With its completion—and a fa-vorable result—we can begin installing the system in the rest of *Commissar* squadron." Tamarkin finished his tea and got up to leave. "I will keep you apprised of our progress."

"Please do, Captain," the admiral muttered. A great deal remained at stake, and Pavlenko wanted nothing left to chance.

Late afternoon, aboard the Meyer

As it had just days before, the ship's wardroom filled quickly. Ensign Vespi entered with Xander and Yuri, tak-ing his seat at the table with them. Captain Neill and Se-nior Chief Richey arrived with Simon Chau, who hooked up the Marine's laptop. Soon the audio/visual equipment tied to the room's monitor began to whir, and the plasma screen above them winked to life. Mike inserted a thumb drive, and with the aid of a mouse, he began retrieving files, provided by Yuri, for the presentation he would host shortly.

With the skipper in sickbay, Commander Towle had joined the gathering, representing the ship's command. Taylor Brisbane wasn't far behind. Looking a little worse for wear, the Australian scientist appeared tired, but focused. Noticeably and painfully absent was Bailee Russo.

Crockett dragged in last. Neill wasn't surprised. The junior officer had slept fitfully and looked it.

"How's the Captain, Michael?" Brisbane asked.

"I can speak to that," Richey announced. "The docs have removed all the shrapnel, and he's on the mend. He's conscious and talking, already issuing orders from his bed in the ship's surgery."

"And the ship?"

"Steaming southwest again," Towle answered. "The aircraft you hear are Hornets from the *Reagan*."

"Elements of the task force have taken positions to the south," Neill told the group. "If you look closely, you can make out their silhouettes on the horizon."

"Might as well address the question on everyone's mind. How do recent events affect our mission, Cap'n?"

Neill turned to Richey, and then to the Ukrainians. "Profoundly, Senior Chief. These circumstances have altered our steps going forward." His eyes swept the room. "Listen, we're all a little numb; some more so than others." A glance at Brisbane, then Crockett, who dropped his gaze. "This ship has lost crew members, and one of our own team is dead."

Taylor's eyes filled with tears. She was still coming to terms with Bailee's death.

"Incidentally, Moscow is claiming this is all a big mistake," Mike continued. "They're saying those MiGs acted in self-defense, after being targeted by *our* radar systems. It's all over Sky News, the BBC, and Fox."

Towle was shaking his head. "I saw those broadcasts in the galley. Those reports are categorically false."

"I know—we spoke earlier with Secretary Avery," Neill went on. "For some of you, what I'm about to say won't come as a surprise."

"That's all well and good. But who's *we*?" The question came from Richey.

The Marine smiled thinly, but he wasn't amused. "Xander, Yuri, and I," he replied.

"With a little help from Ukraine's State Security Directorate, we now have more backstory to share." Neill moved to a bulkhead and dimmed the lights while pointing a remote at the A/V setup. The monitor shifted and now displayed the face of an elderly man with a white beard.

"This is Dr. Radya Zhukov," the captain said slowly. "There are no contemporary photographs of this individual—the image before you has been age-progressed, based on his appearance some thirty odd years ago."

Richey frowned. "A Russian?"

"He's Ukrainian. Pressed into service during the Soviet era. And by all accounts, the man is brilliant."

Brisbane was being drawn in. "Does he have some connection to the pulse weapon being used by the Russians?"

The Marine nodded. "Zhukov perfected it. He's also the brainchild behind our so-called *chimera*, the aircraft discovered by the *Pont Claire*."

"The one on the seabed," Taylor stressed.

"The same." With the push of a button, the image on

the screen changed, depicting a sonograph of the plane that now lay at the bottom of the ocean. "And according to the SSD, Dr. Zhukov is the lead scientist for Project Charybdis."

"Charybdis? What's that?" Chau asked.

"Yes," Yuri spoke up. His English was broken. "Ancient myth. From Greek."

"Alternately described as a sea monster, or a whirlpool swallowing ships," Neill added. "In any case, a hazard to navigation."

Taylor's brow furrowed. "That's putting it mildly, but it would fit what we've seen so far."

"And this Ukrainian—" Malcolm said, "Zhukov—is behind the ekranoplan—*and* the weapon used to bring down the aircraft?"

"I told you he's brilliant. The Security Directorate is also convinced. And with good reason; according to Captain Voskov, they've got eyes and ears somewhere near the mountain ranges of Ust-Kamchatsk. A mole of sorts, working right under Ivan's nose."

"A spy," Brisbane said flatly.

"That's right, Doctor. A Ukrainian agent." Neill used the remote again, and an image of Kamchatka's cliffs came into view. "Zhukov and a team of scientists are operating out of a secret location, a massive hangar complex hidden behind the cliffs on the peninsula."

"Just as Crockett suspected," Brisbane said.

"Hangar—as in a facility for aircraft?"

"It would seem Dr. Zhukov has tweaked his ekranoplan design, equipping the current version with an EMP weapon, using it to devastating effect."

Brisbane pointed to the screen. "This is the same location we saw that day at the Pentagon, isn't it, Captain Neill?"

"Yes, it is. And the SSD has confirmed much of our

conjecture."

Nate looked to the Ukrainians and spoke for the first time. "How long has this spy been in place?"

The group waited for Vespi to translate, and Voskov rattled off something in Ukrainian.

"That's not important," Vespi summarized. "Disclosing that information could get their agent killed."

"You've been in contact with this spy, haven't you?" Brisbane aimed her inquiry at Voskov. "Recently, I would guess."

"Via secure means," Voskov answered. "An encrypted radio signal. He awaits our instructions."

"Can we trust him?" Taylor wasn't convinced.

"I trust him with my life." Voskov's eyes traveled around the table as Vespi relayed his words. "I have been tasked with a mission. And our contact in Kamchatka has provided invaluable assistance."

"What mission?" Richey wanted to know.

"To infiltrate the lair," Voskov breathed, "And to kill Dr. Zhukov."

Neill was taken aback. "Kill him?"

Xander nodded in reply. "His work poses a threat to aircraft and ships at sea. He cannot be allowed to continue."

"But even if Zhukov is dead, that's no guarantee the weapon won't be used again," Chau reminded them.

Voskov shrugged. "Perhaps not. But it would send a message to the Russian Federation. And possibly dissuade others following in Zhukov's footsteps."

"Not to change the subject," Richey interjected, "but you're *certain* the Russians are using another plane— like the one found on the ocean floor?"

Neill nodded. "The SSD's man has witnessed it himself. He described it as massive, the platform for what the Russians are calling the Eye of Charybdis."

Taylor repeated the name softly, and felt a chill run through her body. "What do we do about it?" she asked.

Neill's reply was simple. "Our job now is to disable the weapon."

"Disable?" Richey was doubtful. "That's not something we can do from the safety of the *Meyer,* Captain. You're talking about going into the belly of the beast— sabotaging Russian hardware. That's state-sponsored espionage of the highest order. If they catch you, Moscow will lock you up and throw away the key. Ivan's not going to toss out the welcome mat without having something to say. Did Secretary Avery sign off on this?"

"The Department of Defense is behind us on this. We've been directed to bring back the Charybdis operating system, or the schematics, at the very least. As for your objections, Senior Chief, all of that's true. But look at it this way; Xander was planning to take out Dr. Zhukov. I would imagine his contact on the peninsula has prepared the way—am I right, Captain?" Neill didn't wait for Vespi to translate, choosing instead to speak directly to the officer in his native tongue.

"Access to the hangar is available." Voskov shifted in his chair. "There are tunnels—air shafts to the surface—dug by Soviet engineers more than forty years ago." Once more, the ensign passed along the words for the others' benefit.

"This plan does have one thing going for it."

"What's that, Senior Chief?" Chau asked.

"The element of surprise. The Russians won't expect it—provided it works."

"Those tunnels—is that how we're getting in?"

Neill turned to face his friend. "Lieutenant Crockett, there's no *we* involved here—for this mission, it's just the SSD and myself."

Nate was already shaking his head. "Well, you're not

making this trip without me."

"Can't risk it, pal. You don't speak the language." He gestured to Voskov and Tereshenko. "The three of us do, and in case we're caught, we might be able to talk our way out of things."

"So I'll just play dumb. Or maybe you can teach me some of the basics. Either way, I'm going. I've got a little payback to deliver."

Revenge. Mike had played that card himself in the past. "Keep it professional, Nate. There's no room in this business for grudges."

"Count me in, too," Brisbane huffed. There was resolve in her voice. "But don't expect me to leave my personal feelings behind. Bailee was a good friend."

Neill was annoyed by his associates' volunteerism. But at the same time he was glad to see Nate coming back around to his responsibilities. "I'm sorry, Doctor. It's too dangerous. I can't vouch for your safety."

"You can't do this without me," Brisbane told him. "I doubt you can identify Charybdis, unless you've suddenly become an expert in weaponized pulses."

"She's got a point, Mike," Richey grinned.

"That does strengthen her argument," he conceded. "But this is dangerous." His face was stern, and he turned to Brisbane. "We might not be coming back, Doctor."

"Bailee's not coming back either, Michael," she said hotly. "I won't stay behind while you dash off to make her death more meaningful."

"Why not wait until it shows itself again?" Richey asked. "We could blow it out of the sky and be done with it."

"Because nobody's been able to catch it out in the open. The Russians wait for the fog and use it to mask their movements."

"And destroying that plane won't prevent Ivan from

building another one," Nate pointed out. "We've got to steal the blueprints—or kill Zhukov. Kidnap him at the very least. If both sides have the weapon, then you've got balance of power. Parity, if you will."

"How's this going to work?" Richey asked.

"A lot like Huo Shan." That op included both Richey and Chau.

"So you need a boat. That's risky. How do you plan on getting there without being seen?"

"The same way the Russians do it," Neill smiled.

"We wait for the fog."

Henderson Hall,
Arlington, Virginia

"What's this?"

"Read it," the boss instructed. "It came from SECNAV. He got it from Willis Avery himself."

Master Gunny Etheridge looked at the printed page the colonel handed off. The memo was flagged TS/SCI—top secret, sensitive compartmented information—Special Access Required. Pushing back in his seat, Etheridge scanned two paragraphs before whistling softly.

"Well, dip me in vinegar and call me a pickle." Etheridge would have grinned, but what he'd just read brought a sober look to his face. "It would appear that Captain Neill was right."

Terryton's brow arched. "You've talked to Neill?"

"Not recently. But we've already had this discussion, he and I. He was going on about Peter the Great, and how the Russians expand their empire by adding territory." He held up the message. "You think Neill's seen this intel?"

Terryton smiled to himself. "If the Ukrainians and

Willis Avery know, you can bet the Captain's not far behind."

"Where did Secretary Avery get this?"

"Not sure," the colonel replied. "My guess would be one of our allies, probably Ukraine—the SSD is close enough to the action, and they've got a vested interest in seeing Russia's plans thwarted."

"So Ivan's having a for-real energy crisis," Etheridge went on. "And now they're planning an invasion of our shores."

"Personally, I find that hard to swallow. It's a crazy idea. The thought of Russia landing troops in the United States is extremely unlikely. It borders on ludicrous."

Etheridge considered it. "That's what the Ukrainians thought," he said, echoing Neill's words. "And we've already seen how that worked out."

"True," the colonel allowed. "And maybe Ivan's incursion in the Crimea has emboldened them. But how could they hope to succeed? Alaska's remote, I'll grant you that, but we could deploy a counter-force easily enough to stop their advance."

Etheridge wasn't so sure. "You ever hear of Project WASHTUB?"

"Wasn't that a Cold War operation?"

"Yeah. Back in the fifties, the U.S. was worried that Russia might invade and occupy Alaska. Bear in mind that it was just a territory back then, and not a state."

The colonel's memory had been jogged. "That does ring a bell."

"The plan was to set up a network to keep tabs on the Soviets—if, in fact, they *did* land an invasion force. Would've been very dangerous if they had. Soviet doctrine called for the elimination of any resistance in occupied territory."

Terryton pulled up a chair. "Fortunately Ivan never

chanced it."

"Times have changed. If it's oil they're after, they might just go for a small piece of the pie. A corner of territory, like the Arctic Refuge."

"ANWR?"

"From a tactical standpoint, that's where I'd position my forces," Etheridge told him. "Ivan goes in and grabs the northern slope, then starts drilling. *Viola*—problem solved."

The colonel sported a wry look. "It's not quite that easy, Master Guns."

"Agreed. And I didn't say it would be—"

"—you just *implied* it."

Etheridge ignored that. "Nick, if the Russians gain a solid foothold, it's not hard to imagine them going after the oil rigs in the region. After all, they've been building up their Arctic infrastructure for quite some time now. And the best intel suggests they've got a base under construction close to the American coastline."

"Okay." Terryton was willing to entertain the notion. "Any theories on how they'd go about it?"

Etheridge had already given the idea some thought.

"The key is logistics," he began. "We know the Russians have opened up landing strips at some of their Arctic bases—large enough to handle those big transports, like the Antonovs. The airfields and those planes would be crucial to their supply line, should they take up residence. Of course, their Navy would have to be involved, ready to support ground operations, and to protect the tankers needed to ship the crude back to Mother Russia."

The colonel could almost picture the scenario. "They *do* have the aircraft necessary for the job—but our assets would deny them entry into U.S. airspace."

"That's not a foregone conclusion." The senior NCO leaned forward in his chair, recalling the Pentagon briefing. "If Neill and Avery are right, and Russia does, in fact, have a pulse weapon—"

Terryton frowned. "—they could take down our planes—knock them out of the sky—before we even knew what hit them."

The barrel-chested Marine wasn't done making his point. "Now suppose this EMP thing is set up on their front lines," he persisted. "Ivan could point its muzzle toward American troops, disabling our equipment and repelling every move we make."

Terryton narrowed his eyes, thinking of something else. "Avery suspects the Russians attacked our ship for a specific reason."

"Oh?" Etheridge replied. "And what might that be, 'cause I'm hard-pressed to understand their rationale."

"SECNAV called after the fact." The officer turned toward the window. "He thinks attacking the *Meyer* was a probing attempt, to determine how we'd react if an invasion was launched. The Kremlin figured we'd retaliate more forcefully, launch a full scale assault. By doing so, we'd give them the excuse to counter-punch—and send out their invasion force."

"So they were *counting* on our response, to justify further action?" Etheridge offered.

"Something like that." He waved a hand. "It's thin, I know. But Mark Breese isn't president anymore. Avery thinks Moscow was expecting a more fiery reaction from Charles Cassidy."

"There might be some other reason," Etheridge proposed. "The Russians are just determined to keep this weapon of theirs under wraps.

"Cassidy's contentious in a fight, and he can be stubborn. Must be his background as a surgeon. But he's not impulsive. The United States will have to respond accordingly, and not play into the Russians' hands." Etheridge became somber. "I keep thinking about that Australian woman killed in the attack."

"Bailee Russo?"

"I can only imagine how her death has affected the team." The master gunny stared at his boss. "Did SECNAV say anything else? What's our next move?"

He shook his head. "I don't have a clue. The Secretary was tight-lipped on the subject." His face became a scowl. "But whatever it is, I'd lay even money that Captain Neill will be right in the thick of it."

17

FAVORABLE CONDITIONS

Osbeck Chiropractic Clinic,
Anacostia, Maryland

DANIEL NEILL WAS IN A lighthearted mood, but nervous, nonetheless. The reason for his temperament sat atop a stool just a few feet away.

Dr. Carolyn Osbeck lifted his arm, gently flexing the joint at the wrist and giving it a practiced look. Releasing it, she picked up a clipboard. "Let's review the findings of your MRI. I also have the images from your x-rays."

Osbeck used a desktop monitor, turning it so Daniel could also see. "No films in this day and age," she explained. "We show patients everything digitally now, Mr. Neill."

"Call me Daniel."

"All right." Her tone was very clinical. "*Daniel.*"

Score one, Neill thought.

She tapped a few keys, and a black and white image appeared on the screen. He stood to get a better view. "Here's the first plane I want you to see. Without contrast. Now remember, this process looks at soft tissue."

"Got it. Find anything out of the ordinary?"

Dr. Osbeck examined the display. "Your alignment

and joint spaces appear maintained. The fibrocartilage is also good." She tapped the screen, drawing Daniel's attention. "A small amount of fluid is accumulated, but your flexor and extensor tendons look fine. No soft tissue masses are evident." She turned to face her patient, whose thinking had become muddled by all the medical terms. "All in all, this impression indicates an unremarkable wrist MRI. How does it feel?"

"Getting better," he replied. "And the x-rays?"

"Bones are all good, with no breaks," Carolyn said, putting him at ease. "You've suffered a bad sprain, Mr.—" she caught herself, "—*Daniel*. Give it a few more weeks and I think you'll be fine."

"What about the x-rays of C-One and Two?"

She pulled up a different image, this one showing Daniel's skull and spinal vertebrae. "You present a slight subluxation of the cervical spine. You can see it here." She traced a finger across the screen, demonstrating the angle. "We can fix that with an orthogonal adjustment."

"Will that hurt?"

"It's called gentle chiropractic. You'll feel more discomfort from being positioned on the table." Carolyn flipped through her patient's history. "You've seen your share of trauma. Combat Marine, veteran of Iraq; injured by an IED." She got down off her stool and stood before him. "Is that how you lost your leg?"

"Yeah." Daniel bent his knee, tapping the prosthetic leg he wore. It made a hard, plastic sound, but the limb was composed of carbon fiber composites, covered in a soft foam.

"We'll do the adjustment in this area," she told him, her fingers touching the back of his neck. "I wouldn't be surprised if you have immediate relief from the headaches."

Daniel felt warm. "How'd you know about those?"

"From your chart," she answered. "And given your war injuries, the subluxation has probably existed since the IED blast." She dropped her hands, but didn't back away. "Your service to your country has cost you. You've probably been told this before, but thank you for what you've sacrificed."

He didn't know what to say. "My pleasure, Doc," he muttered helplessly.

Daniel hadn't expected such an outpouring of respect and appreciation. In fact, he had heard those sentiments before, but not from a woman like Carolyn, and certainly not from one standing so close. He felt courage welling up inside, and decided that an opportunity like this might not come again.

"Listen, Doc, can I ask you something?" He felt exposed and vulnerable. "It's kind of personal."

"I'm listening."

"You've been real nice to me," he started. "I appreciate that. And I couldn't help but notice there's no ring on your finger—so I guess you're not married."

"No, Mr. Neill. I'm not."

Uh-oh, he thought silently. She'd dropped his first name. He almost pulled back, but pushed ahead anyway.

"I just wondered if maybe you'd like to have dinner sometime. With me, that is." He cringed. *Of course with you*, he reproached himself.

She stared back, a blank look on her face.

"Are you asking me out?"

Neill nodded his head. "That's right, Doc. I mean, I understand if—"

"I have a rule about that. I don't date patients."

He shifted on his feet, uncomfortable. "Okay. I get it. Can't say that I blame you." He backed away. "I just thought—"

"You're an ex-Marine, right?"

The question caught him off guard. "We prefer '*prior service* Marine'." Ex-Marine or former Marine, they both meant the same thing. And the title had never been rescinded, as far as Daniel was concerned.

"Okay," Carolyn said. "Shores of Tripoli, the Halls of Montezuma, fighting your country's battles and all that?"

"Yes, ma'am." Daniel stood a little taller.

"I didn't think U.S. Marines gave up so easily." Her tone carried mild admonishment, but there was definitely something more—and a sparkle in her eye, Daniel was sure of it.

He frowned, squinting as he did so. "You're gonna make me work for this, aren't you, Doc?"

She gave a shrug. "It's just that when most people want something they don't let a little rejection get in their way. You've overcome everything life's thrown at you—so why stop now?"

"I think I see what you're doing," Daniel grinned. "And believe me, Doc, you'd be doing yourself a grave disservice if you *didn't* accept my invitation."

Carolyn smiled back. "Is that you going after what you want?" Now they understood each other.

The doctor got a wink as part of Daniel's response. "That's me not letting a little rejection get in my way."

Aboard the USS Meyer

Personal reflection suited Neill, and in the hours that followed the briefing the Marine had lots of time for it.

Mike hadn't minimized anyone's feelings when he spoke of being numb. The pain was real enough, and the wounds were still fresh. The ship and her crew had been dealt an injurious blow, and it would take time to recover from the savagery that had been inflicted upon them.

For some, the trauma would never fade.

It was so senseless, Neill mused. All in an effort to further Moscow's aspirations, in a clear bid for energy. He tried to see things from their point of view, defaulting to an analytical approach. *Was their infrastructure* really *worth that much to the Russians?*

Apparently so, he decided.

But how could anyone be so cold and heartless—so *cruel*—dishing out misery, pain and death without a second thought, seemingly without regret? Such a wanton act went beyond the pale. A faceless enemy had struck from the cover of darkness, a darkness of the heart as much as anything else. *What had inspired such evil?* Michael had always struggled with that topic, waxing spiritual each time in his search for answers, but ultimately he thought he knew why.

Scripture was clear on the subject. Such pain wasn't necessary, but in a fallen world, it was all too common.

He could easily empathize with loss, having experienced it during different occasions over the past several years—the first being the death of his parents. About the same time, his uncle had been severely hurt in Iraq. The surviving members of the Neill family licked their wounds and got through their hardships, but Mike and Daniel were still struck by the enormity of their grief.

Michael's own soul-searching always brought him back to one specific event—and the words Ilya Maersk spoke to him on the night Richard Aultman died.

He had always believed that his father was killed by a Chechen separatist during a political rally. The truth was far more sinister, not to mention mysterious. Ilya Maersk—known as REMORA within intelligence circles— had killed David Neill. As an agent for a string of Soviet clandestine services, Maersk had also taken Aultman's life during his bid to kill Viktoriya Gavrilenko. But the assassin was in over his head.

Voskov and Tereshenko had seen to that.

"*He died to save your life,*" Maersk had said. Neill had puzzled over that since Warsaw, the words etched in his memory. And the Russian had revealed something else; Maersk implied that Michael was alive because of a pledge he'd made to his father, a 'professional courtesy between soldiers—in separate causes.'

What had he meant by that?

Neill didn't know, but since Maersk had uttered those words finding answers had become a driving force in the young officer's life.

Nate and the Ukrainians had already regrouped when Mike came in. Using switchblades, the foreign security officers had removed unit patches, name tapes, and other identifiers from their camouflaged utilities, and Xander then produced three additional sets and field jackets from a big duffle bag in the corner of the compartment.

"Take these," Voskov barked.

"SSD uniforms," Neill noted. He and Crockett pulled on the trousers and blouses, sizing up the fit before trying on matching headgear. There were also small rucksacks, fashioned from the same material.

"Those are for Dr. Brisbane." Yuri pointed to the remaining set. "I hope they will fit her."

Nate pulled from his own ruck, choosing items that might come in handy on Kamchatka. Mike did the same, hefting a narrow Bible from his gear. As he did so, something fell from the pages and landed on the deck.

"You've got mail," Nate said, stooping to pick it up. For the moment he forgot his grief, bringing the envelope close to his nose. "Is that perfume?"

"Probably faded by now," Mike answered, accepting it from Nate's outstretched hand.

"Uh-huh." The lieutenant glanced at the envelope as Neill tucked it into his cargo pocket. He couldn't help but notice his friend's name on the front, penned in a woman's handwriting. "Still sealed, too. You plan on opening that?"

"When the time's right," Neill said, his tone guarded. He had a faraway look in his eye.

"This might be your best chance, Mike."

"Could be," he agreed. "But right now I've got something else I should probably do." The captain moved to the entryway. "You three keep packing. And Nate—" he pointed to the extra uniform, "Drop those off with Doc Brisbane. Come get me if Ensign Vespi shows up. I'll be back in a while."

Nate watched him go. "Where you headed?"

"To the SCIF," he tossed back. "I've got a long-distance phone call to make."

Neill exited the room and stepped into the passageway, closing the hatch behind him as he went.

Mike settled into a chair, turning the envelope over in his hands as he listened to the dial tone. Nate might have been on to something; maybe he *should* have read what Christina had written, before going through with this ship-to-shore call.

He weighed that as he looked at the envelope. There was a card concealed within the cream-colored paper, of that he was sure. And undoubtedly Christina has poured out her heart, expressing much of what she'd said to him before boarding the plane at Reagan. Neill had revisited that conversation several times, but in subsequent calls, the two hadn't even brought it up.

The situation was much different now. The mission had changed, and there were things that needed to be said before he left the *Meyer*, exchanging the safety of the ship for an uncertain future on Kamchatka. Recent events had reinforced the fact that life truly was a vapor, that every moment was important, and the people who surrounded him were not to be taken for granted. Neill had barely gotten to know Richard Aultman, and his interactions with Bailee Russo were practically non-existent. Both had died much too young, done in by the twisted conspiracies of the Kremlin.

Those losses and others had changed his heart. He could no longer hold back his feelings, ignoring the importance of friends. Too many things had already gone unsaid; to his parents, to his uncle, and particularly to Christina.

Especially if he wanted to hang on to her.

The dull trilling sound continued. Neill couldn't use his own cellphone; being at sea without service he'd relied on a secure line here in the SCIF. He wondered if Christina's mobile would ID the originator, displaying the number as it was routed through a satellite. If that were the case, she might ignore it, waiting for the unknown caller to leave a message. All of this would be for naught if she chose—

"Hello?"

Neill cleared his throat. "Christina. It's Mike."

"Mike," she breathed. If he'd identified himself by rank, signaling he was in mixed company, she would have been more discreet. "I didn't recognize the number. Where are you calling from?"

He eyed his surroundings. "A secure line. And a quiet little corner of the world. But I can't really say."

Arrens paused, working it out. "So you're not back from your TDY," she chanced. "Is that good news or bad?" She knew he was calling for a reason, and not just to catch up on her day.

"Things are about to get exciting," he told her. "For the better, if all goes as planned."

"Then let's hope for the best."

Hope's not the best strategy when Ivan's involved, he didn't say.

"I've been thinking about you, Mike. And I'll bet the colonel has too, what with everything going on."

Neill knew where this was going. "The attack on the *Meyer*."

"So you've heard." No matter where he was at the moment, Christina knew that Mike would have already looked into the event.

"That has been on my mind," he admitted, stepping delicately around the issue. "And I *can* say it's one of the reasons I called."

"Really?" Christina's eyes narrowed. "You're not in Russia, are you? Because I distinctly recall telling you not to go there."

"No, I'm not in Russia," he answered truthfully. *Not yet, anyway.* "But there are a few things I need to say to you."

"I'm listening."

"Remember what you said at the airport?" he asked.

"I said a lot of things at the airport—namely to stay out of Russia." She was unwavering on that point.

"I think you've already mentioned that." Mike drew in some air. Christina wasn't making this easy. "The *last* thing you said—remember?"

There was a pause. "I remember."

Fortune favors the bold, Captain. "I've been doing a lot of thinking. None of us are promised tomorrow, so what we do today, in the here and now, is what really counts."

"And?" Her heart raced. *Was this the sound of commitment—or something else?*

"I've put this off for too long," Neill continued. He doubled down, his tone forceful. "People died aboard the *Meyer*, Christina. Good people. Some of them were my friends." Neill looked up. From the end of the compartment, Simon Chau had appeared, poking his head through the hatch.

"And you just wanted to tell me how you felt," Christina guessed. She was curious about the friends he mentioned; *who was he talking about*? "And what brought all this on? Have you read my card yet?"

"Hey, hold on a sec." He put his hand over the phone.

Chau closed the door behind him. "You wanted a heads-up. Ensign Vespi's looking for you."

"Gotcha." The Marine dropped his hand. "Okay, listen, I'm gonna have to cut this short."

"Seriously?"

"Yeah. Seriously."

"Just when things were getting interesting."

"Roger that. But duty calls." He smiled. "By the way, getting back to my main point—I think I'm ready to take the next step." He swallowed. "That is, I think *we* should take the next step."

"And that means *what*?" *The man can be cryptic at times*, she thought silently.

"That's a face to face discussion." And it was, Neill reasoned. "Like I said, I've got to go. But there's something I want you to remember."

"I'm all ears."

Here goes. He drew in some air. "I love you."

There was a stunned silence.

"Aren't you supposed to say something in return?"

Christina found her voice and the pause ended. "I'm just relishing the moment," she said, and Mike could almost see the grin on her face.

Neill exited the SCIF and found Vespi waiting in the passageway. The naval officer looked pleased.

"A front's pushing up from the southwest, Captain. Warm, moist air, cooled to saturation. Now the waters here are unseasonably cold, and they're only going to get colder, according to my projections." Vespi was clearly enjoying the lesson. "As that air mass moves into the region, the temperatures will fall, until they match the level of the seawater."

"You're telling me that conditions will be favorable for fog, am I right?"

"There's just one catch; all of this starts in the next two hours, come nightfall. And those conditions will be temporary, at best."

"How long will it last?"

"By dawn the fog will lift and the skies will clear."

"A narrow window. But a window nonetheless. And under the cover of darkness."

"Preferable, I would think," Vespi suggested.

"Very preferable, Mr. Vespi."

Neill gave a nod and turned to go. There were things to do, and it was time to get back to the stateroom.

KAMCHATKA

Part Three

Part Three

18

BOAT TRIP

Aboard the USS Meyer,
Northeast of Arkangel Base

FIVE HOURS WERE NEEDED to properly equip the team before debarkation. Extended briefings and weapons checks took up much of that time as the landing party planned to travel as light as possible.

Being responsible for his team, Neill was more concerned about the weather; but the fog appeared right on schedule, billowing low and enveloping the sea lanes in a blanket of mist that shrouded everything that moved across the face of the waters.

Neill pulled the group together, telling them about what to expect on the peninsula. At Commander Towle's direction, complicit with Willis Avery's orders, they were supplied with electronics and GPS devices, while a minimum of gear—clothing, utility tools, and night vision equipment—was stuffed into their rucksacks.

Brisbane schooled Lieutenant Chau on the gadgets she used to look for EMP fields. With the loss of Bailee, Simon would step in to keep an eye on things, monitoring any Russian activity ashore and relaying that information to Neill, should it become necessary—or even possible.

At midnight the group was nearly ready to go.

"I guess there's not much point in trying to talk you into this," Richey quipped. "But you're missing a chance to get the band back together, you know."

The team had withdrawn to the *Meyer*'s hangar deck, the compartment near the stern used to house choppers like the Seahawk. Their kit was secure, and the enclosed area afforded shelter from the weather and a place for the group to work unseen as they prepared to leave the ship.

"Specific personnel for specific missions," Neill answered. "We have to exercise a little discretion."

"Yeah, but where's the fun in that?" Richey grumped. "At least I'll be at the wheel for the ride in." He waved a hand, gesturing to a watercraft that took up an appreciable amount of space on the *Meyer*'s deck.

She was twenty-eight feet long, with angled surfaces. Fresh off the assembly line, the *Amphibian* was the latest in the U.S. Navy's low-observable boat inventory. The vessel sat atop an oversized trailer, and a handful of seaman and technicians were onboard making adjustments to the craft, fitting her for sea.

Richey nodded at a sailor inspecting the hull. "Petty Officer Calderone will be aboard for the trip," he told Neill. "Just in case I need an extra set of hands."

"Oh—almost forgot." Chau lifted a cardboard box from a workbench. "Cell phones. You'll need to surrender those."

Brisbane resisted. "Can't we just turn them off?"

Chau shook his head. "The Russians can still track them. And that would end your mission real fast."

Nate was intrigued by the *Amphibian*. He stepped closer and peered over her gunwales. "Comes complete with a rigid inflatable boat," he called back. "Like the

Gemini we used to land on Huo Shan, Mike."

"You were very attached to that little dinghy, if I recall correctly," Neill grinned.

"Roger that." Crockett crossed the deck to Brisbane and Chau, who were standing near a pile of rucks.

"Uniform looks good, Doc," the lieutenant complimented. "Those boots okay?"

"A perfect fit," Taylor replied, conscious of her wardrobe. She noted the AK-47 rifles stacked near the boat, and the M4 carbine slung across Lieutenant Crockett's back. "Do I get one of those?"

Neill heard the question. "Not this time, Doc. Best to leave the weapons in the hands of trigger-pullers like Nate. And it's not too late to change your mind, in case you're having second thoughts."

"We've been through that, Captain," Brisbane huffed. "Having me along improves your chances of success."

"You could just tell us what to look for."

"That might work, provided I knew what it was."

"Schematics; technical plans." Neill thought he was being helpful. "Won't it be something like that?"

Brisbane was irritated. The events of the past few days hadn't helped. "It might be that simple, yes. A logic board, or a central processing unit, if we're lucky. But I won't know until we get there. A weapon like this has never been used before—that we know."

Neill softened his tone. "Bailee's death was a blow to all of us—and to you and Nate most of all. I understand why you want to help, but you don't have to do this. That's all I'm saying."

"Good. I think you've said enough. Now what about our itinerary?"

Neill relented. He cast a glance in Voskov's direction. "The contact recruited by the Ukrainians will be waiting for us ashore. I've already got those coordinates locked in." He held up a GPS device. "Captain Voskov radioed him earlier. But for the sake of OPSEC—" his eyes went to the crew members working near the boat, "—I'll give a more detailed briefing once we're underway."

For the first time, Crockett saw the sidearm on Neill's belt. "I hope you're going to carry more than just that."

The captain hefted one of the rifles from the stack and checked the serial number. "Xander brought an extra. I think this one's mine."

"Have you ever fired one of those?" Richey instantly knew better.

"Mike and I got training aboard the *Lexington*," Nate put in. "Familiarization, primarily."

"And I have one at home. My uncle and I fire them quite a bit."

"Do you spend a lot of time at rifle ranges?" Brisbane asked.

"When I can. It's all part of being a Marine, Doc. We like to stay proficient."

She had a worried look. "Are they really necessary?"

"Let's hope not. But it's best to be prepared."

"You're not a peacenik, are you, Doc?" Nate grinned.

"I don't approve of violence, if that's what you mean, Lieutenant," Brisbane replied. The memory of Bailee flashed before her, and the doctor's face became a scowl. "But recently I think I've changed my mind."

Yuri and Xander were taking in the boat, walking her length and exchanging puzzled looks. The sergeant turned to Neill with a question.

"What'd he say, Cap'n?" Richey asked.

"Yuri wants to know how we'll get her off the ship and into the water."

Malcolm waved a hand aft. "We'll roll it out for launch," he explained. "Fixed davits are rigged on either side of the ship. We'll attach lines fore and aft and lower it over the side."

"With us in it?" Nate said.

"We'll disembark using the accommodation ladder. And your Gemini is provisioned with water and MREs."

"Ah," Nate observed. "Meals, Rarely Edible."

"Really?" Taylor almost believed it.

"No, Doc," Richey told her with a smile. "The lieutenant's just using a tactful description of our packaged rations. Some of the euphemisms can be quite crude. But they do fill you up, and they're definitely something to be experienced, I might add."

"I'm looking forward to it."

"Don't," Crockett advised.

Neill caught the Ukrainians' attention, motioning the two toward a corner.

"There's been a lot of talk about your source, but so far he's remained in the shadows." Neill gestured to the rest of the group. "I can't ask these people to risk their lives on a ghost. I need something more definite."

Yuri was forced to agree. "The mission won't suffer by disclosing his identity now. Xander?"

Neill's prodding had the desired effect.

"Our associate was recruited some years ago. At the time, he was a student in Vladivostok."

"He's Russian?"

"No, Mikhail," Voskov answered. "He is Aleut, from the Commander Islands. He speaks four languages that I am aware of. The Directorate has a full dossier. We know him as *Chingkut*."

The Marine was curious. "And how did your people come across an Aleut in Vladivostok?"

"We have friends—and agents—who keep their eyes open in many parts of the world, Mikhail. Beyond that, I can say nothing."

"You've met this individual?"

"On two occasions," Xander replied.

"You said this man has knowledge of Russian military operations," Neill pressed. "Is he working on the inside?"

Voskov shook his head. "Chingkut is a fisherman by trade. He sells his catch to those in the compound, above the base where the aircraft is hidden." He pulled a chart from his cargo pocket. "He will be waiting for us here— on the coastline, at this location."

Neill compared the map with one of his own. "About twenty-five kilometers from Ivan's base. That's a pretty good stretch of the legs, if you ask me."

"Chingkut has arranged transportation," Yuri smiled. "Not to worry."

"And how did you entice this man to work for us?"

Xander chuckled softly. "So full of inquiry, Mikhail. But a legitimate question. Chingkut is a Christian, much like you in many ways. And his family has a certain connection to this whole affair. An historical context, if you will."

Neill wasn't completely satisfied with Voskov's answer. "Can you elaborate on that?"

Xander would only grin. "It's an entertaining story, Mikhail. One best told by Chingkut himself."

Ensign Vespi's forecast was accurate in every respect.

The boat was launched quickly, the air around them was cold, and a heavy fogbank settled in as the *Amphibian* drifted in the *Meyer*'s wake. Senior Chief Richey switched on the power plant. Flooding twin ballast tanks within the hull, they rode deeper, reducing the radar cross section even more.

Richey navigated by instruments. He used a GPS system to guide them, and soon turned the boat on a course that would take them closer to shore. Calderone kept a watchful eye ahead, but the fog had cut visibility dramatically. Neill had counted on that, and was thankful their passage was effectively screened, hidden from any Russian eyes that might be out there.

"What's the plan, Cap'n?" Richey sat at a console amidships, hands on the boat's steering column. Underway for nearly half an hour, the scenery never changed.

Neill produced his chart, then checked the GPS. The team huddled close as he pointed to their position.

"We're here, roughly twenty-five kilometers from shore." He illuminated the map with a red-filtered flashlight. "We'll proceed to a rendezvous point at this location on the beach."

"Where Voskov's man will give us the high sign?" Nate asked.

"According to Vespi, the fog will be thinner along the coastline. We should be able to see his signal."

"Worst-case scenario; suppose he's not there."

"I don't expect that to happen, but if it does, we make our landing and wait. If he doesn't show, we hike out. We're committed, ladies and gentlemen."

Crockett studied the chart. "That rendezvous is quite a distance from our target area."

"About twenty-five clicks."

"We're humping it?" Nate raised an eyebrow. "That's quite a distance, Mike, considering the Doc's with us."

Brisbane seemed miffed. Neill had a ready answer.

"Our contact has taken care of that—or so Captain Voskov tells me. Transportation should be standing by."

"What about the *Meyer*? Where will she be?"

"She'll make her rendezvous with the Japanese research vessel. It's important we keep up appearances.

But we've seen the last of the *Meyer* on this trip."

"Meaning our escape plan lies elsewhere." Dr. Brisbane looked worried. "Let me guess; our contact has that under control, too."

"Sounds dicey." Nate wasn't happy either.

"I know you'd rather be in control," the captain said quietly. "I understand that. I also get that this is a bold move on our part. But people are dying. There's risk involved, no question about that. Remember what Secretary Avery said back at the Pentagon?"

"Yeah," Nate grudgingly agreed. "All that stuff about moral imperatives. I remember that. Something else just came to mind; after we shove off, what happens to the Chief?"

"There's no need to worry about us. We'll be long gone by the time you land on Kamchatka."

"Back to the *Meyer*?"

"Back to the *Meyer*. The pick-up point's already set."

Crockett's eyes went to the Gemini near the boat's transom. "I take it that's our mode of transportation." The inflatable would be a tight fit for the five of them.

"Roger that, El-Tee," the senior chief replied, staring ahead. There was nothing to see, but he couldn't fight the urge to use his senses. "At the moment, we're just another ocean-going vessel in international waters. Once we reach Federation territory, we'll launch you through the back door and you'll be free to make your transit."

Nate raised his head above the windscreen, inhaling the salt air. "How much longer, Senior?"

In the face of a light chop, Richey pointed the *Amphibian*'s bow to meet the waves. He checked his instruments, and was about to answer when something caught his eye.

"Hang on. We've got company." His hands tightened on the wheel. "Fast moving watercraft—making fifteen knots—coming up from the southwest and moving on an intercept course."

"That's not good," Nate growled. "Does that mean what I think it means?"

"I'm afraid so." A frown deepened on Richey's face. "I think the Russians might have found us."

Arkangel Base,
Hangar level

The guardhouse for naval infantry troops had been shoe-horned between two science labs along the eastern wall, in a vacant bay just a few dozen meters from the *Commissar*'s outstretched wings. The space was adequate if not austere; new Russian Marines had only recently been deployed there, and with their sentry post positioned where it was, an unwelcome layer of watchcare had just been added to the underground complex.

Vladimir Baskovich cared nothing for the scientists of Arkangel. He saw them as indifferent and arrogant; snobbish intellectuals who chafed at having troops in their midst, preferring their analytical pursuits *without* the military's oversight.

As a junior NCO, Baskovich thought it just as well that his eight-hour watch began at midnight, when the intellectuals were all asleep. During his short stay on the peninsula, he'd already crossed paths with the science staff in a decidedly antagonistic fashion. Dr. Zhukov had stoked his temper not long after the Marines arrived. Something petty, Vlad recalled; he had been eyeing a few of the technicians with contempt, and was roundly chastened by the old man. He remembered it well, and nursed his bitterness out of disgust for Zhukov—and no small amount of boredom.

Postings like this didn't provide men like Baskovich with many diversions. He would have preferred to be spending the spring in Ukraine, honing his trade with weapons of warfare, advancing Russian causes and doing his part to expand Federation territory. Instead, he found himself stuck here, guarding a bunch of highbrow technicians who—

Baskovich dismissed it. This assignment could be some sort of punishment. On the other hand, his superiors might have provided this tasking as a way to prove the Marines' mettle; a test, as it were. In either case, brooding over it wouldn't change the circumstances.

Duty filled much of the infantrymen's time, but when the workday was finished, leisure presented a challenge. Some stuck their noses in books, or pulled up educational material online, studying the military courses necessary to advance in rank. Off-duty hours were centered one level above the hangar, where the facility boasted a small library, a day room, the enlisted quarters, and a decently-equipped fitness center.

Baskovich was a gym rat and preferred the latter. A big man—even by Russian standards—Vlad stood six feet, three inches tall, and was broad as a barn. His bulk intimidated even his comrades, and he used physical presence to his advantage, skirting more than a few of the rules.

"You're late." Pavel Varushkin's watch preceded that of Baskovich. He stood in the door of the guardhouse, watching a gathering of scientists as they converged on the *Commissar*. Such late-night activity by Dr. Zhukov's staff was unusual, but Varushkin understood its meaning.

Vlad shrugged off his comrade's rebuke, and his eyes went to the technicians. "Only by thirty minutes."

"You'd best be careful," Pavel urged. "The sergeant

of the guard will put you on report."

"You are the sergeant of the guard," the big Russian grinned. He jabbed a thumb toward the hangar. "What are the Einsteins up to now?"

"Another one of their tests," Varushkin said. "Night operations. The first of many to come, from what I've been told."

"So the beast *does* fly?" Baskovich marveled. Since his arrival, the aircraft had left the hangar, but not during his shift.

"It's an impressive sight, Vladimir—watching the plane taxi down to the shoreline, her engines yearning to take flight."

"You should have been a poet."

Varushkin had been at Arkangel a little longer. He regarded the junior sergeant with a critical eye. Vlad was appropriately dressed, but had removed his uniform blouse, reporting for duty in a t-shirt. Sweat stained his armpits.

"You've been hitting the gym," Pavel observed.

"There's little else to amuse me," Vlad snorted. His grin turned wicked. "Although the doctor's daughter might prove satisfying, don't you think?"

"Zhukov's daughter?" Varushkin's eyes went wide. "That's forbidden fruit. You would do well to keep your distance. Colonel Utkin would have your head—" he smirked, "—or worse."

"These scientists are on borrowed time, Pavel. Utkin is waiting for something. Some breakthrough from the admiralty. Zhukov has his secrets, but not for long." Vlad's grin widened. "Petropavlovsk will uncover them, and Zhukov and his team will no longer be needed."

Varushkin had heard that rumor too. Still, he thought it wise to act prudently. The infantrymen were charged with watching the science team, and to report any unusual actions. Defining such activity was left to the discretion of the Marines.

"There she is now," Vlad announced. He turned to face the hangar, his eyes following the lithesome form of Tanya Zhukov.

Varushkin looked up. "She is a tempting morsel," he agreed.

Tanya crossed the floor, stopping to talk with a group of technicians. Radya Zhukov emerged from the *Commissar*, descending a set of steps, his penetrating stare locked on the Russian troops. His look sent an unmistakable message, and then the two stepped off toward the aircraft's nose.

Baskovich watched her go, his leering expression sending a chill up Varushkin's spine.

• • • •

"I don't like those men, *papa*," Tanya whispered, clutching her father's arm. Her attractive features were clouded. "Why are they even here?"

Radya Zhukov inhaled deeply. "Admiral Pavlenko's orders, Tanya. I don't like them, either." Zhukov had his own suspicions, and Pavlenko's character didn't inspire much hope.

At the front of the plane, the old scientist climbed the crew ladder, struggling with his bad leg and taking his daughter's hand as she followed. Reaching the top, Zhukov looked into his daughter's eyes. "And I want you to stay away from the new arrivals."

Father and daughter now stood inside the aircraft, the cargo deck stretching from front to back—or bow to stern, considering the *Commissar*'s waterborne nature. A steep ladderwell led upward to the flight deck.

"You don't have to tell me twice, *papa*." She gave the old man a warm smile, but that faded almost at once.

"There's something about that big one. When he looks at me, I feel shame."

"No, no, no. There is no shame in you, *dochka*."

Some of the electricians were clustered near a bulkhead panel, intent on a series of readouts. Satisfied with what they saw, one of the men gave the Zhukovs a nod.

"All systems are ready, Doctor." Roman Shapoval was Zhukov's chief engineer, and also from Ukraine. A skilled pilot, he saw to the *Commissar*'s pre-flight needs. The two had worked together for more than ten years.

Radya took the cue. "It's time, Tanya. We must take advantage of the weather." He guided his daughter back where they'd come, knowing that the hangar would soon go dark, and the massive door leading to the Pacific would be opened once more.

19

OVERFLIGHT

"IT'S A PATROL BOAT—that's my guess."

Malcolm Richey dropped his voice. It was a natural reaction, in the hopes that through silence the *Amphibian* might avoid detection.

"What's a patrol boat doing way out here?" Nate hissed. "We're far beyond their twelve mile limit."

"Ivan's patrol routes extend into the open sea, Lieutenant. *Past* their territorial waters. They often push beyond, projecting force and creating a buffer zone for their sea lanes."

"How close?" Neill asked. He bent over the console, his face illuminated by the glow of instrumentation.

"About three thousand yards, on the port beam." The radar display bore readouts tied to the incoming vessel. "His bearing is zero-four-five. Ours is converse, at three-one-five."

"Coincidence?" Taylor threw in. "Maybe they're just headed in a direction that will cross our path."

"One way to find out," the senior chief told them.

Malcolm's hand went to the throttle. He chopped the

engines. The dull thrum of the *Amphibian*'s power plant fell off abruptly, and the boat eased forward, bow down, losing speed and settling even deeper.

"How does that help?" Nate asked.

"We want to avoid them, El-Tee," Malcolm told him. "—not cross his path, or reach an intersection point." His eyes never left the screen. "Drifting works to our advantage. If he continues on his present course, and doesn't turn to intercept—"

"Then we'll know if he's seen us or not. Very smooth, Senior Chief. What does the 'scope say?"

Richey waited a full minute, and then a roguish smile appeared on his face.

"Looks like we dodged that one. Ivan's still bearing zero-four-five. But we're not out of the woods yet."

Everyone had become silent. To the southwest, the rolling fog glowed orange, and then was pierced by a shaft of yellow light. The beam was contained in the mists, however, never reaching the *Amphibian*, and just as abruptly, the light was pointed in another direction. In time the glow faded from view, and darkness surrounded them once more.

"Listen—hear that?" Richey whispered.

Neill craned his neck. "Diesel plant," he announced. "Muffled by the ship's hull and the sea, but you can still hear it."

"That was a spotlight, wasn't it?" Brisbane asked.

Crockett answered with a nod. "Do you think they were looking for us?"

"I doubt that. Probably just a standard sweep of the area." Richey reached out and patted a gunwale. "This boat is all about stealth. Virtually invisible to radar. You'd know it if we'd been detected."

Brisbane didn't like sitting still. "Time to go?"

"Not just yet. His propellers will be churning things

up, bringing phosphorescent sea life to the surface. There might be some bored sailor on the stern, taking in the view." Richey shook his head. "No, we'll wait till they're out of range. After that, it's on to Kamchatka."

"And sunnier climes?" Brisbane shivered.

Neill gave her an amused look. "I wouldn't count on that, Doctor."

"Stand by," Richey warned. "We'll be catching some of his wake soon."

He was right. In less than a minute, the boat began a gentle roll as they met the waves produced by the patrol craft. The *Amphibian* rose and fell, and then the sea went flat. Another few minutes passed, and no one could hear the sound of the Russian vessel's engines.

"He's haze gray and out of our way." Satisfied that they were alone again, Richey thumbed a switch and powered up the motor. "Ready to chance it, Cap'n?"

"Whenever you are, Malcolm."

Richey throttled up slowly, urging the boat forward. It didn't take long to cross a patch of ocean flecked with glowing sea life, just as the Navy man had predicted.

The air around them felt cold, wet and close. It was late, and the group was lulled into drowsiness by the boat's forward motion.

The mists grew thick. Taylor imagined that the heavy fog could easily suppress the low sounds made by the outboards. She was struck by the fact that they'd never even seen the Russian boat, and was about to offer a comment when an odd noise reached her ears.

"Do you hear that?" She laid a hand on Neill's arm.

"Not a thing, Doc." The Marine's head was instantly on a swivel. "What do—"

"*Shhh*—" Taylor cautioned. She pointed to the southwest. "*There.* Tell me I'm not imagining it."

In the time it took to speak, Nate had also become aware. "I hear it too, Mike."

"You're not the only ones," Neill returned. Voskov and Tereshenko nodded in agreement, and were growing apprehensive.

"Has the patrol boat turned back?" Yuri asked.

"No; it's a different kind of sound. I've heard it before—"

"Same here," Richey joined in. "High-pitched, whirring. Like—"

"—jet engines. *Big* ones." Crockett's eyes widened, and he gripped his weapon a bit more tightly.

"I should have thought of this—calm seas, all this fog." Neill studied the night. "Conditions are perfect for a test flight."

Before anyone could blink, a deep rumbling filled the air. A shrill whine could also be heard, and with everyone straining for a look, the fog began to change.

Two round orbs glowed dully from within the mists, burning from orange to white. Then the veil split, wrenched violently apart by a broad, dark shape that suddenly filled their view. Coming right at them, the apparition hugged the surface, forcing a compression wave ahead of it as it grew closer.

The obstacle avoidance gear aboard the *Commissar* was better than the patrol boat's. At a distance of one quarter mile, the system began its warbling tone, alerting the pilot that something lay in their path. The aviator cursed under his breath, getting the rest of the flight crew's attention in the process. He then pulled back on the yoke, adjusted the flaps, and added thrust, lifting the plane's body out of the water.

• • • •

"*Get down!*"

Neill's warning was barely heard above the roar of the engines. But his shout was unnecessary; everyone instinctively dropped, and most of the team now lay prone on the deck, hoping the *Amphibian* would be spared.

A wall of sound and spray washed over them. The air itself seemed to vanish, sucked away by the massive airframe as it thundered into the sky. A larger watercraft might have capsized. Brisbane gripped the gunwale, and like everyone else she could feel the deck shudder, but the boat survived the *Commissar*'s passage.

Petty Officer Calderone was another story. Crouched on the *Amphibian*'s foredeck, the sailor was nearly swept into the sea. The updraft tugged at every inch of him. Panic and quick thinking kept him aboard, and he draped himself across the bow, hanging on for dear life. When the plane had gone, the cold waters of the northern Pacific became calm again.

"*Bozhe*," Yuri breathed. *My God*. "Did you see that?"

The Ukrainian's eyes probed the darkness, but the beast was gone, the fog filling the path it had taken.

"Kinda hard to miss, comrade," Neill replied, getting to his feet. His utilities were drenched, and moisture beaded on his face. Looking around him, he saw that the rest of the group had been similarly doused. "Everybody okay?"

Nods all around, and from the bow Calderone gave a thumbs up.

"I'm no expert in aviation," Richey began, wiping seawater from his brow, "But I'd say that was the bird we're looking for."

"That was our dragon," Neill announced. "Anybody see those engines on the nose?"

Crockett chimed in. "I was too busy counting rivets."

Richey had a conspiratorial smirk. "Not our first run-in with one of Ivan's super-weapons, eh, Cap'n?"

Neill grinned right back. "Those were good times, Malcolm. Tense, as I recall, but good."

"And the less said the better," Richey followed up.

Neill's mind went back to the previous year, when the Colonial Rifles had hitched a ride aboard the *Bradford*, one of Her Majesty's fast attack boats. That had been no pleasure cruise. A group of rogue sailors from China had unleashed a Tempest torpedo, threatening everyone aboard the British sub. Only Neill's understanding of the weapon—provided by White Dragon—had turned the tide, and when it was all over, the Chinese crew hadn't fared so well.

Richey's comment didn't go unnoticed, and Neill could feel Taylor Brisbane staring at him.

"You've been in combat—with the Russians?"

The young officer sized her up. Brisbane's hair and clothing were soaked, and she was shivering beneath her field jacket. The Aussie's green eyes were fixed on him.

"If we get out of this alive I'll tell you about it," Neill answered. "Well, the non-classified parts, anyway."

"Those are enough to curl your hair," Malcolm said.

From a stowage compartment, Richey produced a blanket and towels. The team began drying off. Using the GPS, he fixed their position.

"Two miles to the drop-off point. You'd better gather your gear."

"This is close enough, Malcolm. I want you to heave to, before we reach Russian waters. It's time we shoved off."

"Very well." Richey consulted Neill's chart. "Your rendezvous point is thirteen miles due west. Keep a sharp eye and a weather ear, Cap'n; these waters are thick with Ivan's patrols. Still, dawn is hours away, and this fog should conceal you." He stuck out his hand. "Good luck, Mike. And God bless."

The two friends shook on it. "I'm counting on both." From behind, Xander, Yuri and Nate cradled their weapons, hefting their rucks from the deck. "We can use all the help we can get."

Leaving the *Amphibian* was easy enough. The shore party found their places aboard the Gemini while the Navy men lowered the stern gate. With the smaller craft now free, gravity did the rest, and the rigid inflatable passed through the open transom and entered the sea.

Crockett manned the outboard, hand on the tiller. It was a skill he'd acquired from Richey when they'd sailed to the island of Huo Shan. The boat wasn't large, and definitely made for cramped quarters. The Ukrainians sat forward, while Neill and Brisbane shared space amidships. Before Nate gunned the motor, the senior chief gave the group one last wave, and the stealthy *Amphibian* faded into the night.

Brisbane fidgeted, pulling at her hair and tugging at her sleeves. The uniform was still damp, but a cold, stiff wind now braced against them, drying their clothes as they headed west.

She was nervous, Mike realized. And temperatures had dropped. He knew that her exposed hands must be freezing, so he reached into his ruck and pulled something out, handing them over.

"Gloves," she said, sounding relieved as she pulled them on.

"The tactical kind. Should have thought of it before. Probably a little big, but they'll protect your hands and keep them warm at the same time."

Brisbane gave him a sideways look. "You think I'm a tenderfoot, don't you, Captain?"

"Those don't go on your feet, Doc," he said with a grin.

She almost laughed. "You have a dry wit, Michael. Has anyone ever told you that?"

"It's come up on occasion," Neill replied.

Moscow,
The Presidium

Differing time zones made for disjointed communications, Leonid Karpenko thought to himself. In a nation as large as Russia there was no way around that. And it was a good problem to have. Such a dilemma gave the Federation bragging rights over their vast territories, and there were worse concerns for a country to contend with.

The call came late—nearly three p.m. by Karpenko's watch—but even later for the caller. The phone's display told the general who to expect, as well as what the message might be.

"*Dobre veecher,* Admiral," he said to Pavlenko.

The admiral replied in kind. "*Dobre dyen,* comrade General," he said. *Good afternoon.* This was a concession to the hour in Moscow, not Petropavlovsk, where it was midnight. "I trust I'm not disturbing you."

"Your calls are too infrequent for that, Taras." It was an honest reply to an old friend. "Shouldn't you be in bed?"

"I'll sleep when I'm dead," Pavlenko chuckled. "But like fresh milk, glad tidings won't keep until morning, comrade."

Leonid sat back in his chair. "Good news is always welcome. Is that what you bring me?"

"You will find this heartening, I believe. Do you remember Captain Tamarkin?"

"*Kanyeshna.*" *Of course.* "Your aide. The officer charged with unraveling Zhukov's secrets. I remember. Dare I ask, but has he been successful?"

"He and his team are quite clever, General. But you know young people; always ready to meet any challenge."

"And what a challenge it was."

"The latest tests are complete. Captain Tamarkin reports that Zhukov's system linkage dependency is open to us. His secrets are now known."

Karpenko considered that. "Then we need not rely on the doctor's continued assistance, correct?"

"Yes, General. Zhukov's services are no longer required. We have the weapon, and we know how it works."

"You can reproduce the device, then?"

"*Da.* Along with all of its effects."

The senior officer mulled over the consequences of failure—and success. Zhukov had been a necessary part of their plans; unbending, perhaps, for the most part, but inarguably necessary.

Things were different now.

Karpenko regarded Radya in the same way as Kobrin and Malyev. Those two could have caused problems—indeed, Malyev still lived, and continued to be a thorn in his side. Pirogov had been there, and should have made sure that Ivan's life was forfeit. In that simple assignment, the major had failed.

Karpenko reasoned that Pirogov still had a purpose. The man's one mistake, far-reaching though it was, didn't negate that. And Pavlenko had taken steps to ensure that Zhukov and his team would not be so lucky.

Expendable lives were meant to be extinguished; the time for that came when they were no longer useful, and

Radya Zhukov had now arrived at that point.

"Loose ends can be dangerous. We need a solution that precludes that. Do you take my meaning?"

Far away in Petropavlovsk, Admiral Pavlenko knew what he was being directed to do. He'd always known it would come to this.

"I do, comrade General. It will require a day or two to arrange, but I think you will be pleased with the outcome."

"I trust that I will, Admiral. You have your orders."

"*Da,* General. And just the right men for the job."

Karpenko was satisfied with the reply. He cradled the phone, ending the call.

20

THE FISHERMAN

Kamchatka Peninsula

DARKNESS WAS THEIR ONLY cover now. Nearing the coast the fog had thinned, and with less than a mile to go it disappeared altogether.

Neill's hand-held GPS pointed toward a jetty of land with a secluded inlet on the far side. Nate guided them in, eyeing the shoreline as they approached. It wasn't a welcoming sight; the cove ahead was marked by granite boulders, jutting up from the graveled beach. Just yards away, a cliff rose hundreds of feet up, its steep and craggy slopes providing a natural barrier to the top of the ridge. The sky above was black but lit with pinpoints of brilliant starlight.

"So this is Mother Russia," Nate breathed, his voice quiet. He idled back on the motor, slowing the little boat. Breakers formed as they moved into the shallows. "You ever been here before, Mike?"

Neill shook his head. "Not to this part of the country. Several times to Moscow, and a few trips to the southern provinces. My dad used to take us."

"Business or pleasure?" Brisbane asked.

"Missionary conferences. For my Dad it was both."

"Your father's a missionary?"

"He was." Mike set his face toward the shore. "But he's gone now."

Taylor was curious. "Were you born in Russia?"

"Kiev," he answered. "That's in Ukraine."

"I think I know where it is, Captain." She became more blunt. "How did your father die?" It was clear she didn't let tact get in the way of an inquiry.

"Still working that out, Doc."

Another question came to mind, and she started to say more. But from over her shoulder she caught Nate's frown and an unspoken message; *not now.*

"Night vision goggles, everyone," Neill directed. "Comm gear too." He repeated the order in Ukrainian. The team dipped into their packs, pulling NVGs over their heads and plugging in earpieces and microphones. As his vision adjusted, Mike decided that a sniper's perspective would be helpful. "Lieutenant Crockett, pick a spot. Where would you be if you were our contact?"

Nate studied the shoreline. Peering at an outcropping of rock, he waved a knife-hand to the right.

"Two o'clock. Those boulders make excellent cover. And the beach in front is free of rocks, which makes it a good place for a landing."

Every eye now focused on the cove. As if on cue, red lights flashed in the darkness—two short and two long—coming from the location Nate had chosen. It was a moment that affirmed his skills.

"Sweet vindication," he smiled broadly.

"Let's hope so," Taylor added. "I take it that's our contact?"

"We're about to find out, Doc. Like Mike says, we're committed now." Nate added a little gas, and the boat picked up speed on its way to the beach. "Time to go ashore and stretch our legs."

The inflatable surged forward, scraping the bottom as it came to a halt. Yuri and Xander hopped over the sides and landed in ankle-deep surf. They took hold of the bow line and hand-grips and pulled the boat into a secure position on the wet sand.

Brisbane surprised them all by leaping out next. Neill and Crockett followed.

"These are amazing," Taylor marveled. The night vision goggles had opened up a whole new world. "I can see why you're keen on them."

"Stay on point, Doc," someone whispered.

The Marines grabbed their rucks and staged the gear nearby, their rifles at the ready even before landing. Xander and Yuri held their Kalashnikovs loosely, muzzles down. Nate's carbine—nicknamed Iron Mike—was locked and loaded, the selector switch flipped from 'safe' to 'semi'.

"Taylor, put those gloves to use," Neill said in a low voice. He raised the outboard, placing it in the stowed position astern. "Let's get this out of sight."

Brisbane didn't think she could help, but the boat was lighter than expected. In a moment's time the two had dragged it farther up the beach, hiding it in a natural cleft near the base of the cliff. Camouflage netting came next, draped from bow to stern. While they hid the boat, the Ukrainians and Crockett fanned out, forming a perimeter around them.

Nate's gaze was fixed on the spot where the signal had flashed. He was like a bird dog now, his eyes moving back and forth, using the goggles to scan the darkness for movement. Yuri and Xander did the same, and after a time their vigilance was rewarded.

A figure emerged. The team brought up their rifles.

Their contact continued his approach, but more cautiously now, arms outstretched, with palms upward to show that he carried no weapons and posed no threat.

Xander spoke aloud, issuing a challenge. The man before them stopped and gave the countersign. Satisfied, the SSD officer relaxed his grip and began to breathe a little easier. He moved closer, as if he were meeting an old friend.

"Not here," the man said. He was checking the cove from one end to the other. "Follow me."

He turned on his heel and trudged a narrow path between the rocks. The trail wound through several cracks and fissures, and after a few turns they found themselves in a spot hidden from the beach.

Yuri took over. Introductions were made, in Russian for Neill, and in broken English for Brisbane and Crockett. Neither the hour nor the weather were favorable for a warm welcome, but the team got one anyway. Chingkut smiled and faced each of them in turn, his rough, weathered hands shaking theirs.

The fisherman's wide features were framed by a head of thick, black hair, and he wore an all-weather jacket that had seen better days. Beneath that was a wool sweatshirt, dark trousers, and heavy boots of the type worn by outdoorsmen. His voice was deep, and surprisingly enough, he spoke in English now. "This is Kamchatka."

"You live here?" Taylor pulled off the goggles. The air was still, and the sounds of the surf had fallen away.

Chingkut laughed. "Not far," he answered. His tone had a melodic quality, the words strung together without breaks in-between, like the lyrics in a song. "Is your boat secure?"

"It's hidden from view. For the time being."

"Best if it stays that way," Chingkut grunted in approval. He gave them all a once-over. "Now if everyone's ready, I think it's time we found you some shelter for the night."

The Oval Office

"Beer cans and unfinished sandwiches," Avery chuckled, finding a place on the sofa. The President was already seated across from him. "At least that's what Mrs. Reagan claimed."

Charles Cassidy wore a bemused look. "Come again, Willis?"

"I read it somewhere; probably her memoirs. Apparently they came from the previous administration." SECDEF straightened his tie. "Did Mark Breese leave anything behind, Mr. President?"

The question was mostly rhetorical. "There were a few things," Cassidy began. "I could have done without the staggering debt and a defense infrastructure in need of attention." He leaned back on the couch. "And I think we can lay some of today's problems at the former occupant's feet—but that's off the record, Willis."

"I'm not the press, Mr. President."

"Thank God for that," Cassidy said, and he meant every word. Like Avery, his view of journalists was rather jaded.

Avery glanced around him. Since Cassidy had been sworn in, he'd visited the West Wing countless times. "I take it you've met with the National Security Council again?" The Secretary of Defense was a statutory attendee of the group, but couldn't be there for every meeting.

"We did have a late night huddle," Cassidy answered. "We're convening again at nine. I'd like you to be there. Gaming some strategy; spit-balling ideas." He folded his arms, frowning. "I must admit, I've been second-guessing my own actions on this one."

"Reflection is good, but you should have no regrets."

Cassidy swore loud enough to be heard. "If I thought we'd done enough—no, strike that. If I thought *I'd* done enough—"

Avery waved a dismissive hand. "Armchair quarter-backing, Mr. President. And a lot of twenty-twenty hindsight. Don't beat yourself up over it.

"Charles, you've been given a mandate." He seldom addressed Cassidy by his first name. "A charge you've done well with—much better than the last person who held this office. Americans chose you because you represent what they want in a leader. Don't get me wrong. I'm not advising that you cut yourself any slack. No sitting president can do that, because the job demands more."

"But imposing sanctions isn't enough," the President grumped.

"They were pretty effective against Iran," Avery shot back. "Until Breese caved."

Cassidy didn't pout. He was too pragmatic for that. "What's your take on the Council's recommendations?"

"They've got teeth. Sending Bazhenov home says something. Of course, Ivan will retaliate. They'll expel our ambassador. But make no mistake—kicking Russia out of the Group of Eight will sting."

"And our strategic options?"

"We're ramping up our presence in the Baltic Sea; additional ships are en route as we speak. With your permission, I'd like to send more defensive weapons to places like Ukraine. Deploying more brigades in Germany will help. And strengthening the missile shield was a good move, too. Doubling our batteries along Poland's border sends a clear message."

"It's not enough, Willis. No American warship has been attacked like this before. Not in recent memory, in any case."

Avery thought it over. "I guess that depends on how you define *recent*, Mr. President."

A door behind them opened before he could respond. The president's secretary wheeled in a serving cart with cups, saucers, and a carafe of coffee. She got a nod and a smile in return, then retreated back to her office.

The president got to his feet and began to pour. "I'm not sure I follow you. Am I missing something?"

"The attack on the USS *Meyer* isn't without precedent. Fifty years ago something very similar happened. Not exactly a current event, but it's still fresh in some people's minds."

"Involving an American vessel?"

"The USS *Liberty*. The summer of 1967." A shrug. "But that's a discussion for another time."

"And here we sit, while the *Meyer* still has blood on her decks."

"That's the unfortunate truth, sir."

"Politics," he snarled. "It never changes, does it?"

"It can, Mr. President. And you'll be a part of that change." Avery sipped from his cup, raising his eyes to the pediments and mantles around them. "Just do the job you were elected for—and keep faith with the people who put you here."

"They're going to expect more, Willis. Something visceral. Issuing decrees only goes so far."

"Like I said, Mr. President, you've taken solid steps. Some of the bigger ones we've already discussed. I'm hopeful that our more *subtle* response will also pay off."

"Our Kamchatka option," Cassidy said knowingly. "We're taking a big risk on that one, marching into the lion's den."

"The Russians started this fight, Mr. President. Our action on the peninsula is small stuff by comparison."

SECDEF added more cream to his cup. "Politically, no one would begrudge you the course we've chosen."

"The whole region has become a tinderbox. A flashpoint for war. So let's leave political considerations out of it," Cassidy said with distaste. "Tell me about the Marine in charge—O'Neill, is it?"

"Just Neill, sir. I've sent over the file. Makes for interesting reading."

"And this—*Accord*. That was his idea?"

"More like his father's. But the Captain's a key player, yes."

"Provided he's not captured by the Russians."

Avery drew in his breath, letting it out slowly. "Yes, Mr. President. Provided he's not captured by the Russians." *Or worse,* he didn't say.

• • • •

The trail narrowed. Hugging the cliff, it continued northeast for a mile, snaking upward through the rocks. After fifteen minutes of steady climbing the group reached the top, a flat plateau stretching in three directions.

Below them lay the sea. To the south, the ridgeline sloped higher and then vanished in the distance. The night cloaked everything, and even with their goggles very little could be seen to the west.

One object stood out. Parked beside an unpaved road was an ancient Land Rover, its chassis giving evidence of great use. It had a cracked windscreen and a number of dents, and one side panel didn't match the rest.

"It's not abandoned, if that's what you're thinking," Chingkut told them. He spoke in English again, and thumped the vehicle's hood. "This was a gift from the trading company."

"The trading company?"

"The Russians, Captain Neill. That's what my family has always called them."

"And why is that?" Brisbane wanted to know.

"It's not a happy tale. I was born on the Commander Islands. The Russians visited there long before my grandfathers. All they wanted was to trade with my people, or so they said. But they also brought disease and exploitation." His expression was less jovial now. "Our relationship has not been cordial."

"So that's not a term of endearment, then."

"I try my best to get along." Chingkut climbed into the driver's seat. "God is good, and He would have me love my enemies."

"That's not to be underestimated." Neill opened the door on the passenger side. "A little kindness always helps."

"And therein lies the paradox." Brisbane slid across the middle seat next to Crockett, while Voskov and Tereshenko found space in the back.

"Say again, Doc?"

"Christian virtue. It's everywhere I go on this trip. And at every turn I find that it's surrounded by those who want us dead."

"It just seems that way, Doc," Nate offered. "A little dose of religion won't hurt you."

"So don't look a gift horse in the mouth, is that what you're saying, Lieutenant?"

"Something like that." Nate clapped the back of Chingkut's seat, raising his voice. "Present vehicles excepted, of course. The Russians gave you this?"

"A reward for my services," the fisherman replied. With a turn of the wrist he started the engine. "Not as generous as you might think; they had newer models and wanted to get rid of it."

"Does your car have heat?" Taylor was freezing.

"*Generous* is not a word that comes to mind." Crockett noted the distressed interior. "But you roll with it, friend. Where are we headed, by the way?"

"An old Soviet pumping station. It's not far from here."

"Is that abandoned?" Neill asked.

"No, but you'll be safe there for the night." Chingkut eyed the horizon. "The sun will come up soon. You'll spend the day at the station. It's off the beaten path, and you can rest and eat before setting off again."

"Once it's dark."

"That's my recommendation," the fisherman agreed.

Crockett was working it out in his head. "And how far's the hangar?"

"The Russians call it Arkangel. From the station it's eight kilometers by foot."

"So we're humping it."

Their host blinked. *"Izvenityeh?"*

"He means we're going to hike," Neill grinned. "You up for that, Doc?"

Brisbane didn't get a chance to respond.

"That's to the top of the base," Chingkut added. "But only six kilometers to the tunnels."

"Is that how we're getting in?"

"That's how I'd do it." The fisherman switched to Russian again. "What you're planning is very dangerous, Captain. It's my duty to warn you about that. But if you insist—"

"There's no other way."

"Then I have a map. And I strongly suggest that you use it."

The flat plain gave way to rolling hills. Neill's attention was drawn to the south, where headlights could be seen coming from the opposite direction.

"Russian patrol?" he asked.

"Most likely. Much too late for anyone else."

"*Sheesh*. Ivan's everywhere," Crockett muttered.

"Make yourselves small, everybody." Neill got low, hunkering down near the floorboard. "Wouldn't do to be seen."

Chingkut checked the rearview. The Ukrainians had already ducked. Directly behind him, the Australian woman and the American officer followed suit. The fisherman gripped the wheel and drove on, seemingly undisturbed.

21

SAFE HOUSE

The USS Meyer

"HOW'D IT GO, SENIOR CHIEF? Shore party all squared away?"

Richey stood on the port side, supervising the recovery of the *Amphibian*. Calderone, the bosun, and a few able seamen had hoisted the boat out of the water, securing her to the davits.

"You're up late, Commander Towle," Malcolm observed. "Secure that cleat, people. Don't let her swing." Richey ran a hand over his face. Fatigue was creeping in. "Shore party's away, Commander. Couple of hiccups, but nothing we couldn't handle."

The bosun looked their way. "I've got this, Senior Chief. Go below and get some dry clothes."

Towle turned to face him. "You do look a little damp, Malcolm. What'd you do, fall in?"

Richey grunted something in reply and patted his utilities. "I'm dry enough. You should have seen us two hours ago."

"You had a close encounter, am I right?"

He blinked. "How'd you know that?"

"Caught it on radar, flying low and fast. Huge son of a gun, it crossed our wake about nine miles astern. Big as life."

"*Bigger* than life, XO. You should've been there." He shook his head. "It's something I'll never forget."

"Did you get a good look?"

"Hard not to. The thing flew right over us. Could you track it?"

"For a while. Picked up a patrol boat, too."

"We managed to avoid that," Richey told him. The two men headed toward one of the hatches. "Dropped off our shore party not long after."

"They should be on dry land by now."

"Most likely," Malcolm agreed. His thoughts went to the ekranoplan that had rumbled over their heads. "I just hope Cap'n Neill hasn't bitten off more than he can chew."

• • • •

"It's safe now, Captain," Chingkut said. The other vehicle's taillights had vanished. "Our Russian friends are following the road north."

"That was close."

"Not really. Those were base personnel, sneaking off to the village." He pretended to drink from an up-ended bottle. "Arkangel's night life leaves a lot to be desired, from what I've heard."

"Not a patrol then?" Nate asked. He was off the floorboard and back in his seat, checking their six.

The fisherman shrugged. "Might be. But they're out for fun. Stopping us was the last thing on their minds."

"Lucky thing," Taylor said, relief in her voice.

Yuri was looking through the rear window. "How far now?"

"We're almost there," Chingkut announced. He made

a right turn, taking a road none of them had seen. The car traveled away from the ridge and into a hollow. Reaching the bottom, they followed an even narrower lane, a dead end, leading to a building that blocked their path.

"Is this it?" Brisbane asked suspiciously.

"A pumping station," Neill said. "Fresh water?"

A nod, and Chingkut shut off the engine. "This facility supplies the village."

"Do the Russians maintain it?" Nate wondered aloud. "I mean, the place has a custodian, right?"

"That would be me, Lieutenant." Chingkut was grinning again. "No one else wanted the job."

"You have a lot of irons in the fire."

"It's helpful in contingencies like this."

Nate was buoyed by their success so far. "Do you get a lot of paramilitary groups in need of lodging?"

Chingkut didn't answer. Instead, he climbed the steps to the entrance, and with keys in hand took hold of the padlock securing the door.

"It's warm here." Taylor peeled off her field jacket.

Their host flipped a switch, and the light of a single bulb illuminated the space. The team stacked gear and weapons by the door, while Xander and Yuri checked the corners.

But the glare stung Crockett's eyes.

"Mike, if we're going to keep a low profile—"

"Then we should get rid of that light." Neill glanced around them. "Agreed. Too many windows in here. Chem sticks?"

Crockett pulled a few from his pack and flexed them, breaking the barrier inside. He shook the plastic casings, combining the chemical solutions, and the sticks began to glow with a blue light. At a word from Neill, Chingkut extinguished the bulb. The glowing wands produced an eerie luminescence.

"That's better," Neill said, eyeing the room. "Typical Soviet architecture. This place is old."

"Feels like home, right, Mike?"

The blockhouse had an industrial feel—and the pungent odor of fuel oil. It was a small space; big pipes sprung from the floor, painted in a garish green color and filling half the room. Blankets were stacked in one corner.

"The Doc's right. It's downright humid in here." Nate unzipped his jacket. "I can feel the sweat comin' on."

"Boilers, in the basement level," Chingkut explained. "They stay lit through winter, but must be shut down afterwards."

"I'll bet that makes for a lot of cold showers."

"It can't be helped. Our supply of oil is less and less."

That was telling, Neill thought. He wondered if that might partially confirm his theory. "Your English is excellent. Where'd you learn?"

"At the university, in Vladivostok."

"You have a gift for languages."

"Likewise, Captain Neill. Your Russian has a touch of Moscow, but I can't tell about your Ukrainian."

"Kiev," Neill supplied. "And what do your ears tell you about Professor Brisbane?"

He grinned broadly. "Only that she talks funny."

"*Quite,*" she grumped. "That's just my accent."

"You should get out of here." Neill was more formal now. It was time for business. "But before you do I have a few questions. You said you had a map?"

The fisherman produced one; white parchment, folded, and stained with grease. Kneeling, he spread it out on his knee, using his red flashlight to give them a better look.

"Arkangel is here," Chingkut pointed. "But as I said,

the tunnels are closer. That's where you should make your entry—unless you plan on breaching the main gate and shooting your way in."

"I'd like to avoid that, thank you very much." Voskov and Tereshenko crowded closer, peering over the Marine's shoulder.

"Then follow this course." Chingkut traced the route with his finger. "Travel at night, and keep away from the road. You'll be tempted to take the trails, just below the crest." He shook his head. "Don't use those; they're dangerous. Too many loose rocks, even for the most sure-footed."

"How often do the Russians patrol this area?"

"Twice a day, but never at the same time."

"We'll have to be careful, then," Yuri said. "How will we find the tunnels?"

Chingkut returned to the map. "Your path will lead to this point; a volcanic outcropping." A crudely drawn skull marked the spot. "The Russians call it *Scylla's Rock.*"

"More Greek mythology," Neill observed.

"The Russians do love their symbolism," he grinned, circling the location with a felt pen. "The entrance is at Scylla's feet—it's hidden from view, but you'll find it."

"Any security measures? Does Ivan guard that entrance?"

"No, not in recent times," Chingkut answered. Neill translated his words for the Ukrainians. "Soviet engineers dug those tunnels before any of us were born. Some are used as air shafts; others as emergency exits. Many of them run for miles beneath the surface."

Voskov frowned. "And they aren't patrolled?"

Chingkut shook his head again. "They should be. But the trading company has grown fat and lazy. They've forgotten about most of them." As an afterthought, he pulled another sheaf from his coat. "Take these, too."

"What are they?" Yuri unfolded the worn pages before looking up in surprise.

"Tunnel schematics. You'll need them once you're inside."

"*Schematics*? They're hardly that. These are hand-drawn." Yuri was incredulous. "You've been down there?"

"Occasionally. Sometimes wanderlust gets the best of me." The fisherman looked proud of himself. "I made that chart over a year ago."

Nate spoke up. "Then you've seen this aircraft—the plane the Russians are using?"

"The second beast?" Chingkut had a concerned look. "Yes, I've seen it. But only once. From my boat, late at night."

"Never in the hangar?"

He shook his head. "I haven't been that deep in the mountain. The base is heavily guarded on that level."

"The second beast? Why do you call it that?"

The Unangan became silent, stilled by the memory. Voskov saw his hesitation.

"Tell him, *tavarisch*."

Chingkut drew in his breath before continuing. "My father saw the first beast, years ago. He was on the open sea, hunting food for his family." He spoke English now, for Crockett and Brisbane's benefit. "But there were no fish, and no seals to be hunted. The waters were cold and covered by fog, so he turned back."

"And that's when he saw it?" Taylor asked.

He nodded. "He heard it first. A wailing howl in the distance, and then the mists were thrown open." Chingkut's tone had become slow and even, a touch of amusement creeping in. "My father tells the story much better. He's quite the dramatist; you should see him act it out."

"What happened next?"

"The beast nearly took his life. It burst through the fog, rushing past before it dove into the sea."

"Where did this happen?" Neill went for his map. "Can you show me?"

"I can, Captain. It was south of Bering Island."

Nate had a thought. "It was the *chimera*. That's what your father saw. We've seen it too, at the bottom of the ocean."

"*Chimera*?" Chingkut shook his head. "This word I don't know."

"He means the first plane," Neill explained. "It's submerged not far from here. Discovered by an oil company looking for new fields."

"Now the Russians know where it is," Yuri added. "Don't forget them, Mikhail."

"Yeah. Who can forget the Russians?" Neill quipped. "They're like a bad *kopeck*."

"A bad *penny*, Captain. That phrase is familiar." A shadow passed over Chingkut's face. "But you must be careful. Playing with fire has its own reward, and the Russians are not to be toyed with. They regard this weapon very seriously, and will take extreme measures to protect it." He lowered his voice. "There is more to this than any of you know."

"Meaning?" Neill sensed disclosure in the wings.

"Only that the *Rodina* will use this aircraft to protect her national interests."

"We've already had a taste of their resolve."

"The attack on your ship," Chingkut replied. "Russia is desperate. She's facing a crippling shortage—natural resources once taken for granted."

"Let me guess—their access to crude oil isn't what it used to be." Neill was fishing, but he had the right bait.

Chingkut was taken aback. "You knew this?"

"It fits the picture. How did you catch on?"

"It's become obvious. Prices have doubled, our allocation dwindles, and there are rumors everywhere."

"The common man suffers while Ivan funnels what's left into his military machine." Neill considered that. If Chingkut's words were true—and his own theory correct—then invasion was inevitable.

And war, he thought silently.

"My father and I don't always agree, Captain. He is stubborn at times, set in his ways, and he clings to what we might call superstition. Where you and I see an aircraft, he sees a monster, a thing to be shunned. Perhaps he's right; perhaps this weapon is possessed by the spirits—a demon, if you will—I don't know." He stood taller. "I can be stubborn, too. But I am my father's son, and I will honor his beliefs, even if I disagree with them."

"If that's your way of urging caution, then so be it." Neill rested a hand on the fisherman's shoulder. "This isn't a suicide mission. Trust me, we'll be very careful."

Chingkut nodded. "I pray that you will."

Oahu, Hawaii

"I feel bad about this." Christina Arrens turned left onto South Avenue, then put her boot on the clutch and shifted into second gear. White clouds hugged the mountain peaks, the rising sun painted the landscape in hues of orange and gold, and though it had rained overnight, Pearl Harbor now caught the morning rays and looked like a postcard.

Mary Margaret Stillwell gave her friend a puzzled glance. "What's to feel bad about?" She slipped on her dress shoes as they neared the office. "Keep the car as long as you like. You've got farther to go, and I don't like driving, anyway."

Christina gave in. "Well, at any rate, it's only for a few more days. Come Monday I'll be working out of your office."

She was right on that count. Most of Arrens' TDY included a tasking at the NCIS Foreign Counter-Intelligence branch—a billet not unlike the one she filled at Henderson Hall. But her indoc had taken place on the northern side of Oahu, at Marine Base Kaneohe Bay. Christina had been directed to start with the newcomers' platoon, which had lasted just a few days, and now, after some time on the island, she was ready to begin her work at Pearl.

"Be thankful that K-Bay is close to the beach," Mary Margaret put in. Their uniforms contrasted; for Stillwell, working in an office meant service alphas, the business suit of the Corps, while Arrens wore camouflaged utilities.

Christina wheeled into the parking lot. "This is Hawaii, Maggie," she grinned. "*Everything's* close to the beach."

"Got me there," Stillwell smiled back. "Hey, come on in for a few. I'll use my vast resources to look up that number." She saw her friend hesitate. "C'mon, don't be bashful."

"I don't have time for that," Christina protested.

"*Sure* you do. It's Wednesday; how much work can there be? Besides, you admin types are a dime a dozen. So what if you're late?"

"*Oh-two-eleven*," she reminded Stillwell. "*Counter-Intelligence Specialist*—not just admin. If that were the case I'd be stuck in Kaneohe for the duration."

"But you *aren't*, chickee. And Monday's on its way." There was glee in her voice, and Maggie reached out to pinch the side of Christina's face. "*The girl's in Pearl and it's time to party."*

"Cut it out." Arrens found a place to park and killed the engine. "But if you insist—"

"Oh, I insist. Of course, it's practically a boys' club in there; you're bound to disrupt the tranquil environment I've cultivated—"

"Stop it. I've met the agents."

"And believe me, they're still talking about you."

Christina stared at her friend. "For somebody looking for company, you're not selling this very well."

"Oh, whatever." She pushed open her door. "Now get your butt out of that seat and let's go."

It didn't take long for Stillwell to deliver on her promise. Inside of ten minutes the Marine's computer was up and running, and in five more she'd accessed a site firewalled from the general public.

"We're gonna be in *sooo* much trouble—" Arrens moaned.

"Knock it off," Maggie countered. "You have legitimate concerns about your supervisor. We're only trying to determine his whereabouts, and maintain the accountability of military personnel."

"Can you sell that?"

"Only if we're caught. Now give me the number."

"The prefix is Department of Defense, that much I know." Christina fished out her cell. "I'm just not sure about the rest."

"Not to worry." Maggie scrolled to the proper field and entered the digits. With a click of the mouse, the search began. "Should have it in a jiffy."

The screen blinked.

"Wow," Christina whispered. She pulled up a chair and sat down. "That was fast."

The two Marines studied the monitor. "Ship-to-shore

call. You can tell by the first four digits in the series," she instructed. "That last four identify the source vessel."

"Is that a hyper-link?" It was hard to see.

"Yeah. I've got it." Stillwell clicked on it, and her eyes widened. "Well, well—I'd say this probably goes *beyond* classified."

"Classified—as in *not for public consumption*, or—"

Maggie looked over the top of the monitor. No one was watching. "As in, we shouldn't even be here." Her head went from side to side as she quickly logged out. "But now we've got the skinny; that boyfriend of yours is on the *Meyer*."

Christina pursed her lips. Michael's comment about the embattled ship made sense now. She frowned, her worries kindled afresh.

"And I told him not to go to Russia."

"He's on a ship, silly, somewhere in the Bering Sea." Maggie was trying hard to be like a big sister. "Last I heard, the *Meyer* was off the Kamchatka Peninsula."

"The same ship the Russians just shot up." Her angst had become elevated. "An isolated, floating target."

"True. But don't get all worked up. At least he's not in Russia."

"I wouldn't count on that." Arrens' frown deepened.

"You don't know Michael."

22

A LIFE WITHOUT REGRETS

THE PILOT STRUGGLED with the controls, nearly aborting his landing. Winds above the helipad were nothing short of fierce, and they violently buffeted the chopper, the gale whipping up dust, debris, and trace amounts of snow that clung to the mountain top.

But the transport's rotors were resilient in pushing back against nature. Beating the rarefied air, the blades added a man-made touch to the whirlwind. Turbulence on the way in was almost negligible; but now, hovering had become difficult, and the bird was desperate to stay aloft, fighting hard to remain airborne in a sky that threatened to bring her down.

For today's flight, man and machine caught a break, although one of intentional design. A military version of the commercially successful Mi-17, this aircraft had been specifically improved for heavier loads, with beefed up Klimov engines for use in thinner air at high altitudes.

Sweating beneath his mask, the pilot made one last attempt, and the airframe thumped against the deck, her wheel struts absorbing the landing. The chopper bounced once, crabbing a little to one side, her turboshafts at full power. This was a natural precaution, should the pilot deem it necessary to pull up again.

But that didn't happen. There was no further movement, vertical or lateral. The pilot was satisfied. He began throttling back, and the chopper gave in, settling down on the windswept peak.

The hatch opened; a protective detail emerged first, two naval infantrymen, each brandishing rifles with pistols on their belts. Then Taras Pavlenko himself exited the crew door, sunglasses shielding his eyes.

Colonel Utkin was there to greet him.

"Admiral Pavlenko—*dobre ootra*." The ex-aviator forced a smile. His superior's arrival was somewhat unexpected; the naval base at Petropavlovsk had phoned less than an hour earlier, giving Utkin little warning. "How may we be of service?"

"A flag officer's privilege, Colonel." Pavlenko wore a pleasant look but had all the charm of a viper. He surveyed the landscape before them. "All too often I find myself trapped within four walls. But this will be an opportunity to witness your magnificent view, and to breathe in the sea air."

Utkin motioned toward the steps. "Shall we go below? Tea is prepared—"

"You aren't hearing me, Sasha. I didn't come to trade one office for another. This is an unofficial visit; one intended to bring clarity of purpose."

His subordinate swallowed. "In what way, Admiral?"

Pavlenko answered with a question of his own. "Can you provide a tour of the compound? I would prefer to see the living quarters; more specifically, the buildings where Dr. Zhukov and his staff are housed." From behind the sunglasses, he stared at Utkin. "And the children, Colonel. Show me the children."

Utkin found that comment chilling. He stood at nervous attention. "Sir, I have received my orders. I am a dutiful officer. But I must voice an opinion." In spite of the cold, there was sweat on the man's lip. "I have—*struggled*—with issuing your directives. They seem very severe, if I may." He swallowed again. "Are these measures truly necessary?"

Pavlenko said nothing at first, but finally, "Colonel, you understand the need for operational security, do you not?"

"Of course, Admiral."

"It is essential now, and it will be essential in the future." Both men descended the platform's steps, leaving the helicopter behind. "And it must be ironclad, Sasha. As it stands now, Dr. Zhukov and his staff are no longer needed. We can close this off, bringing our enterprise solely within the purview of the military; from logistics, to maintenance and development—and finally to execution." He smiled at the irony of the word. "No outside source is required to complete this mission."

"But what threat do they pose?"

The admiral was prepared for reluctance. "Charybdis cannot fall into enemy hands, comrade Colonel. But that possibility exists as long as there are those who know its secrets. We must be resolute in our determination to keep that from happening. You have received the shipment?"

He nodded. "The Marines have taken charge of it."

"And you have a suitable location?"

"A clean room—our sterile lab, at sea level."

"It can be made airtight?"

"And locked from the outside." Utkin's eyes went across the road to the compound. There was activity at the school. Recess had begun, and the sound of small voices and laughter pealed in the distance.

"And the children, Admiral?"

As a rule, Russians loved their children. In a country still feeling the effects of an oppressive government, there were few other sources of hope available. Yet Taras Pavlenko was different in that respect. Utkin had seen his cold indifference, and his stand-offish ways seemed particularly attuned toward the young. This struck the colonel as a denial of basic paternal instinct. That a senior officer could exhibit this trait flew in the face of good order and discipline. Empathy toward subordinates had always been a pre-requisite for getting results, at least in Utkin's mind, but Pavlenko had somehow risen in rank without it.

Was this a by-product of the old system? Utkin didn't know. Success in those days meant control through fear, and a reliance on punishment to achieve goals. There was no denying its effectiveness, but it did little to foster true loyalty—the kind of loyalty he'd witnessed by those who practiced religion. And since the collapse of the Soviet empire, many of those adherents—the repenters, as they were called—had come out of the shadows.

He considered that Pavelenko's career began before the fall of the USSR, and for the admiral, its tenets had become a source of faith and practice. His orders were frightful, and it was easy to look at the man and see a monster, bent by the remnants of communism. The Soviet Union was gone, yet the authoritarian rule of the State remained, a tangible reminder of how things had been.

And what had filled that void? Utkin often wondered. It certainly wasn't some new morality to replace the rotting corpse of socialism. Nor was it freedom from corruption. There was still plenty of that left, enough to fill the hangar below.

"I should think the answer to that is obvious, Sasha," the admiral was saying now.

"But must they suffer the same fate as their parents?"

"Steel yourself against pity, Colonel. Passing through the veil together is a much more humane solution, don't you agree? To join them in whatever eternity awaits. The alternative is to spend their formative years as orphans." Pavlenko shook his head. "In that circumstance, they become wards of the State, with no guarantee of maturing into productive citizens."

This discussion was morose. Colonel Utkin wanted to change the subject. "There is talk among the officers, Admiral. Is it true that Dr. Zhukov was aboard the first prototype? The one that was lost?"

Pavlenko looked over his sunglasses. "Quite true. I was there when he was fished from the sea."

"And how is it that he alone survived?"

"I have puzzled over that for thirty-five years. But survive he did, and because of it we have achieved great success." He scowled. "The more pressing question is why the prototype crashed at all."

But not the *most pressing question,* Utkin didn't say.

He knew that if he followed orders, there would be a general's star waiting for him, and possibly even a posting in Moscow. Pavlenko had promised as much. That did little to make the tasking less repugnant. In fact, it did nothing at all, and the colonel wondered if it was worth the price of his very soul.

• • • •

Crockett pulled the first watch. The team rested until mid-morning. They'd been awake most of the night, but sleep was difficult. Inside, the room was still, while outside, sunlight poked through birch trees, dappling the blockhouse in shadow.

Neill finally gave up, stirred by hunger. At his urging, everyone broke out MREs, and the Marines demonstrated how to heat them. Xander and Yuri consumed the meals in their entirety. Taylor needed encouragement.

"Eat up, Doc," Neill told her. His eyes moved to each window, but there was nothing to see.

"You sound like my mother," she clucked.

"You'll need the energy. Lots of carbs."

"So it will all go to my hips."

Her dry wit had returned, Neill judged. A good sign. "You'll burn it off come nightfall."

The weapons were checked next, a perennial habit of those under arms. The salt air had left a film; the Ukrainians wiped down their muzzles and lubed the bores. Michael and Nate did the same. The Americans made coffee. Xander, Yuri and Taylor had tea. With their bellies full, the group gathered their gear and took inventory. Crockett moved to the door, rifle in hand, while Voskov and Neill reviewed tunnel diagrams.

The sniper met Neill's look. "Nature calls, Homestyle."

"Behind the building," Mike told him. "What about you, Doc?" He was trying to ask delicately, but fumbled for words.

Brisbane enjoyed seeing him struggle. "While you were sleeping, Captain," she said at last. "The facilities were a bit crude, but I managed." She watched Nate exit the building. In the center of the room the pumps did what pumps do, and the sound of the generator rose and fell. "Why does he call you that?"

"Homestyle?" Neill shook his head. "It's just a nickname."

Taylor pressed him. "An allusion to your homespun values?"

"That's as good an answer as I can give," he replied. Neill folded the drawings and put them away, and the team waited for sunset.

• • • •

Darkness came slowly to the hollow. Hills to the west blanked out the setting sun, extending the twilight, but it was after ten p.m. before the sky went black. The axis of the Earth's rotation accounted for that. At this time of year the complex orbital arrangement made for long days and short nights.

It took some getting used to.

The room had grown dim. Neill unlaced his boots and settled back against the wall. It was warmer now, much more so than when they'd first arrived. And quiet, too. Yuri was nearby, taking his turn at watch, eyes on the windows. He moved every few minutes to change the view. His face was expressionless, and the Marine counted that as a good thing.

Xander breathed deeply in a corner, covered by blankets. He began to snore. Crockett and Brisbane were also asleep, having found space on either side of the pumps. Each of them seemed unaware of Voskov's rumblings.

Neill found himself drifting. He closed his eyes, then thought better of it. His turn was next, and even without checking the time, he knew that Tereshenko would be rousing him soon.

And then the door opened, and no one even noticed.

No one—except Michael David Neill.

He entered quietly, his footsteps unheard, and putting a finger to his lips, David Neill urged silence and stood before his son.

"Dad?"

The younger man had a puzzled look, but was standing now. Nothing else had changed, and Yuri's attention was still on the windows. "You can't be here."

"I'm not, Mike." His face was peaceful, just as it had

been the last time. "You know how this works, son."

"I thought I did. But I'm not so sure anymore."

"You'll find that uncertainty can be a sure thing at times," David Neill smiled.

"Is that something you learned from Grand-dad?"

"No, not really," he answered, looking wistful. "That was your mother." David waved a hand at those around them. "You're in good company, Mike."

"Why did you leave?"

"It was my time. Things needed doing, so I did them." His father's cool blue eyes looked into his. "Sometimes you have to do what's right, no matter the consequences. There are clear choices, and there are right choices. Most of the time they're one and the same. Do you remember John 15:13?"

Mike nodded, reciting the verse. "Greater love hath no man than this, that a man lay down his life for his friends."

"Or his family. Don't forget that, Mike." He turned, taking hold of the door.

"Wait—there are things I need to tell—"

"Don't forget, son," David called over his shoulder.

And then he was gone.

The glow from the chem sticks had long since faded, so Nate cracked a few more. The SSD men used the light to secure their rucks.

"Kit up, everybody." Nate's carbine hung across his back. He tapped Mike's leg with his boot. "Hey, boss. Naptime's over."

Neill looked up, rubbing his face. "How long was I out?"

"Couple of hours."

"What about my watch?"

"I took it. Sleep's over-rated, from what I hear." He lowered his voice. "You okay, Mike?"

"Yeah." Neill wasn't sure. "Why do you ask?"

Crockett looked away. "No particular reason."

"What did I miss?"

"Nary a thing. But we should scoot. I'm gonna check the road."

"Be with you in a minute."

"Don't forget your gloves, Doc," Nate advised. "And zip up that jacket. It's cold out there."

Voskov and Tereshenko were in good spirits, eager to be on the move again. But there were housekeeping matters that needed attention first. Yuri collected empty meal pouches. Mike put aside his dream—if that's what it was, he thought—and policed the interior, stacking blankets back where they'd found them and removing any evidence of their stay. Nothing would be left behind, and anything that didn't travel with them would be buried in the woods.

Xander gave the room one last look. Before exiting, he turned and tossed Neill the padlock. "Secure the door on your way out, Mikhail."

"Roger that." The Marine shouldered his pack and weapon. "Need a hand with that, Doc?"

"I've got it, Captain." Brisbane lifted her rucksack, holding one of the glowing wands. She had all but turned away, but even in the dim light Neill could see her face. What was more, he could hear the anguish in her voice.

"Are you all right?"

She composed herself. "I've had time to think—too much time, in fact."

"Bailee." Neill had guessed as much. It was time for a little compassion. "We were all affected by her death, Taylor."

"But there's more to it." Her eyes were red. "She was

a good friend, and I mourn her loss. But over the past few hours, I've come to realize something more important—that it's her *life* that's affected me the most."

"Not sure I follow you, Doc." Actually he did. She needed to voice her feelings. Mike just hoped things wouldn't become too maudlin; sentimentality could be messy.

Taylor went on, expressing more feelings. "She lived to the fullest. Always finding joy in everything, with nothing held back."

"She was an example to you."

"Yes, in spite of her youth—or maybe because of it, I don't know." She was flustered, but held it together. "I want that kind of life. I want to live, too, like Bailee did—without regrets."

Without regrets. An admirable goal, but Neill wasn't sure that was even possible. "So the academic world is no longer enough," he observed. "And it took a trip to Kamchatka—"

He didn't get the chance to finish. Crockett poked his head in the door, interrupting Brisbane's moment of soul-searching. A pair of night vision goggles were perched on his head.

"Coast is clear, Mike," he announced. His M4 was cradled in the ready position, and the sniper was all business now. "You two need a minute?"

Brisbane didn't hesitate. "I'm ready when you are, gentlemen."

"That's what I like to hear," Crockett beamed. "Now let's steal this monster's thunder and go home."

23

BETWEEN SCYLLA AND CHARYBDIS

"**B**IZARRE." CULL MCKECKNEY was shaking his head, scrolling through a series of color images on his tablet. Some went beyond that descriptive word, touching on creepy. His head came up. "And it's abandoned. Where'd you find this place?"

It was early morning. Willis Avery stirred coffee. "Came with the job," he answered. "Allan Hayes forwarded a list, bases worth keeping an eye on. If memory serves, there were a couple dozen, mostly in Russia. Anadyr-1 was near the top."

Cull had seen this type of thing before. A series of haunting photos came to mind, shots taken at the workers village of Pripyat, Ukraine. It, too, was now abandoned, but for a far more unsettling reason. Pripyat was a so-called nuclear city, planted squarely inside the exclusion zone that contained Chernobyl.

One image from Pripyat had stuck in McKeckney's brain; hundreds of gas masks, unused, littering the floor of one non-descript building. Each had the appearance of a face, with macabre, empty eyes staring back—

"Anadyr-1," Cull repeated. "They name their cities using numerics?"

"Ivan's funny that way," S<small>ECDEF</small> conceded.

"Located in Chukotka, a province to the north. Certainly off the beaten path—but I guess that's the point, isn't it?"

Avery nodded in response. Anadyr-1 was too cold and far too remote to be a tourist destination. Nor could it have been. It didn't show up on any maps, and there were no road signs to mark its location. It was closed, a secret city, off limits to everyone.

And *everyone* meant just that.

In the post-Soviet era, the former missile base was no longer inhabited, though much of its infrastructure still remained; troop barracks, dining facilities, a theater. All of these familiar structures were now collapsing in disrepair.

McKeckney laid aside the tablet and opened a file on Avery's desk. Inside were more photos, satellite imagery labeled by the NRO. These were focused primarily on two locations, Anadyr-1 and Ust-Kamchatsk, and each marked the positions of Federation troops.

"Two brigades of mechanized," he noted. "Another two of infantry. Motor Rifle Companies, it says here. Do we know which ones?"

Avery shook his head. "CIA thinks they've narrowed it down, but they won't commit. Doesn't matter. On the day the *Meyer* was attacked, all four were staged at Ust-Kamchatsk. Now they've fallen back to Chukotka, setting up shop at Anadyr."

"They were waiting for us," McKeckney said. "For our military response—one that never came." *More than that*, he decided; *they were* counting *on it*.

"The old Red Bear mistook our intentions." S<small>ECDEF</small> was also in the mood for speculation. "Karpenko and Rurik figured Chuck Cassidy for a far-right hawk. Fortunately, the president's a little more cautious than that. If he wasn't, we might be at war right now."

"Those troops are still in play. Forward deployed for a reason; a ground force with their skill sets isn't just on maneuvers."

"But they're standing down for the moment," Avery replied. "Walk me through it, Cull. I'd like to know if we concur on this."

McKeckney considered where to start. "Well, you can extrapolate a great deal from their presence at Ust-Kamchatsk. We know the Russians have a base on the coastline not far away. We also know they've housed a large, water-skimming cargo plane in a hangar at sea level. Now add infantry and mechanized troops to the mix." He closed the dossier and dropped it back on the desk. "It's fairly obvious, Mr. Secretary. Ivan planned to launch his invasion from that very spot, and these units would have been the advance team."

"There are probably other locations," Avery allowed. "Karpenko couldn't pull this off with just one aircraft; he'd need several to get the right number of troops in place."

"So we should be looking elsewhere?"

"National Reconnaissance is already on it. We're re-tasking a few satellites, taking a closer look up and down the peninsula."

"A good call," McKeckney said. "And focusing on Chukotka paid off, too. Your instincts were spot on."

Avery wasn't ready to take credit for that. "Conjecture based on Neill's hypothesis, Cull. Nothing more."

"Speaking of Neill," the artilleryman began, "Will I ever get the chance to take a look at his file?"

"The president's got it right now. You can have it next."

"What about communications?"

"You're full of questions, aren't you?" Avery shook

his head. "There won't be any. Not now. He and his team have gone dark."

"You worried?"

Again with the questions. He was a lot like Richard Aultman in that respect, the Secretary reflected.

Worry. "That comes with the job, too."

• • • •

Neill faced east. High above them were the commercial routes trafficked by the international airlines. It was not uncommon to stand on Kamchatka and see their white contrails by day or their running lights by night, wide-body aircraft on their way to the Aleutians and Alaska, or following the coastline of the peninsula southwest to Japan or the Philippines.

Lately many carriers had altered those routes, though not all had done so; there were financial and logistical concerns involved in doing that, and shifting their itineraries was burdensome for the smaller airlines. Still, despite expenses, too many planes had fallen out of the sky, and few were willing to chance the loss of another.

That could hurt their bottom line even more.

With Crockett focused ahead, Neill now looked to the sky. Anything flying overhead would be easy to spot. There were things that would give an aircraft away; the sound of an engine, or the telltale flash of a navigational light. But the Marine wasn't interested in the obvious.

Years earlier, when Neill was a teenager, Ulyanov had told him what to look for. David Neill had formed a fast friendship with the Ukrainian officer; Ulyanov was a colonel then, and like it or not, his days as a jet jockey were over. And one thing was certain.

Andrei Ulyanov did not like it.

His piloting skills were unquestioned, but age caught

up with every man. Ukraine's Air Force needed leaders, and the affable officer was suited to the job of marshaling the next generation. It was then that Ulyanov realized that his choices were limited, and the future unavoidable.

Rank and responsibility had effectively grounded the hotshot pilot. To be sure, he still flew the odd mission, just to prove himself, and to demonstrate to the 'kids' that he still had what it took. But it was time to trade the skies for an office. He parked his somewhat dissatisfied frame behind a desk, and while begrudgingly accepting the circumstances, he was always willing to share his expertise, knowledge built on years of experience.

One occasion stood out to the Marine. Andrei and Irina had come to the Neill home for supper. The colonel had brought wine. After the meal, Jean Neill served tea, while the menfolk engaged in spirited discussion. Michael wanted to hear about airplanes, and Andrei was only too happy to oblige.

"When searching at night," he had said, "Don't try to find the brightest object in the sky. Look for a hole. Shapes darker than anything else in the heavens.

"The planes *without* lights—the ones camouflaged by darkness—those are the ones with something to hide, little Michael."

• • • •

"I'm sorry about Bailee, Nathan." Yuri felt awkward, struggling to find the words. "She was good person."

"The best," Nate answered.

"I wish we could have known her longer."

"You and me both, pal."

The team had long since climbed the hill and were following Chingkut's map to the southwest. They stayed on the eastern side of the road that hugged the ridgeline. Just below the crest, worn footpaths wound between the rocks—rocks large enough to screen their movements.

Nate led the group with stealth and precision; doing so in daylight would have been difficult, as there were stretches of open space along the way. Night, on the other hand, afforded much more secrecy.

There was loose gravel underfoot, just as Chingkut had warned. Crockett steered them clear of that hazard, and kept away from the edge of the slopes facing the sea. His NVGs told him that the escarpment there fell away gently at first, but then angled sharply down to the beach below.

"Third landmark, Mike," he called softly. As point man, Nate had committed the chart to memory.

Neill came up from behind and everyone took a knee. Crockett pointed past the rocks and toward the road.

"Signage," the captain observed. He grinned in the darkness. "Can you read it?"

"My Ivan-speak's a little rusty, but I'll give it a shot," Crockett returned. "*Military installation ahead. No photography allowed. Keep out.*"

"Anything else?"

"Yeah, *Death to America.*" Nate's sarcasm could be biting. "And the usual stuff—about deadly force being authorized. How'd I do?"

"Not bad. You caught the spirit of the message."

Nate shrugged. "Stands to reason. And it still says CCCP at the bottom. That means USSR."

"I've often wondered," Neill joked. "Guess they haven't gotten around to changing it."

"Might be intentional. Moscow's keen on bringing back the old ways; the empire could still rise from the ashes."

"Let's hope not."

Crockett adjusted his goggles, scanning in every direction. "In any event, we're close. Scylla's Rock should be just ahead."

Neill turned to Brisbane. "You're favoring one leg, Doc. Everything all right?"

"Blister—on my heel," Taylor winced. "I'm not used to wearing combat boots, Captain. But I'll manage."

Neill felt bad. They'd covered miles of territory, and just as he'd predicted, they'd also burned a lot of energy. The military men were used to humping it, but he wondered if they'd pushed the Aussie a little too hard.

"You're a trooper, Doc," Nate said at last. "No worries, though—I've got moleskin in my ruck."

"Sounds uncomfortable," she answered drily.

The sniper was amused.

"Good one, Doc."

Scylla's Rock reared up soon enough. It was impossible to miss, appearing right where Chingkut's map said it would be.

Scylla's feet were not so easily seen; ground cover—ajuga, spurge and wormwood—clustered at the base of the rock, and rising higher were thick rows of bugbane and meadowsweet, foliage hardy enough to withstand the cold Kamchatka winters. The plant life served as a natural camouflage.

There were lights in the distance dotting the horizon. Crockett judged them to be a few kilometers away, part of the Russian surface complex. Being this close to unfriendly territory called for even more caution. He and Neill spread out, crouched in positions flanking the stone outcropping. The Marines' heads turned, wary of an unexpected patrol, but again, there was nothing to see, and no movement.

"*Clear on this side*," Neill hissed. "Looks like we picked the right night for a march."

Taking their cue, Voskov and Tereshenko sprung into

action, with Brisbane in tow, pushing through the under-brush in search of the tunnel entrance. It didn't take long. There was rustling out of sight and then silence.

"*Mikhail*," Xander called at last. "It's here."

Neill motioned for Crockett to bring it in. The two began a silent retreat and disappeared into the shrubs. From there it was an easy drop into a narrow, man-made trench.

"This is cozy," Crockett observed. All five members of the team stood in a concrete channel. Framed within the rock itself was a steel door, streaked with rust and secured by a heavy padlock.

"Clever," Neill said, surveying the entrance. "They must've hollowed it out on the inside."

Brisbane wasn't encouraged. She leaned in, trying to see more in the darkness. "Anyone bring bolt cutters?"

"We were expecting this." Neill pulled a gadget from his ruck and swept the doorframe. The digital display was blank. "No frequency emissions of any kind. The other side looks clear."

Nate was nodding. "Makes sense. Our friend Ching-kut got in without a hitch." He tugged at the lock. "But how'd he get past this?"

"My guess? He picked it," Neill said with a smile.

"Nice. The big fisherman's got skills. Unfortunately my breaching methods are less subtle. Wanna try something else?"

"I've got just the man for the job." Neill gave Yuri a nod. "You're up."

"And if the Russians discover our handiwork?"

"We have to risk it. Besides, it doesn't look like they check this spot too often."

Tereshenko went to work. He pulled something from his pack and huddled at the door with Voskov, and in a moment's time a rough, grating sound could be heard.

Nate peered over their shoulders. "Gigli saw," he said approvingly. "Good thinking, Yuri."

"Gigli saw?" Taylor stole a glance.

"Flexible. Primarily used by surgeons, Doctor," Neill explained. "But fitted with the right wire—"

"—it turns steel into butter," Yuri announced. "One last tug . . ."

Something snapped. Xander stepped back, the severed casing in his hand. He held it up for all to see, then stuffed the pieces in his ruck.

"*Vidminno.*" Excellent.

"*Da, tavarisch,*" Nate said, mimicking Neill's Russian. His accent was passable.

"*Da.*" Voskov gave the sniper a toothy grin, and Neill began to think that the two just might get along after all.

While the Ukrainians provided cover, Crockett wrenched open the door. Neill stepped in, his footfalls making a dull, metallic sound. The space inside was pitch black. He snapped a chem stick, waited for the glow, and then waved it before him.

"Stairwell," he announced. "Vertical shaft, narrow, too. Smells like oil or diesel fuel."

Crockett made his entry, the muzzle of his M4 pointed ahead. "Probably fumes from the lower levels. Any ladders? An elevator, maybe?"

They studied the interior. "No elevator, but it looks like there's some kind of dumbwaiter on the far wall," Neill told him.

"How deep does this shaft go?"

The captain shook his head. "Hard to say." The floor beneath their feet was an iron latticework, with open slats revealing the area below. "Can't see that far." Neill walked to the edge of the stairs, gripping the handrail. "Break out your flashlights, people, but keep 'em low.

We're gonna need 'em."

They began to climb down, with Voskov bringing up the rear. No one had to be told to move cautiously. The shaft was bound on all sides by concrete, with half a dozen steps between landings. Their path to the bottom led in a steep, clockwise direction. To Neill's way of thinking, the construction was more fire escape than stairwell, with rickety steel that gave a little with each step.

Crockett felt the same way. Bolts were loose. Each landing groaned under their weight. In some places, the creaking hardware pulled away from the walls, sending crumbling debris falling into the black chasm below.

The group had descended nearly two hundred feet. Only ten minutes had passed, but it felt like much longer.

"This thing's an OSHA nightmare," Nate whispered. "Like beat-up scaffolding."

And that's when the world fell away beneath them. From over their heads came a wrenching sound, metal on metal, and then a startled gasp. Nate's warning had come too late.

Taylor was two landings above them. Xander followed, adding his bulk to where she stood. But the strain was too much, and the Soviet-era platform lurched under their feet. Excessive weight and poor metallurgy did the rest.

Some of the bolts snapped, freeing a section of the stairwell. Still connected to the far wall, those steps swung down in an arc, crashing into the space below and collapsing the next landing.

Brisbane was wide-eyed, teetering on the edge. Voskov reached out, trying to steady her. Instead, he lost his balance, and without the support of the missing steps, the platform gave way.

Taylor slid from the angled dais and dropped into the chasm. From below, Neill turned in time to see her fall.

He took hold of the railing and prayed it would hold.

She fell slowly at first and picked up speed. Neill heard a scream and swung out, managing to loop an arm around Brisbane's waist as she passed. His grasp drove the air from her lungs, and their combined weight, coupled with inertia, nearly toppled them both.

Crockett moved instinctively. He jumped to Neill's side, gloved hands taking hold.

"Hang on, Doc!" the captain gasped. "I've got you."

Taylor was almost breathless.

"I wouldn't dream of anything else, Captain."

Her grip was tight, and as they clung together, she chanced a look into the void. There was little to see, until Xander's flashlight sailed past, falling silently before clattering on the deck below, the beam of light bouncing from wall to wall.

The Americans managed to hoist the doctor safely from the brink. She put her back against the wall, sitting as far from the edge as she could.

"Do you think it was rigged to collapse, Mischa?" Yuri asked. "To deal with intruders?"

Neill gulped air. "That's possible, I guess. Maybe the engineers were just having a bad day." He turned to face Brisbane. "You okay, Doc?"

Addressing him by his rank seemed ungrateful. "I'm fine, Michael. Thanks to you."

"Nothin' to it."

"Far from it, Captain. I could have died."

Neill deflected the comment. "That's a stretch; broken a leg, maybe, but you would have lived." He put a hand to his side; his ribs were sore from the mid-air capture. His eyes went above to where Voskov was perched.

"You all right, Xander?"

The Ukrainian grunted that he was, and a quick inspection of the stairwell offered hope. "The section below is still intact, Mikhail."

Neill pointed his flashlight toward the next landing. There was debris in their path, but nothing they couldn't overcome.

"What about you? Can you get down here?"

"Child's play," Xander scoffed. "And I have rope."

In spite of the resounding crash, no alarms sounded and no Russian troops appeared brandishing weapons. Taylor's adventure forced them to be more wary, and once Voskov climbed down, they set off again.

Neill slowed his pace. Despite cushioned soles, boots on metal made too much noise. The deeper they went, the louder their footsteps seemed to echo around them.

"Almost there," he called. "Another ten feet or so."

He left the last stair step and landed on solid ground. The dark mouth of a tunnel was just yards away. On the deck, he saw a steel A-frame, squat and sturdy, with twin iron beams recessed in the floor.

"A bumper stop and railroad tracks," Neill told the group. "Probably runs the length of the passage." He was about to ask for the schematics, but Voskov had already fished them out.

"This is the main artery," Xander was saying. He clicked on a flashlight, tracing a finger along the hand-drawn route. "It continues due south, and then doglegs southwest for two kilometers."

"With secondary tunnels branching off." Neill put his nose in the air. "Do you smell that?"

Voskov breathed deeply. "That's the scent of brine— saltwater, Mikhail." He referred back to Chingkut's diagram. "To be expected. This passage follows the coastline and leads to the hangar."

"Straight shot?" Yuri asked.

"A few twists, but a direct route, more or less," Neill answered. In the stillness, he could hear himself breathing. "Provided we don't run into any obstacles."

Crockett peered into the darkness. Steel beams and stanchions were irregularly spaced, bracing the walls and supporting the rock above them. "I've been here before, Mike."

The captain blinked. "*Dejà vu?*"

Nate shook his head. "Not literally—and not here."

"Someplace like this, then?" Taylor quizzed.

"Yeah, Doc. The Simserhof bunker, in France. It's an artillery work, combat fortification. Part of the Maginot Line."

Neill glanced up. "When were you in France?"

"After my first deployment. Rented a car and spent a week touring the countryside. I was a sergeant at the time."

"Before you came to the dark side," Neill joked. The two officers almost forgot where they were—deep in a mountain, one controlled by the Russian military.

"Yep. Before the shiny stuff." Crockett tugged at his collar, but his rank wasn't there. And then it came to him.

He was wearing another country's uniform, prepared to commit espionage against a foreign power—an old enemy, one that had attacked an American ship of the line—and taken the life of a special young woman. Nate might have nursed that thought under different circumstances, but this wasn't the time.

He buried those feelings. The present situation demanded focus. So far, the small band of raiders had been fortunate, and Nate hoped their luck would hold. Experience warned him not to count on it.

He was reassured on several fronts; for one, he was well-trained, a sharpshooter, skilled in CQB—close quarters battle. Small arms and resolve were his bread and butter, and he knew he could count on his rifle.

That, and the friends who surrounded him.

He glanced again at Chingkut's map. They were getting closer. But they still had a ways to go.

Nate shouldered his ruck, and the team set off for the tunnel entrance.

They had covered almost a mile. Rounding a corner, beams of light criss-crossed their path, and like a moth to the flame, Crockett drew near. Each was narrow and intense—slivers of red that illuminated the tunnel and made goggles and chem sticks unnecessary. The beams moved every second, shifting in a synchronized dance.

Nate signaled the others with a raised fist. Everyone stopped in their tracks.

"Not good, Mike. Modulating sensors, and never the same pattern. We might have a chance with a static system—we could see which beams to avoid. But these are changing too fast."

Brisbane's voice came from behind. "Motion detectors. Am I right?"

"I wish you weren't, Doc," Nate said over his shoulder. "It's no wonder they don't patrol these tunnels. This is sophisticated, next-gen stuff. Emitters on both sides. Probably infrared, too; break a light source and you set off an alarm."

"Is there another way? An alternate route?"

There was no need to check the chart. Neill already knew the answer to that question.

"I'm afraid not. We were warned—the lower levels are more secure."

"Chingkut's map doesn't say anything about a security system," Crockett grumped.

"Must be recent, then," Neill suggested.

"What does this mean?"

"I would think that's pretty obvious, Doc." Nate's words came in a growl, and he cursed under his breath. "This technology's stopped us dead in our tracks.

"We're not going anywhere."

24

THE BELLY OF THE BEAST

Joint Base Elmendorf-Richardson, Alaska

IT WAS UNSEASONABLY COLD, but there was no snow falling now, and the white-capped mountains grew darker with each passing day. The Alaskan wilderness was coming back to life; black bears and grizzlies foraged with their young, and up and down the foothills moose could be seen, eating the tender shoots of spring.

Nick Tate faced the flight line, his back to the glacier valley rising in the east. Four F/A-38s were parked on the apron to his left; sleek, with sharp angles and dagger-like features. Even chocked and blocked, the warbirds looked menacing. And one of those jets was his.

The door to Air Ops slid open. Christian Prentice stepped through and squinted, then pulled on a pair of aviators to fight the glare; winter was slow to release her grip, but she couldn't hold back the sun.

"What's the word, boss?" the major asked. "Did you see the wing king?"

"Yeah," the colonel grunted. "ARCTIC WRATH is a go. We'll commence ordnance testing as soon as the weapons arrive."

Tate was almost giddy. "Live fire. Hot damn." An AWACS taxied on the runway, and he raised his voice to be heard. "What's on tap till then?"

Prentice eyed the first Hellcat in the neatly spaced row. His name appeared in elegant script below the cockpit, placed there by an unknown employee of Aileron Dynamix.

"Prep the birds. Run a few scenarios." His focus was on the narrow route winding behind the air freight building. "At least the weather's improving. Maybe we can get in a little sightseeing."

Tate had no objections to that. This was his first trip to The Last Frontier. "How do they keep 'em clear? The roads, I mean. And the runways. Do they use salt?"

"For the snow?" The colonel shook his head. "They can't. Not here. Salt attracts wildlife."

"Seriously?"

Prentice smiled behind his Ray-Bans. The major was clearly not a hunter. "Never heard of a salt lick?" He gestured toward the hilltops. "Lots of bear and moose out there. Inviting them on to the flight line's a bad idea."

The pilots headed in the direction of the parking lot, where both had rentals. Rounding the corner they braced against a stiff north wind.

"So no salt. Makes sense," Tate allowed.

Prentice nodded. "Alaska's one state that will try to kill you, Nick. She doesn't need any extra help."

Arkangel Base

The Russian stared blankly, first at the request, and then at Tanya Zhukov.

"CO_2—or carbon dioxide?" Pavel Varushkin said. "Which is it?"

"They are the same thing," Tanya told him. *Stupid infantryman.* She bit her tongue, summoning all her patience. These new Federation troops were Neanderthals.

Pavel's expression remained fixed. He pretended to study the paperwork. "Why do you need it?"

Tanya held back the agitation. She drew in a deep breath and began to explain slowly. "Fire protection, primarily. CO_2 is an extinguishing agent. We use it in the labs, and it's also needed aboard the *Commissar.*"

"And you've run out?" The Russian scanned the page for signatures. It was endorsed by the watch commander, and countersigned by Dr. Zhukov himself.

"Close to it," Tanya said. "It's best to have enough on hand. Like your weapons." She glanced at the rifles arranged on the near wall. "I'm sure you prefer having lots of ammunition, rather than none." Getting permission for simple tasks was a way of life at Arkangel—she'd come to accept that—but of late, the military had made things more onerous.

It wasn't just bureaucratic policy that proved an irritation. On a personal level, Tanya was repulsed. She'd seen the way they stared, their leering eyes always following her. If for only that reason, she despised these troops. Her dealings with them were something to be avoided. And on top of that, on a professional plane, she hated bowing and scraping to these unsophisticated brutes. Pavel's next question proved that point.

"It's not flammable, is it?"

Tanya gave him a quizzical look. "If it were flammable, we couldn't spray it on fire, now could we?"

You really are *an idiot,* she didn't say.

The Russian was rightly chagrined. "I suppose I can authorize this." He reddened, looking back at the request. "These chemicals are stored in the tunnel?"

"*Da*, in the primary passage—Alpha 21," she told

him. "Near the east-west trunk line." There was a chart mounted on the wall, and Tanya pointed. "We have a storage room here."

"But why you? Shouldn't you send some underling?"

I could send you, *mush-for-brains,* she wanted to say, but she held her peace. Tanya smiled sweetly instead.

"It's still early." She waved a hand toward the hangar, beyond the guardhouse. "None of my colleagues are here yet—and I need it now."

"Can you manage it alone?"

Tanya hadn't expected him to be so helpful, but she didn't want him tagging along, either. "I'm taking the UTV. I'll be fine, Corporal."

Pavel soured, irritation in his grumbled reply.

"It's *Sergeant*."

"Where's she going?" Vladimir Baskovich wanted to know.

Pavel handed him the request, and they watched as Tanya got into a service cart. She turned the key, and in a moment's time, the vehicle crossed the hangar and made for the tunnel.

"Supplies. Something for the aircraft." Pavel gave his comrade a puzzled look. "It's your day off. Why aren't you in the gym?"

Vlad ignored the question. "She's going alone?"

Varushkin shrugged. "It can't wait, apparently."

The big Russian exited the guardhouse.

"Disable the sensors," he called back. Vlad had an expression of undisguised lust. "At the far end of the tunnel."

"Near the grotto?" Pavel frowned. "But she's not going that far."

"Just do it," Vlad directed.

• • • •

Crockett checked his watch. Deep in the bowels of the mountain it was his only way of relating to the world above.

"It's daylight, Mike," he announced. "Topside, anyway."

Neill stirred from his position on the floor. His ruck made a poor pillow, but he'd slept nonetheless.

He scanned their surroundings. Nothing had changed since they'd stopped; the security system remained active, the strands of light like a spider's web blocking their path. The beams created patterns on the walls, illuminating the anteroom they were stuck in.

Voskov lay in one corner, sleeping soundly. Brisbane was curled up in the other, unmoving beneath Neill's field jacket. The Marine found humor in that. There was more humidity in the tunnel, but the Aussie woman had complained of being cold, shivering in the depths.

"Are you hungry?" Yuri was heating his food. "Give me your meal. It's time for breakfast." His English was improving.

Neill complied, opening the package with a knife. "I've been meaning to ask you something, Yuri."

"We have plenty of time for that, Mischa." Unfortunately, that was true.

"It's about Xander," Mike began. "What's his background? Personally, I mean. He's a hard one to figure out."

Tereshenko winced. "He's a tortured soul, Mischa. You have seen this, yes?"

"I have. He's suffered loss—am I right?"

Yuri gave a nod. "Xander had a wife. Her name was Anya." He lowered his voice. "They were married for two years, and then she was killed in the revolution."

Neill's mind raced back. "The Maidan?"

"Yes—it was in Kiev, Independence Square." The memory visibly saddened the senior sergeant.

"She was a protestor?"

"No, not protestor." Yuri shook his head. "She was journalist, covering the uprising."

"A journalist?" Neill's eyes widened at the news. "Is that why he's drawn to Viktoriya?"

Yuri poured water into a pouch. "I think in spite of it, Mischa." He chuckled. "If you recall, their relationship had a rough start."

"I remember. It must have been difficult for him."

"I wish you could have known her. Anya and Viktoriya are—*were*—very much alike. Enterprising, idealistic, and noble of heart. Xander misses her terribly, but in this time his life is full again." Yuri tasted his food; it was hot now, while Neill's breakfast had only begun to warm. "After she died—after the revolution, the Berkut were disbanded, and Xander and I were recruited by the Security Directorate."

Neill pondered that but let it go. Voskov wasn't the only one grieving here. Mike turned to Crockett, and in the quiet of the moment, he decided to broach a sensitive topic.

"We haven't had much time to talk since the *Meyer*," he started slowly. "I just wanted you to know—I'm very sorry about Bailee."

There was pain on Crockett's face. "Stow it, Mike. It wasn't your fault."

"It wasn't yours, either. Don't forget that." He was pushing it, but kept going anyway. "If you'd been there, you might've died, too."

"You're not very good at this, are you?" There was an edge to Nate's voice, and he thought it best to change the subject. He tacked in a different direction. "By the way, you haven't said much about our extraction." He waved a hand toward the shifting beams. "That might come in handy, seein' as how our forward progress has come to naught."

"We're not leaving yet." Neill pretended annoyance. "And when did you become such a pessimist?"

"Hey, I'm just sayin'." Tereshenko's food smelled good, and Crockett was getting hungrier by the minute. "Reality's a wet blanket, Mike. I don't like it either, but we might have to rethink things."

Nate expected some kind of a reply, but the captain said nothing.

"There is a plan, right?"

"There's a plan. But it's probably best if we don't discuss it here." Neill tilted his head toward the hall. "If Ivan's got gear like that, who knows what else he might be using."

Crockett understood. "Or listening with," he added. "Operational security. Good call."

Neill started to speak, but something was different. The strobing red beams in the passage had winked out, leaving the room without light. This was unforeseen, and for several seconds no one moved.

Nate's voice finally echoed in the darkness. "*Whiskey tango*—what just happened?"

"I have no idea." Neill clicked on his flashlight and pointed the beam at the tunnel. "But let's make the most of it while it lasts."

"Wait, Mike." The sniper was cautious by nature, especially in tactical situations. "The system just shuts down—for no apparent reason? I'd say that's awfully convenient, wouldn't you?"

"You think it's a trap?"

"Possibly. Ivan might have heard us before, and now he's trying to draw us in."

Neill considered that. He lowered his flashlight and

turned an ear toward the opening. There was nothing to hear, and the passage remained empty.

He made his decision. "We came here to stop Charybdis. If we stay on this side of the tunnel that won't happen."

"There you go, usin' logic again," Crockett deadpanned. "Okay, I'm with you, boss. I say we chance it."

"Come what may." Neill's tone was more exuberant now, and he was standing. "Nate, rouse the Doc. Yuri, get Voskov on his feet."

"What about your breakfast?"

"We'll do carry-out." Neill grabbed the food and stuffed it into his pack. "Now pick up your gear and let's get moving."

25

DEATH IN THE GROTTO

NEILL'S RED-FILTERED LIGHT played along the walls, but there was little to pique his interest. This stretch of the passage was marked by the mundane. Fire extinguishers, sealed doors, and power cables ran overhead. It was dank and musty here, and the scent in the air was a mixture of diesel fuel and seawater.

He related to Crockett's earlier comparison. Bunkers were bunkers, and Mike had visited his share. Most were Soviet emplacements in Ukraine, usually abandoned, and always austere and heavily fortified. None were intended for the claustrophobic. The lowest levels of Arkangel base were no different.

According to Chingkut's diagram they were getting close, and Neill let the beam of his flashlight linger. Some features stuck out, and a few were noteworthy.

"Another sensor array," he announced. "Just like the first one."

"Inactive, thankfully," Crockett added. He couldn't figure why the system was dead. "What gives, Mike?"

Neill didn't have an answer. He stopped and lowered

his light, scanning ahead. At their feet was an inch of water, seepage from porous rock at sea level.

Xander stepped up. "Do you see something?"

Neill cautioned silence. "Faint glow at the far end," he whispered. He gripped his weapon a little tighter. "Signs of life, maybe?"

"Perhaps," the Ukrainian muttered. He turned to his comrade. "Yuri—"

"*Duzhe dobre.*" Tereshenko knelt and pulled a device from his ruck. A wire and ear buds were attached.

"Parabolic microphone?" Nate asked.

Voskov understood. "Yes," he answered. "*Parabolichny.*"

Yuri took point and aimed the small dish forward. He listened for a moment before shaking his head.

"Nothing to speak of, Mischa. Some ambient noise; wind, possibly." He kept the gear handy. "Besides that, quiet as a tomb."

"What's our game plan?" Crockett asked.

Neill studied the far side of the tunnel. "We've got to find Charybdis first. That means getting into the hangar."

"Or a control room. Ivan might have a prototype laying around, something they use for testing."

Neill turned to Brisbane. "What do you say, Doc?"

"To be useful, the test-bed would need to be full-size, or close to it." She shook her head. "We can't walk out of here with something that big."

"All right, then, back to the original plan. We look for schematics or technical orders." Neill had already worked this out in his head. "Worst-case scenario, we download whatever data we find—"

"— and get the heck out of Dodge," Nate finished.

"Dodge?"

Taylor smiled at Yuri's question. "A Western euphemism, Sergeant."

"Very Western," Nate grinned.

. . . .

The passage narrowed. Tanya kept her eyes ahead, and after one more turn, the stores locker came into sight. She parked the UTV and killed its electric motor.

Vlad was skulking in the shadows not far behind. Approaching a corner, the big Russian peered down the hall, spying his quarry some distance away.

Tanya slid out of the seat and tried the door. She frowned. As expected, the knob turned freely; the science staff rarely kept this room locked, and Tanya wondered if that was good policy. There were pilferable items stored inside—some potentially dangerous—and the black market was alive and well. The temptation might prove too great for the new Russian troops, but that was something she'd have to take up with her father.

She pushed through, the ancient steel creaking on its hinges. As the door swung to, Tanya found the switch, and in the glare of the overheads she saw what she'd come for.

Small canisters were arranged on a shelf in one corner. Empties were stacked nearby, waiting for replacements from Petropavlovsk. Several had accumulated, and the resupply truck wasn't scheduled for weeks. That wouldn't do, so Tanya made a mental note—

Her silent musings were interrupted by the groaning of the hatch. She turned in time to see it open before the lights went out—and then the shadow looming in the doorway.

She couldn't say what happened next. Her attacker reached out and pulled her close. Tanya had let down her guard, but now she screamed. Strong arms pinned hers, and one wrapped around her throat.

Deprived of air, Tanya became limp, and the world

around her faded to black.

• • • •

Crockett's attention was suddenly drawn ahead. Things had been quiet, but from somewhere down the hall came a sound none of them expected to hear.

Taylor was the first to speak. "That was a woman's voice."

"No, Doc, that was a woman's *scream*," Neill corrected. "Where are we?"

Xander checked the map, pointing. "We're here, Mikhail." The diagram showed the passage angling west. Hand-written notes filled the margin. "The tunnel branches off just ahead. There's a spur that opens to the sea. Chingkut calls it *the grotto*."

Another cry, more urgent this time, but suddenly silenced. It echoed around them. Crockett was apprehensive, but something tugged at him, and he couldn't ignore what he heard.

"Guns up, people." He checked the safety on his rifle. "Mike?"

"It's on the way," Neill told him. "Let's check it out."

• • • •

Tanya was awake now, and none too soon.

Rough hands tore her clothing, and the young woman's blouse was ripped away. She was on her back, limbs flailing, struggling hard against her attacker. The screams only angered the Russian.

He hadn't counted on this. The doctor's daughter wasn't being the least bit compliant. This only excited him more. He slapped her hard, forcing her head to one side. She cried out again, and this time he put a hand over her mouth.

Tanya was desperate to stop him. She squirmed and

tried shifting her body. In return, Baskovich leveraged his weight. As long as he stayed on top, he could use his bulk to maintain control. But he left himself open. The target was easy to find, and Tanya kicked viciously.

Vlad grunted in pain. The way she fought back enraged him. He groped lower, curling his fingers around the waistline of her skirt and pushing down.

Tanya gave him nothing, fighting hard against her assailant's grip. She could smell his sweat, hear the horrible guttural sounds he made. And in the midst of her peril, one thought came to mind.

Where was she?

She managed to turn her face. The UTV was nearby. The harsh glare of a single bulb brought light, reflecting off a stone wall, and out of sight, she could hear the lapping of water against rock.

The grotto, she told herself. But knowing where she was didn't help. It only inspired more fear.

He'll kill you—then dump your body in the pool . . .

Tanya twisted beneath him. She had to survive. She owed that much to her father. He had lost so much; first, his wife. Before that, the Soviets had stolen any chance for a normal life. All that remained was his work, and under Admiral Pavlenko's rule, he had lost the will to live.

"*Get off me,*" she pleaded.

Surprisingly, he did, but not on his own.

Something had added its weight to the monster on top of her. The force drove air from her lungs. And then the weight lifted, and Tanya—still kicking—saw the big Russian pulled backwards.

Tereshenko had the infantryman in a headlock, the crook of his arm tightening against Vlad's throat. He was smaller than the Russian, but matched his adversary's ferocity. To win, he would have to exceed it.

Yuri held on, tightening his grip and crushing the

man's windpipe. His hold was like iron. Even before he entered the fray, the Ukrainian knew he couldn't let this brute live.

If the Russian survived, the mission was done.

Vlad struggled to breathe, tried to shake his foe, but in vain. He was starting to fade. He now felt a hand on his forehead. The unseen enemy kept one arm in place, using the other to brace against his shoulder, and as the cruel beast drew his last breath, Tereshenko twisted with everything he had.

· · · ·

"He's done, Yuri. Let him go."

Nate and Taylor rushed to the sobbing woman's side. Her torn blouse lay at her feet. She scooped it up and held it close.

Neill approached from the side. It was best to gauge Tereshenko's state of mind before rushing in.

But Yuri heard and understood. He released his grip, and Vladimir Baskovich slumped to the ground.

"I had to stop him, Mischa." His chest heaved.

"It was nothing any of us wouldn't have done," Neill said. He couldn't fault Yuri, and wouldn't, even if he'd had grounds to. "But now we have a problem."

"We've got two," Crockett said.

Nate was right. The girl made for one. The dead man another. In the Russian's case, the circumstances might prove more dire. He wore a uniform, which meant he was base personnel. In time, a roster would be checked, or a formation would be one man short. He'd come up missing. Someone—sooner, probably, rather than later—would notice his absence, and it was only a matter of time before his comrades came looking.

26

LEVERAGE

"**W**HO ARE YOU?" Tanya's eyes were wide with terror. "How did you get here?"

Taylor knelt and tried a woman's touch—soothing words, and then she helped with the torn clothing. It was enough at first, until Tanya saw the body at Yuri's feet.

"He followed me here." Her voice rose. "He would have killed me."

"*Captain Neill*," Brisbane called. She needed an interpreter. "Can you *help*, please?"

Yuri stepped in before Mike could react. He moved forward and took a knee.

"No, no, no, *Meela*. Don't look at him—look at *me*." His tone was gentle, reassuring. He tried Russian first. "He can't hurt you anymore—*panymyoo*?"

Tanya looked into his face. "Yes—I understand."

"You speak Ukrainian." Yuri smiled. Moisture beaded on his face. "*Dobre*—that's good, Meela."

She was relieved when he continued in her mother tongue. "My name's not *Meela*. It's Tanya."

"Forgive me. Ludmilla was my grandmother's name.

She was a fighter, too." Tereshenko's voice softened even more. "My name is Yuri. Do your friends call you Tanya?"

"Yes," she said simply. She looked at those around her. For the moment she was safe, breathing easier now.

Neill marveled at this side of Tereshenko's personality. The change was striking—defender, avenger, and killer one moment, sympathetic consoler the next. Even Voskov was taken aback, but the woman seemed to respond.

Yuri waved at hand at the others. "My companions and I—we would like to be your friends, too, Tanya. Will you trust us?"

There was a pause. *I'll bet the jury's still out on that one,* Neill thought. But what the girl said next surprised him.

She was staring into Yuri's eyes. "You saved my life."

The lanky sergeant reached out. "Give me your hand, then, *Meela*.

"It's time we left this place."

Petropavlovsk

Taras Pavlenko had spent a restless night. It was concern that robbed him of sleep. Despite a long list of accomplishments, he had the nagging sense that something had been left undone, and the admiral needed assurances.

Lingering in bed was pointless. He rose and dressed in fatigues, then summoned a car. The driver was prompt, and the route to the admiralty clear of traffic. The commute to the headquarters building took less time than normal, and once there, Pavlenko watched the dull glow of sunrise from his office.

Hot tea was first, a daily ritual. The senior officer

settled in, impressed by the punctuality of his staff. An intelligence specialist had already stopped by and delivered the morning brief; two paragraphs summarizing overnight developments, clippings from *Pravda* and *Izvestia*, but mostly printed material from the internet. The admiral skimmed them all. Nothing new, he saw, just more of the same knee-jerk reaction he'd come to expect.

But no declaration of war.

The American president was slow to act. No doubt his advisors cautioned against a military response. Moscow had come to expect this from his predecessor; Mark Breese had never served in uniform, and was rumored to despise his own military. In the run-up to his election, Charles Cassidy had voiced a much tougher stand against would-be aggressors.

Given the events of the past few days, Pavlenko had formed a new opinion. The United States was weak, he decided. President Cassidy was still blustering, but in a show of bipartisan cooperation, both houses of the U.S. Congress were crafting new legislation, measures designed to hurt the *Rodina*. Pavlenko snorted at that. *Laws, not action.* The community of nations had already stung them enough, but politics was a blood sport, and Cassidy's constituents wanted their pound of flesh.

It was all retribution for the attack on the U.S. naval vessel. The admiral understood that. The game had rules, and if positions were reversed, his countrymen might demand the same. Truth be told, Taras didn't think the sortie against the *Meyer* went far enough, but it was gratifying to know that his work here in Petropavlovsk—and by extension, at Arkangel—would soon bear fruit for Mother Russia.

Pavlenko digested the analyst's assessment. Sipping the last of his tea, he made the first tactical decision of the day, retrieving his phone and placing a call, giving no thought to the time.

"Comrade Admiral." Captain Tamarkin was an early riser, his office two floors away. "What can I do for you this morning?"

Taras didn't wade in. He charged wholeheartedly. "I require your judgment—on an officer's fitness to command." He sat back in his chair as an aide brought in breakfast, and waited until he closed the door behind him. "I speak of Colonel Utkin."

"Arkangel Base." Tamarkin pursed his lips. "A competent administrator. No blemishes on his record. Why do you ask, comrade Admiral?"

"The colonel has shown some hesitation. A certain reluctance. He may require oversight."

"Of course, sir," Tamarkin answered. *What was this about?* "Has his performance slipped?"

"Not yet."

"But you are worried that it might."

"Some situations call for discretion, Captain. A subtle touch."

"But not all, sir."

Pavlenko sipped from his teacup. "No, not all," he agreed. "As I often say, don't wait for opportunity—"

"—go after it with a hammer," Tamarkin said, finishing his patron's thought.

Pavlenko chuckled. "And so you take my meaning well."

This would be an additional duty, Tamarkin realized. "When should I be ready to leave?"

So much of the captain's value lay in his intuitive responses. Pavlenko liked that in an officer. For one thing, it made for short discussions, free from unnecessary banter. It also reinforced the admiral's decisions. Knowing that his subordinates could anticipate commands, and act accordingly, gave him confidence in his own judgment.

"Two days, I should think, Captain. Possibly sooner." He looked at his calendar. "In fact, I'll join you."

"More leverage, Admiral?"

A job needed doing. *Why not?*

Pavlenko's eyes were on the window. To the northeast, beyond the horizon, was a military base. For some time, its population had been a fixed number, but Arkangel's census was about to change.

•   •   •   •

"You've come for my father, haven't you, Captain Neill?"

The introductions had been made. Names were exchanged. For his part, Yuri was doubly chivalrous; Tanya now wore his field jacket, her arms folded across her chest.

"Your father?" Neill blinked. The name registered now. "Zhukov. Dr. Zhukov—you're his *daughter*?"

The question went unanswered, and Tanya lifted her chin. "If not *papa*, the *Commissar*, then. You seek the *Commissar*."

Neill decided to lay his cards on the table. "I'm not familiar with that name, Ms. Zhukov. We've come for Charybdis."

"*Mikhail*," Xander cautioned.

The team, plus one, stood just outside the grotto entrance. There was a draft here, cool air brought in by sea breezes. At the far end of the cave were the first hints of daylight.

"The *Commissar* is only a plane." Tanya was playing defense. "Charybdis is the weapon itself. Both are out of your reach."

"And why is that, Meela?" Yuri asked.

"There are too many troops," she spat out. "Naval infantrymen. *Marines*. More arrived just days ago."

"Maybe you could help with that," Neill suggested. "We'd very much like to get a look at the *Commissar*."

"To learn her secrets?" She shook her head. "Those belong to my father. Preserving them has kept him alive." Tanya eyed Brisbane curiously. Men with guns she understood, but what was this woman's purpose in coming? "If you're here to kill *papa*, get in line. The Russians would like nothing more."

"We've come to *stop* the killing." Yuri's tone was even. "People are dying, Meela. Innocent people. The Russians have done this, and it must stop."

The Russians, Neill reminded himself. They were ignoring the most likely threat. He turned to Crockett. "Lieutenant?"

"On it, boss."

"Quietly, Nate," Neill advised.

The sniper looked pained. "Is there any other way?"

Crockett set off down the hall, stopping every few meters. He reached the first turn and rounded the corner. The way ahead was quiet, the tunnel empty. It was the same at the next leg. Satisfied with what he'd seen, Nate retraced his steps.

"Clear," he announced, rejoining the group.

Neill gave a nod and faced Tanya. "We're at a cross-roads, Ms. Zhukov," he said, and then asked, "What do you intend to do?"

Uncertainty clouded her thinking, but she made her decision. "I won't turn you in, if that's what you're worried about." She looked to the grotto. "I *can't*."

Xander dropped his voice to a whisper. "She's right, Mikhail. One of their men is dead. The Russians might hold her responsible in some way."

Yuri asked the obvious question. "Then what should

we do with the body? When they discover he's miss-ing—"

"—they'll come looking for him. I know. We can't just leave him." Neill dug at the floor with his boot. "And we can't bury him. This is all volcanic rock."

Xander offered a suggestion. "There are side tunnels, places we haven't explored. One of those could hide—"

"Dump his body there," Tanya broke in. She pointed toward the cave. "In the pool. The tide will do the rest."

Neill looked at the woman. "Water's low right now, but that'll change." He liked the idea, despite its morbid nature. "With any luck, the Russians will never find him."

Tereshenko was worried. "And if they do, Mischa?"

"He slipped and fell. Blunt force trauma." Voskov tapped the butt of his rifle. "Most unfortunate."

Problem solved, Neill decided. *Sort of.*

"Ms. Zhukov, did anyone see you come down here?"

"The sentry, at the guardhouse. I came for supplies."

"You'll have to go back the same way, then—without arousing suspicion. Can you do that?"

"Yes," she nodded. "I can do that."

"Act as if nothing happened," Xander told her. He touched the sleeve of Yuri's jacket. "And you can't be seen wearing this."

"I can change in the storeroom."

"What about us?" Yuri asked.

Tanya glanced at Voskov. "Your friend is right—there are other tunnels in the mountain, places the Russians don't go. If you won't leave—and I strongly suggest that you do—then you should hide there."

"Like I said, we've come for Charybdis."

Her eyes flashed. "That's a fool's errand, Captain. You'll get yourselves killed."

"At least we'll die trying." Neill used a more direct

approach. "Will you help us, Tanya?"

She expected the appeal. And they had saved her life; Tanya was convinced of that. Two Ukrainians—three, counting the *kapitan*; an American—his counterpart—and the woman, whose nationality Tanya could only guess at. Showing up here was foolish, no matter what their intentions might be, but she felt an obligation to this little group. And no other option presented itself.

"Stay clear of the motion sensors," she warned. "Security has grown tight."

"So we've noticed," Neill agreed. "You still haven't answered my question."

He was pressing her, and Tanya gave him a studied look. This one was a puzzle. He spoke Ukrainian like a native, but had a Western name. And somehow he'd managed to lead a team into the very heart of the base.

How had they penetrated the Russian defenses? she wondered silently. *And who had sent them?*

She had one clue to go on; they all carried weapons, except for the woman. This was a military operation, and these five were seeking a target. Everything pointed to the hangar. Her rescuer had been right; people *were* dying. Even though she was cut off from the rest of the world, the plane's purpose was clear. Under the Russian yoke, she had helped to refine it. *Commissar* was a threat, and Charybdis as well.

Tanya had grown to hate them both.

"I'll speak to my father," she said at last. "But I can promise nothing."

•   •   •   •

Pavel Varushkin checked the clock on the wall; nearly an hour had passed, and still no sign of anyone.

Something wasn't right.

The doctor's daughter had gone into the tunnel first,

and then Baskovich. Pavel wore a smirk. He knew why Vlad had followed her. The big Russian wasn't shy about his intentions; he was a loudmouth, with no filter, always broadcasting what he'd like to do to the young woman. He should have been more careful. Instead, he thought only with his—

Pavel's head turned. He heard the high-pitched whine of an electric motor, and the UTV emerged from the narrow passage, bumping across the threshold. Tanya was at the wheel, alone. She drove the little cart beneath the *Commissar*'s wings, parked by the lab door, and hopped out.

Varushkin craned his neck, angling for a better view. He counted three silver canisters in the girl's arms, and to the sergeant's eyes, she was none the worse for wear.

Her errand to the storeroom had taken longer than expected. He wondered about that and eyed the electrical panel. She was back now, but Pavel couldn't reboot the system—not just yet. Baskovich was still down there, and his wanderings might set off the alarm.

He did a quick check of the roster. The big Russian's next shift fell at midnight. He'd be back. Technically, Vlad had time off, and to Pavel's way of thinking, the man wasn't missing at all. Not yet.

• • • •

"What now?"

Nate leaned his rifle against the wall. "Now we wait, Professor. And plan for the what-ifs."

"The what-ifs?"

"Contingencies, Doc," Neill grinned tiredly. "As in, *what if she's lying,* and decides to turn us in? Or, *what if a dozen troops show up with guns*?" He was playing the realist now. "Don't forget, Tanya's first loyalty is to her father. She'll protect his interests before ours."

Brisbane found it hard to disagree. She began to con-
jure her own what-ifs. Fueled by doubt, they were hard
to shake. She didn't mind as long as they were moving,
progressing with the mission, but faced with inactivity—
or waiting, as Crockett had put it—those concerns were
stirred again.

One went to the heart of her worries.

Suppose she couldn't identify the weapon?

That seemed unlikely. The nature of Charybdis was
beyond dispute. It was a known quantity in a fixed location. They knew where to find it. All they had to do was
get close, and that meant a trip inside the hangar.

It was Neill's offhand comment that really got under
her skin. That was a worst-case scenario, but not beyond
the realm of possibility. What if the Russians *did* show
up, guns at the ready? Excuses wouldn't count for much
here; they were deep in Federation territory, and being
on their turf was no 'accident of navigation'.

The most likely outcome involved their arrest and a
trial for espionage. Conviction was a foregone conclusion, but what then? If war was imminent, extradition
was a slim possibility. Taylor pictured a grim gulag, in
some cold, nameless place, spending the rest of her days
as a political prisoner—

And the Marine was *still* talking. "Who knows? Ivan
might have eyes and ears in places—"

Taylor cut him off. Curtly.

"I think I get the gist of it, Captain," she told him.

27

LAYING LOW

SHE DIDN'T FIDGET. That was a nervous tic others might display, but not Tanya Zhukov.

When Tanya was anxious or otherwise preoccupied, her temperament ran in other directions. She became quiet to the point of withdrawal. She sulked, shutting out the world, receding into one of her own making. Some thought her to be overly aloof at times like these, but those who knew her well shrugged it off and gave the young woman her space.

Not so with Radya Zhukov.

"You're not yourself today, *dochka*." Her father approached the workstation tentatively, tenderly. Something had upset her. "Is everything all right?"

Tanya couldn't deny her distracted state. The assault in the grotto had shaken her—the trooper's death even more—but she had managed to keep it to herself. With Pavlenko's goons around, she'd gotten good at segregating her feelings, ignoring the looks from over her shoulder, the close scrutiny of their Russian masters. But she couldn't hide that brooding melancholy from her father.

The shift had come and gone. Another day at an end. Her colleagues began drifting out of the room, bidding the Zhukovs a polite goodbye. Only Roman Shapoval remained, securing a welding hood in the tool locker, his coveralls stained with grease. The chief engineer had a bone-tired look in his eyes.

"Everything is fine, *papa*." Tanya stiffened, forcing a smile, but her hands had started to shake. Two empty CO_2 canisters lay conspicuously on the bench at her side.

Hold it together, she told herself. *You can do this.*

"Would you help me return these to the storeroom?"

Radya gave her a puzzled look. "That can wait. Give them to Sergei in the morning."

Tanya stared back, unflinching. There was something very assertive in her eyes.

"No, *papa*. We have to do this *now*."

Nikolayev, Ukraine

In the aftermath of Soviet domination, much of Ukraine's progress was tied to foreign aid. That had been set in motion early on, and was a strategic decision, as well as a humanitarian one. The West needed an ally in that part of the world, and so, propped up by American financial institutions—many strong-armed into the deal—the republic had prospered. The transition was difficult at first, but now, after years of crushing debt, the buffer between old and new could enjoy the fruits of her labors, a measure of affluence shared with (and fostered by) the United States.

It was popular to think they'd turned a corner, and in many ways they had.

None of that was lost on the general. Andrei Ulyanov had lived it, and thought about it often, usually when his eyes tracked north, tracing the horizon's features as they touched the sky. *And why shouldn't Ukrainians take pride in their newfound good fortune?* Agricultural co-operatives were operating at peak efficiency, and exports were at a record high. Nuclear facilities were much safer in this post-Cold War era, and clean energy sources had started to emerge. Ulyanov's good friend, President Pav-lovsk, had proclaimed an end to the past. Life was good now, and even greater prosperity lay just around the cor-ner.

But that was folly, and Ulyanov knew it better than most.

While some things had changed, many had not. The world truly was different, there was no denying that. Al-liances had shifted—none more dramatic, to Andrei's mind, than the close ties his nation now shared with NATO and the European Union. But every ying had its yang; corruption in his beloved Ukraine was rampant, and the rule of law couldn't go where a change of heart was needed most. Sometimes Ulyanov wondered how Pavlovsk himself had escaped the touch of compromise; or if, in fact, he actually had.

Greed and avarice weren't the worst of the republic's problems. To the north and east, an old adversary lin-gered, a phoenix in the ashes, one determined to absorb Ukraine's vast natural resources. And now the EU was fractured. *What next?* Ulyanov knew the answer to that. The Russians would continue their march across Eastern Europe, expanding their territory—

Enough.

The general pushed those thoughts aside, ending his pointless reverie. There were other matters to deal with. A stack of unfinished paperwork called to him—the bane of his existence. *A small matter in the greater scheme of things*, he reasoned. None of that was going anywhere, and beyond the air-conditioned confines of his office, the flight line offered familiar and comforting distractions.

Ulyanov's attention was drawn to the heart of the air base. There was no shortage of activity there. At one end of the runway was a squadron of six Polish helicopters, Mi-24D Hinds, a venerated platform designed by Soviet engineers. Drifting in from the west—or floating, rather—was a tandem-seat Sukhoi Su-34, hardpoints empty of ordnance, its heavy wheel struts deployed for landing. The fighter was on final approach, but her movements were sluggish, almost inelegant.

Stick time for the navigator, Ulyanov decided. If that were the case, he could imagine the directives being issued in the cockpit. Andrei smiled. He'd been there himself. The pilot would be walking a fine line between trust and oversight, verbalizing a checklist that would put the aircraft safely on the ground.

Watch the control surfaces. Check thrust. Keep your nose up and your eyes—

A light rapping sound, and then the interruption.

"She's escaped."

Ulyanov turned, scowling. It was Dmitri.

"*Who's* escaped?"

Yaroslav's tone suggested bad news. He closed the door behind him. "That Kolvec woman. The one we arrested in Kiev."

The general's brow furrowed. "*Nadia* Kolvec? Boris Isakov's consort?"

"One and the same." He produced a color photo and dropped it on the desk. "Beautiful, is she not? Especially around the eyes."

"Those eyes have seen men die, Dmitri," Ulyanov pointed out. He stepped away from the window. "She was imprisoned at Chernihiv. Occupying Mayakovsky's old cell." That particular irony had struck him.

"But no longer."

Andrei was still wrapping his head around this unhappy news. "One does not simply walk away from a military stockade. How did it happen?"

"She had help," Dmitri growled. He wore his Army uniform, trimmed in the colors of Ukraine's Rocket Forces. "Reports suggest that she and the commandant—the two had a—" he stopped, "—a . . . *physical* relationship."

"It did not end well?"

"Not for Colonel Raviche," Dmitri answered drily. "He was found dead this morning—in Kolvec' cell."

"Murdered." Ulyanov said. It wasn't a question.

A nod. "He succumbed to a knife wound."

Andrei snorted aloud. "He succumbed to more than that. And what of Nadia? Are there any clues to her whereabouts?"

Yaroslav raised a brow and shook his head. "We still had much to learn from her."

"But she never gave up our mole. The Directorate couldn't break her."

That much was true, the major reflected. Maybe she didn't know. Boris Isakov had received material assistance from Moscow, at the state level. It was no small thing if the Federation was collaborating with crime bosses, and Nadia was Isakov's number one. Surely she knew *something*, but short of torture—

The Poles wanted the intel as badly as the SSD. It had become a matter of state security. Ukraine's neighbor to the west didn't like Russian intervention, and her president, Karl Dobrogost, wanted the spy caught.

"A pity. Stealing those codes put the missile shield at risk." Ulyanov narrowed his gaze, regarding Yaroslav with a cold eye. "And I have heard a rumor, Dmitri."

There was a hint of alarm on the officer's face. Yaroslav knew where this was going. He'd heard that rumor too—that the clandestine services of Ukraine had their *own* informant, someone who could draw the net tighter. But the major couldn't speak to that, not even to Ulyanov. Operational security prevented such disclosures.

It was an axiom of intelligence services worldwide; revealing one's hand meant just that—revealing one's hand. The Directorate's information showed promise. Dmitri judged that however speculative the rumor might seem—no matter how abstract—the information gathered so far was completely accurate. State Security was following a trail of breadcrumbs, one that had led to an unlikely location.

"We have received no word from Captain Neill," the major said abruptly. Perhaps it was time to change the subject.

"I didn't ask about Captain Neill," Andrei returned. It wasn't often that he saw Yaroslav ill at ease. "In time, Major. Michael is resourceful."

"And the departure plan?"

"Put your mind at rest, Dmitri. Everything is ready."

"You have a pilot, then."

"Yes, we have a pilot."

Yaroslav chanced another question. "Are you still planning to go?"

"I am," he answered soberly. "I owe that much to his father."

"That's not very advisable, Andrei. Your extraction plan is dangerous."

"Your objection is noted."

General Ulyanov turned to face the flight line once more. Between the maintenance squadron and the tower was a large hangar, sheltering the aircraft of the Mikoyan and Sukhoi design bureaus respectively.

Of late, another plane had come to roost there, an antiquated but reliable transport. It was commonly used by Ukraine's military, and also had commercial applications, but this particular bird had been freshly painted, and now displayed the markings of the Russian Federation.

• • • •

The team gave the space a quick once-over. They had fallen back to an alcove between the grotto and storage locker. It was cold and dark here; condensation dripped from the overheads, and seawater pooled in a corner.

"Only one exit, Mike," Nate observed. "We're boxed in if things go south."

Neill decided it couldn't be helped. This part of the tunnel provided the best cover and concealment, and was far from the nearest sensors.

"This passage isn't maintained, Nate. It's probably unused, but we'll stay close to the entrance. That should increase our options if Ivan comes to call."

Mike found a patch of wall, his AK beside him. The ruck was at his feet, and he retrieved an envelope from the front pouch.

This is as good a time as any, he told himself.

The paper was discolored in places. Christina had sprayed it with her perfume. Neill brought it close and drew in a deep breath, surprised to find that the fragrance still lingered.

He opened it. The card was lighthearted but tender. The first few lines held deep emotion. Like her captain, Arrens valued brevity. She didn't waste words. Her feelings were expressed without being muddled, free of gushing sentiments. Neill was grateful for that.

It's no secret I've been pursuing my degree. By the time I get back, most of my course load will be finished. So what I'm about to say won't come as a surprise . . .

Neill smiled, remembering the last time he'd seen her. The kiss they'd shared. He could still feel the crush of her lips against his, the warmth of her body as they touched. Something akin to loss was tugging at him, and here in this cold pit he wondered why he'd ever let her get away.

I've applied for assignment to Officer Candidate School, through the Enlisted Commissioning Program. Etheridge has been a big help. You taught me to lead from the front, Mike—but don't get the idea that this is all about you.

A zinger. Straight to the heart of his own self-importance. Leave it to Christina to bring him back to Earth. To say that she completed him was too trite, too cliche. Neill disliked that phrase. But the woman could certainly ground his spirit and tether him to reality.

And now she planned to trade her chevrons for bars. She was ambitious, he gave her that. And she was right; he'd been expecting something like this. They'd discussed ways around the regulations, and this course of action would do the trick. They wanted to be together without breaking the rules, and long before their trip to Warsaw, Christina had quietly ramped up her studies.

But this scheme didn't solve everything. In all probability, she'd have to put in for a transfer. The Corps didn't permit fraternization, and relationships within the same command—especially between a senior officer and his subordinate—just wouldn't do.

Neill read further.

I'm doing this for me, Mike; regardless of how I feel about us, I've got to follow my heart, and make career choices in my best interests. I think you can understand that, and I believe you wouldn't have it any other way . . .

The rest would have to wait. There was movement coming from Crockett's side of the room, distracting him. Neill turned. The sniper was using the glow of a chem stick to search his ruck. Yuri did the same.

"Runnin' low, boss. We've got provisions for another two days—maybe three, if we stretch it." He fished out a canteen. "Water's already a problem."

Neill dropped the card back into his pack. He stared at the opposite wall, where the tunnels crossed. *Was that a reflection? Or were his eyes playing—*

"Heads up, people," the captain whispered. He got to his feet, putting the AK's buttstock against his shoulder. There was a light in the hall, and it was moving in their direction.

28

UNINTENDED CONSEQUENCES

VARUSHKIN'S WATCH had ended. *Eight wasted hours,* he grumbled to himself, *tending a docile herd of researchers and technicians.*

Scientists.

Pah!

Pavel was fatigued by boredom. It hadn't taken long to realize that baby-sitting Zhukov's people was pointless. Arrogant, at times, but meek and pliable, sheep who posed no threat. He sputtered a profanity. This assignment blunted a soldier's field skills, and finding new ways to fill the time grew wearisome.

He had one last duty before his relief arrived. Pavel eyed the tunnel again. *Still* no sign of Baskovich. He shrugged it off. Maybe he'd wandered through when Pavel wasn't looking. After all, there were times when duty took him away from the guardhouse; a security sweep of the hangar, walking post around the aircraft, or making a trip to the latrine. Varushkin had done what he could, but if the big Russian was still down there, he was on his own.

Sorry, comrade. Pavel moved to the electrical board. With one last glance at the tunnel opening he threw a switch and closed a circuit.

Perimeter defenses were back online.

The corporal who relieved Pavel had even less to do. The science staff had gone, and he was left minding the largest aircraft in the world. As impressive as the *Commissar* might be, the novelty of the big plane faded quickly.

One thing was different. The sentry was surprised to see the Zhukovs. The doctor was a passenger in the utility cart, while his daughter drove. She stopped at the door, hefting an empty canister.

"Trip to the storage locker." She was informing, not asking. The corporal of the guard nodded in the way sentries did.

Tanya spoke again. "We're doing an inventory. Shouldn't take more than an hour."

Inventory? The corporal thought to challenge that, but the doctor was with her. No, he decided. Best not to rile the old man. He did have unrestricted access to the labyrinth of passageways. That was a concession granted by Admiral Pavlenko long ago.

The corporal relented. He waved them through without a word, watching as the UTV disappeared into the tunnel.

• • • •

Voskov and Tereshenko flanked Neill. Crockett stayed close to Brisbane. The clatter of semi-automatic weapons broke the silence. Muzzles were up and rounds were chambered.

There were two lights, side by side. And a whining sound, one they'd heard before—when Tanya had left them near the grotto. Neill emerged from the shadows, stopping the cart.

Crockett was breathing again. "Well *that* took long enough," he carped to Taylor.

"Dr. Zhukov." Neill stepped forward and stuck out a hand. *I presume* was the natural follow-on, but the Marine resisted.

Radya was wary. His eyes narrowed, adjusting to the darkness. "You were the one who rescued my daughter?"

"No, sir. That would be Sergeant Tereshenko."

"But you're an American."

"Yes, sir, an American. The name's Michael Neill." The captain's rifle was at his side now. He signaled for the others to lower theirs. "And it's a long story."

"You'd better start, then," Zhukov snapped.

Neill did. And the tale was long in the telling.

When he'd finished, Zhukov tapped his forehead. "There is no prototype. It's all here."

Neill interpreted his words for Brisbane.

"No schematics?" she asked. "No test-bed, no design plans?"

Radya ignored the Aussie's question. "You should leave. Every minute you stay increases your risk of capture." His eyes bored into Neill's. "You've killed one of their men, for God's sake!"

She must have told him. He glanced at Tanya, wondering if her father knew *why* the Russian was dead.

"Doctor, we've put you in an awkward position—"

"Awkward? Is that what you think?" Zhukov's voice rose. He fought for control. "Don't misunderstand me, Captain. I'm not ungrateful. But your actions today will bring the Russians down on our heads."

"With all due respect, sir, we aren't leaving without Charybdis."

"It's not yours for the taking!"

"Geez, Doc, inside voice. *Please*." Nate stared at the far end of the passage. Zhukov's words were lost on him, but the volume wasn't.

Tanya spoke up. "*Papa*—they want to see the *Commissar*. Just show them."

"Show them?" he repeated. "March armed men into the hangar? Deliver them into the Russians' hands?"

"*No, papa*. There's another way." She turned to face Neill. "Be ready, Captain. Tomorrow morning."

"With bells on," Neill answered. "Count on it."

"Leave the bells." Tanya gave Yuri a warm look.

But bring your friend, she didn't say.

The Pentagon

The red necktie needed cleaning. The starch in his dress shirt was just a memory. Each was a trademark of the man, but on this occasion, neither hinted at reputation or celebrity. In fact, there were few embellishments to really mark him; just a wristwatch, a wedding band, and an indistinguishable lapel pin.

Cyrano Hatch never considered himself to be handsome, and didn't bother trying to change that perception. He was tall and long-limbed, birdlike in appearance. His glasses were too large for his face, perched on a hawkish nose. The prescription in the lenses was new, but the horn-rimmed frames were no longer in style.

He was an unremarkable man in a pretentious world, and his disassociation from it gave him particular insight into the things he wrote about. There were no sacred cows for Cyrano Hatch.

In many respects, he bookended SECDEF in dress and manner. Each was disheveled, a little frayed around the edges. This was disarming, and cultivated to their advantage. Both men channeled an everyman persona, but with a keen intellect that refuted their dowdy exterior.

The biggest difference between them was age. Hatch was Avery's senior by twenty-five years. The Secretary judged the man to be close to eighty, but that hadn't slowed him down. Hatch was syndicated in dozens of newspapers, wielded a sharp keyboard, and like Willis, was a regular guest and contributor to the cable networks.

"Nice job on the Polk," Willis congratulated. "What was that—number five?"

Hatch put one spindly leg over the other. "Six," he corrected. "But who's counting?"

"You, it would seem," SECDEF laughed. "But after hanging your hat on a Pulitzer or two, there's not much point, is there?"

"It all adds up," the journalist allowed. "Looks good on the résumé, after all."

Avery grunted something. *As if the man needed help.* Of all the reporters Willis knew—and he rubbed shoulders with many—Cyrano's reputation was the most firmly entrenched.

"Thanks for taking time," he drawled. "Especially on such short notice."

"The least I can do. What's on your mind, Cy?"

"I'm hearing things, Mr. Secretary. Scattered rumors, mostly. My contacts in the Philippines are worried about unintended consequences."

"Oh? Related to what?"

"One of your projects."

"Can you narrow that down? We have a number of those in the Pacific."

Hatch was blunt. "Operation ARGOSY."

Avery blanched, but then recovered. Hatch had just crossed the line, stepping into the world of clandestine operations. In the past, fact-finders thought twice about visiting that shadowy realm. But things were different now. In this digital age, the stakes were higher. Information was just a mouse click away, and investigative reporters had become more aggressive, worried some blogger with a laptop might scoop them and stumble over a gem in plain sight.

"ARGOSY?" Willis rose, smoothing his shirt and moving toward the credenza. "Want some coffee, Cy?"

His guest declined. "I've got the broad strokes. I just need clarification on a few points."

SECDEF smiled wanly. "The Three C's."

Clarification, cooperation, and *confirmation*—crucial elements for any journalist working a source. Avery spent a full three seconds deciding if he could stonewall the man, but then thought better of it. While the Secretary distanced himself from most reporters, Cy was different. He understood the need for discretion, and if national security was involved, he'd be the first to impose his own restrictions. Besides, holding him at arm's length had never quite worked out in the past.

For Cyrano Hatch, a good story was a bone worth chewing.

Avery gave in. "All right, Cy. What do you have?"

Hatch lifted a satchel from the floor. He untied a thin folder bound by string. "A psy-op program, paired with some impressive technology. You've been busy."

"And these unintended consequences?"

Cyrano handed over a page or two. "Sounds like Cassidy's listening to the hawks in his cabinet," he began. "I've got nothing firm, but is there an intentional effort to antagonize the Russians, Willis?"

Avery skimmed through the material. The summary paragraph at the top told him all he needed to know. He pushed back in his chair.

"This goes beyond the broad strokes. Do you have anything else?"

"A working theory, without specifics. Maybe you can fill in the gaps."

"No promises."

Hatch pressed on. "All right, then. Here's what I've managed to piece together; ARGOSY's designed to confuse tracking systems. It undermines the ability to differentiate between friend and foe." He watched for some kind of reaction. "Depending on the circumstances, this could be a *good* thing; if your adversary can't tell who's who, he's less likely to fire in anger."

Battlefield optics. Avery was familiar with the phrase. He referred back to Cy's notes. "And you have this on background?"

"*Deep* background, Mr. Secretary. And I'm prepared to extend the same courtesy to you."

Avery understood what that meant. Over the years, Hatch had accumulated a stable of informants, both inside the government and out. All spoke on the condition of anonymity, and Cy was constrained by ethics, and no small amount of assurances, that he would *never* reveal his sources.

"Cy, I'm many things, but first and foremost I'm the Secretary of Defense. I don't trade in speculation or rumor, and I'm not a source for either. What you and I may or may not talk about is completely off the record; you won't be scribbling down notes, you won't be recording any portion of our conversation, and you will *not* leave this room with any quotes attributable to me or this office. Are we clear?"

Hatch didn't bat an eye.

"Had to set the ground rules, Cy. Even for you."

"Then we understand each other," he agreed. *Time to drop the other shoe*. "Let's talk about the Chinese, then. Is it true they've fielded some type of super-plane? A pulse weapons platform?"

"Misdirection," Avery harrumphed. "Come on, Cy. Stop fishing. You're better than that. We both know that none of the chatter's pointing to Beijing."

"The Russians, then." Hatch was pleased with himself. "I know about Flight 778. Your psy-ops project might have achieved a few unexpected results."

Avery frowned. "Are you insinuating some kind of connection?"

"That all depends, Mr. Secretary," Hatch shot back. "Was ARGOSY in play that night?"

For a moment Avery was dumbfounded. Was it possible? Had a developing U.S. countermeasure—one designed to limit casualties in war—somehow been instrumental in causing death?

From inception, ARGOSY's creators had good intentions. The system was designed to operate in an aerial environment, bound by a simple concept; that by blinding enemy aircraft, the dynamics of conflict could be shifted in a different direction. The inability to discern between ally and attacker would create doubt and hesitation, and those who hesitated—

But Hatch had raised the specter of something more heinous. He was suggesting—through meticulous sourcing, no doubt—that the United States was involved, and through the application of new technology, the Defense Department was culpable in the deaths of two hundred and sixty-nine airline passengers.

No. The Russians had pulled that trigger, Avery reminded himself. The blood was on their hands. No matter what role ARGOSY might have played, Moscow had started this fight. Still, Cy's probing created reasonable doubts in the Secretary's mind. *Had* ARGOSY *been operational that night*? *Had the software blinded the Russians*? If that were the case, maybe Ivan didn't know what he was shooting at. Worse still, Avery couldn't answer for it, and didn't know if Cy's theory was correct.

For that, he'd need to dig deeper.

"Are you ready to print this?"

He shook his head. "I'm a patriot, Willis. That sentiment's become *passe*, but there are those who still have loyalist tendencies."

True, Avery conceded. A few in the media hadn't been suborned, seduced by globalist thinking. He nodded gratefully. Cy had already proven his willingness to hold a story—particularly one that might jeopardize an ongoing operation. That was well known within the intelligence community. The first time Hatch had done so was in the seventies. A Soviet submarine had gone—

"But that won't last forever," the reporter continued. "None of us like being scooped."

The Secretary nodded again. "Can you give me some time?"

"How long do you need?"

Avery considered it. Captain Neill still had a mission to complete, and drawing attention to that part of the world might prove disastrous.

"A week," he answered. "Is that acceptable?"

"I suppose," Hatch agreed. "I just hope I don't regret this, Willis. I can't say for sure, but there might be others following up on this."

That was a veiled threat, one that Avery didn't appreciate. "Cy, trust me. In seven days you might have an even bigger story. Maybe an exclusive, if things turn out the way I hope."

Or possibly the DoD's worst intelligence failure in recent history, he didn't add.

29

DRESSED FOR THE OCCASION

Kamchatka Peninsula

"**A**NOTHER UNIFORM CHANGE," Nate groused.

"That's the price of admission, pal," Neill told him. He was already dressed. "C'mon, pick up the pace, Marine."

The sniper tugged at the coveralls, but the sleeves wouldn't reach. Four inches of wrist were left exposed.

"Just roll them up," Yuri urged.

The red coveralls matched those of the hangar technicians. They were worn, smudged with grease at the elbows and knees. Tanya had pulled five sets from the storeroom. Taylor's fit well enough, but she was smaller than the others. The rest were adequate, although Xander's was tight.

Dr. Zhukov peered around the corner. Fumbling with a key from his lab coat, he spied a door thirty meters distant.

"We should go, Captain," he growled. Zhukov glared at Crockett. "Now."

"That sounded like hurry up," Nate muttered.

Neill shook his head. "He's just impressed with your military bearing. I'm the one saying hurry up."

Nate took Yuri's advice and rolled the sleeves. He wasn't satisfied with the fit, but it would have to do. "Bad enough leaving the weapons behind."

"Different role," Mike said. "You're a science jock now. Science jocks don't wander around with carbines."

Crockett didn't like it, preferring a rifle in hand. "A science jock, huh? I don't feel any smarter."

"You don't look it, either."

Tereshenko gave Crockett a nudge and a wink. "You don't worry, *tavarisch*." He lifted his ruck from the deck. "I have surprises."

Nate was grinning now. "Like from a cereal box?"

"We have those now. Just like America."

"Stay on point, people," Neill ordered.

Dr. Zhukov moved down the tunnel. Neill, Brisbane and Voskov hugged the wall, while Tanya and Tereshenko brought up the rear. In a moment's time the door was unlocked and they crowded inside. The hangar wasn't far, and Nate risked one more look at the far end of the passage.

"*Commissar?*" he asked Tanya.

She nodded. "Yes. *Commissar.*"

"Ivan left the hatch open, Mike. I saw landing gear."

"Landing gear?" Yuri repeated.

"Wheels, *moy druh. Aircraft* wheels."

"*My friend,*" the sergeant echoed approvingly. "Your Ukrainian is more good. Keep at it."

The Zhukovs climbed a stairwell. Radya's bad leg made for slow going. This room was dark, but a soft light spilled from a landing two stories higher.

At the top of the stairs was a narrow room. Drafting tables and printers lined one of the walls. Charts, maps and floor plans hung from another. A larger table in the center was littered with coffee cups and blueprints.

"Conference room," Neill observed. He kept to the shadows. A long row of windows ran floor to ceiling and faced the hangar. Something resembling a control deck could be seen on the opposite side.

"There's need to worry, Captain." The climb had left Zhukov winded. "The glass is tinted. No one can see us."

Brisbane studied the diagrams on the wall. "I didn't think these blueprints existed."

Neill started to translate, but the old man took her meaning. "Schematics for the *Commissar*," he explained. "The engineers make constant design changes."

"And the weapon?"

"Charybdis is fully functional," Tanya told them. Her father stayed silent. "*Papa* handles those adjustments."

Dr. Zhukov waved a hand at the windows. "Captain, this is what you came for. Have your look."

· · · ·

Two stories below, the watch commander questioned Varushkin thoroughly.

"Baskovich entered the tunnel; of that you're sure." The officer was stating what he'd been told.

"*Da*, Lieutenant." Pavel swallowed hard.

"For what purpose?"

"He didn't tell me," came the honest reply.

The lieutenant frowned. He wasn't much older than the man he was interrogating. "When did you last see him?"

"This time, yesterday morning."

"But you didn't report his absence." It was a pointed observation, followed by a question. "And why is that, Sergeant?"

Pavel took a deep breath. "Baskovich has been late in

the past, comrade Lieutenant. And he *did* have time off."
He hoped that explanation would be enough. Additional
details would only get him into trouble.

The lieutenant was satisfied with the answer but not
happy about it. Pavel had been right; Baskovich wasn't a
stellar NCO, by any stretch. And as the officer in charge,
he'd already dropped paper on the big Russian, citing a
lack of punctuality.

But this was far different. Duty was involved—faith-
fulness to the *Rodina*. His missing sergeant aside, the
Marines of Arkangel took that responsibility seriously.

Simple tardiness was one thing, being absent from
one's post was another.

"Is it possible Sergeant Baskovich returned without
being seen?" the officer asked.

Possible—but not likely. Still, Varushkin hoped that
was the case. "Yes, Lieutenant. That could have happened."

"Then he may be warm in his bed, or hung over in the
village." He had one more question. "Were all motion
sensors active when he entered the tunnel?"

Pavel nodded. "Perimeter security was operational."
He couldn't admit that the system had been down much
of the day.

The watch commander rubbed a hand over his face.
When Baskovich hadn't shown up, the sentry on duty
was forced to continue his shift, and by dawn, the angry
infantryman buzzed the OIC's mobile, interrupting his
sleep.

The lieutenant shrugged it off. He was the one in
charge, after all. These problems fell to him. And it was
just as well. He'd summoned the rest of the detachment
on his way in, everyone on the day shift. Those men
were now gathering at the far end of the hangar. Rumors
had circulated for days—even weeks—but now the base

commander had given them a new task. It was an assignment for hardened men, those with a stomach for unspeakable brutality.

"We'll give him a few more hours, Sergeant. As of now, he's on report." More important issues required his attention. The officer looked beyond the aircraft, past the big fans that blew constantly. His men were milling about the entrance to the science lab.

The laboratory, he mused. How fitting.

• • • •

Professor Brisbane saw two humps on the plane, straddling the fuselage between the wings. These were large, offset from the center, and one sported a glass aperture several inches wide.

"That's the Eye, isn't it?" Taylor stared ahead and checked the excitement she felt. "That's Charybdis."

Neill translated her words. For the first time, Zhukov looked pleased.

"Yes, Doctor. A tandem-mounted weapons battery." Again, the interpretation.

"Tandem? As in two?"

The Ukrainian nodded his head. "Dual casings. The first rod is the beam exciter. The second amplifies the signal."

"And what about overloads?" The hardware before her was starting to make sense. "How do you prevent the weapon from consuming itself—frying the internal components?"

"A modified Faraday arrangement. It runs the length of the coil." The old scientist smiled mischievously and peered over the frames he wore. "A reducing wave eliminates the compounding destructive elements before they can affect the system."

"And the amplifier counteracts that wave?"

"At the broadcast point, yes." Zhukov liked the Australian. She was catching on fast. "We also buffer the pulse flow. Checks and balances, if you will."

"And such is the source of great power," Brisbane murmured, astonished by what she saw—and now understood. She turned away, but not before Neill saw tears in her eyes, and heard a sob catch in her throat.

"Taylor?"

She fought for composure. "*Checks and balances*, Captain Neill. Bailee suggested that very solution.

"She died before we could test it."

"Are you understanding this?" Tereshenko struggled but managed to make himself clear.

"Over my head," Nate replied. He turned to face the Ukrainian. "You know what that means?"

"The words are taller than you."

Crockett grinned. "Well, yeah. Something like that."

Neither man trusted the windows, and each kept his distance. With the morning shift came new activity. On the floor below, technicians and scientists crossed the hangar, tending to the aircraft in their charge. Maintenance specialists turned wrenches. But it was the movement of another group that caught Nate's eye.

"Troops," he muttered.

Yuri took an interest. He'd seen them too.

"Russian. Naval—your word?"

"Naval *infantrymen*. Marines, *da*?"

"You said it, yes," the lanky sergeant answered.

Nate lifted a hand, pointing. "The one in the center. He's an officer, right?"

"A lieutenant. Probably first shift briefing."

"Sure would like to hear it." Crockett was thinking out loud.

"Truly?" Tereshenko had a gleam in his eye.

"Yeah. Dead Ivan's probably come up missing. We need to know what *they* know."

Yuri took the ruck off his shoulder. "That can be arranged, *moy druh*."

Crockett brightened. "*Parabolichny?*"

"Yes," he smiled. "*Parabolichny.*"

"You were right, Captain. Robust is an appropriate word." Taylor admired the plane from nose to tail. "I've identified the weapon. My job is done—the rest is up to you."

"That was easy," Neill muttered.

"We called the program Seawolf in the beginning." Zhukov seemed willing to talk. "The Cold War was raging. We needed to counter the threat of your president."

"Reagan," Neill said. "But that was more than thirty years ago." He paused. "You had another aircraft—long before the *Commissar.*"

"We tested a prototype, and Charybdis, too; trial runs in the Bering Sea." Zhukov's face was troubled. "That aircraft was lost near the Commander Islands."

"We've seen it," Neill told him.

"It's been found again," Xander added.

"What can you tell us about that plane? It's considerably smaller than this one."

"We crashed," he said simply. "There was a system failure. One of my own making."

"*Of your own making*? What does that mean?"

Zhukov felt the Marine's eyes on him and turned.

"You're asking why it happened."

"You were there, Doc."

Radya seemed relieved to give an answer. "I disabled the Faraday Cage."

"And discharged the weapon?" Neill asked. "To destroy the plane?"

"You make the deed sound noble," Zhukov told him, shaking his head. "But there was no chivalrous intent. I was trying to take my own life." Zhukov patted his bad leg. "I was the lone survivor. God chose me to live."

"Do you believe He orders your steps, Doctor?"

Zhukov answered with a question of his own. "Are you a religious man, Captain?"

Neill gave some thought to his reply. "Faith gives us the power to become what we should be. Grace makes it happen."

The old man looked down into the aerodrome. "And do you ever pray for your enemies?"

The Ukrainian had spiritual substance. It was something Neill hadn't expected. "Not as often as I should. I'm a little selfish in that regard."

"At some point we must all choose sides." Zhukov reached into a pocket and held out his hand. An Orthodox Cross lay in the center of his palm. "My mother gave me this. For luck. I pray to it daily."

The Marine smiled. "There's a little more to it than that, Doc. What happened on the Cross is the source of infinite power, but by itself it's just a trinket."

Voskov was uncomfortable with the discussion. "Are there other aircraft like this one?"

"The Russians are building more," Tanya told them. "Three, we think. At bases on the eastern coastline."

"Are all of those planes armed with Charybdis?"

She shook her head. "The Russians don't know how Charybdis works. Only *papa* can engineer the weapon."

"That won't last forever, *dochka*." Zhukov became sullen. He had already violated several rules by allowing Neill's team to see the plane. The penalty—

He closed his hand around the cross. "There it is, Captain. You've seen what you came for. Now you must leave."

"That's not possible," Xander replied.

"I'm afraid he's right. We reconnoitered the tunnel early this morning. The sensor arrays are active again."

"You can't leave, then?" Tanya asked.

"Not the way we came."

Tanya was buoyed by the thought and worried at the same time. She turned, but the rest of Captain Neill's team had left the room.

Tereshenko and Crockett slipped out unseen. Both were in the tunnel again, moving forward. They stopped short of the hangar entrance and took a knee.

Yuri had a clear line of sight to the assembled troops. He pulled the small dish from his ruck and pointed it toward the opening, then put in the earbuds and frowned.

"Hear anything?" Nate asked.

"Too far. Maybe we should go closer."

Nate didn't like that option. Overheads in the hangar produced a glare. The hall was dark, but moving nearer—

"Can you refine the beam? Turn up the gain, maybe?"

Yuri twisted a knob and smiled. "Done." He listened for nearly a minute. "The Russian's name—*yes*—it was Baskovich—not a good troop, it would seem. The officer says Baskovich is . . ."

Nate waited, his patience ebbing. "Small potatoes? A scumbag? That much we know."

"I missed it." Yuri held up a hand for silence. "Something else—something . . . more important."

The watch commander directed his men away from the science lab, although none of Zhukov's staff were about. Part two of his briefing was delicate. It was something the scientists didn't need to know.

Keeping this impersonal was the best approach. He spoke just loud enough to be heard, choosing cold and abstract terms. It was a speech he had practiced many times since receiving his orders.

When he finished, no one flinched, and no one asked questions. There were no consciences in need of persuasion. This didn't surprise the officer; his men had seen action in the Crimea, and were combat-proven in bloody skirmishes against those who resisted Russian rule.

A huddle of scientists and their families would fare no better.

"Pull back, comrade." Tereshenko removed the earbuds, his face ashen. "I've heard enough."

Crockett didn't argue. Something in the Ukrainian's tone signaled retreat. The two pressed against the wall and retraced their steps to the stairwell.

The sniper didn't like tactical disadvantages. Those were deadly. Comfort and safety meant having a rifle, and Nate would be happier back in the alcove.

Still, he wondered about Yuri's reaction.

"We have to hurry." Tereshenko was more deliberate now. His pace quickened.

"What's the rush? What'd he say?" Nate prodded. He opened the door that led upstairs. "Do they have a plan?"

"Yes," Yuri breathed. He pushed his friend inside.

"They have a plan."

The techs were already at work. They had started at dawn, prepping a new avionics package for installation. Another test had been scheduled for the following evening, weather permitting, and the gear required fine-tuning before *Commissar* left her nest.

Test flights came more frequently now, sometimes twice a week, and while the Russians never gave any reasons, it was clear to the science staff that something was in the works.

Roman Shapoval showed up on time, arriving one hour after the maintainers. He left the elevator and entered the hangar, blinking against the harsh lights above. A quick look around told him that everything was right where he'd left it. It was an acerbic observation, and brought a grin.

Conspicuously present was the *Commissar*, and Shapoval took a moment to admire her lines. The Russians had taken their largest aircraft and redesigned it, giving the bird her sea legs. Roman had played a role in that, and if it weren't for the plane's beastly purposes, he would have been proud. Like Zhukov, he sought redemption, a way to purge the last ten years.

Two things were different on this morning. The Zhukovs missed breakfast. Roman had looked for the two in the cramped dining hall, but the cook told him they'd already come and gone.

The next surprise came from the cavernous hangar. Admiral Pavlenko's troopers had formed up along the wall, opposite the big door that opened to the sea. Roman turned sharply to his right. He didn't like these new infantrymen, choosing to ignore them instead, but not before noting that the watch commander had gathered every man, leaving the guardhouse empty.

And then a double-take. Crossing the hangar, Roman had a direct view into the tunnel. Two figures—in red coveralls, he was sure—used the door, the one leading into—*was it the electrical room*? No, that was closer. He stopped short and gave the passage a second look.

It was the stairwell—the one that led to the second level. And now that door was closed, the figures gone. Whoever they might have been, they were dressed like technicians.

But that wasn't possible, he told himself. Only Radya

had unrestricted access to the tunnel.

Was that the answer? Was the boss back there? Had he taken a few of their people with him?

But Roman had work to do, and traded those questions for an oxy/acetylene rig. He wheeled the tanks beneath the *Commissar*'s starboard engine, and by the time he'd retrieved his goggles, the puzzle was forgotten, lost among the concerns of another busy day.

30

"NO GOOD ODDS"

"**T**HIS IS BEYOND criminal," Voskov snarled. "It's *monstrous*."

The group fell back to the alcove in a hurry. Tereshenko chattered all the way. At times his voice rose; when it did, Voskov or Neill would break in, forcing him to stop or repeat himself.

And the team was not alone. The Zhukovs were with them. Yuri had insisted on it.

"*Papa*—" Tanya began, "How can they *do* this? How could they be so cruel?"

Crockett saw the tears in her eyes. His own darted to a confused Brisbane, and then to Neill. "We're a little in the dark here, Mike."

Neill collected his thoughts. "The Russians are tying up loose ends, Nate."

"Loose ends, starting with Zhukov's people," Crockett reasoned. He didn't need an interpreter to understand

Tanya's raw emotion. "What do—"

"Not just Zhukov and his team; their families, too."

The sniper's jaw went slack. "*Families*? Like spouses; wives?"

"And children, Nate."

"*Almighty God*," Crockett whitened. "I mean, *Jesus*, Mike! How the Sam Hill do they plan on that?"

"Gas." Neill's voice was shallow. "They're going to herd them into the lab. Seal the exits. From what Yuri picked out, it's probably Zyklon-B."

"Same stuff the Nazis used," Nate breathed. "Timetable?"

"This afternoon—before the shift ends."

Yuri wasn't having it. "This can't happen, *moy druh*. We can't let it."

A blaze of glory. That was one option, Crockett decided. They could intervene, try some kind of rescue. It was probably doomed to failure, but they had to try—

"What does it mean, *papa*?"

Zhukov gave his daughter a mournful look. "It means the Russians have the key. They've discovered the weapon's secrets." He shook his head. "Admiral Pavlenko no longer needs us."

Neill shot a glance at the scientist. "Taras Pavlenko?"

"You know him?"

"The name's come up. Career Navy man; politically connected, but not well liked."

"An understatement, Captain. We met long ago, in 1985. He and his men rescued me when the prototype crashed."

"And you've been here ever since?"

"For much of that time, yes."

"Some rescue," Xander snorted. "How many on your staff?"

"There are sixteen of us, including *papa* and myself,"

Tanya answered. "Eight are married."

"Any children?"

She did the math. "Twelve. The youngest—Aleksander—is just four years old."

"Thirty-six souls, Mikhail," Xander declared. "And how many troops does Pavlenko have?"

"At least a dozen."

"Against the four of us," Yuri replied. He spoke in English. "No good odds. No good."

"Any suggestions?" Nate asked.

Yuri knelt and peeled open his ruck. "We make use of these."

Neill's face was stern, and even Brisbane recognized what Tereshenko held in his hands. "You didn't tell me you'd brought grenades."

The sergeant blinked. "You didn't ask, Mischa."

"I'll bet those made you popular on Attu."

Yuri shrugged. "We had authorization—a letter from your State Department. They got over it."

Taylor's head was swimming. "So what's your plan? Blow up the Russians? Engage them in combat? You'll get yourselves killed."

"No, *zhinka*. We use these to disable the sensors—at the source."

Nate was darkly amused. "Nice try, comrade. After what they did to Bailee, I'm tempted, but with the deck stacked against us we need stealth."

"He's right, Yuri," Neill agreed. "We have to be more subtle. Explosives just tell them we're here."

"We take the doctor with us, then." Xander looked at Tereshenko. "And Tanya, too, of course."

"And go *where*? Through the tunnel?" Neill shook his head. "That path sets off the alarm. We can't ask the Russians to turn it off, and we can't blow it up. Even if we got that far, Ivan will be topside waiting for us. And what about the *rest* of Zhukov's team? Are you willing to leave them behind—to write them off?"

"Those people aren't our mission, Mikhail," Xander said testily. "We came for Charybdis."

"But they're *children*." Tanya's voice was pleading. "You *can't* let them die."

It was time to step back. Voskov raised a hand and asked, "How certain are we of this? Perhaps Yuri misunderstood—"

Zhukov broke his silence. "There is nothing to misunderstand, Captain Voskov. These Russians can be quite ruthless. Pavlenko will certainly allow it."

"Of this you are sure?"

"The admiral let my mother die." Tanya tried holding back her feelings. "My father refused to turn over the weapon's secrets. When *mama* became sick, Pavlenko withheld treatment."

Radya stared at his daughter. "You knew?"

"You can't protect me from everything, *papa*."

Neill brought them back to the problem. "So we're left with an unexpected circumstance. How do we get thirty-six—"

"Forty-one," Yuri corrected.

Crockett cleared his throat. "Mike—"

Neill continued. "All right, how do we get forty-one people out of here—and live to tell the tale?"

"Mike," Nate repeated.

"What about the grotto?" Xander threw in.

Neill dismissed the idea. "There's a perimeter sensor on this side of the cave. Listen, people, there's a good chance none of us leaves this mountain alive. Let's do what we can to improve the odds."

"*Homestyle.*"

Crockett had his attention now. The captain turned. "What is it, Nate?"

"Normally I let you come up with the harebrained stuff. You know that, right?"

"What's that supposed to mean?"

"Ask the doc if he's got a pilot."

"A *pilot*?"

"Yes." A broad smile creased Yuri's face. "Yes, Mischa. Ask the doctor if he has a pilot."

Neill studied them both. So did Zhukov.

"What did he say, Captain?"

It was Mike's turn to shake his head. He knew where this was going. He didn't like it, and would have preferred an alternative, but from a practical standpoint—although not entirely tactical—it was the only option left.

"You're both nuts."

"One slice short of a ham sandwich." Crockett threw an arm around Tereshenko's shoulder. "But this way we get to take Charybdis with us."

Brisbane caught on quickly. "And how is that better than taking our chances in the tunnel?"

Crockett had an answer. "For one thing, the Russians won't expect it."

"And how could they?" Yuri asked. "They don't even know we're here."

"But how do we gather everyone—" [1]

"That's the beauty of it, Doc. We don't have to. The Russians will do that for us. We just have to be ready.

"Borrowing an oft-spoken phrase from Cap'n Neill, operational planning begins now."

31

EXERCISE IN SUBVERSION

ZHUKOV DIDN'T BELIEVE in an angry God. An enraged deity could punish him at any time He chose, but that had not been Radya's experience. Far from it, in fact. Through the years, when it seemed most likely—times when even *he* expected some kind of chastening—judgment had always been suspended, instead.

His was not an informed faith. And grace? Another puzzle. The hand of Providence might have been real to some, but the old scientist just couldn't fathom it. Unmerited favor was foreign to him. Nor did he recognize benevolence from the Almighty. When confronted by either, Radya grew suspicious. *Why would God extend compassion to such lowly creatures—to men like himself?* Only one answer made sense, but that ran counter to Zhukov's philosophy.

A God of love wouldn't allow suffering. Certainly no earthly father could stomach the pain of his children;

how, then, could a heavenly father do so? Was that God's will? Or was He, too, somehow constrained, just as much a prisoner of the cosmos as His creation?

Punishment at the hands of the Russians was now imminent. If God did exist, then surely He saw the plight of the innocent. Wouldn't He intervene in the midst of their need? Was He too busy, or given to neglect? Vindictive, perhaps, or cruel? Did He even care? In any case, why endow life, only to permit anguish and affliction?

Love, peace, anger and hatred were things that Radya understood. What he feared most was that God might be capricious.

"Where to, *papa*?" Tanya's voice pulled him out of his reverie.

They had left the tunnel and were back in the UTV. Radya pursed his lips and eyed the hangar. On the far side of the aircraft, Shapoval was using a welder's torch, and sparks fell to the floor.

"To the maintenance stand," Zhukov said, pointing. "Under the starboard engine."

Tanya pressed on the accelerator, steering the cart beneath the *Commissar*'s tail section. "Do you think we can do this?" she asked quietly.

He touched the talisman in his pocket and whispered a short prayer. *A closed fist cannot receive a blessing,* his mother had once said. Her words had always stayed with him.

"We have no choice but to try."

Tanya used some reassurance. "The Americans seem confident."

Radya gave her a shrewd look. "And so does your young rescuer."

She looked away, reddening. "Papa."

Shapoval saw their approach and lifted his visor.

Tanya stopped the cart. "You've finished with the cowling?" Zhukov called up to him. In a distant corner someone used an electrical saw, the high-pitched sound grating in their ears.

"An hour ago." The engineer's face was beaded with moisture. He caught his breath, and asked with a grin, "*Shto, tavarisch*—no time for tea this morning?"

Zhukov didn't answer. "What of the engine?"

Shapoval descended the ladder. "There's no rush, Radya. The test is tomorrow."

The old man lifted himself from the cart. "The true test comes much sooner, old friend." His head went from side to side. There was no one nearby, and Pavlenko's troops had resumed their duties. "Listen to me carefully, Roman. Give no reaction to what I say, and keep your eyes on me. Do you understand?"

"Yes." A pause, and then, "I mean, *no*." He did as Zhukov ordered.

"There are armed men in the tunnel. A small contingent of American and Ukrainian troops."

"American?" Shapoval resisted the urge to stare past Zhukov's shoulder. "Have they hurt you in any way? Have they threatened you—or Tanya?" He removed the wool gloves he wore, suddenly unsure of what to do with his hands. "We should report this, Radya. We should tell the Russians."

Zhukov shook his head, and he leaned heavily on his cane. "No, Roman. We aren't going to do that."

The figures he'd seen in the passage. Shapoval pulled off the welder's hood, fearful now. His hair was matted with sweat. "And why not?"

"Because we're going to *help* them."

"*Papa;* don't forget—"

"Oh, yes. When did you last fly?"

"*Fly*?" Roman wiped the sweat from his brow. He

faced the plane's cockpit. "During the initial trials, last year. Of course, the Russians watched me like hawks."

"Think carefully. *Can you do it again*?"

"The *Commissar*?" His eyes fluttered. He was confused, but then a smile crossed his face. Illumination and hope came with it.

"Yes, Radya, I can do it again. When do we leave?"

· · · ·

"You're putting a lot of trust in that old guy, Mike," Nate observed. "Is that smart?"

Neill chucked some gear from his pack. The others followed his example. "Are you asking because he's an old guy?"

"Not at all. I'm asking because he could use *us* to his advantage; if he squeals, Ivan might go easy on him."

"That's not in his best interests," Taylor announced. She pushed a handful of red hair up under her cap. "The Russians aren't interested in rewarding him."

"Hey, the Doc gets it." Mike began disassembling his weapon. "Got room for your rifle in that ruck?"

"If I break it down, sure."

Neill glanced at Yuri and Xander. They were already finished. "Break it down, then."

"How's Zhukov getting us into the hangar?"

"He's got something in mind."

Crockett worked the takedown pin on his weapon. "Let's hope so."

Brisbane gathered the discarded supplies. From her own ruck she retrieved one last MRE. "You do have some trust issues, don't you, Lieutenant?"

"I've got my share," Nate defended.

· · · ·

Pavlenko's chopper was heavier this time. That was

good. The added weight helped with stability, and the pilot brought the aircraft down with little more than a gentle *thump*.

The passengers on board waited for the rotors to stop before exiting. A security detail dismounted first, and then Pavlenko and Tamarkin jumped from the crew door. Six members of the Federation's science and technology group trailed behind.

A strong gust nearly claimed Tamarkin's cover. He looked out to sea; dark clouds rolled in from the east, a gray band that stretched across the horizon, and sheets of rain had begun to fall. It was tempting to think that the gods were displeased.

Colonel Utkin trudged up the platform to greet them. Tamarkin smiled ruefully. Like the gods, Utkin didn't look pleased, either.

"Your men are ready, yes?" Pavlenko asked him. He wore a Makarov pistol on his hip.

Utkin gave a grudging reply. "They are, Admiral."

Taras looked at his watch, and then faced the compound. The wind carried the sound of laughter to his ears. Utkin saw the expression on Pavlenko's face and winced.

"The children, Admiral. It's their first recess of the day. They have two—one in the morning, and another in the afternoon."

"After lunch," Taras announced coldly. He could see them playing now. "You needn't be a party to this, Sasha. Your infantrymen are quite capable."

Utkin caught the smell of brine in the air. "I am the commander, Admiral. I should be present."

"As you wish, Colonel." Taras accepted that answer, and approved.

They would take the elevator in groups of four. Utkin would play host, serving tea to his guests, and eventually a meal. Pavlenko's scheme was ghastly, but if his troops were efficient, the deed would be done, and Sasha could put this behind him. He might even be able to accept the admiral's justification, but he suspected there would be many sleepless nights before that day would come.

• • • •

Zhukov entered the guardhouse. The corporal on duty got to his feet.

"We need more acetylene," the doctor announced brusquely.

"Acetylene." The enlisted man blinked. "And where is that kept, Doctor?"

"In the stores locker. Where else would we keep it?" Radya feigned impatience. It wasn't difficult.

"What is it used for?" *The old man was testy today.* The corporal looked past him. Zhukov's daughter and chief engineer waited outside.

Radya heaved a sigh. "We're repairing a worn panel. One of the turbofans." Roman had already finished the repairs, and tin snips would have been a more appropriate tool, but the sentry didn't need to know that.

Zhukov used his thumb, gesturing toward Tanya and Roman. "My daughter will fetch what we need."

The corporal gave Tanya a brief but admiring glance. "Of course, Doctor. Will she be long?"

Zhukov checked his watch; half an hour before the corporal took his lunch.

"As long as it takes, Sergeant." The corporal didn't seem to mind the upgrade in rank. "Shapoval will accompany her. He needs to calibrate the mixture in the tanks." That was another lie, but a convenient one to further Lieutenant Crockett's plan.

The infantryman eyed the clock above the door. Still plenty of time before the big show. *Let them go about their business,* the lieutenant had said. Best not to give the impression that something was amiss.

"Very well, Doctor. Your people are free to enter the tunnel."

Zhukov didn't bother to thank him. He turned to give Tanya and Roman a wink and a smile.

The two hopped into the cart, and Radya watched as they entered the passage. Despite the danger involved, he was beginning to enjoy this exercise in subversion.

• • • •

"Right on time," Neill told the group.

The UTV rounded a corner, headlights illuminating the hall. Tanya stopped the cart just short of the alcove, and introductions were quickly made.

Shapoval seemed cautious. "Dr. Zhukov says we can trust you—that you are our friends."

"We'd like to think so." Neill shook the man's hand. "You're the pilot? You can fly that plane?"

"My skills are rusty," the engineer hedged.

"I'm sure they're better than ours."

"What about your weapons?" Tanya asked.

"Stowed in our packs."

She stared past the Marine. "Are you ready, then?" The warm look in her eye was meant for Yuri.

"We're ready, Miss Zhukov." Neill gave Tereshenko a friendly smirk. "*All* of us."

She ignored him. "Put your equipment in the back. Roman will take it to the plane."

"How do we get aboard, Meela?" Yuri was all charm.

"You'll enter the hangar a few at a time. Don't worry; *papa* has promised a diversion."

"The lion's den." Voskov's face darkened. "That will be risky."

She gave a shrug. "We can't avoid it. The coveralls

will help; you're all dressed like us." She studied Brisbane's appearance. "I'm afraid the professor complicates things."

"How's that?"

"We have women on the science staff, but no female technicians. The men will spot her immediately."

Shapoval smiled for the first time since they'd met. "I have a solution, when the time comes." He reached into the cart and handed Nate a clipboard. "You, on the other hand, should carry this."

"What's that for?"

Roman rattled off something else. Neill laughed.

Crockett was suspicious. "What's funny?"

"He suggests you hang on to it," Neill replied. "Nobody *ever* hassles a guy with a clipboard."

"Or a measuring tape," Nate grinned. "Just like our military, Mike."

• • • •

Like many cargo aircraft, the *Commissar* had egress doors fore and aft. In flight, they provided a pressurized environment. On the ground, they were lowered and used as stairs. A wire-framed handrail was another feature, extending from the fuselage when the doors were deployed.

Zhukov descended the ladder at the rear of the aircraft. This was always cumbersome with his debilitated leg. He reached the floor and turned. The *Commissar*'s auxiliary power unit—the APU—droned in his ears, giving life to the plane, powering electrical and hydraulic systems. It was also required to start the engines.

What's next? Radya ticked off a list in his head and then crossed the hangar. The corporal in the guard shack would be hungry, anxious for his lunch. It was time for the next phase of their scheme.

"I want to show you something, Sergeant," Zhukov thundered, entering the cramped post.

The infantryman corrected the old man. "It's *corporal*, Dr. Zhukov."

Radya grunted dismissively. "Come with me."

The scientist did a fair job of spinning on the ball of his foot, cane notwithstanding. He began moving away from the tunnel, toward the big hangar door. The corporal had trouble matching his pace.

Zhukov stopped abruptly. He tapped an instrument mounted on the wall.

"Do you know what this is, Corporal?"

The sentry studied the device. For all his time at Arkangel, he'd never paid it much attention.

Zhukov peered over his glasses. "This is a hygrometer. Are you aware of its function?"

"Is that like a barometer?"

Did the old man just roll his eyes? The Russian was almost certain of it.

"That's a reasonable guess," Zhukov admitted. "A barometer—like this one—" he stepped to his right, "—measures atmospheric pressure. It's also useful in predicting the weather."

"And what does the hygrometer do?" Humor this Ukrainian, the corporal decided.

Zhukov waited before answering, then looked to his left and gave an imperceptible nod.

Tanya stood at the tunnel entrance. She watched her father's animated ramblings and waited for his signal. When he gave it, she turned to face the open door.

"Go," she told Shapoval.

Tanya set off toward the plane. With the bill of his cap pulled down, Yuri followed. Shapoval drove out of the tunnel and made for the tip of the *Commissar*'s wing.

Taylor was next to him, wearing the welder's hood. The visor was up, so as not to attract too much attention. Roman made a wide arc and parked just meters from the rear of the aircraft.

Brisbane got out, looking neither left nor right. *Walk like a man,* Neill had told her. She took his advice and trailed Roman into the plane. Once inside, she relaxed.

Tanya and Yuri meandered a bit, making a show of inspecting the landing gear, and Tereshenko positioned his boot under a wheel.

"Say the word."

Tanya made sure no one was watching. "The coast is clear," she told him.

Yuri slid his foot forward, pushing the chock out of the way. "And the other side?"

Tanya nodded. "All the drive wheels are blocked."

They moved beneath the plane's tail section. An ambling turn and the two repeated the action on the right side.

Neill and Voskov carried cardboard boxes, hugging them close to their chests. Both wore dust masks. Crockett marched behind them, the last to leave the tunnel, glancing at the girders overhead and squinting in the harsh light.

Focus, he told himself. *Don't get sidetracked, Nate.*

He faced front again, but not before being noticed by one of Pavlenko's more ambitious troops.

"A hygrometer measures moisture content," Radya was saying.

"Humidity?"

"*Da,*" he answered in Russian. Zhukov touched the face of the gauge. "This reading—do you know what it means?"

The corporal didn't, and decided it was best to admit

that. "No, Doctor."

"Too much condensation." In truth it was elevated, but not egregiously so. "Far too much. Not even the fans will reduce it."

"How is that a problem?"

"Moisture fosters oxidation, *molodoy chelovek*. Rust. The *Commissar* is the sum of many parts. All are sensitive." He waved a hand toward the plane. "We must protect her."

"Corrosion." The corporal understood. Or thought he did. "But it is Spring. The weather is becoming warmer."

"All the more reason to act." Zhukov pointed toward the massive door. "Water is already pooling—I can see it from here."

Air in the hangar was bottled up, noticeably dank. It needed refreshing. "We could open the door," the Russian suggested.

"That would help. Can you make it happen?"

A smile spread across his face. "I do have *some* autonomy, Dr. Zhukov."

The corporal moved to a control panel nearby. He flipped a toggle switch marked in red. Then came the whirring of motors from above and below. The big door began rolling upward, and lights on either side flashed a warning.

"You, there."

He was a mere private, one of the newer troops, but buttoned-down, with an authoritative voice.

"I say, *you there*."

Crockett groaned inwardly. He turned, catching sight of Neill in the corner of his eye.

"*Da?*" The sniper pretended indifference.

The private walked up to the three. "What's in the boxes?"

"Tools," Voskov answered.

"—and spill kits." Neill moved closer, slapping the box and sending dust into the air. The effect was better than he'd hoped. "Caustic chemicals. Bad for the lungs."

"What kind of spills?"

"Oil, gasoline. Dangerous solvents. We keep a supply aboard the plane for mishaps." He stepped forward. "Would you like to inspect them?"

It was clear that he didn't. The man drew back. These technicians were wearing masks, and he didn't want to take any unnecessary risks.

"Get on with your business, then." He turned to go, making a hasty exit. "And be careful with that stuff."

Neill grunted a reply and kept walking. He wore a cautious grin that no one could see.

"Nice recovery," Voskov mumbled. The Russian was gone now. "Fortunate that he didn't want a closer look."

"I gambled that he wouldn't," Neill admitted.

"Do Christians do that?"

"You'd be surprised."

Nate looked happy. "Ivan bought it, Mike. I spoke in Russian and he didn't even blink."

"Congratulations. You're a linguist now."

A quick glance overhead. The door had stopped its creaking movement, and now rested in the girders above.

"The doctor did it, Mikhail," Voskov kept his eyes ahead. "The path is clear."

Neill looked past the front of the plane. The hangar was now open to the sea. It was nearly noon, but the sky beyond was dark, and thunder clapped in the distance.

32

A BEAUTIFUL CONCEPT

Joint Base Elmendorf-Richardson, Alaska

IT WAS THE KIND OF day fighter jocks dreamt of; a clear sky, excellent visibility, and no sign of commercial traffic from nearby Anchorage. That wouldn't last, Chris Prentice told himself. Murphy's Law being what it was, he knew that a score of aircraft would soon crowd the skies, probably long before HELLCAT Squadron was even airborne.

It didn't matter. The big blue van carrying the pilots wheeled south on the apron and parked. Prentice jumped from the front seat. Major Tate and two other officers— Lieutenants Elsketh and Settles—spilled from the back. A short distance away, the fighters waited in a neat row on the tarmac, with ground crews making final adjustments.

One group caught his eye. Ordnancemen attached weapons to the planes' hard points and wingtips, snapping the last AIM-9 Sidewinder into place. But Aileron

Dynamix had another dog in this fight; each Hellcat was also armed with a complement of four Helius missiles, a weapons system recently advanced by the company and built specifically for the F/A-38s.

And like the Hellcats, Helius was also on probation.

Prentice gave the crew chief an approving nod and started his walk-around. From the ground up things looked good, and he and his pilots climbed the ladders and strapped in. One by one the canopies of each aircraft were locked in place. Lines were connected to pressure suits and cool air flowed as the environmental systems spun up. Pre-flight checks came next. Flaps and control surfaces. Auxiliary power and oxygen. Hardware and software.

And juice; Prentice powered up the engine, idling to one-quarter thrust before easing off. The crackling of static in his helmet told him the comm gear was also good to go.

"Hellcat Lead, Tower." The air controller's voice came in a monotone. She gave instructions for rollout, followed by weather. "Winds are ten knots, south-by-southwest. Ceiling unlimited. You're first to tee off, Colonel."

"Tower, Hellcat Lead copies."

"Nice job yesterday, sir."

A *professional* compliment. Prentice smiled behind his oxygen mask, his mind going back. The Hellcats had spent the previous day in combat against an 'aggressor' squadron of six F-16s. They were outnumbered, but that was always the possibility in a real-world scenario. In the first encounter, he and his pilots held their own, but they were just getting warmed up. In subsequent 'battles', the F/A-38s had bested the Falcons two out of three.

"You catch the hot wash?"

Her tone was more lively now, pleasant. "All of day

shift did, yes, sir," she told him. "Nicely done."

For the new Hellcat, Defense wanted more than just the standard after-action. Aileron had delivered. Tied to radar and real-time satellite returns, software apps recreated the dogfights. Presented on a plasma flat-screen, the animation made for an impressive display, complete with lighting effects and modeling. Christian likened it to watching cartoons.

But today would be different. *Real* weaponry hung on their wings, ordnance that would be brought to bear against unmanned drones, aircraft controlled by junior officers from cubicles on the ground. This was no simulated furball; today would be metal on metal, a tactile exercise.

True, this was just practice, and their adversaries wouldn't be shooting back, but that was also a possibility in a real-world exchange—especially given the Hellcat's standoff capabilities.

One last check on fuel and avionics. The other pilots signaled ready. Prentice got the nod from the tower and released his brakes, leading the formation to their launch point. He applied thrust and was airborne moments later, climbing above the Chugach mountain range before angling to the south.

• • • •

"Worthless?"

Neill nodded sympathetically. "Apart from faith, it's just a piece of jewelry."

The group hid aft of the *Commissar*'s flight deck. A small space behind the cockpit held bunks and a lavatory for the plane's crew. Xander, Nate and Yuri reassembled their rifles near the hatch, and Tanya gave Brisbane a tour of the weapons compartment.

"Just a talisman? Nothing more?" Radya Zhukov

closed his hand around the cross. The hard edges dug into his palm. "But how can that be? She told me—she *promised*—"

Mike saw emotion in his eyes. "Your mother wasn't *wrong*, Doctor. She just didn't have the full story."

Zhukov wasn't willing to believe what he'd been told. But there was an undeniable sincerity in Captain Neill's words, a straightforward quality that the old man couldn't ignore.

"All this time," he began, "I've believed a lie."

Neill shook his head. "No, Radya. You're not *listening*. You hold the truth in your hand, in the simple shape of The Cross. And what The Cross represents is far from worthless."

• • • •

"Where are we *going*?"

The elevator was cramped and humid. Aleksander held his sister's hand, moving closer as they started to descend. The wide-eyed boy stared up at the Russian Marine and then looked away. The man never smiled, and the rifle in his hands frightened him.

"Anushka," he whispered again, "where are we going?"

The girl was eight years old, twice Aleksander's age. She hushed her brother and tightened her grip.

"To the hangar. We're going to the hangar, Aleks."

That pleased him. "To see *papa*?"

"And mama," Anushka told him. The other children in the car jostled against them, fidgeting in the enclosed space. "It's a field trip. To see the laboratory." She was proud of herself; Anushka had only just learned that word, and liked to show off by using it.

"But where's teacher?" Aleksander looked up once more. Their Russian schoolmarm had not accompanied them, and scary soldiers with guns *never* took them on field trips.

"*Shhh!*" she warned. The trooper gave them a stern glance. "Be quiet, Aleks!"

The doors slid open. Six children left the car, herded forward by the infantryman. Half a dozen more were corralled nearby.

"Is that the last of them?"

The corporal came to attention. "*Da*, comrade Lieutenant. Everyone is accounted for."

"And their parents?" the officer asked.

"I've double-checked the roster. Most are in the lab. A few are in the aircraft with Dr. Zhukov."

There was a rushing sound, and the lieutenant's eyes were drawn away. "Why is the hangar open to the sea, Corporal?"

"To counteract condensation, sir. Moisture degrades the aircraft's function." He looked beyond the fuselage to the fans lining the far wall. Indeed, every blade now turned, creating an updraft. "Dr. Zhukov says that the fans are not always sufficient to keep the air dry."

"Reducing humidity is our responsibility, then?"

"Dr. Zhukov thinks so," the corporal snorted.

"And what of Sergeant Baskovich?"

"I have not seen him, Lieutenant."

The watch commander grumbled. The missing NCO would reflect badly on him. After dealing with Zhukov's people, he'd send his men on a proper search, but for now there were just too many other details requiring his attention.

He faced the hangar opening. Standing at the yawning mouth was a single figure using a mop and bucket. Outside, sheets of rain fell, and in the distance lightning flashed.

"Very well then, Corporal. Fetch Dr. Zhukov and the rest of his team." The time had come, and there was no need in prolonging this. "We have our orders."

The infantryman stepped off briskly.

"*Da*, comrade Lieutenant!"

Roman Shapoval took his time with the mop, edging closer to the wall. At the entrance was an electric generator used to raise and lower the door. Rainwater had collected beneath it, and Roman diligently swabbed it away.

The engineer cursed under his breath. The coarse strands had tangled, caught in the bolts at the motor's base. Roman knelt and tugged. After some effort the mop head came free.

But it wasn't only the mop that was liberated. Roman reached into the housing and pulled on a handful of wires. He cast a casual glance across the floor. No one had seen him. He tucked the wiring back into the mounting, grabbed the mop handle and got to his feet.

• • • •

"Sacrifice." Zhukov understood now. "The giving of one life for others."

"For *all* others," Neill corrected gently. "*For what I received I passed on to you as of first importance: that Christ died for our sins according to the Scriptures, that he was buried, and that he was raised on the third day.*"

"That's from the Bible." Even Radya knew that. "My mother had one. I don't know what became of it." He gave the Marine an odd look. "You have committed this book to memory?"

"Not all of it," Mike grinned. "Blame my dad; he was the missionary."

"But not the only one, Mischa," Yuri called out. He

slapped a magazine into his rifle. "It would seem that's a family tradition."

Zhukov touched Neill's arm, intrigued by what he heard. "And His death was enough?"

He nodded. "Yes. *For by one sacrifice he has made perfect forever those who are being made holy.*"

"*Holy.* How can a man be made holy?"

"By putting faith in Him, Doc. By trusting Christ."

"Nothing else?"

Neill was shaking his head. "There's nothing you can add to it. The work's already been done."

Voskov looked elsewhere. He'd been silent, listening to every word, but now braced at the sound of clattering on the stairwell. Roman Shapoval appeared and was met with a muzzle pointed his way.

"Radya—it's time." Xander lowered his weapon, but the engineer was only partially relieved. "The Russians want everyone downstairs."

"And the children—have they brought them?"

"In the hangar. With the admiral's troops."

"Taras won't be far behind, then," Zhukov muttered. He got to his feet and faced Neill. "Stay here."

The Marine nodded. "Remember the plan, Doc. You might have to improvise, but you can do this."

A tired smile, but hopeful. "I must do this, Captain. And don't forget your role—all of you."

"We'll be ready. Count on it."

Yuri and Xander nodded in agreement. The old man turned to go. Reaching the ladder, he stopped.

"Sacrifice, Mikhail. What a beautiful concept. What a completely selfless and beautiful concept."

And before Neill could answer, Zhukov was gone.

33

FIELD TRIP

"**W**HAT'S THIS, THEN?" Zhukov strode forward, hobbling on his cane and challenging the young officer. Shapoval was at his side.

The watch commander turned. "We wondered if the children might enjoy something different today, Doctor." A dozen young faces stared up at him. "A chance to see where their parents spend so much of their time."

"A drafty hangar?"

"No, Doctor. The science lab."

A school trip. So that's how they're selling it, Radya mused.

"This is not a playground, Lieutenant. "

The Russian shrugged. "A photo of the group, then. With all of your people, and their families." An infantry-man standing nearby held a camera. "The admiral would like to document your work."

Some of the scientists drifted out of the lab, curious, and one of the machinists approached from his work-bench. His son was among the group of children, and he eyed the gathering with suspicion.

"Radya—what's the meaning of all this?"

"Admiral Pavlenko has an outing in mind, Sergei." There was a touch of sarcasm in his voice. "But the lab is hardly the place for an excursion." Zhukov struggled to take a knee. Gripping his cane, he looked into the eyes of the children and smiled. "Now then—who would like to visit the plane, instead?"

There was wide-eyed enthusiasm for this. Radya's audience erupted in shouts. Several raised their hands— a few cried "Me, me!"—and the youngest among them jumped at the prospect.

Zhukov was also pleased. This was exactly the response he'd hoped for.

The watch commander frowned at the old scientist. "Doctor, I think it would be best—"

"Don't spoil their fun, Lieutenant," Radya admonished him. He could be most persuasive. "You wouldn't want to disappoint the children. Besides, we can tour the lab later—after we've seen the *Commissar*." He smiled warmly at the officer. "By all means, bring a few of your men—most have never been aboard, am I right?"

"That is true," the lieutenant was forced to admit. He considered the idea. There was no harm in delaying the inevitable, giving them all a few happy moments aboard the plane. Forcing them into the lab now would only arouse suspicion. A quick look-see, and then his men would herd them back—

Zhukov took charge. "Sergei," he called to the machinist. "Bring everyone from the lab. And be quick about it." A mischievous grin. "The photographer looks anxious."

• • • •

Crockett waited by the crew door, the muzzle of his

weapon pointed at the cargo deck.

"What if the old boy can't persuade 'em, Mike?"

Neill's sidearm was unholstered. "We improvise."

He leaned back into the bulkhead, hidden between the *Commissar*'s rib-frames. The interior lighting was subdued and gave him further concealment.

"You get a good look at the hangar? Place looks old."

"Positively ancient—everything but the plane," Neill agreed. He spied movement on the floor. "Heads up, pal. We've got incoming."

Nate melted into the shadows. "Friendlies?"

"Zhukov's in front," Neill breathed. "Kids. Parents. Shapoval, too." Everything was going according to plan—so far.

"Any troops?"

"Three naval infantry."

"The gang's all here."

"Almost," Mike answered. He faced right. "Are you ready, Tanya?"

"I'm ready," she swallowed.

"Okay, get the kids as far forward as you can. We'll take it from there. *Safeties on*, people—this could get dicey."

The young woman edged closer to the egress door. Yuri and Xander crouched on either side of an instrument pallet, weapons in hand. Brisbane waited upstairs.

Footsteps on the stairwell. The tapping of Zhukov's cane. Aided by Shapoval, the doctor crossed the threshold and stood by the door, ushering the children inside. They needed little encouragement; there were smiles on each face, and the first ones aboard gaped in wonder at the *Commissar*'s cavernous bay.

Tanya played her part effortlessly, welcoming the youngsters with a broad smile. Quick hugs for a few, and then she took them by the hand and guided them toward the front of the plane.

"Radya—*why are we here?*"

Zhukov could see puzzled looks as his team climbed the steps. Everyone was accounted for. The old scientist felt little surprise. After all, he reasoned, the Russians were very thorough.

Radya laid a finger to his lips and urged silence.

"In good time, Sergei," he whispered.

• • • •

"Enough tea," Admiral Pavlenko announced. He placed the cup on the conference table and stared at his watch. "We should go below."

"How long have you known Zhukov, Admiral?"

Pavlenko stared at Utkin. He was struck by the odd nature of the question—and its timing. Was Sasha trying to sway him? Was he making an appeal to moral restraint, maneuvering him to reconsider?

"Since Soviet times, Colonel. My patrol boat fished him from the sea following the loss of the first plane."

Utkin had a smirk, and Taras regarded the expression as impertinent. "*Your* patrol boat, Admiral? Were you in command of the *Gromov*, then?"

Tamarkin hadn't expected a contest between the two men. He looked on with interest.

The senior officer glared. "I was the *Gromov*'s political officer. As such, I shared the captaincy with another patriot of the motherland." To his own surprise, Pavlenko couldn't recall the man's name. "Do you have any other comments, Sasha?"

"No, Admiral." Utkin seemed unusually cool.

"Then this discussion is over."

Pavlenko got to his feet. Tamarkin also stood, the last remnants of a meal before him. Colonel Utkin pushed back his chair, and together with the admiral's protective detail the group moved to the door.

• • • •

For their part, the Russian troopers embarking on the giant plane received a less than cordial welcome.

The watch commander boarded behind his men. His eyes were drawn to the right; two of the red-garbed technicians lingered by the door, facing the front. It was only when they turned that he saw their weapons.

One of the infantrymen brought up his rifle. Crockett stopped him with a butt stroke to the face. The man's head snapped back; he grunted and dropped, his weapon clattering to the metal floor.

But his comrade was faster. He raised his AK, pointing the barrel in Zhukov's direction and managed to squeeze off a round. The shot was wild, and the rifle's report caused chaos, sending most of the alarmed Ukrainians crouching for cover.

Nate slammed his carbine into the Russian's gut. He doubled over, and Yuri pounced, disarming and knocking him to the deck in one swift motion. After a moment of inaction the watch commander found his wits. He reached for a sidearm, but before it cleared his belt a pistol was jammed against his temple.

"Arms at your side."

The Russian braced and swung an elbow. This earned him a knee to the groin. Neill's 9mil was now in his face.

He checked the Russian's collar. "Don't test my resolve, Lieutenant. At this range I won't miss." Neill's concern was for the passengers. "Anybody see where that round went?"

Shapoval was having trouble standing. He sat down abruptly. Zhukov gripped his arm, eyes wide.

"I think I've found it, Captain."

He said nothing else, his face as white as Roman's.

• • • •

The admiral's entourage left the hall and stepped into the hangar. Six Russian infantrymen were nearby. They were indifferent until the officers arrived.

Pavlenko stopped cold. Something wasn't right; the lab was open, and the space inside was empty—with not a Ukrainian soul to be seen. And then came the sound of gunfire.

But from where?

"Sergeant," he barked. His eyes swept the room. "Where is your lieutenant?"

Pavel Varushkin braced. The fans made hearing difficult, and he raised his voice. "He's aboard the plane, comrade Admiral."

"And Dr. Zhukov?" Tamarkin demanded. He could see the darkened sky. The rain was heavier now.

"Also aboard the plane, sir."

Why was the hangar open to the sea? Taras felt bewilderment and alarm. "The Ukrainians, Sergeant. The children; where are they?"

Varushkin grew nervous. "Sir, everyone is on board."

Pavlenko blinked. He'd given strict orders, and his troops were hand-picked; battle-hardened infantry, most fresh from the field. They knew the price of disobedience.

Radya was behind this, he was sure of it. Did the old man know? Had someone tipped him off?

"Every member of Zhukov's team—*including their families*—is aboard the aircraft," the admiral snarled. "Is that what you're telling me, Sergeant?"

And then he saw the landing gear.

Where were the wheel chocks?

"Sergeant, bring two men and come with me."

• • • •

"Yuri—Nate," Neill snapped. "Get the door."

The watch commander's hands were behind his back. Electrical tape covered his mouth. He managed a glance to his left. Kneeling beside him was the man Yuri had subdued.

A rifle lay next to the man with the broken nose. Neill kicked it away, then gagged him and secured his wrists with a plastic tie. He wiped sweat from his brow. "Let's get Roman upstairs, Doc. We've got to make this fast."

• • • •

The door was halfway up when Pavlenko got there. He reached high, clawing the edges, trying to pull it down. Yuri and Nate struggled on the other side.

"Nathan—" Yuri called out. "*Let it go!*"

And so they did.

Crockett saw an opportunity too good to pass up. He flipped the selector switch on his weapon to 'semi'. Pointing the barrel through the open door, he fired one round at Shapoval's oxy/acetylene rig.

The tanks exploded. Pieces of the shredded bottles flew in every direction. Two of Pavlenko's men were hit by shrapnel. Two more dove for cover, but Nate's well-placed shot created more distraction than injuries.

Yuri's ploy had worked; the door see-sawed, moving in the other direction. Gravity did the rest. Taras found himself falling backward, his body slamming to the floor. On the way down he lost his grip.

Tamarkin was at his side instantly. His weapon was drawn, but someone on the *Commissar* yanked hard on the handrails, and the Russian officer—along with his winded admiral—watched as the door lifted and the plane was sealed from the inside.

34

TRAINING FLIGHT

"**T**HAT WAS a *gunshot*, wasn't it?" Taylor focused on Nate as he came up the ladder. "Did you fire on the Russians?"

"They were shooting at us, Doc," Crockett answered. He turned, taking hold of Roman's arm. Neill popped up next, steadying the engineer from behind. "Shapoval's been hit."

"*What*?" Her eyes widened. She rushed forward, and then doubled back, finding a place for the injured man. "How bad is it?"

"Bad enough." The two Marines guided him toward the row of seats. Shapoval was conscious, but his breathing was labored. Blood stained the right side of his coveralls. The Ukrainian fell into the chair, gasping.

"I'm all right."

"Shut up, Roman!" Tanya chided. She had nearly reached the top. Radya followed her, climbing one step at a time. "Let them help you."

Neill knelt, checking the wound. "Lower torso—" He ran his hand along Roman's back. "And an exit wound. Through and through." He applied pressure in front. His palm was covered in blood. "Doc, find a towel or something—anything to stop this bleeding."

Brisbane rummaged through one of the rucks. She found a rolled up t-shirt. "*Here*—use this."

"No, not me, Doc—*you*. Get over here and keep your hand on this wound."

"I'm not medically trained!"

"It does say doctor in front of your name," Crockett pointed out.

"You're not helping, Lieutenant," she glared.

"I'm not asking you to perform surgery. Just help me keep this man alive." Neill faced Zhukov. "What about it, Doc? Can we still do this?"

The scientist frowned. "It will be difficult without a pilot."

"All this fuss over nothing," Shapoval grunted. He tried getting up. "I can still fly the plane, Radya."

"Sit *down*." Brisbane pushed him back. "*Michael*—"

Crockett found his ruck. "Hang on—I've got a pouch of QuikClot and some gauze in here someplace."

"Do as she says, Roman," Neill said. "We can't have you bleeding out."

"No, Mike—lay him flat," Nate advised. He helped Taylor get him to the floor. "Basic first aid—keep his airway open. We'll need to watch his breathing, too. He's probably going into shock."

"This man needs proper attention."

"Probably not the best place for that, Professor." Crockett tore open the pouch and poured the contents into Roman's wound. "Ivan's not likely to be handing out band-aids."

• • • •

Captain Tamarkin had to give it to the Old Man.

Pavlenko must be pushing sixty, he reasoned. Yet he was agile enough—and bold enough—to rush ahead of his protectorate, to challenge whatever waited for him aboard the plane.

And he'd almost made it.

"The egress doors." Tamarkin pointed to a recessed pocket. A handle inside was marked RESCUE. "They can be opened from this side."

Pavlenko waved him off. His body ached, but he pushed through the pain. He was already bouncing back.

"Zhukov intends to escape. We must prevent that."

"But our men are still aboard," Tamarkin reminded him. "Surely—"

"Our men have been compromised, Captain," Taras spat out. "Otherwise Radya could not have taken control of the aircraft. You there—" he called to his Marines, "Get beneath the plane; put those chocks in front of the drive wheels." He stared at the girders overhead. "Colonel Utkin—have your troops secure that door."

"But does he have a *pilot*, Admiral?" Tamarkin objected. "Otherwise, Zhukov couldn't possibly—"

"Zhukov is a desperate man, Nestor. There's nothing he won't try now."

• • • •

"We're wasting time." Dr. Zhukov crossed the floor and moved toward the front of the plane. "Captain Neill, come with me."

Mike was also giving orders. "Nate, go below and give our friends a hand. Make sure the Russians don't find some way to breach the doors."

"Roger that, boss." Crockett was off like a shot.

"Now, Captain." Radya was insistent.

"On my way, Doc." Neill turned to go. "Tanya, stay with Shapoval; cover him with a blanket and do what you can to help." He held a fist to his chest. "Stay strong, Roman."

He managed a feeble grin, one that faded as soon as Neill left the passenger compartment.

• • • •

"Sit there," Radya directed. He was seated on the right side. Neill sized up the space. It was larger than he expected, and the instrument board was a curious shade of aquamarine.

"That's where the pilot sits," Neill observed.

"Yes, Michael. That's where the pilot sits." Zhukov began toggling switches. Systems whirred, and the cockpit glowed with red, orange and green light. He worked the manual controls for other systems. "Are you ready to test your skills?"

Neill's expression was blank. "You said we couldn't do this without a pilot."

"I said it would be difficult," Zhukov shot back.

"I'm a *ground-pounder*. Not an aviator."

"You're an officer."

"That's not enough." He regarded the controls as if they were a snake. "What about some other member of your team?"

"Roman is the only one with flying experience—no one else." Radya motioned to his left. "Take your seat, Captain. I can guide you through the basic functions. Tanya can handle navigation."

The Marine offered one last protest. "Radya, you're not hearing me; I don't have the training. *I'm not a pilot.* I'm analog in a digital world."

"That's perfect, then," Zhukov said. "In case you haven't noticed, most of the controls *are* analog." He reached overhead, but the panel was too far. "Would you mind? That control—far left."

Neill stepped forward and moved the switch to the 'on' position. Something rumbled on the right side of the nose. "What did I do?" he asked.

"You just started engine number one," the scientist answered matter-of-factly.

• • • •

Tamarkin looked up. There was a low roar just ahead; the turbofan near the cockpit drew in air, forcing it into the combustor. Ignition came next, and hot exhaust flowed from the nozzle assembly.

The light had changed; control surfaces on the trailing edge of the wing moved, blocking the glare. Flaps. Ailerons. The stabilator at the rear.

Pre-flight checks, Tamarkin surmised correctly. *He's preparing for take-off.*

Three of Pavlenko's infantrymen had crawled under the landing gear. The sound of the turbine almost forced a panic.

"He can't move with only one engine," Tamarkin shouted. At least he hoped that was true. "*Now get those chocks in place.*"

The infantrymen understood. Lying under the *Commissar*'s belly, they kicked at the long wooden blocks, wedging them under the massive wheels.

• • • •

"Here." Zhukov tossed a small booklet Neill's way. "That's the pilot's checklist. Start-up procedures are in the front; read them aloud."

Neill leaned back in the seat. He turned the laminated pages and started working through the list. Zhukov answered as he called off each item.

"Ivan's not going to just let us waltz out of here, Doc. Shouldn't we fire up the other engines?"

"Stay focused, Captain." Radya studied the control panels before him. "For routine flights, we use a warehouse tug to haul the plane to the entrance."

"No time for that," Neill replied. "Can we move this beast under its own power?"

"We have to try." Zhukov's brows knit together, eyes moving from left to right. "We need to start the rest of the engines in sequence, and then add thrust. Now keep reading."

"Accumulator power?"

"Operational."

"Pneumatic systems?"

Zhukov found the gauge. "Also operational."

"Pneumatic rotation—on all turbines?"

"Check."

"APU cutoff." He frowned. "Won't we need that?"

"One engine is already running. It can supply power for the rest."

"If you say so. Electrical fuel pumps?"

Zhukov searched but couldn't find it. "Skip that one. Go to the next."

Fuel mixed with air and was fed into the combustors. The rumbling increased. Ten engines shuddered with life, four on either side of the nose and the two hanging under each wing.

"Time to leave, Captain," Radya said quietly. "You may release the brakes."

"Where?"

"Your right knee—that handle, yellow grip."

Neill pulled. "Got it."

"Now add power." He pointed to the center console. Two sets of levers were positioned between the pilot and co-pilot seats. "Ease the throttle forward."

Neill pushed on the controls. The gentle vibration became more pronounced, and there was an increase in sound. But no movement.

"Nothing's happening," the Marine observed.

"Check the brake handle. It might be stuck."

Neill worked it back and forth and throttled up again.

"Negative. Still no-go."

Zhukov cursed under his breath. "Pavlenko's discovered the chocks."

Shapoval shouted from the back. "Radya, angle the nozzles. Thirty degrees."

"You can do that?" Neill asked.

Zhukov tripped more switches, cantering the thrusters. A motor hummed. A string of lights went green.

"Try now, Captain."

Neill pushed. Still nothing.

Nate's voice came up from below. "Why aren't we moving, Mike?"

"Workin' on it, pal." The captain clenched his teeth, imagining Russian troops crawling all over the plane's exterior.

• • • •

Flight-Ops called for his supervisor.

"Sir," he rose from his chair. "We have an unauthorized engine start in the hangar!"

In the midst of everything else, the officer in charge was already aware. The floor beneath his feet shook, and he marched to the windows.

A weapon—*or weapons*—had fired. Scuffling on the floor, and some kind of explosion. Now this.

What the devil—?

"Radio those in the cockpit," he ordered. A quick glance at the mission board; no tests were scheduled until tomorrow, and the *Commissar*'s pilots were elsewhere.

Someone waved from down below, someone he recognized. *Captain Tamarkin.* He waved again, pointing up at the girders. The message was clear.

"Any response?"

Flight-Ops shook his head. "No, sir. No response."

"Never mind."

There were protocols for these kinds of situations. Closing the hangar door was the first order of business. A round red knob sat squarely on the operations console. The officer hit it with an open palm. He stared at the ceiling, waiting. Nothing happened. Again, with the same result.

The door remained frozen in place.

"Sound the alarm, Sergeant." He swore. "Where are the manual controls?"

"Downstairs." Flight-Ops raised a hand and pointed. "Southeastern corner, at ground level."

• • • •

Tamarkin's eyes were fixed on the engines. Waves of exhaust rippled the air, distorting his view.

Pavlenko was also watching the plane. So was everyone else. "You didn't even say goodbye, Radya," he said aloud. His voice was without emotion.

"Would you have done so?"

There was anger in Pavlenko's reply. "I told you to close that door, Colonel."

"Let them go, Taras."

Pavlenko faced his insubordinate officer. He was surprised to see that Utkin held a pistol in his hand.

One of the guards started forward. Utkin was undeterred. He chambered a round.

"The children are innocent, Admiral. You have no right."

"Put the gun down, Sasha."

Utkin shook his head. The smell of jet fuel was in his nostrils, and the fumes stung his eyes. "When the plane is away. Not before."

"You've been *helping* them, haven't you?"

"I'm helping them now."

A klaxon sounded. It was enough to pull Utkin's eyes elsewhere.

Pavlenko leveled his Makarov and fired.

• • • •

"Gunfire in the hangar!" Flight-Ops drew back before peering below. He was pointing again. "By the plane, sir."

"I see it, Sergeant."

The weapons discharge brought more naval infantry running. They bunched around Pavlenko, eyes searching for threats while Tamarkin bent and touched the still form of Colonel Utkin.

"You saw what he did." Taras tried excusing his actions. "The man was ready to shoot me."

With five rounds in his chest Sasha wasn't prepared to argue. Captain Tamarkin rolled him over. There was little blood; the colonel's heart had stopped pumping before the volley ended, even before he slumped to the deck.

Tamarkin released his grip. "He won't be making that mistake again, Admiral."

• • • •

The plane roared, rocking forward and then back, but was held fast, like some great tethered bird.

Tanya took her eyes off Shapoval. "*Papa*," she cried. "We need to go."

"Use the *rockets*, Radya," Roman called. He pushed

up on one elbow. "And turn off the transponder—"

"Rockets?" Neill's head came up. "What rockets?"

"Jet-assisted take-off," Zhukov answered. He did as the engineer instructed. "Short burn boosters; the *Commissar* has them on both sides."

"Will that work?"

"Yes." A shadow entered from behind. "It will work, Captain." Roman was in the cockpit now, leaning on Tanya and Brisbane for support.

"So you've got your own Fat Albert," Neill grinned.

Zhukov frowned at both men. "I don't understand."

"The American Blue Angels," the Marine explained. "Part of the Navy's demonstration team. Fat Albert had rockets, too."

"Same principle." Shapoval was at Neill's side.

"Now get out of my seat."

• • • •

"We could disable the aircraft," Tamarkin suggested. "Small arms fire, directed at the engines. Or the landing gear—"

Pavlenko considered it. Near the opening, his men struggled with the chains and pulleys used as a backup for the door. These were never used, and the gears had long since seized.

It wasn't surprising that no one heard the plane's servomotor. The big fans stirred the air, but even those were drowned out by the sound of the engines. On both sides of the aircraft, pods snapped free of their lateral mounts. Arranged symmetrically, each casing held eight thrusters pointed at the deck. The admiral and his troops stood just meters away.

"No!" Pavlenko howled. He gripped Tamarkin's arm and pulled him toward the wall.

A repetitive clicking sound cut through the din. The

rocket motors were primed and ignited. There was a flash of intense heat; fire blazed, scorching the hangar floor, momentarily blinding everyone. Most of the infantry-men scrambled, but one of the Russian Marines moved too slow, his legs and trousers singed before he managed to escape.

There was more than enough thrust to make the jump now. The burst of power jolted the fuselage. Graceless on the ground, the aircraft hopped over the obstacles and bounced, then accelerated forward, freed from her restraints. The boosters still burned. Pavlenko shielded his eyes from the glare. Cowering by one of the fans, he and Tamarkin watched as the plane surged toward the entrance.

She was building speed. Two of the admiral's men came to their senses and fired short bursts. The rounds peppered wing joints and flashed against the hull but had no effect. The *Commissar* kept moving. Her nose dipped; she was on the ramp now, splashing into the shallows, rain pelting her skin as she pushed out to sea.

35

THE EYE IN THE STORM

Arkangel Base, hangar level

THE *COMMISSAR* WAS LONG GONE, passing through an angry sky, her path now erased by sheets of falling rain and the black clouds that hung just above the waves.

Pavel Varushkin stood near the boundary separating storm from hangar. The barrier between wasn't hard and fast; at times, gusting winds drove the downpour inside, soaking the concrete floor. Pavel often wondered if anyone out there could see the interior when the big door was open. Probably not, he decided. Russian aircraft and coastal patrols kept prying eyes away, and the hangar was rarely open to the sea. Of course, there was nothing the Federation could do about *satellites*—

He lifted his chin and put his nose to work. The smell of salt was in the air, but the stench of jet fuel was gone, pushed out by the fans and claimed by the gale whipping the coastline. Pavel turned and looked over his shoulder. The Nest was stark and unoccupied. It felt odd to see it that way, the wide expanse just a void, vacant and empty, and Pavel wondered if he would ever see the plane again.

A new sound reached his ears, something other than the spattering of rain on cement and the rolling breakers.

"The wiring's been ripped out," the corporal of the guard reported. He'd just come from the generator. "One of Zhukov's people must have done it."

"Can it be fixed?"

The enlisted man shrugged. "I'm not an electrician, but I think so."

The wind sent spray across the ramp. Saltwater was hardly a proper lubricant for any firearm, so the two men stepped away, shielding their rifles. They watched the waves for another moment before the corporal spoke again.

"The admiral wants us to take Utkin's body to the infirmary." His tone was solemn, almost reverent. And Varushkin knew why. The corporal was showing defer-ence, but not for the dead colonel. It was intended for him. "You do know that you're in charge now, Pavel."

The sergeant grumbled something that was hard to hear, but the corporal was right. Their lieutenant—and two other Marines—had been spirited away by the *Com-missar*, leaving Pavel as the next in line for command. A new officer would be sent in short order, to be sure, but until that time, Sergeant Varushkin was bound by duty and rank to take charge.

It was not a career move he had expected.

"Put someone to work on the generator," Pavel in-structed. "I want that door closed before the storm pass-es. Take three others and carry Utkin upstairs." He eyed the open floor; two of his troopers stood over the colo-nel's body, but Pavlenko was not to be seen. "And we'd best be quick about it."

There was no immediate response. Lightning flashed

and thunder pealed over their heads. The corporal's attention was drawn away, but then he pointed; something rolled at the water's edge, nudged by the surf. Something man-shaped, wrapped in the colors of a Russian Federation uniform, bloated by exposure.

"*Pavel—*"

The tide had found its way back, depositing a grisly piece of flotsam. Vladimir Baskovich had come home, and Varushkin realized that the dispensary would receive two bodies today, not just one.

• • • •

It wasn't hard to gauge the admiral's next play. He led the group to the second level gallery, bounding up the steps two at a time. The control center stiffened as he came through the door.

"I need a direct line to the admiralty," Pavlenko growled. "And I need it *now*."

The operations officer nodded curtly, his face lined with angst. He motioned to the *starshy serzhant* manning the communications console. This man was less cowed in the presence of a three-star, and the connection was quickly made.

• • • •

The *Commissar* shook in the face of a strong headwind. Shapoval and Zhukov fought back, wrestling with the yoke and lifting the plane's nose.

"You're free to maneuver." Tanya studied a display. "We've cleared the shallows—almost five kilometers now."

Brisbane steadied herself by holding on to the back of a seat; the storm thrashing the plane did little to blunt her spirits.

"Are we really away?"

"Temporarily—but that won't last," Neill warned. It was time to consider immediate threats. In Ukrainian he asked, "How long before Pavlenko sends the alert aircraft?"

Zhukov was quick to reply. "I would imagine those orders have already been given."

"This will not sit well with the Russians," Yuri explained in broken English. "They will try to stop us."

"How?" Taylor's concern was growing.

Shapoval broke in. "What course, Radya?"

"A good question. One we dared not consider, until now. Captain?"

"I guess that depends on gas. What's the range of an aircraft like this?"

"Fully fueled? Eight thousand kilometers."

"Did anybody top off the tank before we left?"

Radya peered over his glasses, checking a readout.

"Our current capacity is fifty-four percent," he said. Rain slapped at the windscreen, and the sky was a gray mass. "Which means we have several options."

"Follow the Aleutians, then. Steer for Alaska."

The doctor didn't argue. "The Americans probably won't shoot us down," he agreed.

"*Probably?*" Tanya's voice pitched high. "I'm glad you're so optimistic."

"Your father's right," Neill told her, and he hoped so. "Our side wants to get their hands on Charybdis."

Tanya was kneeling next to Roman, pressing against his wound. "Your side will see a big Russian airplane, Captain. What's to stop them?"

"We'll cross that bridge when we get there. Can you navigate this thing?"

"Yes."

The Marine scanned the consoles. "Which station?"

"Here." She motioned to Taylor, and the two women traded places. Tanya moved to the navigation panel. "Alaska?"

"Works for me."

A sigh. "*Where* in Alaska?"

From far beneath them came a dull thudding sound as the belly of the plane slapped against whitecaps. Neill saw sweat on Shapoval's brow.

"Anchorage. Can you put that in?"

She used a keypad, typing in the destination name to call up a set of coordinates. "It's done." To Roman she called, "Navigation's locked. Auto-pilot at your discretion."

"Not yet." Shapoval's eyes were glued to the radar scope. He steered in a northerly direction, following the coastline. "We have a rendezvous to make first."

The *Stenka*-class patrol boat was a simple affair, but robust, a green water navy vessel, lightly armed and barely forty meters long.

PSKR-235 belonged to the Russian Coast Guard. She stayed close in, harassing uninvited ships and skirting the littoral zones within sight of the shore. Her course today was southeast, but the wind and waves were treacherous, and the pilot steered into the teeth of the storm, trying to avoid the rolling swells.

"New contact, Captain—starboard quarter." The officer of the watch was a young midshipman on the cusp of promotion. He had no sooner made the pronouncement when his eyes were pulled back to the position indicator. "*Captain*—!"

The sailor's tone screamed alarm. The boat's captain faced right and aft, field glasses in hand. He stared into the murk but saw nothing.

"Distance?"

"One kilometer." The man's voice caught. No, that wasn't right. "*Comrade Captain*—now *half* a kilometer!"

"I see it," the captain answered. His grip tightened.

It wasn't a ship, but he already knew that. The contact's speed was too great. It had to be an aircraft, flying at sea level.

Literally.

"Brace for impact."

The calm, dispassionate voice the captain heard was his own, but even he thought the order was comical. In this circumstance, there was no suitable preparation. Colliding with the approaching leviathan would be fatal for everyone on board.

The giant plane seemed to split the sky, parting the rain in its path. Navigational lights blazed in the soup. Engine noise filled the air. 235's bridge crew instinctively ducked, and only the boat's captain didn't flinch.

His eyes were closed.

A deep shadow passed over the wheelhouse, lingering as the *Commissar* soared above. The hull shook, and the weather abated, briefly shunted aside by the plane's presence. But there was no collision, and as quickly as it had appeared, the beast was gone.

It was the aircraft from Arkangel Base. The captain had seen her before, and so had most of his crew. All of their previous encounters were under the cover of darkness—never this close, and never in daylight. Which made him wonder—

The communications officer burst through the hatch. "Captain! We have traffic from the Fleet!"

"We've just seen the traffic, Lieutenant."

"*No*, comrade Captain," Comm sputtered. He looked around him. Every eye in the compartment was trained to port. "I'm talking about *radio* traffic—from the Fleet office in Petropavlovsk."

"From the admiralty?" The winged apparition was gone, so the captain relented. "And what does the Fleet require from us?"

"They want information," Comm answered breathlessly. He lowered his voice. "The whereabouts of the *Commissar*. Course and speed. The request has gone out to every ship in the sector."

The captain was struck by that. *Why was Petropavlovsk looking for her*? She wasn't lost—the plane had just flown over their heads—and given her great size, the *Commissar* was certainly hard to miss. Surely they knew where she was.

"Something easy for once," the captain grumbled. He checked the compass, but that was unnecessary. "Course is due north. *Officer of the watch*—do you concur?"

The midshipman nodded his agreement. "I concur, comrade Captain. The plane's course is due north."

"Speed?"

"At the point of intersection her speed exceeded two hundred KPH."

"*Kharasho*." *Very well.* The officer was pleased. He was also quite happy to be alive. "Radio the Fleet and give them our answer."

"*Da*, comrade Captain." Comm was already on his way through the hatch.

• • • •

The obstacle avoidance system had gone from soft buzzing to full shriek. Now it was silent again. Neill stared out at the horizon, but there wasn't much of one to see.

"You nearly clipped his mast."

Shapoval countered with a crooked smile. "Do you think they saw us?"

"That was deliberate. You're giving them a false trail

to follow."

"Yes, Captain," the engineer chuckled. "Two more kilometers. Maybe three. Then we change course—and hope they take the bait."

Neill looked at the navigational display. "This route puts us over dry land."

"We aren't going that far." Roman's hand dropped to the throttle. He eased it forward, adding thrust. "We need to use the storm for cover, and steer clear of the shoreline."

"You don't want to be seen again."

Roman shook his head. "Not once we've turned."

"And then?"

"Then we climb—*above* the storm. Twenty-thousand feet should be sufficient."

Neill was confused. "I thought the *Commissar* was a sea-skimmer. Wing-in-ground effect and all that."

"We've progressed much further than that, Captain Neill." Zhukov's mood had brightened, and there was a lilt in his voice. "Roman and I have managed a few adjustments to the airframe."

"Do the Russians know about those?"

The Marine's gut told him they didn't. He certainly hoped so. It might provide a crucial advantage and buy them some time, but neither Zhukov nor Shapoval would give him an answer.

36

ABOUT THE CLOUDS

Control Room, Arkangel Base

"**S**URFACE SHIPS will do no good."

Pavlenko studied a sheet of Plexiglas fixed to the wall. It was marked with a grease pencil, triangles and squares showing the positions of Russian naval vessels. "The *Commissar* will only evade them."

Captain Tamarkin agreed, but there was a finer point to be made. "That depends on your goal, Admiral. Is it your intention to chase after Zhukov—or simply to find the plane?"

Taras looked away. "Both," he replied. To his way of thinking there was little distinction.

The room hummed around them. The plane's unexpected departure had brought Arkangel to life. Enlisted men bent over consoles, monitoring their radar screens. Comm tried again, but the *Commissar* ignored all transmissions. The officer in charge moved from one station to another, trying to be useful. He mulled over what he should do next. It was best to be proactive in the admiral's presence, especially in light of what had happened.

This was an unprecedented event, he brooded. The lieutenant had been dazed by what had happened over the course of the afternoon. *Everyone* had. Colonel Utkin was dead; three infantrymen—including the watch commander—had been snatched away; the body of a fourth had washed up on the ramp.

And the largest aircraft in the world had been stolen.

"Finding the *Commissar* could prove a simple task. But what then? Do we convince the doctor to return?" Tamarkin shook his head. "I'm sure we can make a most persuasive argument, but in the end, Admiral, such an outcome is unlikely."

Pavlenko took his meaning. The word had gone out to scramble fighters from Yelizovo Field, but none were readily available. Two flights had just returned from a mission, but as luck would have it, their ordnance was spent. The task of refitting the planes was underway and nearly complete, but the admiral was growing anxious.

"Finding the *Commissar* will hardly be simple, Captain," Taras sneered. "The sea is vast. And Radya has disabled the transponder. What's more, he knows our capabilities. He will fly low—under the radar horizon. Indeed, the plane is designed to do just that."

"A coordinated effort, then," Tamarkin suggested. He tapped the board with an index finger. "Between surface ships and aircraft. Our naval vessels will sweep the skies, while our planes employ downward-looking radar." His eyes fell on one of the displays. "What about transmitting over the horizon? The ionosphere could—"

"Admiral—" The sergeant at the comm desk raised a hand. Headphones covered the man's ears. "The Fleet reports success; one of our patrol craft was just overflown by a large aircraft—a very large aircraft."

"Where?"

The sergeant pecked at a row of keys. His monitor jumped, and a map appeared on the screen. He pointed.

"*Here*, sir."

"He's headed north," Tamarkin observed. "But where can he go? Karaginsky Island? The gulf, perhaps?"

"The gulf makes more sense," Pavlenko replied. "Radya might try ditching the plane on some stretch of coastline. Or he could cross the peninsula and make for Penzhina Bay." Taras shrugged. "A dozen options are possible, but if he hopes to succeed, he'll need help."

Tamarkin turned on his heel, facing the plot board again. "What about guided missile cruisers? Are there any in the gulf?" The captain envisioned a worst-case scenario, one where the plane would be shot down.

"The *Ustinov* is tied up at Petropavlovsk," Pavlenko told him. "And the *Nakhimov* is steaming south of the Commander Islands. Both are well out of range."

The sergeant with the headphones broke in again. "The alert aircraft have been resupplied," he announced. "They can be airborne in minutes."

Tamarkin stabbed at a point on the board. "Send the fighters north, Lieutenant.

"Tell them to start here."

•   •   •   •

Shapoval added power and eased back on the yoke. The control inputs were very responsive, and the *Commissar*'s angle of attack changed as her nose came up. The view was different now, and the gray veil beyond the windscreen was thinning.

More importantly, the clotting agent from Crockett's ruck had done some good.

Without warning, daylight filled the cockpit. Everyone shielded their eyes, but the engineer only squinted.

"We've broken through the ceiling. What does the altimeter read, Captain Neill?"

It took a moment to find the gauge. "Five thousand feet. How are you feeling?"

Roman began a slow banking maneuver to starboard. The plane continued to climb, buffeted by turbulence. "I can manage until we reach a higher altitude. Then we'll set the autopilot."

From the navigator's seat, Neill gave Zhukov and Shapoval the eye. "You two are full of surprises."

"Oh?" Roman smiled faintly. "What do you mean, Captain?"

"The West's knowledge of this plane is based on certain principles," he began. "But you've just blown those out of the water—no pun intended."

"The wing-in-ground effect?" Radya volunteered.

"That's a start. And the engines, *above* the fuselage."

"To protect them from seawater."

"But what about the turbofans under the wings?"

"What about them?" Zhukov seemed to be enjoying their banter. "The engines on either side of the nose pull the *Commissar* forward. For official consumption, the other two do the same, but they also supply lift—allowing us to climb."

"And Ivan hasn't figured that out?"

Radya shrugged. "These Russians aren't the sharpest knives in the drawer." He peered at the altimeter. "Approaching ten thousand feet, Roman."

"Seawater's corrosive. I get that. So what are they made of?" Neill was trying to take Shapoval's mind off his injury. "Glass carbon? A metal polymer?"

"You've done some research."

"But you're not going to tell me, are you?" The old man was being cagey.

"I can't give away *all* of my secrets, Captain Neill.

Besides, you haven't been properly vetted."

"Sarcasm," Mike laughed. "What about this rescue? Doesn't that count for something?"

"It's a mark in your favor," Radya conceded with a chuckle. He leaned forward in his seat, looking for back-scatter on the radar display. "We've been fortunate, up to this point. Nothing on the scope."

"So Pavlenko's not giving chase?"

Radya frowned. "Not yet, Michael."

Near the Aleutians

Shifting to F-16s was a natural progression in the world of target drones, with Falcons replacing the depleted supply of rapidly aging F-4s, and 'natural' because Phantoms were getting harder and harder to find.

The single-engine Falcons, derided by some as 'lawn darts', were chosen to fill the gap. Most were pulled from the boneyard at Davis-Monthan, in Arizona, and while these birds were unmanned, they were not unpiloted. That job was left to a select group of aviators cooped up in air conditioned portables on the ground. To seasoned veterans like Chris Prentice, they were mere youngsters with good hand/eye coordination and a penchant for video games, but he had to admit to a begrudging admiration for their skills.

"Targeting pods are working nicely," Nick Tate observed. "IDM modems integrating well, too." He checked his radar, spotting a contact to the south. That would be the command and control element—BALLPARK—a Boeing E-3 Sentry loitering in the distance. The AWACS plane—for *airborne warning and control system*—provided an overview of the battle space, plus weather surveillance and communications. A KC-135 from Elmendorf was standing by for fuel replenishment.

The major considered painting the Sentry with his fire-control radar. Maybe a little practice to shake up the drivers, but then he thought better of it. There were plenty of other targets in the sky; Hellcat Flight had already downed two of the fighters-turned-drones—their appearance had come as a surprise, calculated to test their reaction—and they hadn't even reached the exercise grid yet.

The voice of Colonel Prentice came over the radio. "Nice shot, Hellcat Three." He'd almost called the pilot by her first name.

"Thank you, sir."

Eager to learn and eager to please, Lieutenant Gwendolyn Elsketh had trained at Vance Air Force Base in Oklahoma, and was recruited for the Hellcat program because she had little to unlearn as a pilot. The young woman's flying prowess was another qualification. She'd proven those skills just minutes before, splashing a Falcon near Unimak Island in the Aleutians. Making the kill had been exhilarating for her, but she wasn't alone in her enthusiasm; the fourth member of the flight was Litt Settles, an officer hailing from Tyndall Air Force Base in the panhandle of Florida. Settles had loosed an AIM-9 earlier, knocking a drone out of the sky and earning bragging rights for drawing first blood.

Major Tate checked Elsketh's wingtip. The left rail was empty, but she still had a Sidewinder on her right, in addition to four Helius missiles in the internal bays. Arctic Wrath had gotten off to a good start, and there were other engagement opportunities waiting in the target-rich environment of the proving ground.

"Bring it in, Flight," Prentice directed. "Screenplay wants us downrange."

Tate and the others recognized the phrase from the morning briefing. Screenplay was today's byword for

Shemya Island, the land mass near Attu, and more specifically, Eareckson Station. SCREENPLAY was hosting the op on the ground, calling the shots in tandem with the Boeing AWACS plane.

The Hellcats drifted closer, forming up around the lead aircraft. Prentice pointed his jet toward Nikolski. He dipped his wing, gazing below. Clouds hugged the island chain as far as the eye could see. The colonel added thrust and climbed to twelve thousand feet, and the rest of the group joined him as they raced to the southwest.

• • • •

Two flights of eight Mikoyan MiG-29s covered the distance from Yelizovo to Ust-Kamchatsk in twenty minutes, following the jagged coastline and buzzing Arkangel Base at a low altitude. The squadron of navy aircraft was collectively known as GUARDIAN Flight. Humidity was thick, made more so by the westward moving storm, and the fighters climbed higher to avoid the denser air.

Senior Lieutenant Anton Kritchkov lifted his helmet visor and stared ahead. The Kamchatsky District jutted out to sea and passed beneath the fighters quickly. Spread out before them now was the wide expanse of the Gulf, while farther on was Karaginsky Island and the Litke Strait.

Kritchkov could guess at what he would find there. He swept the regions ahead with forward-looking radar, banking the Fulcrum for a look below. Winter had only begun to release her grip, and chunks of ice littered the emerald-green bay. From village ports, fishing boats pushed out from the mainland, dotting the surface. A Federation corvette patrolled the shallows, her wake trailing for half a mile, and not far behind a pod of Orcas hunted for food.

But the one thing Kritchkov didn't see was a large

aircraft flying north.

The officer keyed his mike. "Arkangel Base, GUARD-IAN Lead—no contacts at this time."

Given current weather and atmospheric conditions, Kritchkov's radar could interrogate targets at a distance of two hundred kilometers. He'd radioed the rest of the squadron, but the results were the same; none of his aircraft had detected a large body fuselage nearby—or anywhere in the immediate sector, for that matter.

Pavlenko hadn't expected this. Radya had somehow slipped away, covering his tracks. The admiral's eyes were on the plot board again, tracing the coastline of the bay to the inlet near Pakhachi. The Federation had a listening post there in the form of a radar installation.

Taras tapped the location and shot a glance at the operations officer. The man understood, nodded, and then placed a call while Pavlenko lifted the microphone from the console.

"GUARDIAN Lead, Arkangel." His voice was low and deliberate. "Sweep northwest. The plane might be making for the mainland—or even the Gulf of Shelikhov."

"Already done," came the terse reply. It was the second sortie of the day, and Kritchkov was tired. "We've also ranged east—without reflection."

Pavlenko heard the irritation in the pilot's voice. He decided to identify himself; such a disclosure might yield better results.

"Pilot—" he began, "—do you know to whom you are speaking?"

The lieutenant's attention was piqued. There was a pause as he considered the question. The voice did sound familiar.

He had met Pavlenko on two occasions; once on the tarmac at Yelizovo Field, and again in Petropavlovsk, at his own promotion ceremony. Kritchkov brightened.

Now he had an opportunity to serve not only the *Rodina*, but a flag officer, as well—and the latter might prove more beneficial.

"How may I be of service, Admiral?"

Much better. Pavlenko was satisfied with this reply.

"The aircraft in question is stolen property—we have reason to believe the perpetrators of this crime will seek refuge to the north or northwest." His grip on the microphone tightened. "I rely on you to hinder them."

"It's the *Commissar*, then?" the weary pilot asked. There was only one aircraft at Arkangel.

"It is," he admitted. His body stiffened. For the first time, Taras felt embarrassment at the situation.

"And is it their intention to escape, Admiral?"

"Yes, that is our conclusion."

Desertion, defection—or even theft. However one might define this occurrence, whoever stole the plane intended to make a getaway. Kritchkov was a true huntsman, and a different strategy came to mind. "Then I suggest a more plausible pattern for our search."

"I'm listening."

"Escaping to a country you're fleeing from is hardly liberation. Such an act would not accomplish the desired goal."

Across the room, the operations officer finished his call and cradled the phone. He turned to the admiral and shook his head; Pakhachi Station had seen nothing.

Kritchkov continued. "Should I steal such an aircraft, I would offer it up for its tactical value—to those who could ensure my safety."

Pavlenko could see it now. *The Americans*, he fumed.

Radya was colluding with the West.

Until now he'd resisted the idea. Turning over the plane to the United States would be dangerous for Zhukov, but no less so than remaining behind on Kamchatka, or being overtaken by a squadron of interceptors. Still, this pilot was right. And if Radya could convince the Americans of his intentions, the tactic might work.

"Southeast, then," Taras muttered. Prudence dictated a flight path that followed an appreciable land mass; the Aleutians offered both refuge and cover, and were the stepping stones to a safe haven in the United States. "Do you agree?"

"*Da*, comrade Admiral."

Kritchkov relayed his instructions to the squadron. One by one GUARDIAN Flight broke formation and banked right. The lieutenant was the last to turn; he pointed his radar to the west and north for one last sweep of the skies. Still nothing. The sun was high, and he slewed his fighter to the east, following his wingman on a course that would take the Fulcrums across the cold stretches of the Bering Sea.

37

EN ROUTE

"How's Shapoval?" Nate called. The plane had leveled off and was continuing northeast.

"He's stable enough to fly," Tereshenko answered back. He descended the narrow ladder, taking the steps two by two. His ears popped, and he flexed his jaw and swallowed to alleviate the pressure.

"So?" Voskov looked up. "What's our destination?"

Yuri jumped from the last step and laid a finger to his lips. He pulled his colleagues aside before saying anything else. Nate guessed at the reason; strapped into a row of seats were the Russian infantrymen, gagged, hands secured behind their backs, out of earshot but not forgotten.

"North America," Yuri told them. It was hard to catch his words. The droning of the engines filled the compartment.

"Alaska?"

Yuri nodded. "That's what the man said."

"North America," Xander repeated. "I've never been there."

Yuri grinned. "And why should you?"

Neither of the two had ventured far from home. Poland, Belarus, the Baltics; an occasional visit to Russia—discreetly, of course—but traveling to a Western nation was not in either man's résumé. Only their work with the security services afforded a chance for travel, and those excursions rarely took them beyond Eastern Europe.

But that was not the case now.

On either side of the aircraft were the scientists and their families, strapped into center-facing seats. Yuri wondered at their state of mind, sensing a range of emotions among them. Most felt anger for their former captors, and wrestled with the urge to act on those feelings. But there was also elation at being free, although short-lived; as reality sunk in, so did their fear—fear of the unknown, and the terror of reprisal.

It dawned on most that Arkangel would not give up without a chase.

Yuri waved a hand at their Russian prisoners. "What will we do with our guests?"

Crockett had his own ideas. "I say dump 'em in the Pacific, but the plane's already pressurized. Besides, Mike would probably object." He pointed his weapon in the Russians' direction—and made sure they noticed. "Most likely scenario? Our State Department questions them before they go back to Moscow."

That thought amused Tereshenko. "That would be—*awkward*, yes?"

Crockett smiled wickedly. "Sometimes humiliation's the best form of punishment."

· · · ·

GUARDIAN Flight raced south of the Commander Islands, instruments pointing ahead in search of a contact. There was nothing of interest for some time, but passing Medny—

"He is following the commercial routes," Lieutenant Kritchkov announced. The pilot studied his heads-up display; at the outer limits of his radar coverage was an immense aircraft, the return suggesting something much larger than any wide body airframe. He checked the distance; one hundred and twenty-eight kilometers, twenty-two thousand feet, give or take.

His wingmen saw it too. Their acknowledgements rippled across the net.

"He's much higher than expected," one of the junior officers noted.

Kritchkov was forced to agree given what he knew of the plane. Ekranoplans were knap-of-the Earth ground-hugging vehicles, but technology rarely stood still, and the contact before them was the only one in sight. This object *had* to be the *Commissar*.

The lieutenant pushed past the fatigue he felt and sent a new message. "Arkangel, large contact ahead. Please advise."

"Close and confirm, pilot."

"And the thief, Admiral? Does he have a name?"

"*Da*. He has a name."

Pavlenko's focus was on the plot board again. He had something special in mind for Radya. One way or another, the *Commissar* would not fall into American hands.

How that played out was entirely up to Zhukov.

Hellcat Flight

Two of the QF-16s were already up, streaking across the skies between Adak and Amchitka.

"Take the one on your right," Prentice directed. He was speaking to Lieutenant Settles in HELLCAT TWO.

They were still more than twenty miles out, but Settles had range and bearing almost immediately. "Tickling the patient," he acknowledged, using the colonel's phrase for interrogating a target. "*Fox Three!*"

An active-radar Helius jumped from the plane's open weapons bay and zoomed ahead. The pilot on the ground was good, but there was no escaping the missile's advanced targeting suite. The rest of the flight watched the impact, and the Falcon plummeted to the sea, a streaming fireball of jet fuel and twisted metal.

"Splash two," Settles chirped happily.

The other fighter banked east to evade the F/A-38s. Colonel Prentice was just lining up for a shot when his radio came to life.

"Hellcat Lead—" It was Ballpark. "We have a request from ground control. Can you provide assistance?"

Prentice was mildly irritated. The interruption had broken his concentration and cost him the shot.

"Send your traffic, Ballpark."

"Screenplay is monitoring multiple inbounds—one large heavy on a southeast track. He's got five—" Ballpark looked at his radar. "—make that eight aircraft on his six, trailing at fifty kilometers."

"Tactical formation?" Ivan might be conducting an exercise, Prentice thought, much like their own.

There was a pause. "Hard to say, Lead—hence the request. You game for a look-see?"

Prentice wasn't opposed to it. USPACOM—the U.S. Pacific Command—was on heightened alert since the attack on the *Meyer*. Forces in the region braced for the next shoe to drop, and the eyes and ears of the American military were tuned to any and all unusual activity that might be instigated by the Russian Federation.

"What's the location?" Prentice asked.

"The big bird is due north of Camel Train—" that

was the exercise name given to Attu Station, the larger island west of Shemya, "—following the bread crumbs back home."

Home meant Joint Base Elmendorf-Richardson. The radar officer on the Sentry consulted the rules of engagement; CARAVAN was the code-word for the Aleutians.

"Very well, BALLPARK," the colonel replied. ARCTIC WRATH would have to wait. "We'll extend and take a look. Stand down the exercise and give us a vector." To the rest of the Hellcats he issued a different order— *weapons hold.*

Prentice smiled to himself. The last time he'd uttered those words was in the skies above Poland, near the so-called Kaliningrad Corridor. In that instance, his Polish wingman had loosed an air-to-air missile and brought down a Russian Flanker. It was undeniably provocative, one that might have created an international incident— had the Federation not already caused one of their own.

With tensions running high, the colonel didn't want to repeat that performance.

• • • •

"You should lie down, Roman." Neill was anxious for the engineer to give up the controls. He didn't want the man to start bleeding again.

"I won't argue with you," Shapoval answered weakly. With Tanya's help he lifted himself out of the pilot's seat. Dr. Zhukov gripped the yoke a little more tightly, and Roman was amused.

"The auto-pilot is on, Radya. You don't need—"

Shapoval didn't finish his sentence. Threat receivers buzzed in their ears, filling the space, the insistent sound impossible to ignore. Warning lights flashed on the consoles. What came next was even more alarming.

The plane's automatic pilot took over. *Commissar*

banked hard to the right, dumping Shapoval back into his seat. Tanya almost fell but got low and managed to keep her balance.

Neill's eyes were on the windscreen. From above and behind something sailed past—a cylindrical object with a burning end.

"Missile." Zhukov had seen it too.

His voice was almost toneless.

There was chaos on the cargo deck. The scientists were strapped in, but Crockett and the SSD operatives were thrown against the plane's bulkhead and landed in a heap.

"Hey, keep it *steady* up there!"

Nate disentangled himself from the pile. He gripped Voskov's forearm and pulled him from the floor, noting that none of the three had dropped their weapons.

Yuri collected himself. "It's Shapoval. Has to be."

"One way to find out. Stay here."

The plane leveled off again. Nate turned and bounded up the ladder.

· · · ·

"Where did that come from?" Neill's eyes went to the display in the center console. He got his answer soon enough.

Zhukov tapped a finger on the screen. "I count eight aircraft. Interceptors, Captain—probably Navy MiGs from Petropavlovsk." He shook his head. "I was hoping your military would find us first."

Far beyond the windscreen, the missile dropped out of sight, falling toward the ocean. There was a flash and then a rumbling sound, followed by a shock wave that barely nudged the aircraft.

"The warning receivers are sluggish. We should have seen that coming." Roman reached out and turned a dial.

"I'm attenuating their range."

"Too late for that. Ivan's already found us."

"That was a warning shot," Zhukov declared. "We present an easy target. The next one won't miss."

"What's their range?"

Shapoval returned to his instruments. "Twenty kilometers and closing."

"Should we contact them? Seek terms?"

"Terms? That's a negative," Neill advised. "They'll try to contact *us*. Stay off the net—a little radio silence just might buy us some time."

"Time for what?"

"I wish I spoke Russian," Brisbane weighed in. The dialogue around her was hardly illuminating.

"It's Ukrainian." Crockett appeared from the hatch in the floor. "But don't sweat it, Doc. You can barely speak English. What gives, Mike?"

"We've got company," Neill breathed. "Multiple bad guys on our six."

"Does this thing have defensive weapons?"

Neill repeated the question to Dr. Zhukov. He turned away from the console, a dour look on his face.

"None at all—" he started. But then his expression changed. "—however, we do have something for *offense*." Radya fairly jumped from the chair, surprising Neill with his agility. "Take my place, Captain. Roman can't do this alone." He marched past Taylor. "Professor Brisbane—*pishly zem noyu*."

The Aussie blinked—Zhukov had spoken to her.

"Go with the Doc, Doc," Neill ordered.

"But where?" She was on her feet now.

"You wanted to know more about Charybdis," Radya called over his shoulder. He was moving aft, past the passenger compartment. "This might be your last chance."

38

OVER THE ALEUTIANS

GUARDIAN FLIGHT HAD located their quarry dead ahead—there was no mistaking the wide body transport with a boat-shaped fuselage. Kritchkov ordered his group to tighten their formation and the planes left the boundaries of the Bering Sea for the northern Pacific.

At Arkangel, Pavlenko walked to the map, flight ops personnel moving aside to give the senior officer space. The admiral took a grease pencil and marked the interceptors' last position. He studied the chart, eyes narrowing. The planes were well past the Commanders and fast approaching the Near Islands of Attu and Shemya. The *Commissar* was reportedly north of that position, traveling on an easterly path, and by now Zhukov was probably approaching Kiska.

Far too close, Taras thought. Radya was virtually in the enemy's camp. He needed to be stopped.

"No response, Arkangel," Kritchkov reported. "The *Commissar* ignores our transmissions."

Pavlenko was not at all surprised. "Persuade him to turn, pilot. Make him listen this time."

"By what means?" To this point the rules of engagement were non-existent.

The admiral considered the pilot's question. There were only two possible outcomes to Zhukov's gambit. Taras would have preferred to keep the plane intact, and to see its safe return to Kamchatka, but that seemed unlikely now. Radya would have weighed his options and decided on a course of action.

The man had made his choice. So be it.

"Pilot's discretion," the admiral growled. "But make him alter course. I want the *Commissar* back in her nest before nightfall."

Or in twisted pieces on the ocean floor, he didn't say.

• • • •

"They'll try to jam us," Neill said to Shapoval. "Can you squawk a distress call?"

"To the Americans?"

"Yes. On the guard channel—do you know the frequency?" Neill didn't.

Roman's brow furrowed. "It's two-hundred megahertz—I think." He reached out, adjusting a different dial and wincing in pain. "What should I say?"

"Try sending Mayday—or S.O.S. Anything." Neill looked behind him. "Nate, take my seat."

"I'm no pilot," Crockett objected.

"But you are an officer."

"Big deal—that doesn't mean I can fly." Zhukov had used the same rationale, but like Neill, the sniper wasn't convinced.

"Maybe not, but you've got better reflexes. Just help Roman steer." Neill kept his hands on the yoke and got to his feet. "And go *easy*—the control inputs are sensitive."

"Like a hair trigger?"

"Now you're catching on."

"Where you going?" Nate slid into the pilot's seat.

"Back there—to give the Docs a hand." He was already moving aft.

"I can do that!"

The captain shook his head. "Uh-uh. You don't speak Ukrainian."

"Neither does Brisbane!"

"Exactly," Neill called back, and then, "Try not to crash, okay?"

• • • •

Lieutenant Kritchkov switched armament controls to gun. He could see the contact clearly now, lumbering ahead and bearing Russian Federation markings. He tried the radio again and got no reply.

"Climbing," he told his wingman.

Kritchkov pushed the jet's nose up and added thrust, then leveled off at a vantage point above the giant plane. He banked left and trained his sights on the *Commissar*'s starboard pontoon. He'd have to be careful. Most of the ekranoplan's fuel supply was stored in her wings. Kritchkov wanted to send a message, but he wasn't ready to create a fireball just yet.

Hellcat Flight

Ballpark was on the line again.

"Hellcat Lead, be advised. Ground is reporting a high order detonation north of Kiska." The officer on the AWACS plane studied his instruments. "Bearing is two seven zero—due west—your position."

"That's a good copy, Ballpark." Prentice chewed on that. "What do we have on that sector? Is Ivan running an op?"

"No word on that, Lead," the Sentry replied. "Detonation is—ouch. Different altitude, but same location as the heavy. I'm not there, but from where I sit that's a little close." He was having second thoughts.

If Ivan was in the middle of a live-fire exercise there was no upside to being involved. The incident with the USS *Meyer* came to mind; the Russians certainly showed no reluctance when it came to firing on her.

"Break off, Lead. This isn't our show."

"Negative, BALLPARK," Prentice barked.

The Russians were in America's backyard. They had no business being there. Ivan was up to something, and the colonel wanted to know what it was.

· · · ·

Kritchkov lined up for the shot and loosed a three-second burst from the thirty-millimeter cannon in the Fulcrum's wing port, walking the rounds into the target. The effect was devastatingly immediate, and the *Commissar*'s pontoon splintered in a flash of metal, the shattered fragments erupting in a trail of debris behind her.

The cockpit rocked. Everyone lurched in their seats.

"*Shto tse bulow*?" Tanya cried.

Nate craned his neck for a look outside. The smooth edges of the wing were now shot through and through, creating drag, and the *Commissar* pulled to the right.

"Ivan's shooting at us. Roman—what now?"

Shapoval didn't have the proper English word for *prayer*. Nor did he have the time. The plane was unbalanced. The engineer struggled with the yoke, fighting to keep them from nosing into the Pacific. He tried the radio again, but got only static.

The interceptors were jamming his signal.

• • • •

Xander and Yuri found empty seats next to Sergei and his family. Four year old Aleks stared up at the two men, sizing them up quickly.

They're almost as scary as the Russians, he thought.

Xander saw the fear in his eyes. "What's your name, boy?"

"Aleksander," the child gulped.

Voskov softened his tone. "That's my name. And are you afraid, Aleksander?"

"A little," Aleks replied. In spite of his fear, this gruff soldier hadn't dampened his curiosity. "Do you know where we're going?"

"Yes." Xander cinched the seatbelt at his waist, then reached into a pocket. "We're going someplace where you'll be free."

He held a Velcro patch in his hand and tossed it into the boy's lap. "It's a flag—the flag of my country. Blue at the top, for the sky, and gold below—like fields of wheat."

"Wheat?" The boy had never heard of wheat, much less seen it.

"As far as the eye can see," Voskov answered.

The plane dipped and shuddered again. Aleks didn't seem to notice. He turned the patch over in his hand.

"Is this your home?"

A nod. "Soon it will be yours, too," Xander told him, and he was surprised at the warmth in his own voice.

"Admiral Pavlenko is trying to get our attention." The doctor's bushy eyebrows twitched. He steadied himself by grabbing a seat back.

"He's got mine," Neill grumbled. The Marine shot a glance at Brisbane. She blanched as the plane shook. "Just some turbulence, Doc," he tried reassuringly.

The three found themselves in the plane's weapons compartment, positioned beneath the rounded nodes housing Charybdis. Zhukov flipped switches and dials. Equipment began to hum, and a variety of control surfaces glowed in a spectrum of color. Neill couldn't make heads or tails of any of it, but the Aussie woman was catching on.

"You're building up a conducted current." Taylor's pale expression faded. Her voice was full of wonder. "Repeated waveforms—am I right?"

Radya spoke very deliberately. "We don't have much time, Professor. Do you have the will to fight?"

Neill interpreted his words. She smiled at Radya. He smiled back.

"Show me the target. I'd be happy to."

• • • •

"The tail section!" Pavlenko demanded. "Aim for the tail section!"

Taras composed himself and reconsidered. They still had options. Destroying the *Commissar*'s ability to fly was a last resort; after all, the MiGs stalking her might yet be able to salvage this situation.

"Belay that order, pilot," he bellowed. There might be a better way to persuade Radya—something to prove they meant business.

"Put some lead through her spine."

Kritchkov muttered something and then dove on his target, spraying cannonfire at the *Commissar*'s widest point.

• • • •

The sound was like sheets of tin being ripped apart, but amplified a hundredfold.

Xander reacted, wrapping his arms around Aleks,

shielding the boy as a dozen rounds pierced the *Commissar*'s outer hull. A few lodged in the plane's bulkheads while others rattled around the cargo bay. Oxygen masks dropped from above as the cabin lost pressure.

• • • •

The weapons suite was wedged into a cubicle directly beneath Charybdis. The targeting device was a vibrant green monitor flanked by readouts. Digital icons moved on the screen; these were the radar images of the Mikoyan interceptors hounding them.

Taylor sat at the console, eyeing the display. A joystick controlled the gunsight, a cursor that looked for all the world like the crosshairs from a video game. On top were several buttons, while mounted in the grip was a red switch.

"Do I use this?" she asked Radya.

The plane convulsed; Kritchkov's attack shook the deck under their feet. The scientist recovered and took inventory of the instruments, then laid a hand on the casing rods above their heads.

"Exciter and amplifier—almost there," he mumbled. "The casings are active—coil charge at thirty percent."

"When can we fire?"

"Minimum capacity—" Zhukov tapped the readout. "It must be green—forty-two percent."

The Marine didn't like what he saw. "We're still in the red, Doc."

"Yes, Captain. I know."

• • • •

Kritchkov swooped in again, taking aim at the *Commissar*'s port side wingtip. He dove and squeezed the trigger, and the remaining pontoon was obliterated in a hail of gunfire.

Fragments reflected the sun and tumbled in midair, falling into the sea below. The pilot hadn't been so cautious with this volley. The thirty-millimeter rounds ignited fuel, and the wounded aircraft now trailed smoke and fire.

Yet the giant bird still flew, showing no signs of turning, continuing on her eastward course.

The plane shook again, and Brisbane took hold of the joystick.

"What are we waiting for?" she asked impatiently.

Zhukov studied the display, his brow lined. *Not quite forty percent*, he noted. Still—

"For maximum effect, center the crosshairs over the *group*—not an individual target," Radya directed. "*Now*, Professor."

Neill interpreted. Taylor faced the screen again. She moved the cursor across the display and squeezed the trigger.

The casings above their heads vibrated, and a rumbling sound reverberated throughout the plane's interior. In the weapons compartment—and everywhere else aboard the *Commissar*—the lights winked out, and the steady tumult of machinery faded completely.

That effect was repeated in the skies behind the giant plane. The results were magnified.

Pilots in four of the MiGs now stared at blank instrumentation. Displays went dark; air flowing through pressure suits stopped, and radios became silent as the percussive wave of an electromagnetic pulse swept across the aircraft.

Most alarmingly, the engines of each Fulcrum simply cut out. Thrust died completely. Inertia carried them for-

ward just a bit further, but without power, the interceptors began to lose altitude.

One by one they started to fall.

• • • •

"Did you see that, Lead?"

Hellcat Flight was due south of Amchitka, and Major Tate watched his screen. He did a double-take, not
trusting what his eyes told him.

"Copy, One," Prentice answered.

The F/A-38s had front row for the drama, approaching the Rat Islands at an oblique angle. There was a reason for that. Vectoring in head-on wasn't advisable; the
Russians might take that for provocation, and the colonel
didn't want to risk his small squadron unnecessarily—
especially under the current circumstances.

The E-3 Sentry had warned them about a detonation;
now the AWACS was reporting an exchange of gunfire,
a barrage directed at the largest contact. That aircraft appeared to be in distress. It was hard to confirm, but its
heat signature indicated that something was amiss—a
fire, maybe. And now four of the smaller planes were
falling like rocks.

Ivan was clearly having a bad day.

"MiGs," Tate announced. "Harassing the larger—"
They had visual now, and his eyes widened. "—*Jesus,
Mary* and *Joseph*! You getting dimensions on that bird?"

A black smudge hung in the sky behind the lumbering transport. The American pilots could see it clearly
now; the big plane *was* on fire.

"Ease off, One." Prentice squinted through his visor,
his attention drawn to the smaller shapes dotting the sky.
Three of the Fulcrums had popped their canopies. He
saw chutes opening. The fourth plane plummeted into
the ocean ahead of the others, smacking hard into the

dark blue surface and leaving a splash of white to mark the impact.

But before any of that, sensors aboard HELLCAT Flight had registered a massive pulse emanating from the midst of the action.

This is no exercise, Prentice knew. Another question came to mind; could this be the giant-killer—the weapon used in multiple attacks over the past few months?

The colonel did a head count. Three more MiGs were scattered elsewhere, flanking the larger aircraft on either side. Another paced the plane at a lower altitude.

"Stay sharp, Flight." The colonel's quiet professionalism drifted across the net. Ivan had pilots in the drink, and his first thought was to radio the Sentry to launch CSAR—combat search and rescue. He fired off the request and got back to his own.

"Countermeasures up and stand by," he told his people. "Warning yellow—weapons hold. *I repeat*; warning yellow, weapons hold. Confirm."

HELLCAT Flight acknowledged, confirming the order. This was no ordinary day at the office, and each pilot could feel the adrenaline starting to flow.

Aboard the Commissar

As abruptly as it had faded, the power had returned. Lights had begun to flash on the instrument panel. Crockett rose from his seat, peering through the windscreen.

"Fire on the port side wing!" he shouted.

To his left, Shapoval reached above, pulling handles. Self-sealing tanks kept the blaze from spreading. A fire suppression system installed in the voids and wing spaces did the rest.

Charybdis. It had to be. Radya had used the weapon.

Which meant—

Tanya had the same thought. "Try the radio." She looked twice; Roman was pale, his movements halting.

But he managed to slip on the headset for a listen.

Clear air. The static was gone. The planes jamming them must have been disabled, done in by the discharge. Were there any left? he wondered. Had Charybdis dispatched all of them—or just a few?

They needed to make that distress call. Surely the Americans were tracking them by now. Mayday? S.O.S? Those were for *maritime* emergencies, but that didn't matter. Shapoval needed to make himself understood. He couldn't do that in English, and in the end he opted for Morse code . . .

"We lost power—is that normal?" Neill asked. The hiccup had passed, and the *Commissar*'s electronics were back online.

"Completely normal, Captain. Charybdis interrupts non-essential systems to amplify the pulse. The primaries are unaffected." Zhukov's face crinkled in a smile. "I should have warned you."

"The primaries—by that you mean the engines?"

"Engines, avionics and the like." He stretched out an arm, patting the casings affectionately. "Even at low charge, Charybdis is effective."

"But we've got other contacts," Neill announced.

Radya stared over the Australian's shoulder. The display before her had changed; the interceptors Brisbane had targeted were gone, but to the southeast were four more blips approaching at high speed.

"The other MiGs. Could they have gotten in front of us?"

Zhukov's brows twitched again, his heart sinking. Admiral Pavlenko had undoubtedly dispatched another squadron. The *Commissar* was boxed in and wounded, and the Russians were closing in for the kill.

Radya checked a gauge; power in the weapon had dropped to just eight percent. There wasn't enough charge for a second salvo.

• • • •

Kritchkov's slashing attack brought him below the *Commissar*. From this position he watched in anger as four of his comrades fell into the sea.

So the rumors are true, he brooded. Pavlenko's monster was a decidedly lethal weapon—a weapon that had just downed half of his flight.

Zhukov was fighting back.

• • • •

"Radio traffic," Major Tate announced to the rest of the Hellcats. "On the guard channel."

Colonel Prentice heard it too—an audio message, but not vocal. He tried to piece it together.

"That's Morse."

"It *is* Morse." Tate had reached the same conclusion. He listened as the signal was repeated. "What's '*O-S-O*' supposed to mean—is that Russian?"

Prentice grinned. "Negative. Definitely not Russian, and not *O-S-O*. Big bird is signaling distress—but he's mixed it up.

"We're dealing with an amateur."

• • • •

Kritchkov's eyes were drawn to the sea. Far below, a Russian support ship was steaming west, her antennae reaching skyward and relaying their chatter back to Kamchatka.

The pilot looked at his radar display. What he saw

brought fresh concern; there were more aircraft coming up from the south, following the Aleutian Island chain.

"Americans directly ahead," Kritchkov declared.

That made perfect sense; the renegades would need help to carry out this plan. Zhukov must have found some way to contact the West, enlisting their aid in delivering not only the plane, but the weapon his *tavarischi* had fallen victim to.

Kritchkov keyed his microphone. "Guardian Flight, check in."

The other pilots responded in succession. And then a familiar voice came over the net.

"I see them, new contacts approaching at high speed. What are your orders?" It was Guardian One. His wingman was still alive.

"New vector," Kritchkov announced. His teeth were bared. They would meet the Americans in force—give them something to think about, warn them off. "Break with the *Commissar* and steer one-five-zero."

But that was not to be.

"Negative, pilot." It was Pavlenko who broke in now. "Ignore the Americans."

On the peninsula, the admiral stared at the plot board. With jaw set, his mouth had become a thin gray line. Zhukov's actions were entirely predictable. He had used the weapon once, and if he had the chance, he would do it again.

This wasn't turning out the way Taras had planned.

Commissar and Charybdis were the feathers in his cap, and now both had been wrenched from his grasp. Much of his career had been tied to the scientist's projects, and on the day Taras meant to sever their association, the old man had gotten the better of him.

He cursed aloud before letting the rage pass. All was not lost; the *Rodina* had the rest of *Commissar* squadron, and Captain Tamarkin's team could now replicate the weapon. For Zhukov and his associates the end was very near.

Pavlenko's choice had already been made. The plane would not be allowed to reach the West. "Your target is the *Commissar*. Bring her down, Lieutenant." His voice filled the room and was transmitted to the interceptors in the skies over the Aleutians.

39

<u>FINAL APPROACH</u>

K RITCHKOV FLANKED THE *Commissar* on the right side. His wingman took up a position on the left. At the lieutenant's command, both MiGs added thrust and streaked ahead, climbing to a higher altitude.

Kritchkov turned for a look. The squadron had tried, but intimidation wasn't working; the giant plane still flew, pushing east and trailing smoke. She had become a pitiful sight; both pontoons were gone, drag tugged at the aircraft's twisted wingtips, and chunks of aluminum and metal came free.

It was time for GUARDIAN Flight to finish the job.

Not many aircraft could handle what Kritchkov intended, and those that could were mostly Russian in origin. One was a variant of the MiG-29, like his own. A few more had been designed by the Sukhoi Bureau. The Chinese had a stealthy fifth-generation fighter, but that platform's capabilities were a mystery; not even the Russians knew its secrets.

There was one notable exception, but Kritchkov ignored the American F-22. After all, he reasoned, he wasn't going up against Raptors.

Just a large transport.

"Execute," Kritchkov ordered.

The MiGs pitched up in a tight arc, the loop's diameter exceeding each plane's length by only meters. The somersault decreased airspeed and brought the Fulcrums to the point of stall before they went up and over.

Kritchkov regained control as the jet completed the loop. His wingman wasn't so skilled, aborting in mid-flight, but recovering quickly enough. They leveled off, and with air flow restored, the pilots found themselves behind the *Commissar*.

GUARDIAN Lead used the targeting device in his helmet and lined up for another shot. He reacquired and fired again.

• • • •

"Frolov's Vortex," Lieutenant Elsketh declared. She had watched the maneuver, and knew it by name.

Colonel Prentice was impressed. "You been paying attention in class, Three?"

The young woman didn't get the chance to respond. HELLCAT One interrupted with an observation of his own.

"More cannonfire, Boss." Major Tate's sensors were active. What was more, he could see bursts from the two MiGs badgering the damaged aircraft. "Targeting those nacelles topside."

Tate had excellent eyesight. Prentice focused on the engine mounts on either side of the heavy's nose. The cowlings on the outer turbofans blew out. The gunplay brought more smoke and fire, and the nose of the big plane began to dip.

"Death by a thousand cuts!" Tate said gruffly. "We gonna let this slide, Lead?"

Prentice could tell when he was being goaded. He didn't like this any more than his wingman. Ivan was in the process of shooting down a *Federation* transport, and he'd chosen to do so by violating U.S. airspace.

Prentice wasn't about to let that stand.

"BALLPARK, be advised," he called. "Russian aircraft have engaged one of their own in an offensive action. HELLCAT Flight is pushing out to render assistance."

Tate grinned behind his mask. *Now you're talkin', Boss.* But he knew this wouldn't sit well with the Sentry supporting them.

Prentice didn't seem concerned by that. He barked a question. "Elsketh—what do you know about Fulcrums?"

"Hard to beat, inside of ten miles," she came back. "With an almost unmatched turn rate."

"Almost—so he's pretty good in a knife fight," Prentice summarized.

A voice came across the radio. "Stand down, HELLCAT Lead!" BALLPARK ordered. "ROE is firm. I say again—"

Prentice couldn't hear him, but that was intentional. He turned down the gain, cutting off the AWACS. An aircraft in distress was pleading for help, and the colonel was duty-bound to answer that call, rules of engagement be damned.

• • • •

Tereshenko came up through the hatch from below. He looked forward. Sunlight pierced the flight deck, and he saw the silhouettes of Tanya, Crockett, and Shapoval seated in the cockpit.

"Meela—!" he called out.

Tanya was glad to see him. "Yuri—help me with Roman. He's bleeding again."

Shapoval gave a reply, sweat beading on his brow. "Not yet." He eased back on the yoke, struggling to keep the plane level.

The sound of something new surrounded them—something tinny, like metal caught in a fan or a piece of machinery. All at once the clamor came to a halt.

Lights on the panel glowed red. "We've lost number four on the right, and seven and eight on the left," Roman informed them. "And we're leaking fuel."

"Doesn't sound good," Nate guessed. He could feel the plane start to vibrate as he gripped the controls.

"Mechanical difficulties," Yuri deflected.

Crockett offered a half-hearted grin. "You have a gift for understatement, comrade."

A new volley. The *Commissar* shook and slewed to starboard, laboring to maintain speed. Shapoval's eyes went back to the display.

"Number nine, below the wing." He shook his head. "The Russians will force us down—nothing can stop that now."

"Go higher." The order came from Nate. "The air's too thick here, right?"

"Yes. But not *too* high—we've lost pressure below."

"Okay, but if we gain altitude, that's one less thing working against us, right?"

Yuri repeated the words in Ukrainian. The engineer pushed the throttles forward, and the plane began a slow but steady ascent.

Radya stared at the gauge, willing the numbers to climb. But the readout still hung in the red.

"Twenty percent," he told the others. He wasn't happy sharing the news.

Neill wasn't happy getting it. "That's not enough."

"No, Captain." The deck beneath their feet pitched, angling up. "Not nearly enough."

The *Commissar* clawed at the sky, trying to free herself from the denser air.

Kritchkov watched from a thousand meters behind. Another man might have felt something for the wounded beast, but not the lieutenant. He had a job to do, a nation's secrets to protect.

The contact before him rose slowly. Crosshairs were projected on the inside of his visor; distance, speed, and altitude. Kritchkov cued his weapons through line of sight imagery. All he had to do was look at his intended target, line up for the shot, and then press the firing switch.

It was obvious that only three of the plane's engines were functional on the right side. The one under the wing was also gone. Kritchkov's comrade in the other MiG would soon destroy the turbofan on the left.

He was ready to squeeze the firing switch, but his action was interrupted. Something had caught his eye, and he tracked back to the radar in his display. The MiG's proximity alarm warbled softly as four Americans dropped out of the sun and crashed the party.

• • • •

The F/A-38's formation stretched half a mile across. Elsketh and Settles sailed up and over the *Commissar*'s nose and jetted north. HELLCAT Lead eyed the Russians and chose the Fulcrum pouring the most lead. He buzzed the MiG at a distance discouraged by most flight manuals.

"Stay sharp, Flight—and weapons hold." He added a warning. "Close-in combat is this bird's best friend."

Prentice had brought HELLCAT Flight to distract Ivan, to lure the Russians away from their victim. To do that, he would swing around and make sure he had their attention.

• • • •

"Those are our guys!" Nate followed the Hellcats as they shot across the sky. The fin flash of each bore the red white and blue. "They're Americans!"

"Americans," Roman repeated. That was good news. He hoped.

Nate was thankful for the company, but concerned at the same time. They were in a Russian aircraft encroaching on American airspace—trading one group of trigger-happy pilots for possibly another.

He picked up the radio. The dial was still set on the guard channel. "Better tell those guys not to shoot." The comment was directed to no one in particular. "Not at us, anyway."

Lieutenant Kritchkov ordered the surviving members of GUARDIAN to break off their attack. The *Commissar* was limping now; she couldn't hope to get far. In fact, Kritchkov fully expected the plane to ditch at any time.

He pulled back on the control column and veered away, adding power and angling in the direction of the fighter that had spoiled his shot. He had a visual almost instantly and began to pursue.

He checked weapons status. Guns were favorable, given the circumstances, and Kritchkov focused his eyes on the rapidly fading intruder, puzzling out the type of aircraft he pursued.

The sky was bright and cold in the upper reaches. He studied the Americans. Not Raptors, he decided. And not F-16s. Despite his familiarity with Western airframes, the Russian couldn't identify them. But Kritchkov didn't nurse that thought for long. He put his foot in the throttle and closed the distance, squeezing off a dozen rounds as the MiG thundered across the sky.

Threat receivers warned Prentice that an attack was underway. He pulled up and banked right—directly into the path of the incoming munitions. He winced as three of the rounds sliced through a wing.

He grumbled, cursing; it was not a shining moment for the colonel's instincts.

That was uncalled for, he growled under his breath. Ivan was getting bold—too bold, with deadly effect. First, the attack on the *Meyer*, in international waters. Now they were here, in U.S. airspace, taking potshots at more Americans. And that had raised his ire.

He made his decision. If the Russians had come this far spoiling for a fight, Prentice was determined to oblige them.

"Weapons free, HELLCAT Flight! I say again, weapons free!"

Major Tate had wheeled around and watched as the boss took fire. He didn't know the Russian's intentions—no one did. Nor did he need any coaxing. He dove, accelerating, condensation flashing from his wings as he pulled out of the dive. Tate's master arm switch was hot. At less than two thousand meters his gun mounts erupted, sending a burst in the path of the attacking MiG.

Kritchkov could see tracer rounds punching through the sky ahead of him. He flinched, shoved the stick forward and pointed the Fulcrum's nose at the deck, banking hard to the right.

Elsketh had turned away from the *Commissar* and dropped below. Ahead was the colonel's attacker at a distance of one mile. She'd seen him coming, seen the Russian shower the boss's plane with several rounds. The young woman gave free rein to her emotions, and her blood began to boil.

That was the wrong response. Anger had clouded her

reflexes, but with seconds to spare she drew a bead on the rapidly closing aircraft.

Too late. Kritchkov had loosed a Vympel air-to-air missile. The weapon's search and track suite had a lock, and the medium range rocket left his wingtip and began streaking in to the target.

Proximity fuse. The thought pounded in Elsketh's brain. HELLCAT Lead was right; she had paid attention in class, and knew that to survive she would have to evade the missile—before it got close enough to detonate and shred her plane. She pulled up, popping flares to draw the heat seeker in another direction. She would make Ivan work for this one, forcing the inbound missile into a series of twists and turns that would deplete fuel.

But Kritchkov wasn't done. As quickly as the first missile had jumped from the rail another was launched. The ripple tactic was a common one for Russian pilots. Elsketh saw the flash in the corner of her eye. She knew Ivan's game; by climbing higher, she would forfeit air-speed, making her Hellcat an easier target. The heat seeker would zero in on the jet's engines, fly up her tail-pipe and end the engagement.

Lieutenant Settles saw it too. He thumbed the switch on his radio, sending a warning on the guard channel. "You've got incoming, Three! *Get out of there!*"

Not so fast. With the flip of a dial Elsketh increased the output on her own gear, blunting the Vympel's track-ing suite. The first missile lost its lock, but the second arced up and began to climb. Elsketh pitched the plane over on its back, adding thrust in a desperate attempt to lose number two.

The threat alarm wailed in her ears but then went si-lent. She banked again, rolling to the left now, chancing a look over her shoulder.

Relief.

Settles had dropped in behind and was tight on the Russian's six. Elsketh looked below; another flash had caught her eye. Sunlight glinted off the second missile as it fell tumbling into the sea.

One of two things had happened. Either the tactic worked, and the Vympel ran out of fuel; or Settles had blasted the rocket with a wave of his own countermeasures. Her instruments confirmed the latter, and Elsketh whispered a prayer of thanks for her wingman's intervention.

But that consolation was unmercifully brief. Another look back told her that the Russian was still there.

● ● ● ●

Kritchkov was ready to switch to guns. He needed to drop the fighter weaving desperately in the skies ahead—and return to finishing off the *Commissar*.

But now he had a new problem; another mystery plane had appeared, dogging his tail, and try as he might, Kritchkov couldn't shake him.

Settles was determined to keep him occupied, sending a hail of cannonfire over his wingtip. The Fulcrum jagged right. Another burst from the Hellcat, but the Russian continued his pursuit of Elsketh.

Enough is enough, Settles decided. He used the sight in his helmet and put the crosshairs between the MiG's vertical fins. A steady tone sounded in his ears; fire control had a firm lock.

"Fox two!"

Settles toggled the master switch and squeezed the trigger. The clamps on the wingtip retracted. The Helius dropped, its rocket motor igniting, the sudden combustion pushing the missile forward.

It was a snap shot without any wiggle room. The air-to-air missile streaked ahead of the Hellcat on a course straight and true. Settles followed it in, watching the bare wisp of an exhaust trail before turning sharply away.

The distance between them was so close that Kritchkov had almost no warning. The Helius slammed into the Fulcrum's starboard engine, detonating inside the housing and ripping most of the tail section away from the fuselage. The MiG suffered catastrophic loss, her control surfaces shearing away from the airframe and twisting violently as the plane began to disintegrate. Tungsten fragments, jet fuel and engine parts filled the air, mixing in a jarring explosion that put the forward section into a flat spin. The cockpit was vaporized in a fireball of black and orange, and Kritchkov died instantly.

· · · ·

Zhukov stared at the monitor. Something had changed; the radar contacts from the south were mixing it up with Pavlenko's interceptors, chasing them off, and Radya felt encouraged for the first time since the air battle had begun.

"Come with me."

"What about those fighters?"

The doctor was moving toward the cockpit. "Those are American aircraft, Captain. It would seem that your countrymen have finally arrived."

· · · ·

Guardian One watched helplessly. His squadron commander's plane was reduced to shattered pieces, a thick bloom of smoke and fire falling from the sky.

He looked away, banking right and choosing a target. The closest was the plane Kritchkov had fired on, its wing punctured by thirty-millimeter rounds. GUARDIAN One raced in, his multi-function display feeding data to the air-to-air missiles hanging on the wings.

Major Tate was a thousand feet below, but not far behind. He pushed up, pointing the Hellcat's nose at the Fulcrum's underside. A trilling sound filled his ears, the tone telling him that the targeting device had a lock.

Tate climbed and kept his eye on the MiG. He increased speed and overshot the Russian, stitching Ivan's fuselage with armor-piercing shells as he rocketed past. GUARDIAN One continued to fly. Then came the alarms; lights tied to the annunciators flashed red, signaling a variety of system failures.

He was resolute in bringing the wounded bird home, but hadn't counted on the tenacity of his opponent. Elsketh was now in front, and a Helius slipped from her weapons bay.

The missile streaked ahead, sliding into the MiG's intake, the resulting explosion splitting the plane in half. Both wings were severed. Engine mounts broke free. The cockpit canopy shattered and popped like a cork. Folding in on itself, the Fulcrum came apart in the air.

Yet the pilot was lucky. He managed to punch out. Tate's gunsight camera caught the plume of red and white nylon as the Russian's chute was deployed.

· · · ·

"They're turnin' tail," Crockett announced, his voice rising. He twisted his head from left to right; their Russian attackers had broken off, the sleek silhouettes peeling away and angling back to the west.

"They have little fuel," Shapoval told him. He was right; the MiGs had been stretched beyond their limits.

Neill, Zhukov and Brisbane found their way into the cockpit. The space now felt crowded.

"How are we doing?"

"Still in the fight."

"Keep your head on a swivel; there's another squadron out there. The doc thinks they might be American."

"They are, Mike. Two of 'em flew in front of us. "

At a word from Radya, Yuri helped Roman extricate himself from the pilot's position. They moved aft, and the scientist wedged himself into the seat and took the controls.

"What can I do?" Neill asked.

"Tell the doc to chop our air speed. And lower the landing gear. I've already radioed our friends in the Air Force."

"I think you're getting the hang of this."

"Hardly."

Neill relayed his words to Zhukov. The doctor gave a nod and pulled back on the throttle, slowing the *Commissar* significantly.

The plane convulsed and yawed to the right. They dropped almost a thousand feet. Zhukov gripped the yoke tightly. Crockett did the same.

"Another engine gone. We're losing power." Radya checked the instrument panel and struggled with the wheel. "The damage is greater than I feared."

Crockett caught the edge in his voice. "Hang tough, Doc," he put in.

"Who's the hotshot pilot now?" Mike forced a smile. He stood, peering through the windscreen. "Think you can bring this bird in?"

"On time and under budget. But we're losing altitude—and there's an awful lot of water down there."

"Then you can't miss, can you?" Taylor encouraged. The Aussie was more nervous than she let on. She tried humor. "Did you bring your pool noodle?"

"Pool noodle?"

The *Commissar* dropped again. The sea grew closer, filling the horizon. "Hollow foam. Flotation devices used by children."

Crockett was amused. "Good one, Doc."

• • • •

"You buying that, Colonel?" Elsketh had reservations about the voice on the radio.

"Sounded like one of our guys," Prentice responded. And it made sense; what other reason would the Russians have for shooting at one of their own? He keyed the mike. "Pilot, maintain your easterly track. We'll escort you someplace safe."

"She's going in, Colonel," Major Tate called. "Droppin' like a rock."

HELLCAT Flight stayed abreast of the giant plane, and now the pilots watched as the Russian heavy began to fade from the sky.

Prentice soared above, surveying the *Commissar*'s wounds. Her wingtips had been shot away, the pontoons gone. Holes riddled the plane's hull, and most of the engines were failing; two of those were now just twisted, blackened shells. Jet fuel spilled from joints in the port side wing. Even to the untrained eye she was dismal to behold.

A large land mass lay just ahead—this one part of the Fox Islands, more stepping stones in the Aleutians. The big transport was making for the shallows south of Umnak. Prentice called BALLPARK and gave their position.

"She's at five hundred feet," Tate said.

Prentice admired the Russian's lines. The plane had all the features of a flying boat; aerodynamic, but with a clean hull for sea landings.

"Stick and rudder, pal," the colonel muttered. "Stick and rudder."

"Come again, Lead?"

"Choppy seas, One," Prentice answered. "Big bird's in for one heck of a ride."

• • • •

The air was thicker as the *Commissar* dropped. The very elements battled against them, and a cross wind tugged at the airframe.

Crockett and Zhukov were white-knuckled. The two men fought to keep the nose up—but not too much. Lift was still critical, and pitching too high would stall the plane, collapsing what control they had left.

The caterwauling of the engines from the starboard side abruptly shut down. The *Commissar* crabbed to port, dropping further. Brisbane's stomach was in her throat. From below came a new vibration as the hull slapped the waves.

They were too close to shore. Umnak's beaches lay half a kilometer to the north. The shallows were just that, and the depth of the waters didn't give the ekranoplan enough draft for an optimal landing.

And Zhukov was no pilot. He tried to compensate, dipping a wing too low; the shattered ends caught the waves and held on, then plunged below the surface. On the left side, the remaining engine was wrenched free, along with half the wing.

Spray splashed across the windscreen and the *Commissar* spun. She struck the surf at an angle. Below, terrified children screamed. Everything not strapped down moved forward. Noise filled the cockpit; scraping, tearing, deep groanings from below. The enclosed space shook, and Neill's chair was knocked from its mountings. He was thrown against a console and blacked out.

The sudden arrest had an even worse effect aft. Stabilators and ailerons came free. The rudder snapped and cartwheeled into the breakers. The plane's massive bulk displaced more than a hundred tons of seawater, and as the *Commissar* came to rest in the shoals, her tail section broke in half, flooding the cargo bay . . .

EPILOGUE

Washington,
Near the Pentagon

MID-MORNING traffic wasn't heavy at all, which was odd for D.C., and Avery's limousine followed Independence Avenue west before merging with Maine. The Secretary looked right. The Tidal Basin (once known as Twining Lake) was in full view, calm and placidly serene, and beyond the reservoir was the Jefferson Memorial, where dozens of tourists spilled out of the portico and onto the basin promenade.

Cherry blossom trees ringed the banks, but visitors who had come to see them bloom would be disappointed. It was far too late in the year for that. Such was the gamble; flowering usually took place in Spring, between March and April, and accurate forecasting was always hit and miss.

Much like divining the whims and impulses of men and nations, Avery considered thoughtfully. He smiled. Unpredictability was an inevitable force of nature, and change, as the saying went, was always a constant.

As he had done so often in the past, Avery's driver approached the Pentagon's river entrance from one of three different routes. The car was waved through, parking close in a reserved spot, and the Secretary and his escort took the elevator to the building's second floor and his E-Ring office.

•   •   •   •

"This might require a little intervention."

Cullough McKeckney wasn't comfortable with what he was about to suggest. He approached Willis Avery's desk cautiously, tablet in hand. "Have you seen this?"

The Secretary of Defense sipped from his coffee and eyed the image on the screen, peering over his glasses. He found bifocals an annoyance, and could never adjust to progressive lenses.

"You mean the video of the *Commissar*?" Avery had already received one briefing and the plane's name had reached his ears. "Caught it last night. Wouldn't mind seeing it again, though."

Cull laid the tablet before his boss. It was a short clip, less than two minutes long. SECDEF watched it twice and then pushed back in his chair.

"It's getting a lot of airplay on the networks. Social media, too," Cull explained. He walked to the fridge and cracked the seal on a bottle of water. "Shouldn't we have pulled the plug on this before it went viral?"

"Who posted it?" Avery didn't seem alarmed.

But McKeckney was. "Deckhand on a crab boat. Just happened to be near Umnak when the plane ditched." He wore a puzzled expression now. "Can you *ditch* an ekranoplan?"

"I think that was more of a controlled crash," Avery chuckled. He shook his head. "Intervention won't work now, Cull. That ship's already sailed. The Navy's recovered every piece of the plane, and the Russians know we have it. They also know we've got Charybdis, which gives us leverage. And there are strategic advantages that go along with it."

McKeckney understood that concept all too well. "Balance of power—between East and West. But what about disclosure? Do we tell the world Moscow's been knocking down commercial airliners?"

A pensive look. "That's certainly not off the table," the Secretary answered. The real question was *why*, and that had dogged Avery for days. Something just wasn't adding up, and the Russian attack on the *Meyer* was at the top of the list.

Willis went back to the tablet again, staring at the frozen image of the aircraft. SECNAV's theory had merit; maybe the assault was a probing attempt, a prelude to invasion. The *Commissar* was suited for that purpose, and with a squadron of such planes, and the Federation troops spotted at Ust-Kamchatsk, the idea was entirely plausible.

Avery shook it off, looking at the clock on the wall. "There's a meeting in the Oval Office at noon. The president, Joint Chiefs and myself. We'll discuss our options then."

"Exposing the Russians would be a net gain," the younger man conceded.

"And it wouldn't hurt us in the court of public opinion, either," Avery agreed. "The president's advisers are already stressing that point, Cull, and I'll give him my own recommendations. We'll just have to see what he decides."

"What about Zhukov and his team?"

"We'll offer asylum, but I can't imagine any of them accepting it. After all, they are citizens of Ukraine."

"So we'll expedite their return?"

"It's always good to keep peace with an ally," Avery smiled.

"And our friends in the media?"

The man with the unruly hair frowned. True journalism was largely dead, in his opinion, and he didn't like reporters as a rule. "We have a very large Russian plane on our hands. That's all they need to know for the moment."

"But they'll start asking questions soon," Cull pointed out. "They already have."

Avery grunted. "Can't be helped. Anything else?"

"I got an email from Personnel and Readiness. The position has been approved—along with the salary and title. I suspect you're happy about that."

"I am indeed. With a few other arrangements, I can present the final proposal to the president." He grew thoughtful, and then frowned at the younger man. "Why the long face?"

McKeckney hesitated.

"Spill it."

"You recall our discussion? About covert tactics—with hidden motives?"

SECDEF dredged his memory. "False flags," he muttered. *Had Cull been puzzling over the same questions?* "What about them?"

"You described them as operations carried out secretly—designed to muddy things and protect the real perpetrators of a crime."

"That's one definition. Is there another?"

"Yes, sir—any deception that brings us into war."

Avery was silent. It wasn't like McKeckney to chase rabbits. Still, his statement raised the hair on the back of his neck. *Why*? He didn't know.

"What are you driving at?"

"An aspect of Neill's analysis," he answered. "He might have been wrong on one point."

"Which one?"

"The assessment regarding Russia's crude oil supply." He had the run of the table now. "We've been led to believe their reserves are depleted. But in recent years they've become one of the world's biggest exporters. What changed?"

Avery blinked. "You're suggesting it's all a ruse?"

"Yes, Mr. Secretary. To push two nations into war."

"But who benefits from that? Not us—and certainly not the Russians."

"Who *always* benefits from war?"

Cull waded in slowly at first, but before he finished, his water bottle was empty, and the last of Avery's coffee had been drained.

"I think you need to talk to Cyrano Hatch," SECDEF told him at last. "He's written a few things along those lines."

"I can be discrete," McKeckney added.

"You'd better be," Avery boomed. He had lost one right hand man. He wasn't about to lose another.

673rd Medical Group Hospital,
Joint Base Elmendorf-Richardson

Nathan Crockett strode into the room, boots clopping on linoleum. He had traded one uniform for another. The camouflage of Ukraine was gone, replaced by the woodland pattern of Marine Corps utilities, and for the first time in days he was clean-shaven.

Taylor was with him. Her tactical garb had also been replaced. She wore something much more feminine now, a cotton blouse and denim, and her red hair fell to her shoulders, no longer captured in a pony tail or pushed up under a cap to hide her appearance.

"How's the leg?"

Captain Neill tried sitting up in bed and regretted it. The pain in his ankle reminded him why he was there.

"I won't be running a PFT anytime soon, that's for sure. Three screws near the joint," he told them. "Anterior fibula, or something like that." He tapped his forehead. "Plus a minor concussion."

"Yeah, well, I wasn't gonna ask. Your head's too hard to do any damage there."

Neill smiled at the taunt. "Hey, Doc, nice duds."

Brisbane reddened. "I was a bit grotty before, thank you." She smoothed the front of her jeans. "Lieutenant Crockett took me shopping."

"The BX," Nate added. "Command Post even loaned us a car."

Neill waved a hand toward the window. "Bring that box over, will you? There's somethin' inside you two might like to get back."

"Get back?" Nate echoed. He crossed the room and rummaged inside the container. A smile creased his face. "Our phones. Where'd you get these?"

"The Navy sent them—Richey or Chau, most likely. Got here this morning. The rest of our stuff's being held by the Air Force."

"Zoomies got our gear?"

"There's not much to *get*," Neill reminded him. They had left very little onboard the *Meyer*.

Returning the group's personal effects wasn't a priority. The dignified transfer of the ship's dead was. The *Meyer*'s casualties were handled by a mortuary affairs team at Eareckson Station, and the eight sailors killed in the attack had been flown to Elmendorf by chopper. Bailee Russo's body arrived with them. To spare his friends' feelings, Neill thought it best not to mention that detail.

"Nice job bringing in the plane. I doubt Doc Zhukov could've done it without you."

"Not something I'd care to repeat anytime soon. Hey, what about the Berkut boys?"

"Yuri and Xander have been debriefed by the DIA. Zhukov's people, too. Oh, and Shapoval's next door. He lost some blood but they tell me he'll mend. What about you, Taylor?"

"I'm catching a flight to Sydney in a few days—after I get a closer look at Charybdis."

"I know you're looking forward to that." Neill was in a thankful mood. "You did good, Doc. It's been a privilege to have you along for the ride."

"But she'll be going home without Bailee." Nate's pain was still fresh, and Taylor's emerald eyes lost a little of their light. "That's not the way any of us planned it, Mike."

"I know, pal." Neill couldn't think of anything better to say, and he kicked himself for it.

"And Christina? You call her yet?"

Neill appeared to blush. "The DoD's flying her up. Special dispensation from Secretary Avery."

Crockett gave a nod. "Yeah—must be nice to have friends in high places."

"It doesn't hurt," Neill quipped. "What about you? Homesick for Lejeune?"

The sniper's eyes went to the floor. "I'll go back," he said at last. His voice was low. "But just for administrative reasons."

Neill didn't like where this was headed. "And that means—exactly *what*?"

"I've been doing some thinking. Probably too much. And a lot of soul-searching." Nate turned away. "I'm no good at this anymore. I couldn't keep Aultman safe. And now I've lost Bailee."

"None of that was your fault."

"Tell that to their families," Nate scoffed.

Neill's mind raced. A friend was hurting, and by every measure of leadership he should have seen it coming. Had he missed it? If that was the case, it said little about his command qualities. From a professional standpoint, officers were trained to take care of their people; it was a primary tenet, and he chided himself for dropping the ball.

"Don't you think we should talk about this?"

Crockett shook his head. "I'm done, Mike. I've disappointed too many people." He drew in some air. "I'll stick around till you're on your feet. Help write the after-action report, if you want. But when I get back to Lejeune I'm resigning my commission."

Edgewater, Maryland

She hadn't baked in months; ages, so it seemed, and couldn't recall the last time the oven light had been on.

Amber Aultman peeked through the glass. The dough had started to rise, and the small dollops were looking more like cookies. Toll House, Richard's favorite—with added vanilla extract, more than the recipe called for. She smiled at that. It was a guilty pleasure she'd never been able to argue with.

A couple more minutes for this batch. Why she was making them she couldn't really say; there were two dozen cooling on the countertop, and enough ingredients left in the bowl for at least two dozen more. She'd never finish them; her sweet tooth would be satisfied after just a few, and the rest would grow stale.

But they were an indulgence for Richard, and she

wanted to do something for him, even if he wasn't there to enjoy it. It wasn't at all practical, but she knew that. And she reminded herself that the cookies wouldn't go to waste; the family next door had kids, and what child didn't like chocolate chip?

Baking represented a return to the real world, but something so simple would have filled her with anguish only weeks before. Now the persistent melancholy was gone. Her pain was fading, and she was almost happy. Did that mean the old adage was true—did time really heal all wounds?

Amber stepped out of the kitchen and into the den. Windows lined the room on every side. In one corner of the yard, Richard had planted two varieties of apple, and their branches moved in the breeze. The young widow had always enjoyed a crisp red delicious, but so far the trees hadn't yielded any fruit.

Her gaze lingered. The sky was orange, almost pink now, coloring the fence line with the hues of sunset. She'd cut the grass earlier; the lawn was her domain, always had been—even when Richard was alive. The task had taken the better part of two hours. She had color on her cheeks and arms. The sun on her skin felt good. Summer was fast approaching, and after a bitter winter—and a bleak spring—she looked forward to being outdoors again.

The timer pulled her back to the kitchen. Amber removed the cookie sheet and set it aside. She started for the spatula when something on the floor caught her eye.

It was the size of a business card, leaning against the baseboard next to the wastebasket. She stooped and picked it up, surprised, realizing immediately how it had got there. *Hadn't she thrown this away?* Of that she was sure, but the tears flowed freely that morning, and her recollections might have been clouded.

Lieutenant Nate Crockett. She read everything else the Marine had scrawled; his unit's name, cell phone number and email address. She recalled the young officer's visit—the feelings he'd stirred—and stopped cold. It was much too soon, but to be honest, he'd crossed her mind more than once.

Was that what he'd planned?

That was hard to say, she decided. She hadn't known him long enough to gauge his intentions. But that wasn't the real question, and as long as she was being candid, Amber faced up to her own feelings.

She was warm in a way that had nothing to do with the sun. She found her purse and put the card carefully inside. Another smile. She wouldn't use it just yet, but in time Crockett's number would end up in her phone's directory.

She would get through this, of that she was sure. Her memories of Richard would comfort her. The pain wouldn't last forever, and she'd make it to the other side. Amber knew what she'd find there, too. Just what Crockett had told her.

Hope.

And maybe even a new friend to help her enjoy it.

Look for the next book

in the Michael Neill Adventure

Coming Soon!

Look for the next book

in the Michael Neill Adventure Series.

Coming Soon!